Praise for *Fangs for Nothing*

'Like *Midsomer Murders* and *True Blood* had a delicious, delicious baby. Who wouldn't want to solve a murder mystery with a vampire that looks like Aragorn's hotter brother? *Fangs for Nothing* is a sexy, kooky, gothic good time.'

Sam Hall

'I cackled my way through this kooky vampire rom-com. The romance is swoony, the feel-good vibes are immaculate, and it all comes wrapped in bonus gothic castle aesthetic. An absolute delight!'

A.J. Lancaster

'*Fangs for Nothing* is like the perfect cup of chai latte – rich, comforting, and with just the right balance of sweetness, mystery and spice. I couldn't get enough of our brooding vampire Alaric and professional organiser Winnie who together create a delightful brew that keeps you hooked until the last sip.'

Bea Paige

'Swoon-worthy, spellbinding and impossible to put down. A fang-tastically charming romance that you'll immediately fall in love with.'

A.K. Mulford

'Cute, cosy, sassy and spicy! Steffanie Holmes writes with wit, whimsy, dollops of humour and a delicious flair for the macabre.'

Iris Beaglehole

'Cosy, hilarious and a little bit spooky, *Fangs for Nothing* is my favourite comfort read!'

Lee Savino

STEFFANIE HOLMES

ATRIA BOOKS
New York · Amsterdam/Antwerp · London · Toronto · Sydney/Melbourne · New Delhi

This story is for those of us with an emotional-support pile of half-finished craft projects.

FANGS FOR NOTHING
First published in Australia in 2025 by
Atria Books Australia, an imprint of Simon & Schuster (Australia) Pty Limited
Level 4, 32 York St, Sydney NSW 2000
Previously published by the author in 2024.

New York Amsterdam/Antwerp London Toronto Sydney/Melbourne New Delhi
Visit our website at www.simonandschuster.com.au

A catalogue record for this book is available from the National Library of Australia

ISBN: 9781761633911

Map © Fred Kroner 2025
Cover design: Covers by Aura
Interior design: Midland Typesetters, Australia
Cover images: Coffee pot/alenagonik, blood/stas11, smoke/Seamartini (all via Depositphotos)

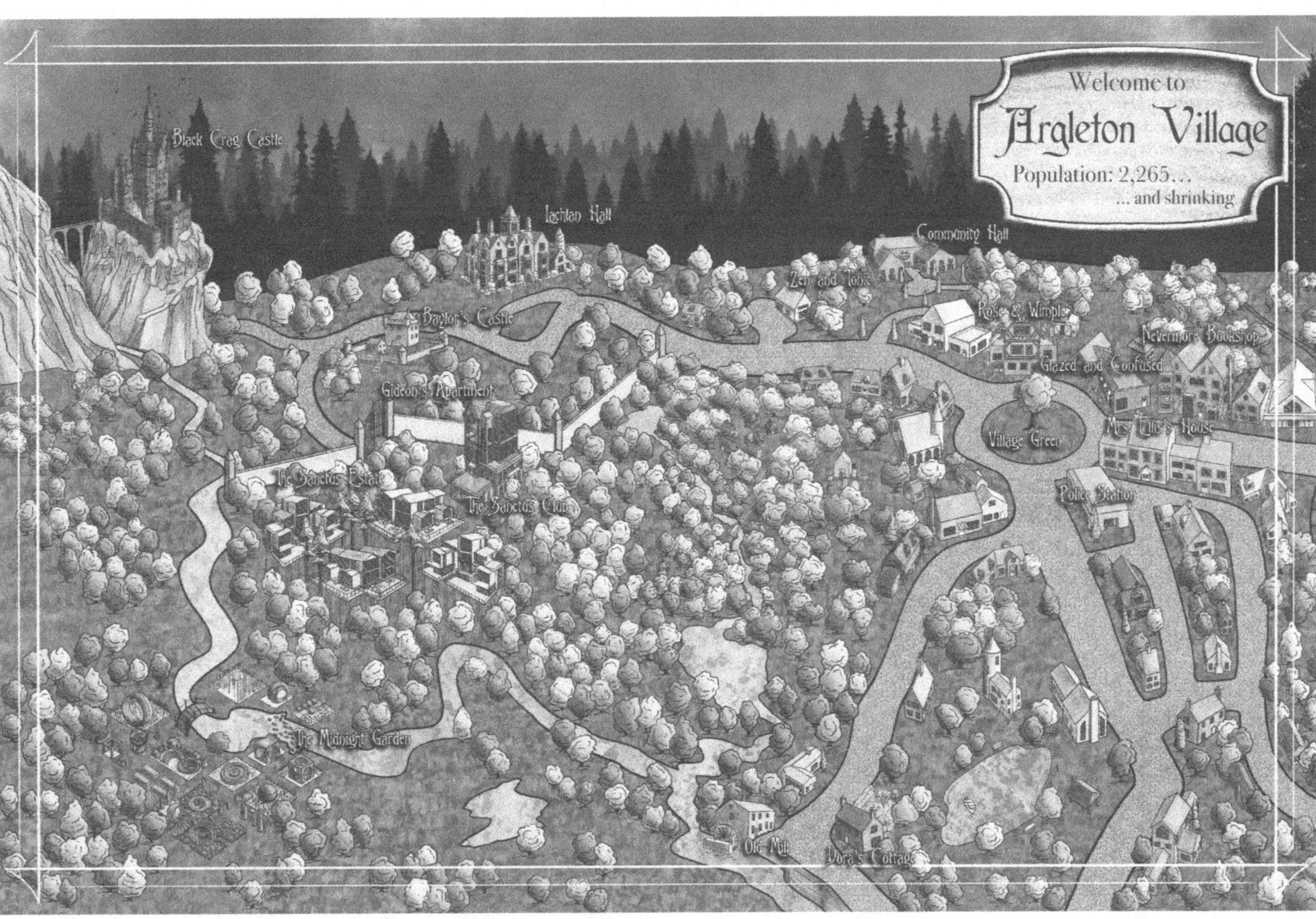
Welcome to
Argleton Village
Population: 2,265…
… and shrinking
Black Crag Castle
Lachlan Hall
Community Hall
Zen and Tonic
Baylor's Castle
Rose & Wimple
Nevermore Bookshop
Glazed and Confused
Gideon's Apartment
Village Green
Mrs Ellis's House
The Sanctus Estate
The Sanctus Club
Police Station
The Midnight Garden
Old Mill
Dora's Cottage

1

Winnie

Mum: Winnie, I got back from the shops and found the note you stuck to the telly. I can't believe you just left for the countryside without even saying goodbye! If you'd told me in person, I could have shown you the lovely sundresses I picked up for you at the charity shop. I think you'd look very fetching in this sunflower one. Perhaps if you had the dress, a man could be taking it off you right now. Think on that.

"I'll have gin in an IV," I mutter to the bartender as I slide into a seat, water dribbling off the end of my nose onto the pristine wooden bar. I roll up my sleeve and present her with my wrist.

She flashes me a sympathetic smile. "I'm clean out of IVs, sorry. How about with ice and tonic?"

"That'll have to do." I brush my ruined, sodden hair out of my face. When I lean on my elbows, my best lightweight wool coat squelches.

"Bad day?" The bartender raises a perfectly tweezed eyebrow as she fixes my drink.

"I don't know what gave you that idea. Today's been wonderful. I thought I'd try the new Supersize Baptism over at your local church." I point out the window to the white Presbyterian steeple towering over the flooding village green. "I figured you can never have enough of the god juice."

I drop my ruined leather tote on the floor at my feet, wedge my purple suitcase in the corner of the bar, and drape my cashmere scarf over the top of it. Maybe if I lay it out nicely, it won't dry all misshapen.

I notice the bartender adding a double shot to my drink. She slides it across the bar to me. "At least if you're doused in holy water, you'll repel any vampires in the vicinity."

"Honestly, bring on the vampires. An eternal bite sounds brilliant right about now." I tug down the neck of my shirt. "This drink is excellent. I shall have another. And a plate of something unhealthy and delicious, ideally with cheese."

"Cheese does make everything better. Another G&T and a basket of loaded wedges, coming up."

She goes off to the other end of the bar to put in my order, while I drink my G&T far too quickly and curse my own stupidity. Today's disaster is entirely my fault. I'm always the responsible one, the one with the checklist and the Instagram-famous organisation system. I never mess up.

But I've been messing up everything lately.

I've spent the last two hours waiting in sideways rain at the train station in Argleton, Loamshire for my new client to pick me up. It was only after I checked my phone for the gazillionth time and pulled up the email from Reginald, Lord Valerian's personal secretary, that I realised I got the date wrong. Somehow, I, Winnie Preston – the woman who gets paid to clean up other people's chaotic lives – showed up for my new job a whole day early and was waiting in the pouring rain for a client who wasn't expecting to pick me up until tomorrow.

How did I get it so wrong? I studied Reginald's emailed instructions a hundred times. I wrote the dates in my calendar. I colour-coded them according to the Clutter Queens colour chart.

If I'm being honest with myself, my head's been filled with cotton wool ever since Patrick. And Claire. And my mother and her terrifying sundresses don't help – in the photos she sent me, I could see that one was covered in red splotches, more a crime scene photograph than a fashion choice. The other had bright yellow flowers with terrifying beady eyes in the centres. They were awful, and I think that she knows that.

The sundresses will join the two breadmakers and the antique apothecary cabinet she bought me yesterday, and the twenty-two pairs of men's socks from the day before.

No matter how many times I tell her not to, she still buys me these "gifts". Nothing I say or do will stop her, so I will accept the breadmakers and the creepy sundresses and the apothecary cabinet and the socks and I will throw them away, and the ordeal will begin again next week.

I stare at her text message as raindrops continue to roll off the end of my nose. I had initially debated hopping on the next train and heading back to London. I'd be too late to find a hotel, so I'd have to crash at Mum's, but maybe it wouldn't be so bad this time, and then I could flat hunt in the morning before catching the train I was *supposed* to catch …

But some defiant part of me whispered, "You escaped, Winnie. You escaped London and that cursed house and all those horrible memories. Don't go back now."

So I did what any self-respecting girl would do in my position. I squared my jaw, smoothed down my frizzy hair, and headed for the pub.

Which is where I find myself now, staring at the bottom of a G&T glass. How did that get empty so fast?

The bartender places a new drink beside it.

"You deserve a knighthood. Is there a B&B or hotel nearby?" I say, as I take a sip. I nearly choke. She made this one even stronger than the last.

This girl's got my back.

"We have a couple of rooms upstairs." She pulls a pint for a customer further down the bar. "Nothing fancy, mind, but the pillows aren't lumpy and we throw in a roast dinner."

"Sold." I glance around the pub. It is just on dinner time, and the place is starting to fill up. It's a typical country pub, with a community noticeboard, quiz team draws and sepia-toned photographs of horses on the walls, and paper coasters advertising a locally-brewed cider. It's a far cry from the glitzy cocktail bars I used to go to with Claire, where we'd yell gossip to each other over pounding music and try to get Claire laid.

By contrast, all the alcohol I've consumed in the last three months has been done in my empty flat while lying on my IKEA rug and raging along with the angry music pounding out of my speakers until my downstairs neighbour bangs on the ceiling.

And now I can't even do that.

Something about this pub makes me let out my breath. People here aren't in such a rush. They greet each other as they walk in the door. There's a group of women my age crowded around a table in the corner, cackling like a coven of witches. Everyone knows everyone. There's a whole community here – people who'll look after you when something shitty happens. I wish I had that. I *thought* I had that, until Claire and Patrick—

My wandering gaze grinds to a halt as I clock the man at the end of the bar.

Holy Aragorn, heir of Isildur. My breath stills in my throat.

I can't explain the sensation that washes over me as I drink him in. I came to Argleton to get lost from my shitty life, but as I watch him, I wish more than anything that I could be found.

For one thing, he looks about as pleased with life as I do. His broad shoulders slump over a glass of red wine. Eyes the colour of anthracite, flecked with ripples of silver, study the contents of the glass as though they contain the secrets of the universe. He wears an exquisitely tailored jacket that's about two centuries out of fashion.

Period clothing in a country pub is a *vibe.*

And that vibe is *sexy AF.*

I'm aware that I'm staring, my jaw wide open like I'm a Venus flytrap with a ravenous hunger. I quickly turn back to my drink just in time to see an unremarkable man with a skeevy smile slide onto the stool next to me.

"Can I buy you another drink, love?" The man's arm brushes against mine, too close for a stranger.

Instantly, I become a cat protecting my personal territorial bubble – back rigid, hair raised, ready to scratch out some eyeballs if required.

"I'm meeting a friend," I say quickly, my stock-standard response for when creepy guys try to hit on me in bars.

"When your friend gets here, she can sit on my knee." He leans in close. I cringe away from the beer-and-mouldy-cheese scent of his breath. "Or *you* can sit on my knee, if you like."

"I'm fine, thanks." I turn away from him.

"My name's Danny. What's yours, love?" Danny leans in even closer. I jerk away as his stubble brushes my cheek. "I want to know what name I'll be screaming later."

"I'm not interested, thanks."

"I heard you tell our lovely barkeep Lilac that you're going to be staying above the pub tonight. Lucky for you, I'll be down the hall. I could sneak over later. You can be my Republic of Ireland, since lookin' at you my penis is Dublin." He leers at me with a smile that I suspect is supposed to be charming. "I want you to taste my lucky charms."

"Leave me alone." I try to scoot out of the other side of the seat, but he grabs my thigh.

I freeze.

"You're an uptight bitch, aren't you? Think you're too good for someone like me?" Danny's fingers dig into my flesh. He latches onto my shoulder with his other hand, trying to force me to turn towards him. My heart hammers in my chest. I shrink away from his leering face, his cheeks flush with liquor. Every self-defence lesson I've ever had flies straight out of my head—

"Excuse me," a deep voice behind me says. "My darling, I'm sorry I'm late. Is this man bothering you?"

Danny's hand drops from my shoulder.

I whirl around. My surprise catches in my throat.

The voice belongs to the shadowy stranger at the end of the bar. Only, he's no longer draped in shadow but standing right beside me, his stance rigid, protective. He places a hand on the small of my back, and, unlike Danny's unwanted grope, the touch of his fingers lights a fuse in my stomach.

His eyes lock with mine, his full lips quirking up on one side with an unasked question.

Understanding dawns. *Hot sulky Aragorn is saving my arse.*

"Hello, um, *darling*," I manage to choke out, pretending that there is a universe where someone as beautiful as this man could possibly be dating me. "I didn't see you there. I tried to save this seat for you, but—"

My rescuer fixes his anthracite eyes on Danny. Beneath the low lighting of the bar, the flecks of silver at the edges of his irises appear to glow.

"Hey mate, I don't want any trouble." Danny raises his hands in mock surrender. "I was just chatting with your girl."

"It didn't look like you were chatting. It looked as if you were touching her when she specifically told you that she wasn't interested."

How does he know that? He was sitting too far away and the pub was too noisy for my voice to carry.

But I'm not about to question my knight in period clothing, not with his fingers rubbing a reassuring circle on the small of my back that makes my skin feel like I'm being invaded by an army of fire ants, but in a *good* way.

"She never said she wasn't interested—" Danny's eyes narrow. "Hey, I know you. You're that recluse who lives in the big house outside of the village—"

I've stopped listening to Danny because Aragorn is peering intently at my face. His hand grazes my cheek, making my skin tingle. He seems to be steeling himself for something.

He tips my head back and kisses me.

Woah.

What is happening right now?

His lips are cool, probably because he's come in from the freezing weather outside. But the way he holds me with casual possession makes my whole body burn. For a single heartbeat, the kiss is chaste. But then he pushes against me gently, then a little harder, to force my lips apart with his tongue.

I open for him, and his tongue loosens something inside me that's been tied up in knots for too long. My heart hammers against my chest and I'm worried that I'm doing everything wrong, that I've forgotten how to kiss.

Surly Aragorn is a method actor, fully committing himself to the role of my devoted boyfriend. His hand cups my cheek as he tips my head back to deepen the stroke of his tongue. He tastes of winter spices – cardamon and ginger – and something else. Something delicious.

It's the kind of kiss that Taylor Swift would write a hit song about.

I'm dimly aware of Danny shouting some more and stomping out the door. The rest of the pub has hushed to watch the scene, but I don't want to think about them because that will mean the kiss will be over. This man will go back to being a stranger and I'll go back to being boring Winnie Preston who never does anything spontaneous or wild.

But I feel wild now – wild and untethered. I reach up and run my hand through his dark curls, letting the silky threads fall through my fingers. He tugs at my lip with teeth that are a little sharp, and a throaty moan erupts from my throat.

Did I just make that noise?

Yes. Yes, I did.

And I do it again as his lips lay a trail across my jaw, along my neck. He pauses, scraping his sharp teeth over my skin. I feel his body tremble, as though he's on the edge of control. And I find myself melting against him, begging him for something I don't understand …

He draws back, his features tight. "He will not bother you again," he says, his voice formal, as if he wasn't still kneading the skin of my back with his fingers.

My skin burns with embarrassment. He's just being nice, and I'm ready to climb him like the property ladder.

"Thank you so much." I wave to Lilac. I need another G&T to burn off the mortification of this moment. She hurries over and I turn back to my mysterious rescuer. "Can I buy you a—"

But he's gone.

Vanished into thin air.

I glance towards the door, but I can't see him. He's not moving between the empty outdoor tables or splashing across the village green.

How did he manage to sneak off so stealthily?

I shuffle into the corner and pat the stool where he'd been sitting before he came over to rescue me. His wine glass has disappeared. The stool is ice cold, as if no one had sat there for some time.

"Did you see where that man went?" I ask Lilac as I settle into the vacated seat. She sets down a basket of wedges loaded with cheese, bacon and a generous dollop of sour cream.

"What man?"

"The one who saved me from Danny? He had a glass of red wine. He was standing right there, and then … poof." I wave my arms around to indicate the empty space. "He's gone, like magic."

Lilac slides a new drink across the bar to me. "If I were you, I'd forget that you ever met him. He's more trouble than ten Danny O'Hares, you mark my words. Now, how about I get you that roast dinner to go with your cheese wedges?"

2

The Killer

Danny O'Hare leaves the pub in a hurry, the collar of his coat pulled up over his head in a vain attempt to protect his mop of ginger curls from the downpour. Danny loves to fuss over his hair. He thinks it's his best feature.

I disagree. His best feature is the sweet nectar that flows in his veins.

I crouch down low behind the bins, trying to ignore the smell of stale beer and rotting fish and chips that assaults my olfactory sense. My thighs burn from crouching, but I know I need to time this perfectly. I need to take him by surprise and get him quickly away from the street. I don't want him discovered until later, when I'm far away from this spot.

As I predicted, Danny turns down the alley towards me on his way to his favourite spot for a smoke. I've hurried out of the pub to get to my hiding spot ahead of him. Luckily, Lord Valerian distracted the woman with his mouth. Very chivalrous. And effective.

As Danny stomps past the bins, singing a reel under his breath, I reach out and grab his ankle. My fingers close around his damp sock. His body jerks and he goes down, crying out as his knees crack against the cobbles and dank water soaks through his jeans.

I step out from my hiding place and kick him in the ribs. "Roll over," I command him, placing the weight of centuries behind every word.

He groans as he rolls onto his back, his eyes widening.

"*You*," he hisses. "Why—"

His words cut off as I lean over him, my hand circling his throat. It takes nothing for me to squeeze so tight that his air cuts off. "You're a naughty boy, aren't you, Danny? You should have learned by now not to mess with women."

His throat pulses beneath my fingers, the blood rushing through his veins. This close, the salty scent fills my nostrils. I lean in closer and take a deep sniff, savouring the palate.

Then I bite down, and feast.

3

Alaric

Gideon: Allie, you'll never guess who's called me this evening. Your mother. That's right, Lady Callista of the Blood Valerian, darling of the Nightshade Court herself, demanding that I set aside my work on Sanctus to plan an elaborate ball at your place in six weeks' time. A BALL, Allie? Have you got high off your paint fumes? What possessed you to agree to this madness?

"DID YOU HAVE A PLEASANT EVENING, MY LORD?" REGINALD ASKS as I slide into the car seat behind him.

"It was positively wretched," I snap as I brace myself for Reginald's erratic driving. My phone beeps in my pocket. Gideon again, no doubt. He's the only other person who messages me, and I wish he wouldn't. "You should have a word to Lilac about her vintage. Her blood tastes as if it's watered-down with badger piss."

"Of course, my lord." If Reginald is surprised by my crass language, he doesn't show it. This is wise, since the torment of my weekly visit to the village pub is entirely *his* fault.

I lean back against the seat as the vehicle speeds out of the village, taking deep inhales of the cold, musky air of the car. I cannot dislodge the taste that lingers on my tongue.

Strawberries and sunlight. The taste of *her.*

My stomach blooms with warmth from all the blood I've consumed this evening. Or perhaps it's from the memory of that delicious little moan.

I noticed her the moment she walked into the pub. At first, it was her scent that captured me, like nothing I've ever smelt before (which, in five hundred years, is quite a statement), but then it was the way she slumped over her drink, her damp hair plastered to her face.

She looked exactly how I've felt many times in my life, as though existing in the world had become a burden and the glass of alcohol in front of her was the only thing stopping her from throwing herself into a fairy circle and yelling, *Take me away now!*

When I saw that man harassing her, something stirred inside me, something of the old Alaric who stained the dirt red with the blood of his enemies, who wants to do good things but doesn't know what good is anymore.

I meant only to frighten away the rat, but when I pulled her close and that scent rose from her skin, the monster in me took over.

It's been so long since I've felt the warmth of a body pressed to my skin.

I touch the sharp tip of my fang, shuddering with pleasure at the memory of scraping it along her soft skin, horrified at how close I came to piercing her—

By some sorcery, that scent still clings to me. My skin throbs with the heat of her living flesh. My ears ring with the delightful sound of her voice.

I am sick. All this exposure to humans is turning me mad.

"I saw you speaking to a lovely woman at the bar before I left to bring the car around," Reginald calls over the rushing wind. He likes to drive with the windows down because he is a masochist. That's probably also why he still works for me.

I don't answer him.

"That's good, my lord! Six weeks ago you couldn't walk into the pub without hunger overcoming you. Remember that fellow in the men's toilets on the first night? We're lucky he was too drunk to recall why his neck was bleeding. Now you're talking to humans like you're one of them."

"I don't want to be one of them," I grumble. "They're annoying."

Not her.

She's … enchanting.

And that's all the more reason for me to return to my castle and never speak to another human again. But it seems I can't host this gods-forsaken ball without one.

"You don't think *I'm* annoying, my lord."

"My opinion of you has lessened since you decided to put me through this ordeal."

"If there were vampires who did this kind of work, I'd have hired one." Reginald yanks on the wheel, sending me sliding over the bench seat. "The organiser arrives tomorrow, and I think you're ready. I'm sure you'll be able to resist one human. I've made up their room in the tower, so you shouldn't smell them during your slumber, and I'll be ever at your side if you need me."

Yes, the organiser. Because Reginald is determined to test my immortal patience, he decided that preparing for my mother's visit was beyond even his capabilities, and he hired a human to help us tidy my things and arrange the castle while Gideon – my only friend and the darling of the local vampire community – plans the actual event. Reginald says it will look good to our guests of honour if I'm seen interacting with a human.

I don't care what my guests think. I don't want a human in my castle. I don't want to take these trips into the village to "train" myself not to devour their stupid faces.

And most of all, I don't want a ballroom filled with snooty vampires quaffing my finest blood and acting like they're so fancy that their coffins don't rot.

But what I want is of no concern when Callista Valerian is involved.

As long as the organiser doesn't smell like that woman at the pub, I will endure their presence. And the sooner they leave my castle and my mother hosts her ridiculous ball, the sooner things can go back to the way they've been for five hundred years – quiet and perfect.

4

Winnie

Mum: Winifred, I still haven't heard from you! You must be very busy with that job of yours. I left those sundresses in the hall to give to you next time you visit, along with a beautiful wooden rocking horse. I saw it in the charity shop window and I think it's just perfect for when you have kids. You will be having kids, won't you? You only have so many years before your eggs are no longer viable. If you had the sundresses with you, you might be pregnant already.

I LIE ON THE BED IN MY CREAKY PUB ROOM (LILAC LIED – THE pillows have more lumps than an elephant with chickenpox), staring at the crooked ceiling beams, contemplating the mess that is my life and wondering if the hot guy from the bar ever really existed, until sunlight streams through the flimsy net curtains.

Every time I remember that needy, wretched sound I made, my face flares with shame. I thought that when I moved out of Mum's house and got my life together, I'd never feel shame like this again. But ever since Patrick left me, it's been living beneath my skin, flaring up whenever I dare to believe that I'm worthy of good things.

Of *course* a guy like that wouldn't be interested in me. Of *course* he was just being kind. Of *course* I moaned like a pornstar in a pub full of people. No wonder he ran off into the night.

I'm a *mess.*

You have to get your shit together, Winnie. You're meeting the new client today, and they mustn't know you're an abject failure at life.

When I hear staff wandering around downstairs, I drag my arse out of bed and into the shower. I make liberal use of the surprisingly-fancy bottles of shampoo and body lotion from a local company called Zen and Tonic, and wrap myself in fluffy towels like an Egyptian mummy. Today is a new day, and I'm a new Winnie. I'm out of London, and I'm off to meet a new client who will think I'm absolutely wonderful, and no one will remember me as the girl who caused a scene in the pub.

I throw open my suitcase, admiring the neat rows of packing cubes, each one containing the components of a different colour-coordinated outfit. Yesterday's carefully chosen "impress the new client" outfit is hanging dripping wet from the curtain rail, but lucky for me, I'm Winnie Preston and I'm always prepared for any eventuality.

I pull out my backup "impress the new client" outfit – a pair of Max&Co purple tailored trousers and matching jacket, a pale grey blouse, and a scarf covered in bright squares from a Mondrian exhibit Patrick took me to at the Tate Modern. I swipe on some makeup, fluff my blonde hair, and smile at myself in the mirror.

This is why Faye wants you to do the jobs. Because you have a way with the clients. The Winnie Wins System will triumph once again.

I blow myself a kiss and head downstairs. Lilac is nowhere to be seen, but an older lady named Emma is setting tables in the restaurant and making coffee for the handful of customers demolishing their full English breakfasts. She offers to store my suitcase for the day, and since I'm not due to be collected from the station until this evening, I gratefully accept.

After the barrel of alcohol I consumed last night to obliterate my shame, the thought of a plate of greasy sausage and baked beans makes me feel as though life is still worth living, so I scarf down a big breakfast before setting out to explore the village.

Yesterday's rain has eased back to grey skies and on-again, off-again drizzle. I wander around the shops that circle the village green and discover that Zen and Tonic has a whole store filled with cute soaps and beauty elixirs, as well as a schedule of weekly yoga classes. I buy a mountain of delicious-smelling things with spurious health claims from a fresh-faced blonde named Beth who forces me to drink a free sample of dirt-flavoured tea while giving me a sixteen-minute lecture about the detoxifying powers of dandelions.

Buoyed by my toxin-clearing purchases, I decide to test the dandelion tea's efficacy with a fresh date scone slathered in butter, jam and clotted cream from a bakery called Glazed and Confused on the corner. I wander around the flower-lined churchyard, sucking in lungfuls of fresh, scented, un-smoggy air.

I may have made a silly un-Winnie-like mistake coming to Argleton a day early, but honestly, I'm not sad about it. Every street I walked down in my London neighbourhood reminded me of Patrick or Claire, and Mum's been driving me crazy, trying to convince me to move back in after I lost the flat. This job is exactly what I needed.

Besides, it's hardly going to take six weeks. Our clients always think their mess is worse than it actually is. My last London job was just three days standing in a rich housewife's state-of-the-art scullery, helping her put labels on bamboo containers of quinoa and activated charcoal. When you're rich enough to hire a professional organiser, you don't have the kind of life that gets messy. But this client paid a huge bonus in advance, and, as Faye pointed out, I have nowhere else to go.

Six weeks or six days, I don't care. I'm away from London, from my mother and her piles of stuff, from the memories of Patrick and Claire, from my beautiful flat that's being bulldozed to make way for an ASDA, from all of it …

I may be a hot mess, but at least I'm a *fun* hot mess, like a runaway train filled with glitter and Jammie Dodgers.

I wander down a narrow lane beside the butchery and come across a strange and beautiful building. A three-story architectural sampler tin with Medieval, Tudor, Victorian and art nouveau details, little dormer windows in the attic, and a hexagonal turret on one corner. Fairy lights flicker from the depths. A window display beside the narrow front door shows an arrangement of spell books and witchy fiction arranged around a bubbling cauldron.

The sign above the door reads "Nevermore Bookshop".

I stop in my tracks. As a kid, I used to love bookshops – I adored the neat rows of books organised by subject and genre and author names, each one a window into a new, different world. I loved the smell of all that paper – heavy with history and possibility.

But my mother loves bookshops, too, especially the charity ones where you can buy a box of old paperbacks for three quid. She loves books about murder and books about romance and books that are broken and need love and books that are new and smell like a specific memory from her childhood and books that remind her of me and things I liked, and especially books that my father would have loved if he was still here. She loves these books so much that they all have to come and live with us.

After she stacked our downstairs hallway and bathroom so high with books that the small amount of floor space, piled with damp paper, squelched between my toes like wet sand, we had to abandon the rooms altogether. And after the angry letters from neighbours in our mailbox, I simply cannot love books anymore. I haven't purchased or read a paper book since I left my Mum's house at eighteen. If people give them to me as gifts, I buy them on my Kindle and donate the hard copy. If Claire or Patrick ever wanted to visit a bookshop, I'd fake a stomach ache and wait outside.

But something about Nevermore Bookshop calls to me. *What's the harm in one little look?*

I push open the door and step inside.

I find myself in a long, narrow hallway, made even narrower by the towering shelves of books on each side and the piles strewn across the floor. I breathe through the rising panic.

For a moment, just a *moment*, I am back in my mother's house, drowning in stuff.

But then, I see the traces of organisation – shelves divided into genres and sections, signs explaining to customers where to go. The relief of order in the chaos. This mess is not my shame, and it is part of the bookshop's beauty.

As bookshops go, Nevermore is particularly striking. Strings of fairy lights outline each shelf, and more lamps and lanterns are shoved into every space not occupied by books. Every inch of wall space is filled with strange and wonderful artwork. On the end of one bookshelf, someone has placed a smashed Kindle on a wooden shield, as if it were a hunting trophy.

I think about the gleaming Kindle in my bag, the virtual bookshelf arranged in folders by genre and author surname. I'm not sure I'm welcome in this place.

I hear female voices laughing, and I pass under an archway into a large room stuffed with even more books on shelves and tables. A large desk occupies one corner, practically buried under even *more* books and an ancient till, upon which sits a large black raven who watches me with intelligent, fire-rimmed eyes.

Behind the desk, a brown-haired woman around my age shuffles through a stack of blank card sheets without looking at them, her fingers tracing over little raised dots on the surface. *She's blind.* She chats with two other women on my side of the counter. One is dressed in workout clothes, her waist-length black, wavy hair pulled back into a tight ponytail that accentuates her soft brown skin and huge dark eyes. She beams at her friends with the softest smile I've ever seen. The other – a shorter white woman with a penchant for purple velvet and the kind of curves that sinks ships – bunches up a wild tangle of dark red curls and shoves them through a scrunchie before clasping her hand on the blind girl's shoulder and shaking her friend with excitement.

"Mina, you have a customer. Hey there!" The redhead waves to me, her voice bubbling with enthusiasm in a way that reminds me uncomfortably of Claire.

"Oh, hello!" the brown-haired woman named Mina calls out to the room. "New customer, announce yourself! Get me away from these two witches and their meddlesome ways." The other two giggle. "Can I help you?"

"I'm just browsing, thanks."

Their faces fall a little, but they go back to their conversation. I study the rows of books on the poetry shelves, now feeling like I'm intruding on their private gossip session.

"—all I'm asking is that we dig up some dirt on him," the black-haired woman is saying. "Just one *teeny tiny little* sex scandal to topple him from his throne. Maybe you could give him a little hex, Isis? Nothing too major, just make him grow a wart on his nose or only speak in a Basil Brush voice. That man is ruining my life!"

"Augustin Durant is hardly ruining your life, Komal, just because he opposes your parking solution for the Midsummer Festival—"

"The fair is our main tourism event for the year. If we don't have parking, how does he expect people to attend? Are they going to beam down from their starships? And this is the *fifteenth* proposal of mine he's opposed—"

"That's probably because you sit on every committee in town. Heathcliff has forbidden me from sticking my nose into any more village mysteries," says Mina. "But I *do* enjoy a good hex . . ."

Okay, scratch that. I'm *definitely* eavesdropping. But it's because their conversation is so damn fascinating.

"I have just the spell to sort him out." The red-haired one rubs her hands together with glee. "I've been working on this curse that will give him an itch between the shoulder blades that he can never quite reach."

Spells? Hexes?

"Or perhaps he can always step on a wet spot after he puts on fresh socks?" Mina shudders. "I *hate* when that happens."

I shudder too. I *detest* stepping in a wet patch in fresh socks. It reminds me too much of my mother's house.

"If Dora would get involved, I bet we could dig up a sex scandal in ten seconds flat. I know she's my sister and I should respect her decision, but I've wanted that kind of power ever since I knew what it was, and she doesn't even care," the redhead sulks, playing with the lace on her purple velvet dress. "She thinks it's a *curse*."

"Personally, I think that it would be a curse to hear what's going on inside people's silly heads," Komal laughs. "People are dull enough when they speak with their mouths. Imagine having to endure their thoughts. I'd rather poke out my eye with a rusty spoon."

"She doesn't read minds, Komal. Have you even been listening? She has visions of the future. And all I can do is mix a few measly herbs together and bake a decent cheese fondue."

"Your teas *are* special," Mina reassures her friend. "And your cheese fondue is literal *magic*—"

I wish I had friends who made cheese fondue …

Six weeks. I'm only going to be here for six weeks, and then I'll never see these strange ladies again. Why would I—

I clear my throat.

The three girls whip their heads back toward me. My heart thunders in my chest. "Hi again, sorry for interrupting. I'm new to the village. My name is Winnie. I'm going to be working up at Black Crag Castle. I wondered if you could help me find something to read?"

The blind girl beams. "Sure, Winnie. I'm Mina Wilde, purveyor of books. These are my friends, Komal and Isis." The two girls wave. "What do you like to read?"

Komal beams at me and I feel as though I've been kicked by a unicorn. And Isis sounds like the name of a village medicine woman, which is exactly what she looks like, right down to her wide emerald eyes and the clanking crystal necklaces hanging around her neck.

"True crime, psychological thrillers, anything with a bit of murder," I say. "And … um … romance."

I admit it. I'm a bit of a hopeless romantic. I used to devour one or two romance novels a week – give me all the burly mountain men, clever professors with kinky proclivities, spoiled billionaires, wild motorcycle gangs or sexy vampires, as long as the hero is broody, grumpy and possessive, with a schlong that has to be checked as oversized baggage on aeroplanes, I'm in.

I've been in a reading slump ever since the whole Patrick/Claire thing, but maybe this kooky bookshop can change that. And I can return the paperbacks after I've read them for the secondhand section.

"We love romance novels, too. Especially the smutty kind." Mina gestures to the shelf behind her desk. "You'll find all the new releases here, and another shelf of favourites in the room opposite. We even have a book club that meets here at the bookshop once a week—"

"It's not *just* a book club," Isis pipes up. "It's the Nevermore Murder Club and Smutty Book Coven."

"The … what?"

Komal laughs. "No one could agree on whether we were meeting to read smutty books, do a bit of amateur sleuthing, or investigate strange supernatural goings-on in Argleton. So we decided to be all three."

"We just say the Nevermore Coven for short," Isis adds.

Nothing they're saying makes sense to me. "What do you mean by strange goings-on?"

"You're working at Black Crag Castle?" Komal tightens her ponytail.

"I am."

The three women nod sagely.

"You'll find out soon enough." Isis claps her hands together, jangling the crystal bracelets around her wrists. "Black Crag Castle and its owner, the mysterious Lord Valerian, are at the centre of some of the strange goings-on in Argleton."

I want to ask more, but the shop bell tinkles as a busload of tourists crowd through the door, exclaiming over the perfectly quaint interior. The redhead looks at her phone. "I'd better go. Spell The Tea is probably swamped already, too. Dora will kill me if she has to help them pick out healing crystals on her own. See you ladies on Wednesday!"

She winks at me as she hurries past, disappearing in a cloud of patchouli.

"And I'd better get to yoga class. Beth will be pissed if the only Indian girl is late. It makes her look like she's culturally appropriating.

I'll see you on Wednesday, Mina. A pleasure to meet you, Winnie." Komal bounces off, her gym bag slapping her thigh.

"See you both on Wednesday!" Mina calls after them as she swipes books off her desk and shoos the raven off her till. "We host the Nevermore Murder Club and Smutty Book Coven meeting every Wednesday night here in the shop, 7 pm till late. It's mostly local girls about our age. Would you like to join us?"

I can't help but grin back. I might only be here for six weeks, but it would be nice to make some new friends. "I'd love to."

"Great. Then I'd better help you pick out some smutty books! We can't send you to Black Crag Castle without a lifeline. Working for Lord Valerian will be … interesting."

Worry stabs at my stomach. "How so?"

"He's a bit of a recluse, hardly ever leaves his castle. I've met him once, and he's …" Mina shrugs. "It's hard to explain. You'll just have to wait and meet him yourself."

I rush across the village to make it to the train station by 6 pm – finally the date and time I'm actually supposed to be there – weighed down by my Zen and Tonic purchases and seven new books Mina convinced me I absolutely *must* read. When I dash into the pub to pick up my suitcase, I'm surprised to find it empty, although there are a couple of police cars and a group of people milling around outside. I don't have time to stop and see what's going on.

By the time I make it onto the platform and pretend that I've just stepped off the train, a willowy man in a natty suit is already waiting for me, holding an ornately handwritten sign that reads MS WINIFRED PRESTON.

"Hi, that's me." I hold out my hand to him. "Most people call me Winnie. And you must be Reginald—"

He sweeps his arm across his body into a deep bow. "A pleasure to meet you, Ms Preston. I am Reginald, Lord Valerian's personal secretary."

"Do you have a last name, Reginald?"

"Just Reginald, Ms Preston. Please allow me to take your bags. I shall escort you to the car."

Before I can protest, Reginald whisks my bag from me and scurries away towards the parking lot. Passengers on the platform leap to get out of his way.

I follow him, admiring the cut of his old-fashioned uniform. I've had several rich clients in London who had me deal directly with their assistants, but not one asked their staff to wear a coat and *tails.*

And not a one has ever picked me up for a job in an *antique.*

I gape at the vehicle as Reginald grunts and twists my bag to make it fit into the tiny trunk.

The car isn't just vintage, it's *ancient.* Its probably the same vehicle King Tut used to drive around the desert to pick up nubile young concubines. Reginald has to jiggle the door to get it to open for me. He offers me his arm as I climb up onto the footplate and settle myself onto the bench seat.

There are no seatbelts.

The roof is made of canvas.

Where are the *windows*?

How is this even legal?

I'm reaching for my phone to call Faye and tell her I'm pulling out of this job when the car sputters to life. Reginald aims the long nose in the vague direction of the parking lot exit and hits the gas.

And by hitting the gas, I mean, Reginald goes balls out *pedal to the metal.* The car jerks forward with a roar like a pissed-off cougar. The radio comes on, blasting loud hip-hop. Reginald sings along, slapping the steering wheel. I grab the door and hold on for dear life as we hurtle through the village.

The group gathered around the pub has grown larger. The tourists I saw at Mina's bookshop wave at us from the tearoom as we puff around the village green. Reginald tips his hat to them and blasts the car's foghorn while I grip the edge of the seat. Their cameras flash in my eyes.

Somehow, Reginald picks up speed as we hit the country lanes. Branches from the towering hedgerows reach in the open windows, their spindly fingers tickling my arms as we fly past. My carefully chosen "impress the new client" outfit is now covered in leaves. I shuffle to the centre of the bench seat, wrap my arms through the back of the seats in front of me, and pray to any god who will listen that I won't die.

As we rocket along, Reginald keeps up a steady stream of commentary over his loud music about the homes and farms we pass and the people who live there. I barely hear two words of it. I'm becoming increasingly uneasy about the distance we've travelled from the village. I was told when I took on this job that I wouldn't need a vehicle, but how am I supposed to get back to my accommodation in the village in the evenings?

Reginald yanks the wheel hard around. I scream as the car goes up on two wheels before bouncing back onto the road. We rocket under a pair of crumbling stone pillars, through an open wrought-iron gate, and past a wisteria-choked gatehouse that Reginald tells me is his "bothy". As we round a sharp corner of the winding drive, I gasp as it comes into view.

Black Crag Castle.

I expected a stately home – all Regency finery and rambling white roses. But Black Crag is pure medieval *grimness.*

This is a castle that has *seen some shit.*

It stands rigid upon a jagged rocky outcrop overlooking the valley, on all sides a sheer drop into the woods below. I count no less than eight turrets piercing the violet sky with blackened oriels, like the fangs of a mythological beast trying to devour the dusk. One whole wing has crumbled down the cliff – the rooms open to the elements, rotting carpets still clinging to broken beams.

"It's made from a local volcanic stone quarried further up the valley," Reginald yells. "The minerals in the stone give the castle that unique black colour."

"Lovely," I manage to choke out.

Reginald steers the car onto a walled bridge that leads across to the stone outcrop. The bridge is only wide enough for a single vehicle, so when I glance out the window I look down, down, down into the nothingness of the valley floor. Water rushes somewhere far below, and a cold breeze whips up, stinging my cheeks. I notice a narrow stone staircase snaking around the edge of the cliff, towards the source of the water. I hold my breath until we reach the other side and pass beneath the portcullis.

Reginald parks in a small inner courtyard and leaps from the car, seemingly unaffected by the fact that we're about to fall to our deaths from this crumbling heap of blackened stone. He holds my door open for me, and I long to curl up into a ball on the backseat and demand he take me to the train station.

I wanted to get out of London, but this is *not* what I signed up for.

But then I think of Patrick's sad eyes when he told me that he was leaving me for Claire. *We never do anything spontaneous, Win. You've organised all the fun out of our lives. When I'm with Claire, I have the freedom to be myself.*

I think of my old landlord doing his final inspection of my perfect Crouch End flat. *You're very neat, aren't you?*

I think of my mother's texts blowing up my phone, and her neighbours begging me to go back and help. I think about my three boxes of stuff sitting in her living room, being slowly buried by the detritus of her disease.

I think about all the reasons I don't want to go back to London.

I'm curious, too. What kind of toff lives in this medieval villain's lair?

If Dracula visited Black Crag, the infamous vampire would step back in disgust and tell the owner: *Cool it with the gargoyles, dude. No one's* that *goth.*

I slide from the car, seeking purchase for my trembling legs. I square my shoulders and follow Reginald to the front doors. He shoves open one of the imposing wooden slabs and wheels my suitcase inside. "Follow me, Ms Preston."

"Coming." I tear my gaze from the turrets. "I was just admiring the next cover of *Architectural Digest*. Why are you bringing my suitcase in?"

He squints at me oddly. "Black Crag *is* remarkable, but you'll have plenty of time to explore her secrets. I don't want to keep my lord waiting."

As I step inside, I'm greeted by two warring sensations – the sound of Louis Armstrong's gravelly voice blasting at top volume from somewhere deep within the castle, and the scratch of dust getting up my nose.

My client must be an older man – a quirky lord who has allowed his estate to go to rot and now needs a professional organiser to help him get on top of things. I suck in a breath as the familiar sinking sensation washes over me.

Don't be intimidated by the ramparts and gargoyles, Winnie. You've dealt with this type before. The Winnie Wins System can work for anyone (except your mother).

It's never as bad as you fear. You can do this.

It takes my eyes a few moments to adjust to the gloom. The entrance hall is decorated in what I'll now forever refer to as "Medieval Stabby Chic". Several dusty suits of armour glare at me from around the perimeter of the room. Weapons cover the walls and ceiling – swords fanned out like peacock feathers, knives and spiky things arranged like works of art. Everything is covered in dust and cobwebs. The only light comes from candles flickering in dirty sconces.

Two things are out of place – an empty, dust-free plinth and square on the wall where some items have been removed recently, and a small shelf under the grand staircase. It's stuffed with teddy bears of various sizes and states of fluffiness, each one dressed in handmade clothes – a chef, a firefighter, a plague doctor. There are more bears than space to hold them, so several are piled on the floor beneath the shelf, giving the impression of a teddy bear army storming the castle doors in a bid for freedom.

Curious.

Reginald leaves my suitcase at the foot of the stairs. "Lord Valerian would like to meet you before I take you to your lodgings."

From his tone, I get the distinct impression he thinks that once I meet Lord Valerian, I won't want to stay.

I follow Reginald to the left and along a grand corridor. At least, the corridor *would* be grand if it weren't crowded with stacks of newspapers, piles of boxes, lumpy, misshapen candles sticking out of ornate iron candelabras, and display cases jammed full of what look suspiciously like model trains. There are several more square gaps on the walls where paintings once hung.

My breathing grows shallow as a familiar dread twists in my gut. The haphazard stacks of things, the disorder, the smell of dust and decay …

Please, don't let this be what I think it is …

Reginald picks his way through the mess, showing me a path through the detritus. Beneath the piles of stuff, I see the antique furniture and gilt objects I'd expect from such a grand home, all of it hidden and neglected beneath Lord Valerian's junk.

"My lord?" Reginald calls out.

"I'm in the green drawing room," a faint voice calls back.

The music swells. Louis' trumpet soars through the vaulted ceilings.

Reginald leads me down another snaking hallway. Oddly enough, this hallway has electricity. Modern lamps on either side illuminate stacks of oil paintings and more strange gaps where objects and artwork have been moved. I peer into room after ornate room, each one stuffed to the brim with … stuff.

What I've seen so far isn't as bad as Mum's house. At least … not yet, but only because the castle is so *large*. As I inspect the piles, I sense an internal order to the chaos, the same connections between disparate things that my mother can see and I never can.

If Faye had known what waited for me at Black Crag, she'd never have accepted the job.

That's not true, a voice niggles in my head. *Faye doesn't care what you have to do on a job if it means more money for her designer handbags and celebrity brunches.*

But maybe …

... maybe I can save Black Crag.

This is going to be *so* much work, but already the old castle is speaking to me, whispering that beneath all the dust and grime and stuff is *real* treasure. Even though this place looks like a junk store had a drunken hate fuck with a Jackson Pollock painting, it has a personality, a vibe, a *presence*. And I could be the one to bring it to life.

I can't stop my mother from filling her house with rubbish, but this Lord Valerian called *me*. He *wants* my help.

Maybe I can save him.

Despite the dust and the dinginess and the tightness in my chest, I can't *wait* to get started.

I practically skip into a gloomy room after Reginald, who bows deeply at a shadowed figure behind a large table. "My lord, may I present to you, Ms Winifred Preston, from the Clutter Queens."

I step forward, extending my hand at the shadow. "Good evening, Lord Valerian. You can call me Winnie. You have a beautiful home, and I'm here to help you make it shine. I'm so excited to get stuck in and clean up your—"

As the shadowy figure lifts his head from a desk covered in paints and brushes to fix me with a withering glare, my words die on my lips.

It's *him*.

The stranger from last night. The one who saved me from that creep and kissed me as if he needed me to breathe.

He's my new boss.

5

Alaric

REGINALD, I AM GOING TO *DESTROY* YOU.

6

Winnie

Claire: Winnie, I know you're ignoring my messages because you're still angry at me, and you have every right to be. I just wanted to see if there was anything I could do? You mean the world to me and I want to fix things. Just tell me what I can do, please.

NINETY PERCENT OF MY BODY FREEZES AT THE SIGHT OF THOSE anthracite eyes fixed on mine, revealing none of the surprise that I feel.

The other ten percent of my body – my feet – doesn't get the message. They collapse from under me. I stagger forward, trip over a large model locomotive, and go flying.

"Argh!"

I sail through the air, limbs twisting as I try to stop myself from falling on what looks suspiciously like a glass terrarium filled with cacti. But no amount of acrobatic talent I do not possess will save me from my spiky doom, so I close my eyes and brace myself for pain.

But no pain comes.

Instead, something cool and hard slides beneath my arms, lifting me from the ground.

I open one eye.

Lord Valerian holds me beneath my armpits like I am a clumsy child he's rescued from disaster, which isn't that far from the truth. Those dark, fathomless eyes regard me with ire, and the corner of his mouth quirks up in what could be annoyance or amusement.

How did he move so fast?

His desk is on the far side of the enormous drawing room, yet somehow he crossed the distance in less than a blink, and is now holding my entire body weight with no visible signs of strain.

I search for those eyes, a thousand unanswered questions bubbling up inside me. But he's pointedly staring at the wall behind my head.

"Are you quite alright, Ms Preston?" he says in that deep, ragged voice of his, the one that hums through my body as if someone has melted down ten of Louis Armstrong's trumpets and then poured that molten metal into my veins.

"I tripped on a train," I say lamely.

"Quite so. Here, let me—"

"No, I can—"

Lord Valerian sets me down gently. I get my feet beneath me and stand upright, dusting off my clothes and trying to rid my body of the tingling sensation from where he touched me. Like last night at the pub, his touch is surprisingly cool, but I figure that's what happens when you live in a draughty medieval castle.

He's dressed in tight-fitting trousers, knee-high leather boots, and a loose white shirt dotted with paint. His dark curls flop over his eyes, making him look more like a seventeenth-century poet than a rich toff. Where does he get his clothing from? His great-great-great-great-great grandfather's steamer trunk?

I expect him to smell of dust and paint, but his scent is the same as it was at the pub last night – winter spices and haunted groves. The kiss brushes my memory again. I can *taste* him on my tongue. My hand flies to the spot on my neck where he raked his teeth over my flesh, feeling the roughness where he left a small scratch …

"I got the wrong train," I blurt out as a lone butterfly slams against the walls of my stomach. "I came here yesterday by accident, so I stayed the night at the pub and then met Reginald today, but it was a one-in-a-million mistake and in no way reflects poorly on my organisational abilities. I mean, it *does*, obviously, but I swear that I really am quite good at cluttering cleaner. I mean, cleaning clutter—"

"Let us not mention it." Lord Valerian clears his throat, and I know he's talking about more than my awkward fall. "Mrs Winifred Preston, I apologise—"

"It's Ms," I say. "Always Ms."

His eyes whip to me then, and my breath stills.

"*Ms* Preston, I apologise that you've come all this way for work that is so obviously beneath your skills. All I have is a few canvases and art supplies lying around, nothing to be concerned about, but we are hosting a ball at the castle in six weeks, and my valet is convinced that my things will develop sentience and devour our guests."

One thing I've learned from Mum is that people like her are in denial about how bad things are. Their stuff isn't just stuff – it's a precious dragon hoard, and my job is to help them protect it from filthy hobbitses. "This is my job, and I enjoy it. I'm happy to be here. Why don't you explain to me what you'd like to achieve during my visit? I've read the brief from Faye but it was quite vague."

"Very well." He sweeps an arm around, indicating the vast room that I think might've once been called a study, judging by the enormous desk, piles of books, and dusty globe in the corner. All fancy rich people's studies have the same globe. I reckon Elon Musk hands them out for free so people will be his friends. "I live here alone, save for Reginald. Over the years, I have acquired several … distractions. These activities keep my mind active and bring me joy, but recently, Reginald has been watching a programme on the television and is convinced I may have a disease. Now, normally, this idea would be preposterous because I cannot become ill. Reginald believes

I am suffering from a disease of the mind, one called 'hoard'. Is that right, Reginald?"

"Hoarding, sir," Reginald replies. "I think he might be a hoarder, ma'am."

"He found your company on the computer. Your website said you could clean any mess, big or small. Well, I have a mess in my castle, and an even bigger mess in my head, and Reginald believes you may be able to help me."

Deep breaths, Winnie.

That word, *hoarder*, punches me in the gut. People toss it around affectionately to describe their little collections of frog figurines or the messy desk in their office, but nothing about hoarding is funny.

If Lord Valerian *is* a hoarder then … I am going to work even harder. It's going to test the very limits of the Winnie Wins System, but I know I can help him. I *have* to help him.

I plaster a smile on my face and indicate the half-finished locomotive that attacked me. It's almost large enough for a person to sit on.

"I noticed the model trains. And you're painting?"

Lord Valerian sweeps his arm dismissively at his desk. I step over three more model trains and a broken record player, shuffle around another pile of teddy bears, and step up to the antique desk beneath the window where several canvases rest on paint-splattered easels.

I gasp.

The paintings are beautiful.

No, beautiful is not the right word. They're *arresting*.

Lord Valerian has been painting the landscape he sees from the towering, mullioned window on various nights. Tonight's effort is streaked with deep violet, the moon a cold eye glinting off the water in the stream winding below. Others show wind-tossed trees and tempest clouds, or crisp, midnight-blue summer skies and spindly, foreboding trees.

"You're talented, Lord Valerian."

He frowns. "They are hopeless scribbles. I have many years of practice ahead of me before I'll be happy with them."

I study his porcelain features and steady anthracite eyes, trying not to blush as I remember those soft, full lips on mine. He's young, perhaps a few years older than me. He's *too* young to be holed up in this castle trying to become a master painter.

"You said you had other hobbies?" I need to get a full sense of what I'm dealing with. The biggest part of being a professional organiser isn't actually the cleaning up – it's getting to know your client so you can understand how they think, and then you design a system around that. I've learned that the way to get people like him to open up is to get them talking about the things they're passionate about.

Of course, the only thing most of my clients are passionate about is designer shoes.

"Yes!" Lord Valerian's face lights up. It's as though someone has flicked a switch inside him, and he goes from being a grumpy gothic villain to an excited schoolboy. "Come. I will show you."

He holds out a hand to me. The gesture is so oddly intimate, so at odds with his stuffy cadence and ramrod-straight posture. I find myself staring at his lips again.

You're here to help him, Winnie. It doesn't matter that he's the most beautiful man you've ever met and he kisses like the hero of a smutty romance, he's your boss now and you can't think of him like that.

I step around the teddy bears and over the trains and place my hand in his.

His cool fingers envelop mine, squeezing a little in his excitement. He pulls me to the other side of the room and snaps at Reginald to light the candles.

Does this part of the castle not have electricity?

Reginald rushes around, lighting candles in sconces on the walls. He hands Lord Valerian a candelabra, which he sweeps dramatically over a table.

"This is one of my model train sets. I was quite enamoured with trains for a time. Something about the way they connect places, how once there were no trains at all and the next moment, they were the centre of life, commerce and adventure. They interest me."

I gasp again. I know I'm starting to sound like the heroine of a gothic romance with all this gasping in the castle, but I can't help it. On the table stands a perfect scale replica of Argleton village – all the shops I perused around the village green are there, including Zen and Tonic, Glazed and Confused, and the Nevermore Bookshop. The pub even has little meat pies and baskets of chips sitting on the outdoor tables. A model of the London train I arrived on waits in the station as a line of people board, and a goods train sits on the tracks outside the village, pulling several tanker wagons and containers. There is even a replica of Black Crag Castle overlooking the wooded valley.

Lord Valerian barely gives me a chance to take in the details before he drags me across the hall into the next adjoining room. "Here is my pottery studio."

Another grand drawing room has been haphazardly filled with potters' wheels, bags of clay and pigments, racks of tools, and an entire wall stacked nearly to the vaulted ceiling with shelves and racks of pots, mugs and vases in various stages of finishing. Lord Valerian flicks on the lights – this room must be one of the few with electricity – and the bright-coloured glazes pop before my eyes, sucking me into a delirious world of colour.

I gaze around in awe. "There's a *kiln* under the window. Isn't that a fire hazard?"

"Quite possibly. Come, come." He drags me around several bolts of fabric and flings open the doors to a magnificent ballroom. "Here is where I keep my loom."

His *loom*?

Sure enough, all the fancy antique furniture had been pushed to the side of the room to make way for an enormous contraption that fills the entire marble floor of the ballroom. Warp threads stretch between two enormous rollers, while the floor is littered with discarded wooden shuttles and threads of wool, silk and glittering gold. A half-finished tapestry sits in the machine – a herd of wild horses dances across a brightly-coloured landscape filled with wildflowers, their bridles stitched with gold thread, as waves in shades of jewel and azure roll beneath their hooves.

"You … you made this?" I reach out to run my hand over the threads, unable to believe something so beautiful is real.

"It needs so much work." He nods disdainfully at several rolled tapestries resting against the wall. "I intended to finish it so I might master the Flemish technique, but instead, I became enamoured with painting, so it waits here for my enthusiasm to return. However, according to *some*, one cannot host a ball with a loom in the middle of one's ballroom, so it has to go."

How does one man have the time for all this? From the intensity with which Lord Valerian speaks of his "distractions", I get the sense that they aren't simply hobbies, but passions that consume his every waking thought.

"Lord Valerian—"

"Alaric, please." He nods formally, which gives me no confidence that I should stop calling him Lord Valerian.

"Forgive me, but these … distractions of yours … I think you're being quite hard on yourself. You're not a hoarder." The word sticks in my throat. "At least, not yet. You're an artist. You have a brilliant creative mind, and you have the time and space to indulge your creative pursuits. You are not hurting anyone, and the castle, if a little cluttered, isn't dangerous to you or others. Why do you wish to wipe all of this away when it makes you happy? You could hire another venue for the ball—"

"I'd happily host the tedious affair at the bottom of the river," he snaps. "But my mother insists it must be at my castle. It will be the first time she's visited me here."

His voice cracks a little.

Ah, a difficult mother.

I can relate.

The vice that's gripped my chest ever since he said the "h" word loosens, and a slow smile creeps over my lips. "You called the right woman. I'll help you get this place in order before your mother's visit, and I can show you my Winnie Wins System to help you manage your hobbies after I'm gone so things don't get quite this bad in the future. When does she arrive?"

"Six weeks from today, the evening before the ball."

I wince.

Lord Valerian nudges one of the tapestries with his boot. It slips against its friends and the entire pile topples over and rolls across the marble floor. Lord Valerian looks back at me and smiles coldly.

"You are wearing an expression that suggests you do not believe you can achieve this task."

I peer around at the rolled tapestries, the trays of lopsided ceramic pots, the bloody *loom*. "I can do it. But I'm going to need your help."

"I have work to do."

You're a bloody peer. You've never worked a day in your life.

I indicate the mess. "*This* is your work. You can put down your paintbrush for a few hours each day and help me out."

He narrows his eyes at me. "As you wish."

Why does the way he says that, in that gravelled voice of his, make my knees shake?

I beam at him. "Let's do this."

His shoulders relax a little. Do I imagine the tug at the corner of his mouth is a half-smile trying to assert itself? "We may begin immediately, if you are not too tired. I keep nocturnal hours, so I will be awake for some time yet. If you require any supplies, simply provide Reginald with a list and he will procure them for you. Reginald," he calls out. "Show Ms Preston to her rooms."

"Hold on, my rooms are *here*?"

"Why, yes. You'll be staying in the castle with us. It will save you making the trip to and from the village every day. Is this agreeable to you?"

I'll be living in the castle?

When Faye said the job included accommodation, I assumed she meant I'd have a room like the one above the pub.

It's highly inappropriate for me to stay in my client's home, but I don't exactly have anywhere else to live for the next six weeks, and when faced with Lord Valerian's half-formed smile and fathomless eyes, I find myself unable to protest.

"No. Yes, I mean, that's fine." I order my racing heart to sort her shit out. "Show me to my rooms."

Reginald appears silently in the doorway, carrying another candelabra. "This way, Ms Preston. I've already taken your bags up to the tower."

I follow Reginald back down the winding corridor to the Stabby Chic entrance hall. We ascend the staircase. As we climb, the castle changes around me.

We pass through a library that leaves me breathless. Carved mahogany shelves reach to the high ceiling, each one packed haphazardly with books. More books sit in tall, dusty stacks on the floor, and in the centre of the room beneath a glittering crystal chandelier that has been electrified, sits a circle of mismatched armchairs.

This library can't be frequented by Lord Valerian. Between becoming a potter, mastering tapestry, model trains, becoming an accomplished painter, and – I now suspect – a maker of adorable teddy bears, he doesn't have the time to read all these books. These must belong to an ancestor – one who also doesn't believe in organising.

Odd that there are no ancestors on the walls. Some hunting scenes and landscapes remain, but everywhere I look, portraits and statues have been removed. In my experience, the peerage love being surrounded by monuments to their bloodline, but Lord Valerian clearly doesn't want to be reminded of his.

My fingers itch to start pulling books off the shelves and alphabetising them. I love touching other people's books because, at the end of the day, I don't have to go home with them. I glance at the huge window at one end of the library, which holds a view down the valley only partially obscured by towers of books, and I imagine curling up on a sofa in that exact spot with one of the books from Nevermore Bookshop and a glass of wine …

I'll be too busy scrubbing and sorting to have a moment to enjoy this place. But at least Lord Valerian will have a beautiful ballroom by the time I'm done.

Reginald hurries me through the library and several more dusty reception rooms that don't appear to have been touched for some time.

"This way, Ms Preston. Mind your step."

He starts to climb a narrow, winding stone staircase into one of the towers. The stairs are uneven, the edges worn away by centuries of use. I keep a hand on the inner wall and work my glutes harder than a hot yoga session to keep up with Reginald.

Up and up we climb, until my head spins. There are no windows in the staircase, only thin arrow slits that let in slivers of pale moonlight. The only other light is Reginald's flickering candelabra.

What have I signed up for?

Finally, we reach the narrow wooden landing. Reginald throws open a door. "I hope these are sufficient accommodations. Lord Valerian and I worked hard to prepare them. He used to store his stamp collection in here, but we've moved those into the corridor downstairs. We had electricity run up here, although you'll need the candelabra for the staircase. Please, let me know if you need anything at all."

I step into the room, and discover I'm not done gasping at the surprises this castle throws up.

The circular room is right at the top of one of the turrets, beneath the conical oriel. Two paintings of moonlit forests hang over the bed – Lord Valerian's work, judging by their gloomy palette and bold, assertive strokes. The bed is made up with bamboo and linen sheets in soft grey and piled high with throw pillows. Through an arched wooden door, I can see a modern bathroom that I hope has running water. I am happy to accommodate most clients' strange whims, but indoor plumbing is a necessity.

Tall, arched windows overlook the valley below on three sides. I step up to the largest one and vertigo claims me as I peer down at a sheer drop. A small wrought-iron table and two chairs sit in front of the window. Upon the table is a basket of pastries and chocolate bars, and a collection of drinks in an ice bucket.

My stomach rumbles. I haven't eaten since lunchtime. I grab a pastry and bite down. Strawberry cream explodes on my tongue, and the pastry disappears far too quickly.

Reginald points to a wooden panel with a button on the wall beneath the light switch. "This is the call button. You will find one in all the rooms in the house that have electricity. I am used to my lord's chaotic whims, but you may wish to keep a more regular schedule. If you are ever hungry, or if you need anything at all, please ring for me and I shall come running."

He says this in a friendly way, but his eyes flicker over my face, and something like fear bristles there.

"Thank you, Reginald." I set down the second pastry I was about to devour. A cold sense of unease settles in my chest, pushing out my excitement at meeting the beautiful Lord Valerian again and the challenging job he has for me.

Nothing about this house or this job or my new boss makes sense.

How has Lord Valerian had time to acquire all these hobbies, all this stuff?

Why would a young, beautiful toff lock himself away in this castle like a vampire hiding from the light?

How did he stop me from falling on that terrarium?

Why is he afraid of his mother?

Why does he keep "nocturnal hours"?

And, most importantly, how did he leave the pub last night without me seeing him?

No, *actually* most importantly, does he want to kiss me again?

Why do I feel like Jonathan Harker when he first arrives at Dracula's castle? I feel as though I'm being lured into a trap, like a fly caught in a web. But maybe there's a part of me that is excited to meet the spider …

The Nevermore Murder Club and Smutty Book Coven Group Chat

Celeste: Does anyone know what all the commotion is about over by the pub? There's quite a crowd gathered. I want to go over but I can't leave the bakery until these sticky buns are glazed.

Isis: Komal found us a new murder to solve.

Celeste: WHAT? Who got murdered?

Maisie: Danny O'Hare. Komal found his body!

Komal: I did. It was awful. I was taking the shortcut behind the pub to yoga class, and there he was, sprawled out behind the bins. This is going to be terrible for tourism, and we have the Midsummer Festival coming up.

Beth: Hmmmph. The things Komal will do to get out of my yoga class.

Celeste: Oh, well, no need to solve his murder. Simply an act of public good.

Mina: Did he have a woman's stiletto jammed into his eye socket? That's always how I imagined he'd go.

Maisie: Nope, but he was wearing an expression of abject horror, which honestly looked similar to the expression most women in this village had after they spent any time with him.

Maisie: I'm on the scene now, trying to get some details out of the cops for the paper. They're being awfully evasive, and there's something strange and possibly supernatural that I'll tell you about at the next book club meeting. We can decide if it's worth our effort to investigate further.

Celeste: Maisie, do you need me to bring the coppers some sticky buns? That usually gets them talking.

Dora: You're all going to hell.

Komal: As long as I can get Celeste's sticky buns in hell, I'm fine with that.

7

Winnie

Faye: Hi Win, are you at the new client's house? You're an absolute star to take on this job. You know how much I detest the countryside. I'm having lunch with Jennifer from ITV tomorrow and I'm telling her all about how amazing you are. Don't forget to get some great photos for the gram! And can you get the accounts done by tomorrow? I know it's supposed to be my month to do them, but I'm flat out. Ta, doll!

Reginald leaves me in my room. I scarf down the pastries and skull a bottle of raspberry-infused water and feel a hundred times better about life.

Okay, so I'm living in the tower of a definitely, *absolutely* haunted castle, and my new client is profoundly strange and incredibly talented, and outrageously hot. *And* he might be heading down the path to becoming a hoarder.

I should call Faye immediately and yell at her for signing me up for this job. I should tell her to shove the accounts and demand to get on the next train back to London.

Instead, now that my belly is full, I can't wait to get back downstairs to help Alaric … er, Lord Valerian.

This job is why I became a professional organiser in the first place. To work with hot lords—I mean, to save someone else from having to live the way I grew up, drowning beneath piles of rubbish.

I throw on a black hoodie to ward off the castle's chill, grabbing my candelabra, phone and Winnie Wins kit (comprising of a portable speaker, wet wipes, Clutter Queens branded gloves, a purple Moleskine and matching pen) before heading back downstairs. I reach the first landing before realising that I have no idea how to get back to the other wing.

I spin around in circles, trying to remember. I strike off in a random direction, crossing my fingers that I won't get lost in the castle, because Alaric won't notice I'm missing until he smells my decaying corpse. As I step through a narrow doorway into a drawing room that doesn't look familiar at all, someone squeaks behind me.

I whirl around, but there's no one there.

"H-h-hello?"

"*Mrrrrrrew*?"

A black cat with white paws like tiny socks steps out from behind a dusty futon and regards me with regal disdain.

I exhale with relief. "Hey, kitty. You don't look like you're lost. I wonder if you could help me get back to the Stabby Chic room?"

The cat lifts her head, demanding payment. Beneath her chin is a small smudge of white fur. It almost looks as though Lord Valerian has dried his paintbrush on her by accident. I dutifully reach down and scratch her chin until she purrs gently against my hand.

"*Meow*!" The cat withdraws a few steps, throws me a look that indicates how much of an idiot she believes me to be, then turns on her little socks and stomps off.

"Wait—kitty!"

"*Meorrw*," she calls from deeper in the house, as if she's saying, *Keep up!*

I hurry after her, following her down winding staircases and through cavernous rooms packed with even more racks of pottery and rolled-up tapestries. This is definitely not the way I came with Reginald.

Finally, we pass through another drawing room onto the main corridor. My shoulders sag with relief as I recognise the pile of teddy bears.

Alaric emerges from his office, a fresh paint smudge across his forehead. My fingers itch to wipe it away. "I see you have met Mirabelle."

"*Meorrrw,*" says Mirabelle, clinging to Alaric's trousers.

"She helped me find my way."

"I'm not surprised. Mirabelle is the true mistress of Black Crag." He bends down and scratches her behind her ears. She butts his hand and eyes me smugly, as if declaring that Alaric is hers. "I have put down my paintbrush. Where do you wish to begin?"

Where indeed? I gaze around the room Alaric has claimed for his study, and I can already picture it after I whip it into shape. We can use racks of open industrial metal shelves along that wall, so that the bare stone is visible behind them. Storage boxes for each project so that he only has to pull one out. A circular table in the centre of the room will display his locomotives with spotlights to highlight the fine features, and soft lamps over a pair of chairs beneath the window where he can sit and think, provided we can get electricity in here …

And we're *definitely* moving that terrarium.

I'm getting ahead of myself. If I only have six weeks to present the best side of Black Crag to Alaric's – Lord Valerian's – mother, I have to focus on the most important rooms.

"Tell me which rooms we should prioritise for the ball and your mother's visit," I say. "We won't be able to tidy every space. We'll need the ballroom, obviously, and the drawing rooms adjacent for catering and seating? I presume your mother will stay in the guest room in the tower where I'm sleeping? That seems to be the tidiest room in the house—"

"No, no, that room won't do for her," he shakes his head. "My mother will stay in the guest quarters in the west wing, near my rooms. She will wish to use my study for her correspondence, as well as the two drawing rooms and the ballroom for her infernal gathering, as you suggest."

"What about your dining room?" I've been to enough rich people's homes to know they go nuts for fancy dining settings. "Actually, where *is* your dining room? I haven't seen it yet."

Alaric frowns. "Don't concern yourself with the dining room. I gave it over to a … rather *unusual* distraction. We keep that room locked."

Am I imagining things, or are his porcelain cheeks darkening a little?

Alaric looks away, and I'm dying to ask him what's in that room, but respecting client privacy is rule number one of the Clutter Queens' Five Tidy Tenets of Client Happiness.

"Okay, then. We'll focus on your mother's bedroom, the study, two drawing rooms, and the ballroom. If it's alright with you, I'll start work in your study. It's the smallest of the rooms, and I think that if we can knock it out quickly, it will give us some momentum to tackle the other jobs."

Alaric nods.

"The biggest challenge is going to be the loom. We'll have to hire an expert to move it—"

"I will arrange that. I was the one who placed it there, after all. I designed it, so I know how it comes apart."

Wow.

Okay.

I decide to brush right over Alaric's casual "I built a loom" confession. "Do you have another room where you would like to set it up?" I ask. "I passed a yellow drawing room on my way from the tower that wasn't nearly as crowded as these."

My unwilling student lets out an ennui-filled sigh. "I shall move the loom to that room."

"Good. Then we'll have heaps of room for stage one of the Winnie Wins System."

"… The what?" Alaric's eyebrows approach his hairline.

"The Winnie Wins System. It's my special system for helping my clients get clean and stay clean. It's four words, the first letters of which spell 'WINS', so it's easy to remember. It's so good that I trademarked it. Well, technically, the Clutter Queens trademarked it, but I'm one half of the Clutter Queens—" *The half that does all the work.* "The first stage is W – Whirlwind. We whip through these rooms like a storm of tidiness."

Alaric looks like I've just suggested he jump into a bath of razor blades.

But I can't stop. I'm on a roll. "We move all the items in the office to the centre of each room – that way, we can see exactly what we've got, what's junk and what's art, and how to categorise them. We toss the rubbish and sort everything into groups of like items, and decide where those items live. I'll need to purchase some containers. Make that a *lot* of containers. And get some shelves made to fit the office wall. I have contacts who can get us a decent price. Do you have a budget in mind?"

"Money is no object," he says. "You'll need to speak with Reginald about the funds. He may need to sell some of my gold."

Ooooookay.

I shrug. "That's fine. As long as the bills get paid on time."

"Would it be agreeable to you if I move the loom another day? I'd like to assist you with the tornado."

"The Whirlwind. And absolutely. I need you to tell me what's junk and what's special to you. I can't make those decisions for you. But fair warning, I like to play music while I work," I say.

"As do I."

I recall the jazz music he'd been playing when I arrived. We have different tastes. I open my kit and drop my phone and portable speaker on the corner of his desk. "Do you want to pick the playlist?"

He lifts up his hands in a gesture of surrender. "I'm sure whatever you enjoy will be … educational."

I can't help a cheeky grin as I flip through the playlists on my phone. Alaric watches over my shoulder, that delightful corner of his mouth quirking up as he takes in the names of all my playlists.

"'Tunes for Drunken Wallowing'?" he asks. "'I Hate Patrick' playlist? 'Naked Shower Dancing Songs'?"

"I have a playlist for every occasion." I am a professional organiser, after all.

I push play on my "Getting Shit Done" playlist, which is a mix of old-school metal and bangin' singalong pop tunes. The opening riff of Amon Amarth's "With Oden on Our Side" blasts from the speakers. Alaric leaps back, his eyes wide with terror.

"It sounds as though the Vikings are invading," he yells.

"That's accurate." I turn it down a notch. What kind of man is afraid of a riff? "Better?"

"Much."

"Okay then, now that we have our soundtrack, it's time to attack this room. We're going to make three piles: Keep and display. Keep and organise for future art projects. And junk to throw away. By the end, you're going to love the Winnie Wins System, I guarantee it. Now, this misshapen lump of metal: junk or modern art?"

From the Clutter Queens Website: The Winnie Wins System

Our unique Winnie Wins System was created by Faye's business partner and organiser extraordinaire, Winnie Preston. Winnie created this system to help our clients declutter and stay organised long after we leave.

***Step 1: Whirlwind** – Winnie arrives at your house as a whirlwind of positive energy. You can't help but be swept along with her bubbly enthusiasm as she blows through your untidy garage or cluttered closet, sorting your belongings into what to keep and what to get rid of.*

***Step 2: Intention** – This is where Winnie helps you to set an intention for your space. She'll guide you on a visualisation exercise to help you see a positive future for yourself. It sounds a little bit woo-woo, but we swear it works!*

***Step 3: Neutralise** – During this stage, you have to get rid of all the barriers that stand in the way of staying neat and organised and achieving your vision for this space. Winnie helps you build a system you can stick to.*

Step 4: Sustain *– We've done the hard work, now it's up to you to keep going with the plan! If you think you need additional support during the sustain stage, you can book a Winnie Wins Sustain package – get 20% off when you book with Faye's Picture Perfect Home Makeover package.*

Show off a before/after reel of your space on Instagram and tag #fayearnolddesigner #winniewinssystem – we love to see your progress!

8

Winnie

Unknown Number: Winnie, it's Ken, your mother's neighbour. Love, are you coming over soon? She's getting out of hand again. There's a giant pile of plastic dolls by the letterbox – Barry came home from work late last night and nearly had a heart attack when he saw them leering at him. I'm afraid we're going to have to call the council again.

With my playlist blasting, Alaric and I get into an organising groove. By the time I glance at my phone screen, we've sorted over half the enormous pile and it's past midnight. As if on cue, my stomach rumbles. All I've had since lunch was those pastries in my room.

I stifle a yawn. "I think we should call it a night."

"Of course – your feeble body requires rest."

I roll my eyes at him.

"Who are you calling feeble? I moved all those heavy locomotives by myself, thank you very much." Although Alaric was fitter than I expected, lifting antique tables with one hand and rushing about with cacti-filled terrariums without ever being out of breath. I try not to imagine the muscled, fit body beneath those stuffy, old-fashioned clothes, but I fail. I smile at him. "You need rest, too."

"I prefer to rest during the daylight hours." Alaric glances out the window, his expression unreadable as he regards the moon.

"Even so, it's not easy to be ruthless with your stuff like this, but you've done amazingly well tonight."

He really has. With the exception of my mum, who doesn't count, Alaric is the messiest client I've ever had, just a few rungs below full-on hoarder. But unlike many clients, he's engaging with the organising process. Once he got over his initial grumpiness, he genuinely seems to enjoy making decisions about his stuff. We already have several bags of rubbish – mainly broken tools and materials he'd been keeping "just in case". His mind enjoys categorising things, but living all alone in this huge castle has allowed him to get so distracted by his imagination that he hasn't noticed things piling up.

I've been surprised at how fun it's been for me, too. A lot of my clients are condescending and defensive about their habits. Most of my first day is spent convincing them that I'm not judging them.

But Alaric's face lit up whenever I held up a train or painting that he was particularly fond of. He placed them lovingly in their respective piles, sometimes offering me details about their construction that he was particularly proud of. Honestly, I never found trains particularly interesting until tonight, but Alaric could talk about paint drying in that deep voice of his and I'd listen.

Actually, he *did* talk about paint drying for a bit.

It was surprisingly hot.

So hot that I'm still awake at nearly 1 am, and this is usually around the time when …

"I am heading to the sitting room for a nightcap," Alaric says stiffly. "Would you care to join me?"

"I'd love to." Immediately I regret how over-eager I sound. I stand up, brushing dust and bits of train off my purple suit. My stomach rumbles again. "Will there be food?"

Alaric rings the call button on the wall in the hallway and speaks into an intercom. "Reginald, I am ready for my nightcap. Ms Preston will be joining me, and she requires sustenance."

A weird way to phrase that, but Alaric's odd, old-fashioned way of speaking has endeared itself to me over the evening. I follow him as he shows me into an opulent bathroom to wash my hands (Electricity! And running water! Such luxury!), and then escorts me up a narrow flight of stairs to a small sitting room decorated in jewel tones and hung with some of his intricate tapestries.

The room is surprisingly bare of Alaric's hobbies, with only a small stack of ceramic mugs and a couple of half-finished embroidered cushions on a folding table beside the blazing fire. A wobbly pile of books teeters beside it.

Alaric folds his long, lean body into a well-worn wingback chair beside the fire and indicates for me to take the chair opposite. I sink down gratefully, not realising until this moment how tired my limbs are and how cold I've become. Castles aren't exactly designed to capture the summer sun. I turn my hands to the fire, enjoying the warmth soaking into my bones.

"You were cold." Alaric frowns.

"Weren't you?"

"I do not feel the cold as you do. Ms Preston, you must tell me when you feel a chill. I will have Reginald light the fire in my office when we work tomorrow."

"That would be brilliant."

Reginald appears in a blink, as if he were hiding in the shadows the whole time. "I have prepared dinner, Ms Preston. It is not much, I'm afraid, but I hope it will suffice. Would you like a red or white wine, or do you prefer a hot drink?"

"I'll have a white if it's going, thank you, Reginald."

"My pleasure." He turns to Alaric. "Your usual, my lord?"

Alaric nods. Reginald slinks back into the shadows and appears a moment later with two bottles of wine. He uncorks the white and pours a generous amount into a crystal goblet for me. He then moves to Lord Valerian's side and pours him a red, the wine sloshing nearly at the rim.

I raise my glass to Alaric. "Here's to the first successful day of Operation Organise Alaric's Life."

He raises his glass in return. "To many more such evenings to come."

Beneath the intensity of his stare, the butterfly in my stomach dances a little jig.

Reginald arrives and places a tray over my knees.

The food is nothing fancy – roast beef with a dark gravy, vegetables and salad – but the flavours dance on my tongue. The vegetables are so perfectly cooked that they're caramelised around the edges, and the salad is made with grains and sharp goat's cheese. I don't recognise a single one of the herbs Reginald has used, but everything tastes incredible. I finish the plate and wonder if Alaric will think I'm rude if I lick the rest of the gravy.

I look over at him. He has one of his books open on his knee, those fathomless eyes devouring the page with a hunger that makes me wish I was made of paper and covered in diagrams of locomotive engines. The cat, Mirabelle, luxuriates across the back of his chair. He raises an eyebrow at me and sets his book aside.

I notice he doesn't have a plate. "You're not eating?"

"I am not hungry."

"How can you *not* be hungry? We just sorted enough stuff that we could open our own eccentric art gallery and model train museum. I'm so starving I'm going to eat this plate."

He laughs, the sound startling for its unbidden mirth. I beam back at him. This guy is *nothing* like my other clients. Too bad there's no permanent job out there for organising castles filled with art for eccentric, grumpy, hot AF peerage, because I think I'd nail it.

As quickly as his laughter began, Alaric snaps his lips shut. "Forgive me, Ms Preston. I was not laughing at you. I merely …"

"You don't have to apologise for having a good time. This work is quite personal. I'm digging around in the objects that make you who you are. It helps both of us if we can be friendly."

That's why I'm having dinner with you, even though it's wildly inappropriate. Even though I've never eaten dinner with a client before. It's for the good of the job. That's the only reason.

It has nothing *to do with the way you kissed me at the pub.*

"So you live here by yourself?" I ask. "Just you and Reginald in your medieval bachelor pad? No … Mrs Brooding Artist or Mr Sexy Jazz Fan?"

I shouldn't be so flippant with a client, but, in my defence, he laughed at me first.

I like it when he laughs.

Lord Valerian doesn't acknowledge my wit. His mouth forms a firm line. "I have sworn an oath never to marry unless it be for love, and it is difficult to fall in love in a lonely castle."

"Are there *other* reasons to marry?"

"*Obligation*," he growls. "Political alliance. Punishment, if you have a family like mine."

"You might be surprised." I dig my fingers into the soft leather of the chair. *He's a peer. You can't even imagine his life.* "You could try the dating apps. I'm sure there's someone out there who loves dusty old castles and model trains. I could help you with your profile if you want. I write all the marketing copy for Clutter Queens." *What am I saying?*

"That is enough about me. I wish to speak no more of things that cannot be. Tell me of yourself, Ms Preston. How did you come to do this work?" he asks me. "I didn't know Professional Organiser was a métier until Reginald found your website."

"You mean all little boys and girls don't dream of tidying up after rich people?" I smile to hide the blood rushing to my face. I'm not used to clients asking about *me*. "I went to university to study archaeology. I loved history, exploring different times and places, and how people lived. I *thought* my calling was to explore dusty tombs and dig up skeletons and solve the mysteries of the past."

"But it was not?"

"Ew, nope. Too much dirt." I screw up my face. "But I had this professor I adored. Professor Lewicki. She was brilliant, but she was hopelessly disorganised, always late to class and losing her phone or important pieces of paper. I won a summer scholarship to work as her research assistant, and nearly had a heart attack when I stepped into her office on the first day. It was a complete shambles, with papers and books everywhere. She couldn't find a thing."

I shudder, remembering the piles of paperwork in Professor Lewicki's office and other, much taller piles that had taken over my mother's kitchen, and the way the floor sagged and squelched beneath every step from the water damage.

"I knew I couldn't work the whole summer in that mess, so I offered to organise everything for her. I've always liked things to be tidy." I suck in a breath as the old shame comes flooding back. *Just because he saved you last night doesn't mean he cares about you. He's merely being polite.* "I don't like owning a lot of stuff. I thought I could help her. I spent the first week of my internship cleaning her office and researching ways to help her stay organised. She was so impressed that she told me I had to meet a friend of hers, Faye, who was starting her own interior design business.

"I dropped out of uni the next week, and I became Faye's first employee, and then later, when I created the Winnie Wins System, we became business partners. In the early days, we worked out of a pokey front room in Faye's Fulham flat. Faye's parents are dignitaries and she has lots of wealthy contacts. I helped the clients organise their designer shoe collections and create Instagram-worthy children's bedrooms, and Faye did all the design work and schmoozed the clients. A couple of years ago, we did a penthouse design for a celebrity influencer, and she and Faye hit it off and started creating design and organising content together. Now Faye has more followers than that influencer, so she focuses on building our online brand profile while I'm in charge of the design and organising team."

And everything else.

I shove the accounts out of my head.

"Influencer? Content? Brand profile?" Alaric's lips twist as he takes another sip of wine. "None of these terms are familiar to me."

"That's right, I forgot that you live in an Edgar Allen Poe story and eschew technology." He rolls his eyes, but laughs all the same. "Influencers are people who make a living posting about a certain topic on the internet. My boss, Faye, makes videos showing people how to organise their designer purse collections or use scheduling software to make sure they don't miss a single Botox appointment. I bet there are model train influencers on TikTok arguing about who built it best, Stephenson or Brunel."

"There's no argument to be had," Alaric says, not a trace of irony on his stern features. "It's Brunel, all the way."

It's my turn to laugh. "Exactly. *And* Brunel had the best fashion sense. Why stovepipe hats aren't still in style, I'll never know. You know, you could be an influencer yourself, if you ever fancy a career change from brooding, reclusive lord of the manor. You could make videos about your hobbies, like learning how to weave and—"

Reginald appears suddenly to take my plate. "Reginald, that was delicious. I refuse to believe you simply whipped that up from left-overs you had lying around. Would it be possible to have that hot drink now?"

"Certainly, ma'am. I can offer you coffee, a selection of teas, or hot chocolate made from a recipe my grandmother passed down to me."

One never passes up an opportunity for fancy chocolate. "I'll take the hot chocolate."

Raw pleasure crosses Reginald's face. "I'm so happy. I hardly get to make Granny's hot chocolate these days. I'll be right back."

Alaric and I settle into a comfortable silence, until Reginald returns with a steaming mug.

"What time would you like to begin tomorrow?" I ask, raising the hot chocolate to my lips. "I'm here to work with you, so I'll fit into your nocturnal schedule."

"I usually arise around 5 pm."

Wow, he wasn't kidding about being a creature of the night.

"It might take me a few days to adjust to that time." Especially given my sleep issues. I long to ask Alaric why he has chosen those late hours, but he's my client – it's none of my business why he does the things he does. I'm paid to indulge his whims.

I sip the hot chocolate. It's *amazing*.

Before I can stop myself, a small moan of pleasure escapes my lips.

Exactly the same sound I made at the pub when he kissed me.

Alaric jerks back, his dark eyes flashing. His wine splashes down the front of his old-fashioned shirt. He does not attempt to wipe it. Instead, he glares at me as though I'm some wild creature who has found its way into his castle and he doesn't know what to do with me.

My cheeks flare with heat. I slam my hand over my mouth, but it's too late. The moan hangs in the silence between us.

"Ms Preston," Alaric says stiffly. "You should retire to bed."

"I'm not tired!" I insist, taking another sip of hot chocolate. It's spiced with flavours that I don't recognise. As I drink it, my eyelids droop. "It's like battling jet lag. I've gotta stay up so that I can reset my body clock …"

Alaric rises from his chair just as my eyes fall completely shut, and the world fades into shadow and slumber.

9

Alaric

Callista: Alaric Valerian, answer your phone! We have important matters to discuss prior to my visit. Word has reached me about a murder in your village – the body has been husked. You may have chosen to shut yourself away from the world, but you represent the Nightshade Court and this is a violation on your watch. If you don't do something to find this aberration and bring them to justice, I will.

Winifred's head slumps against her shoulder. She must have been tired from her day, as it is well past normal human bedtime. Mirabelle leaps down from my chair and prods Winifred's eye with a white-socked paw.

"Don't do that," I caution her, pushing her off Winifred's slumbering form. "Winifred doesn't want to play with you right now. She needs her sleep."

Poor Winifred. I have asked so much of her. She is here, in my castle, even though she is afraid. I can smell the fear in her blood, mingled with other scents that make me struggle to focus. She is helping me, even though I fled from her in the pub and say things that make her sigh and curse under her breath. She is touching my things, bringing order to the chaos of my mind.

I am not used to kindness from humans.

I am not used to the way her kindness makes me feel.

She has no clue of the danger she's in. At least she will be long gone before my mother arrives.

I stare down at her as she slumps in the chair, her sleek, impossibly straight blonde hair falling over her face like a silken veil. She may wake shortly – humans don't sleep as soundly as vampires, for ours is a dreamless sleep of the dead. She will regret slumbering with her neck at that angle.

Before I can remind myself how wrong this is, I slide my hands beneath her and lift her into my arms.

She is warm. So warm. Her blood pumps beneath her skin, coursing against me where I hold her, beckoning me. She smells like sunshine, like strawberries. Like things that are not for me.

I cradle her head against my chest, her ear right against where my beating heart would be if I still possessed one, and I begin the long walk to the tower.

Mirabelle trails behind me, keeping up a steady stream of cat chatter about our new houseguest. I trudge through room after messy room, a wave of mortification hitting me. Winifred has been so polite about my mess, but she must think me an animal, the way I live.

She's not wrong. I live like what I am – a dreaded creature; a monster.

I only allowed Reginald to employ the Clutter Queens because my mother will make my life miserable if the castle looks like this for her ball. But now that Winnie is here, singing along to her horrible music under her breath as she dances around my study, treating my distractions as though they are precious, as though *I* am precious …

I find that I want her to love Black Crag as much as I do.

You are sick. Too much exposure to humans is addling your mind.

I hold her head against my chest as I climb the narrow stairs to the tower room. Sometimes her feet scrape against the stone, but she doesn't wake. When I enter her room, a wave of heat engulfs me. Reginald has lit the fire here, too, knowing that Winifred will feel the bite of Black Crag's chill. I'm pleased that one of us remembers what is required to keep a human alive.

I lay Winifred on her bed. Her shirt has come untucked from the purple trousers that hug her hips in a way that makes my undead heart clench beneath my ribs. I catch a glimpse of the flesh of her stomach and a whiff of her sunshine scent. I have to look away as I pull the blankets up to her chin.

I whirl around and race for the stairs. I must get as far from her as possible before the monster inside me takes over.

I pace in front of the fire, my nerves taut as bowstrings.

A book lies open on my chair: a history of the laws of the Three Courts.

Thou shall not lie with a human or invite them to share your life, outside of the bonds of the blood rite. This is to prevent the begetting of the corrupted Dhampir. Thou shall not reveal the secrets of the Immortal Upyr to humans, except as required from the blood rites. A betrothal between a human and vampire is forbidden. A vampire may petition their court for permission to turn a human, but only if—

I thought that reminding myself of the shackles that bind me would stop this pulsing, keening *want*, but it's only made the hunger worse.

After the kiss, I thought the monster in me hungered for a taste of her, like an epicurean salivating over a particularly delicious dish. But after spending the evening with her, I know it is more. I cannot stop thinking about her golden hair and honey eyes, and the laugh she drew unbidden from me.

I haven't laughed in …

I'm not certain I've ever laughed. I shall ask Reginald.

"My lord."

I whip my head to the doorway. Reginald stands rigid, his forehead furrowed with concern.

Reginald should not be worried for me. I'm not the one in danger here. "She has settled?"

"She is sleeping soundly, my lord. The fire is warm and Mirabelle has snuggled on her pillow."

I slump back into my chair, the hunger burning.

This whole evening has been … taxing. Winifred is the first human I've been around in decades apart from Reginald, and as we are tied by the blood rites, he doesn't count. I thought with my training in the village I'd be able to spend long periods with her without my hunger making a beast of me. I thought I'd been doing well. I'd even managed to tear myself away from that arresting woman at the pub, though I hated leaving her alone without explanation.

But that was before the *same* arresting, delicious-smelling woman moved into my castle. Before she began to sift through my stuff, placing her delectable scent upon everything that I hold dear. Before I got close enough to hear the blood rushing in her veins or that damned *moan* issuing from her perfect lips.

Before I started to imagine all the forbidden things I'd like to do to her …

"You wish to say something," I say to Reginald.

"I believe that you should tell her the truth, my lord."

"I haven't lied to her." I've not hidden my nocturnal proclivities or the centuries of distractions scattered about my castle. I've even allowed her to share a drink with me. Callista would say that I am tempting the gods, but I don't care.

However, I cannot break our laws and tell her the truth.

"She is going to be living in the castle for six weeks," Reginald says. "We have never had to hide ourselves around a human for this long. She'll figure out the truth."

"I don't see how. She has accepted everything so far with her human logic. She thinks I'm … what's the word she used?" I screw up my face. "Odd."

"She will become suspicious when you do not eat, and when you refuse to leave the castle during daylight. She will discover what you hide in the dining room. Or you will succumb to the hunger and ..."

"I will *not*." I spit the words, and my fangs begin to descend with my anger.

Reginald lurches away. I incline my head in remorse, my fangs sliding back into place. I rarely lose my temper with him.

I sigh and hold out my glass. "I cannot reveal myself to a human."

"The laws are wrong." Reginald shifts uneasily as he moves to refill my drink. "But you *can* reveal yourself under certain circumstances. I think she would agree if you—"

"I will not ask *that* of her. I have hired Ms Preston to organise the house for my mother. That is *all*."

The hunger rages.

"As you say, my lord." Reginald kneels on the rug at my feet, his fingers trembling as they grip his knees. His knuckles are white. "But you need to keep your strength up. You appear even paler than usual."

"I've told you before, I won't take from you. That is the end of this discussion."

Through the haze of strawberry, I smell something else – his hunger, his *desperation*.

I hate it, but it's necessary.

I need Reginald as much as he has come to need me.

I draw back my cuff as my fangs slide down again. I slice a small hole in my wrist, squeezing until three droplets of blood bead on the surface of my skin. Reginald's eyes blow out, his tongue snaking out of his lips at the anticipation of his reward.

Reginald takes my arm in his, bringing my wrist to his mouth. He sucks and licks, drinking his fill of my blood, tasting immortality on his tongue as he kneels in thrall.

I allow it, this curse, this violation, because it is what we have always done. To be a monster is to make a choice – I had a choice forced on me the night I allowed my mother to gift me the Kiss, and another the night I fled the Nightshade Court for this lonely, crumbling castle.

I've come to understand that I cannot survive here without Reginald, and thanks to the poison in my veins, he now cannot survive without me.

My head pulses as I turn over my mother's latest text message and the news article I'd briefly glanced at while Winifred was in the bathroom. Out there is another vampire, hunting and *killing* on my territory, one who has made a different choice. One who has embraced the monster within. *Husking*. All that separates him and me is my high walls and my thin veneer of control.

And Winnie Preston has proven that she can shatter my defences in a single evening.

10

Winnie

Harudha: Winnie, I'm texting because you missed your appointment yesterday, which isn't like you. I know you're still having the nightmares but I think we're making real progress. Also, when you reorganised my desk, do you happen to remember where you put my stapler? I can't find it anywhere.

I'M WALKING THROUGH A MAZE. THIS ISN'T A FUN CORN HEDGE MAZE or the minotaur's prison, but a maze of towering stacks of paper, books, clothing and toys, unopened boxes from Amazon and rusting kettles, stacked so high that I can't climb over them. I have to go through.

I'm searching for my school rucksack. It's bright red with characters from Hotel Transylvania. I love that rucksack, and I'm worried that it's been swallowed by the maze, that I'll never see it again and I'll have to carry my things to school in a hessian sack.

I turn myself sideways to move through a narrow gap.

"Mum!" I call out. "Mum, I have to leave for school. Where's my rucksack?"

"It's in the kitchen, of course." She sounds defensive, as if I were blaming her for my bag going missing. "I made you lunch. Your favourite – peanut butter and honey sandwiches."

I haven't been able to eat peanut butter since I was seven and I opened the jar to find a rat inside. But Mum always forgets. Sometimes when she looks at me, it's like she doesn't see me. She still sees a baby girl in my dad's arms.

I twist and turn through the tunnels. Papers rain down on my head. The floor sways and buckles beneath my feet, warped from water damage and the squashed, rotting piles of newspaper that cover it. Things move in the piles around me, the scurrying sounds growing closer. I swallow down my fear and press on.

I get down on my knees to crawl through a tunnel between two old washing machines. I put my hands into the newspapers and they become covered in brown, sticky sludge. I emerge in the kitchen – or rather, what might've once been a kitchen. The counters are covered in boxes of food that wobble and crunch as the rodents inside them chew their way through. There's blackened sludge in the sink, and the refrigerator, cupboards and bright yellow kitchen table are buried under piles of stuff. I spy my rucksack on top of a stack of National Geographic magazines that Mum saves for me because they have articles about archaeology. My Elsa lunchbox is sitting on top. I open the bag to shove it inside …

… and scream.

Huge black bugs with beady eyes and long scratchy legs pour out. They crawl up my arm, their tiny legs scratching my skin as they swarm over me. More bugs crawl out of my bag. They're in my hair, my ears, burrowing into my nose. I cover my eyes, zip my mouth shut, and swallow my screams as I curl into a ball on the damp floor. There's nothing I can do as they start to bite …

I wake, sweat-drenched and scratching, my skin covered in thousands of tiny, invisible bugs. Mirabelle yowls in protest as I throw myself out of bed, flick the light on, and practise the deep breathing my therapist taught me as I check my phone. 4.32 am.

"Meeerw?" Mirabelle regards me from her new spot on the windowsill.

"Don't mind me, kitty. I'm going crazy. I'm sorry for tossing you out of bed."

I've had these nightmares ever since I was eighteen. I had the first one the day I moved out of Mum's house. My therapist, Harudha, says they're a way for my brain to process the trauma now that I'm in a safe place, away from the piles. I thought I had them under control, but as we got closer to the wedding, they came back. I haven't slept through the night for months.

I rub my eyes. I don't remember coming up to bed. The last thing I recall, I was sipping hot chocolate and talking with Alaric, and then …

I glance down at myself. I'm wearing the same clothes I had on when I arrived. My mouth tastes of roast beef and chocolate.

Horror dawns on me.

I fell asleep in front of the fire.

Someone carried me up here.

Argh!

The breathing exercises aren't helping. My skin itches and now my lips are tingling. Tiny bug legs crawl up my nose, squirm in my ears and creep over my clothing. I tear off my clothes and hurry into the shower. I'm pleasantly surprised to find a modern bathroom with a black-and-gold tiled shower. I stand under the three jets, allowing the hot water to sluice off the embarrassment of last night and the horrible dream.

I scrub my skin until it's red and raw. I put on my fresh, clean pyjamas. Then I pull off the sheets, throw them outside the door, and replace them with fresh ones I find in a blanket box at the end of the bed.

Under the sink in the bathroom are some cleaning supplies. Mirabelle cleans between her toes and watches me scrub the floor, the bed frame, and every surface in the room. By the time I'm done, my eyes sting from the chemicals and I need to take another shower, but at least the bugs have stopped crawling over me.

I climb back into bed, exhausted but knowing that my eyes won't close now. Mirabelle settles into a furry ball against my hip. I pick up one of the romance novels in the stack Mina sold me.

I fall into a world of brooding, epically-schlonged vampires and read until sunlight pours through my windows. Mirabelle's back rises and falls as she sleeps. I try not to be jealous of the cat.

I fail.

I finish one book and get five chapters into another before hunger drives me from bed. I throw off the covers again, forgetting about my little furry bedmate.

"Meorrw!" Mirabelle glares at me with indignation as she clings to the blanket for dear life.

"Sorry, sorry!"

I glance at the clock. Nearly lunchtime. Still too early for Alaric's nocturnal schedule, but my body clock isn't wired to sleep all day, especially when there's organising to do.

I pull on one of my favourite organising outfits – a burnt orange romper with wide-legged pants, and a slouchy pinstriped men's jacket I wear with the sleeves rolled up. I swipe on some lipstick and mascara.

I want to make a good impression on my client. That's all.

I grab the candelabra Reginald left for me and light the candles before padding down the crooked stairs, gripping the metal in one hand and pressing my other palm into the wall. Mirabelle winds around my feet, meowing loudly about how she's a poor, starving orphan who hasn't been given so much as a morsel of gruel.

I allow the cat to lead me downstairs, past the rooms we're cleaning, past the dining room with its padlocked doors, to the kitchen – a large, rough-stone room near the rear of the house.

"Reginald?" I call out. "Anyone?"

Mirabelle leaps onto the kitchen table, bats off a mesh fly cover with her paw, and drags a wedge of roast beef from a plate. The table is laden with food: a platter of cold meats and slices of cheese, fresh fruit, hard-boiled eggs, a selection of jams and fresh honeycomb, a loaf of sourdough, and another basket of delicious pastries.

A note is taped to the top of the loaf.

Dear Ms Preston,

I figured you'd be up before Lord Valerian, so I've left out some breakfast things that you may enjoy. Please help yourself to anything you like in the larder or scullery. There is a coffee machine on the counter opposite, and tea in the containers beside the stove.

Lord Valerian is not to be disturbed until the evening, when he will be ready to begin your work. You may not see me today, as I have chores to do around the estate. Use the call bell if you need anything.

Yours,

Reginald

My stomach growls.

How long has Reginald been awake to get all of this done?

I have so many questions.

But first, coffee.

I feed Mirabelle another chunk of beef, shove a handful of fresh strawberries in my mouth, and set about making a giant cup of black coffee. Alaric may enjoy his medieval trappings, but I'm thankful that his coffee machine is modern and expensive and runs on glorious electricity and not steam power or five guinea pigs on a treadmill.

I sip my coffee as I circle the table, picking at all the delicious treats on offer.

I cut a slice of sourdough and slather it with honey, but realise too late that Reginald has forgotten to leave me a plate. I glance around the kitchen, wondering where they might keep the crockery. I slide open a couple of drawers, but they're filled with what I suspect are the tools of a discerning sous chef.

At least, I hope that's what they are. One cannot be certain of anything at Black Crag Castle.

I take a bite out of my bread as I wander through a doorway at the end of the kitchen into the larder. I pull up short.

Odd.

I expected to see shelves stuffed with dry foods, baskets filled with produce and plaits of garlic drying from a ceiling rack. Instead, the scullery shelves are practically bare – only a handful of open boxes and a container of honeycomb in the corner provide any indication that food is stored here at all.

How does Reginald conjure a delicious breakfast spread when the cupboards are bare? I open a few drawers, still searching for a plate, but they're all empty.

This huge kitchen is designed for a master chef, but there's hardly any food. There has to be an explanation. Maybe it's shopping day? Perhaps that's one of the chores Reginald was referring to in his note.

On the back wall of the larder I spy a narrow door hidden in the wood panels.

Ah, I bet that's the scullery for crockery and mugs and stuff. When I was in the Duke of Harrington's summer house, he had a whole room for his scarf collection. Rich people have more rooms than sense.

I tug open the door and fumble on the wall for a light. I flick it on …

… and gasp.

Instead of the dark cupboard I expect, I'm standing in an impossibly long room with a high, vaulted ceiling. Rows of wine bottles nestle in wrought-iron frames along each wall.

There must be thousands of bottles in here.

I take a tentative step into the room, admiring the bright labels and immaculate rows. I suspect I've stumbled upon another of Alaric's "distractions". From the way he swirled his wine last night, I have him pegged as a wine guy.

Patrick was a wine guy, too. He swilled and snorted and sniffed every glass someone handed to him, and loved to impress people with his knowledge of crop projections and obscure New Zealand vineyards. People thought he was brilliant but honestly, it all seemed a little unhygienic to me. He would flip out to see this collection. I bet these bottles are all old and expensive.

No, I'm not thinking about Patrick, or the fact that since he dumped me I've become a "wine girl" – as in, drowning my sorrows with a £9.99 bottle of plonk more evenings than not, just so I can get a full night's sleep.

I'm drawn to a rack of bottles in the corner beside the door. They're all red wines, and each one is nestled within what appears to be a temperature-controlled sleeve. The gaps in the rack indicate that someone has been enjoying these wines. I remember the glass of red dangling from Alaric's long fingers yesterday evening, and I wet my lips for reasons that I don't want to think about.

I'm curious about him. That's all this is.

I step towards the shelf and draw one of the bottles from its protective sleeve. A light on the sleeve blinks red. I peer down at the bottle. The label is like nothing I've ever seen before – it's written in what appears to be French, and covered in stamps and wax seals and maker's marks. It looks far older than anything in Patrick's collection.

I pull out another bottle, expecting to see a similar old style, but this label is modern – a dark garden of blood-red roses on a black background. It's also written in a language I don't recognise, and none of the markings make sense for what little I know about wine—

"Ms Preston."

I whirl around, shocked by the harshness of the voice.

Reginald whips the bottle from my fingers before I drop it.

"Reginald, you startled me. I was looking for a plate—"

"I don't think you should be in here." Reginald slides the bottle back into its sleeve and settles it lovingly into its cradle. "I didn't mean to frighten you, but some of these bottles are quite old, and my lord is very particular about his wine. I'll show you where we keep the crockery. Will you be starting work shortly, or do you wish to return to bed until Lord Valerian rises?"

As Reginald talks, he herds me towards the door, his gaze flicking back to the red wine bottles, eyes narrowing in concern. I know I've done something wrong, but I don't understand what it is.

"I can't sleep anymore. I'll need more than a day to adjust to Lord Valerian's nocturnal schedule," I babble. In the kitchen, Reginald shows me a narrow door near the stove that leads to the scullery where I find shelves filled with delicate, dust-covered china. "I'm glad you found me. I need to place an order for some shelves and containers. If you can get me set up on the castle wi-fi, I'll do that and then I'll get started in the ballroom. Lord Valerian can join me when he wakes up."

"Very well, Ms Preston. I shall leave you to your breakfast. The castle network is named 'LAN Helsing', and the password is 'cantstakeme', all one word." He pauses when he sees my expression. "Lord Valerian's humour. He was most aggrieved at having to install the internet, but now he cannot live without it since he discovered he can order art supplies without having to set foot in a store."

I can't help but smile. "I believe it."

"Write me a list and I'll order anything you require." Reginald's eyes flicker over me. "And perhaps when you see Lord Valerian this evening, don't mention that you were in his cellar."

"Okay. I won't."

Reginald hurries away. I load my plate with food, but as I sit down to eat it, I find that I've lost my appetite. I peer over my shoulder at the scullery and the hidden door to the wine cellar.

What did I just stumble upon?

11

Winnie

Mum: Would you believe that Ken picked up one of my boxes of magazines from the front walk and put them out in the recycling! How DARE he! It was a box of TIME issues I've been saving for you because I know how much you love the articles on archaeology. And now they're gone forever! To make it up to you, I bought you another sundress.

"MY LORD, YOU HAVE A VISITOR!" REGINALD YELLS OVER MY music.

Alaric's head snaps up from a box of locomotive wheels he's sorting. He has a piece of cobweb stuck to his unruly dark curls. "Reginald, if this is your attempt at a joke, I'm not amused."

"I'm a little amused," I say, turning down the volume on my Get Shit Done playlist. "Why would a visitor be a joke?"

"Lord Valerian doesn't have visitors at the castle," Reginald explains. "Apart from delightful London organisers with appalling taste in music. But I'm afraid these visitors are quite insistent on seeing you. It's the police."

Why are the police here?

My mind immediately swings to a memory of five years earlier, when the police showed up at my flat to explain to me that my mother's hoarding, her screaming fits at the neighbours, and her reluctance to let council inspectors into her home, constituted anti-social behaviour. Has something happened to my mother?

Surely, someone would have rung me instead of coming in person to a remote castle to tell me that Mum's in trouble again?

But then, what's the alternative – is *Alaric* in trouble?

The dent between Alaric's eyes becomes a chasm. "Send them away."

"You can't send them away without talking to them. They're here to ask you about the murder in the village."

What?

"Hang on, someone was murdered in the village?" I leap to my feet. "How did I not know this?"

Being at Black Crag is like stepping out of time. I'm still getting used to all the normal, everyday things (Taylor Swift and Netflix) that Alaric has absolutely no clue about. My phone reception here is so bad (and the castle wi-fi is rather temperamental) that I haven't been checking the news. Or my emails. Or my mother's texts, although that last one is more about self-preservation than shoddy internet service.

"A man's body was found in the alley behind the Rose & Wimple," Reginald explains.

At the mention of the pub, my treacherous brain immediately replays my memory of Alaric's cool lips against mine, his long fingers pressed protectively into the small of my back as he tilted my head back …

My cheeks flare with heat, and my hand flies to the small graze on my neck from his teeth. What might've happened if he hadn't run away? "The same night that we …"

"Yes," Alaric says stiffly.

It's as close as he's come to acknowledging that night. I search his face for a reaction, but Lord Alaric Valerian is made of stone.

So I guess if I was wondering if he felt anything when he kissed me, I have my answer.

Not that I was wondering. At all.

"Should I show them to the sitting room?" Reginald asks.

"They're not coming in. If they insist upon intruding, they can stand in the hall. And don't you even *think* about offering them tea." Alaric shoves the box aside and unfolds himself from the floor, unfurling like some kind of dark, exotic plant. I dust off my favourite jacket and follow him and Reginald to the Stabby Chic hall. Two detectives stand in the doorway, peering at the weaponry and teddy bears with pursed lips and wide eyes.

An older man with salt-and-pepper hair and kind eyes holds up his warrant card. "Lord Valerian, I'm Inspector Hayes, and this is Detective Sergeant Wilson. We're grateful you can give us some of your valuable time. We're investigating an unfortunate crime in the village and we'd like to ask you about your movements on Sunday evening."

"If you must." Alaric lets out a beleaguered sigh. "My personal secretary, Reginald, drove me into the village so I might have dinner at the Rose & Wimple. I went inside. Nothing on the menu took my fancy so I had a glass of wine and left. That is all."

He whips around on his heel and storms off down the hall.

"I did have some more questions," Inspector Hayes says.

"I think what Lord Valerian *means* to say is that he didn't see or hear anything strange at the pub, but he'll be happy to assist with your inquiries," Reginald squares his shoulders. "However, now's not a good time. Perhaps an appointment—"

"I'd like to make it a good time. I have eyewitnesses who saw Lord Valerian speaking with a woman at the bar—"

"I might be able to help." I give a little wave. Wilson's eyes snap to mine. "I'm Winnie Preston. I was the woman Alaric—er, Lord Valerian was talking to at the Rose & Wimple."

She raises a slightly bushy eyebrow. "Eyewitnesses report that you were doing more than just talking."

"Er … yes. Lord Valerian kissed me," I mumble.

Reginald's eyebrows shoot waaaaay up.

Wilson scribbles on her pad. "You and Lord Valerian were on a date?"

"N-n-no. He was sitting at the end of the bar, and I was in the middle. I was having a drink when a guy came over. I think he said his name was Danny—"

"Danny O'Hare?"

"That's him. Danny was getting too close, making suggestive comments, just making me feel uncomfortable. Lord Valerian pretended to be my boyfriend so that Danny would leave me alone." I rub my neck, my cheeks flushing with heat as Reginald studies me. "The bartender, Lilac, can confirm that story. She saw the whole thing."

"We'll check with her." Wilson scribbles frantically. "And what time did you and Lord Valerian leave together?"

"No!" I shout, my cheeks burning. "I mean, no. I'm not here because … I'm a professional organiser. I've come down from London to help Lord Valerian clean out his castle. I didn't know he was my client when I … um … when we met that night."

This is the universe punishing you for moaning against your client's lips.

"I drove Lord Valerian back to Black Crag. We left the car park at 9.15 pm. He was alone," Reginald says.

DS Wilson scribbles this down in her notebook.

"What was the crime?" I ask. "I hope nothing happened to Lilac. She knew I was having a bad day and made sure my G&T was eighty percent G. The woman deserves a knighthood."

"We're not sharing any further information at this time." Wilson hands me a card. "If you remember anything else about that night, anything unusual that occurred after your liaison with Lord Valerian, you let us know."

Well, he did disappear into thin air, but I'm sure that was just the eighty per cent gin making me miss his graceful exit.

Right?

The Nevermore Murder Club and Smutty Book Coven Group Chat

Mina: Don't forget about book club tonight! We have a guest so everyone needs to be on their best behaviour. This means no talking about the supernatural – that scared off our last two prospects. Instead, Maisie is going to tell us all about Danny O'Hare's mysterious death.

Dora: Because gruesome murders won't scare off our new prospect?

Mina: But then what else would we talk about?

Dora: Maybe this week we could discuss the book we're reading?

Komal: A book club that ACTUALLY discusses the book and doesn't devolve into village gossip, amateur sleuthing, the consumption of enormous amounts of junk food, and hexing our exes? What kind of heathens do you take us for?

Celeste: I'll bring the cupcakes!

Isis: I'll bring the hex bags!

Maisie: I'll bring the horrifying murder facts.

Arabella: I'll bring myself. On time.

Komal: You won't.

Celeste: I'll believe it when I see it.

Dora: I'll bring my disapproving face for when we get off-topic.

Dora: Also, some Jammie Dodgers.

Beth: I'll bring this week's Zen and Tonic class schedule. I think Dora needs to sign up for some relaxing tai chi.

12

Winnie

Mum: Winifred, you'd be so proud of me! I sat down and sorted through some boxes and I took a bag to the charity shop today. The house looks so much better. I can't wait for you to see it!

Ken from next door wants me to get rid of your old dolls, but of course he's a man so he doesn't understand about saving things for the grandkids! When am I getting grandkids?

"Reginald, what do I do if I need to go to the village?" I ask on Wednesday evening as Reginald hurries into the kitchen from outside, stomping his muddy boots on the rug. Mirabelle dashes past his feet and leaps onto the counter beside me.

After the police left yesterday, Lord Valerian and I worked until past midnight. A nightmare woke me at 5 am, but I managed to finish another book before falling asleep again, and I didn't get up until 1 pm today. We finished sorting the office, moving the terrarium to a nice display table and leaving everything in piles ready for when my shelves and containers arrive, and we moved onto the ballroom, which is a much bigger task. We need to clear away the tapestries before we can even think about moving the loom. It's going to take the strength of all three of us to shift around those heavy bastards. I'm grateful for the distraction of the Nevermore Murder Club and Smutty Book Coven meeting tonight so I can put it off as long as possible.

"Why would you need to go to the village?" Reginald frowns at the empty plate in my hands. "Have I not been feeding you properly? Is there some comfort you require that I have neglected?"

He looks so distressed that I feel guilty.

"Everything you've done for me is wonderful." I take a bite of one of the berry tarts he left for me in this morning's breakfast spread in support of my point. Honestly, Reginald's food has been amazing. Alaric and I sat beside the fire again last night and Reginald brought me an incredible venison stew. Once again, Lord Valerian didn't eat a single thing. "It's only that I've been invited to a book club at Nevermore Bookshop this evening, and I thought that sounded like fun."

Reginald makes a face like he stepped in something foul. "Is that Isis Meriwether's coven?"

"It's a book club. I think she's a member, yes." The redhead was named Isis, I remember.

"How have you been in Argleton only four days and you're already mixed up with Isis Meriwether and her ilk?"

"Are they the village bad girls? Do they ride in cars with boys and wear skintight leather cigarette pants?"

Reginald doesn't seem to realise I'm joking. "They're not *bad*, merely troublesome."

"Okay, then."

"Troublesome is far worse."

"How so?"

"They have a reputation in the village – Isis runs the local magic emporium and is convinced that every strange happening is linked to the supernatural, and Mina Wilde, who owns the bookshop, fancies herself an amateur sleuth. She's put more murderers behind bars than the entire Loamshire police force, and they're none too happy about it. Some people say that Beth Duncan's tinctures and treatments are magical, although I think it's a load of codswallop. Komal Ahuja has her finger in every committee in the village, and she flies helicopters for a living. I don't trust people who don't have two feet firmly on the ground." He stomps his boots for emphasis. "And the less said about Arabella Lestrange, the better, because that woman is terrifying. The only sensible one amongst them is Isis's sister, Dora."

"Wow." That's the most Reginald has ever said in a single conversation. "You really don't like them."

"You may think that you're attending an innocent book club, Ms Preston, but you'll soon find yourself sneaking about the village at all hours, spying on suspects and conducting naked rituals in the forest." Reginald sighs. "Of course, I'll be happy to drive you to the village. I'll pick you up again when your book club finishes."

"I don't want you to have to go all the way just for me. Is there a car I could borrow? One that was built *after* the last world war?"

"I won't hear of you driving this dangerous road by yourself. It's my job to make sure you're comfortable during your stay, and if that means taking you into the village so you can become Isis Meriwether's latest project, then so be it."

I beam. "Thank you, Reginald."

Now I'm even more curious about the Nevermore Murder Club and Smutty Book Coven.

My ride arranged, I head into the ballroom to continue sorting Alaric's junk into various piles. I dump yet another slightly crooked sword onto a towering pile.

Why does a man require so *many* swords?

And what's with all the crucifixes? Alaric doesn't strike me as a religious type, but every time I move something in this house, I come up with another crucifix. I've been tossing them into a bucket for him to sort through when he wakes up.

As I work and sing along with Iggy Pop at the top of my lungs, I find myself glancing at the doorway, hoping that Alaric will wake early. I set aside several items that I want to discuss with him. But he doesn't appear until the sun falls beneath the horizon.

"Good evening, Ms Preston."

"Good even—" I turn to the door and my words catch in my throat.

Alaric stands beneath the gothic arched doorway, clad only in a pair of his tight, impeccably-tailored trousers and his high leather boots. His upper torso is naked, gleaming with beads of water that roll down the kind of perfectly-chiselled alabaster chest that would have Michelangelo's David reaching for the kettlebells. The only dent in his perfection is a white scar that extends from beneath his left armpit.

He flicks a wet curl from his forehead and regards me with those dark eyes, pressing his lips together as the corner of his mouth quirks up in what might've been a lordly smirk if Alaric Valerian were capable of such things.

Maybe he is. There's a warmth at the edge of his coal-dark eyes I haven't noticed before.

He tilts his head to the side, regarding me as I struggle to put out the fire in my ovaries. "Winifred, are you quite okay?"

"I ... um ... forgot ... what I was going to say." I run my hands through my hair, searching for a coherent thought. "Why are you damp?"

"I begin my evenings with a swim." He rubs his hair, and I try not to drool. "There is a path down to a beautiful spot I like to go. I could show you—"

"I can't swim," I blurt out.

Wait, why did I say that?

Because he's standing there all naked and wet and perfect, that's why.

"You cannot swim?" He looks confused. "Everyone should learn to swim. It's a basic survival skill."

"I don't disagree. But at my school, you needed a parent to sign a consent form before you could have swimming lessons. My mother said she'd sign it, but then the permission slip disappeared somewhere and—"

I snap my mouth shut. I can't believe I said all that. I've never,

ever spoken about my mother to anyone except Claire. I barely know Alaric and here I am starting to spill one of my most horrific secrets.

"I understand, Ms Preston," he says. "I too have a difficult mother, as you may discover if you are still here when she arrives."

"Winnie," I say. "Please, call me Winnie."

"I'll call you Winnie if you call me Alaric."

"But you have a fancy title. If I had a fancy title, I'd make everyone use it."

"Would you like a fancy title?" The corner of his mouth quirks again. "I believe I have the power to bestow them. Would you like to be 'Empress Winifred, Lady of Light and Laughter and Terrible Music', or perhaps 'Her Royal Highness Winifred, Grand Poobah of the Clutter Castle'."

I giggle despite myself. "You are ridiculous."

"The Very Very Reverend Winifred, Mistress of the Storage Containers."

"Stop!"

"Galactic Czarina Winifred? Witchfinder General Winnie?" He taps his chin. "I'm certain there is a title that will convey all of your beauty and brilliance …"

"Just Winnie! Please!" My stomach hurts from laughing. "Alaric."

At the sound of his name on my lips, both corners of his mouth crick up into an unmistakable grin. I catch a flash of perfect white teeth before he wipes the smile off his face and strides towards me, all seriousness. "Winnie, I hope you haven't been waiting for me too long. I'm eager to begin our work."

The way he says this, his eyes locked on mine with the same raw intensity he usually reserves for his art, makes me self-consciously check that I definitely, *absolutely* remembered to put clothes on this morning.

I swallow, running my fingers over my shirt buttons and totally, *definitely* not thinking about what his long fingers would feel like unbuttoning them. "You'll be working by yourself tonight. Reginald is taking me into the village for a book club."

He lifts an eyebrow. "Are you certain it's wise to go out by yourself? With a murderer still on the loose?"

I swallow. "You don't need to worry about me. I won't be by myself. I'll be in a room with several other women armed with books."

"Books may be wonderful, magical receptacles of knowledge, but they can't protect you from a killer."

"That's where you're wrong," I grin. "If that killer dares to crash our book club, they'll suffer death by a thousand paper cuts. I'd like you to sort out these crucifixes."

"Done. They can all go. They're Gideon's idea of a joke. He likes to hide them around the castle for me to find."

"Gideon?"

Alaric doesn't elaborate. I wave my hands at the pile of swords.

"Can these go, too? You have a whole gallery of stabbing in the entrance hall. You can get rid of these imperfect ones. Maybe there's a local museum or re-enactment group who'd like them."

Alaric glares at the pile of broken, warped and bent swords as though he only just noticed it.

His body stiffens. The warmth in his eyes flickers out.

"I ..." He swallows. His shoulders slump. He looks so *lost.*

"I mean, keep the ones you like." I hold up a thin blade with a bunch of glittering rubies embedded in the hilt. *Are those real? Is it normal to have a bunch of expensive jewels stuck in a sword?* "But this one is all bent. Do you need to keep the bent ones?"

Alaric takes the sword from me. "Mortimer's Cross," he murmurs.

Mortimer's Cross? Why is that name so familiar? Isn't that a famous battle?

Alaric has been so decisive with his belongings up until now. But he stares at the sword in his hands, lost to a memory.

Suddenly something occurs to me. "Alaric," I say. "Did you make these swords?"

He nods.

"Years ago, I built a forge in one of the outbuildings," he says woodenly. "You don't want to go in there. I surrendered it to the spiders. They are the forge overlords now."

Even that doesn't explain his reaction. Alaric is so critical of the things he makes that he's consigned many of his projects to the rubbish pile for the smallest imperfections. But these swords are hard for him.

I move beside him, reaching out to touch his arm. He shrinks away.

Shame burns in my chest. "I'm sorry. I didn't know they were important to you. You should keep them."

Alaric shakes his head. "You're right, they are broken, useless things. Toss them all."

He turns his head away from me.

"You're allowed to keep them." I swallow, upset with myself that I've made him feel like this. "It's okay if you're not ready to part with these things."

The sword falls through his fingers. Alaric turns back to me, his chin raised, eyes clear and cold. "I wish them gone. I shall have them removed by the time you return tonight, with the exception of this." Alaric draws a long, curved blade from the pile. "Take this with you. For protection."

"And put it where? Drat my luck, I left my sword-concealing pants back in London."

Alaric rolls his eyes, tosses the blade over his shoulder, and picks out a short dagger. "This one, then."

"I don't know. I've never carried a weapon around before. What if I sit on it and accidentally eviscerate myself?"

"Please, Winnie. It would ease my mind."

I can't refuse him after I upset him, especially not when those onyx eyes are brightening again.

"Fine."

As I reach out to take the blade from him, my hand brushes his finger.

Alaric's skin is exactly as I remember – cool to the touch, impossibly smooth and soft. I put the coolness down to wandering the halls of this huge, draughty castle after his swim.

Alaric's eyes burn into mine. He doesn't draw his hand away.

No.

What am I doing?

He's a client. He's technically my boss. And I've already made a complete fool of myself in front of him more than once.

I close my fingers around the hilt of the blade and drop it into my tote. "Thank you for the knife."

~

An hour later, I leave Alaric in the ballroom tossing even more swords into the growing rubbish pile, and huddle beneath the portcullis, wrapping my arms tight around my body as the wind howls through the ancient stones. The car huffs and burbles as Reginald brings it around. I climb in, bracing myself for the drive into the village.

"Reginald?"

"Yes, Ms Preston?"

"Alaric is throwing out his swords."

"Yes." Reginald's hands on the wheel are white.

"Can you make sure they don't end up in the skip? Hide them in a cupboard or something. I have an idea."

"As you like, Ms Preston."

By the time we pull up in front of the bakery at the top of Butcher Street, I'm a human limpet from holding on for dear life. I manage to un-jellify my legs enough to slide out of the ungainly vehicle, and Reginald gives me his mobile number and says that he'll be having dinner at the Rose & Wimple, and to call him when I'm done.

I walk along, listening to the sounds of merriment from the pub across the village green and thinking about the poor person who got murdered the same night I was moaning into the mouth of my future boss.

Lights blaze through the windows of Nevermore Bookshop. In the gloom, the building appears even more strange – the different architectural styles piled on top of each other as if the building is caught in some kind of temporal rift. (Patrick was a big Doctor Who fan. He thought the Doctor would enjoy his favourite Riesling.)

I step up to the door, but stop when I notice the CLOSED sign pasted angrily across the mottled glass window.

Oh no. Maybe I have the wrong night?

"Croak."

I jump. "Who's that?" I glance all around, but there's no one else on the street, except …

A large, black raven sits on a planter filled with dead flowers next to the door, peering at me with large, fire-rimmed eyes.

"Croak?" The raven inclines his head toward the door.

"I'm here for the Nevermore Murder Club and Smutty Book Coven," I tell him. "But I think I might have the wrong night. The shop's closed."

Why am I talking to a bird?

The raven flaps his wings and flies at the door. He grabs the corner of the sign with his beak and flips it over.

The other side also says CLOSED.

"Oh."

The raven grips the handle in its talons and yanks sharply. The door swings open, revealing the long, narrow hallway. Someone has turned on all the lamps and fairy lights that line the shelves, so the hallway glitters like the entrance to a fae realm. The raven swoops down the hallway and disappears around the corner, croaking at the top of its lungs. From somewhere deeper in the shop, I can hear voices and laughter.

"Hello?" I call out.

"Winnie, is that you?"

Mina appears around the corner, with a handsome golden retriever at her side, wearing a white and yellow harness. The raven is now sitting on Mina's shoulder. Am I imagining it, or does that bird look smug?

"Quoth told me you were here." Mina pets the raven's head. It nuzzles her hand, making a *nyuh-nyuh-nyuh* sound in the back of its throat. She beckons me to follow her. "I'm so happy you made it. We thought we'd scared you off."

"Nope, but I did get confused by the closed sign on the door."

"Sorry about that. That's my husband Heathcliff's idea of a joke. Or maybe it isn't. He doesn't like customers, which I understand is a silly thing for someone who runs a bookshop, but that's Heathcliff – a master of contradictions." Mina leads me through the main room I'd seen last time. "Come on through. This is my guide dog, Oscar. We're almost all here now. Arabella is late, but that's nothing new."

Mina pushes open a door and leads me into a large event space. The walls are hung with impressive artwork. I recognise scenes from *A Midsummer Night's Dream* and *Grimm's Fairy Tales*. This is the room I could see from the street, but as my eyes adjust to the twinkling of even more fairy lights, I realise that what I thought was a hexagonal turret is actually a pentagram shape, which strikes me as irregular for Victorian architecture … but what do I know? That corner of the room is mostly in shadow, but the turret appears to contain only a lumpy object on some kind of plinth, covered with a purple cloth. A couple of bookshelves in the opposite corner display a small selection of romance and fantasy novels, and the rest of the space is taken up with a circle of mismatched chairs, an overstuffed Chesterfield, and several beanbags arranged around a table groaning under the weight of cakes, sandwiches and open wine bottles.

Several women around my age already occupy the seats, steaming cups of tea or glasses of wine in their hands, and books scattered about their feet. Suddenly I worry I'm intruding.

"Winnie, you came!" The redhead – Isis – leaps to her feet and throws her arms around me. She's wearing a red cottagecore dress with bell sleeves that's covered in a print of what looks suspiciously like poisonous plants. She has purple streaks in her hair now that perfectly match the purple lumpy thing in the corner. "Have you read this week's book? We're discussing *Butcher & Blackbird* by Brynne Weaver. It's Komal's pick. That girl may look innocent, but she can't get enough of dark romance."

"Sorry not sorry," pipes up the black-haired girl who flies helicopters, according to Reginald. She flips her long plait of shimmering dark hair over her shoulder. "I always crush on the villains."

"Me too," I say, daring a smile that I hope doesn't wobble too much from nerves.

"Take my word for it, you wouldn't want to be married to them," Mina pipes up. "Fictional villains may leave your enemies eviscerated and your knees weak, but they're more trouble than they're worth."

The women laugh. I force a smile, knowing that it's a private joke. Perhaps they're poking fun at Mina's husband being named after *Wuthering Heights*'s swoony gothic villain.

Personally, I'm more of a Dracula-stan. Maybe I've duelled with London property prices too long, but I love a man who owns his own castle.

"Next week's book is something more lighthearted, although just as spicy. And there's lots of juicy murder." Isis tosses me a paperback called *Lords of Pain* by Angel Lawson and Samantha Rue. "Let me introduce you to everyone."

Isis sweeps her arm around the room, indicating each member of the club. "You've already met Mina and her dog Oscar. He's the only man allowed in our club."

"Croak!" the raven protests from its perch above the chamber door.

Isis rolls her eyes. "Apart from Quoth, of course. Although a little word to the wise, whatever you do, don't quote any Poe around him. He doesn't like it."

I peer at the raven with renewed interest. "What does he do if you quote Poe?"

"Trust me. You don't want to know." Isis makes a face and everyone laughs again. Even the raven makes his *nyuh-nyuh-nyuh* sound. "Next to Mina is Maisie Collins. She's a reporter for the Argleton Gazette and the best Aunt Sally player in the county. Then there's my sister, Pandora—"

"—Just Dora," Isis's sister mumbles, pulling her blanket tighter around herself. I see the family resemblance. Both Meriwether sisters have a wild tumble of red hair and heart-shaped faces with huge, pale blue eyes. But while Isis bounces around the room with her loud clothing and even louder voice, Dora looks as though she longs to fade into the woodwork, swimming in a scratchy-looking jumper that's as cosy as it is unfashionable.

She's also the only woman in the room apart from Mina wearing a wedding ring.

"Fine, just Dora. Just Dora works with me at Spell The Tea – the best magical shop in all of England. And she hates every minute of it, but with Mum gone, I need the help. Next to my gloomy sis is Celeste Lucas. She's the village baker, owner of Glazed and Confused at the top of Butcher Street, and provider of most of our fabulous spread. But be careful around her – she's like a drug pusher for sugary goodness."

"Lovely to meet you, Winnie. You *must* try the peanut butter cookies. And the honeycomb and white chocolate doughnuts." As Celeste shoves a platter under my nose, the fairy lights highlight bright red streaks in her short, textured brown bob.

I take a doughnut with a grateful smile, but leave the cookies alone. Peanut butter still turns my stomach.

"And last but not least is Beth Duncan, the village beautician and yoga instructor." Mina gestures at the standing lamp next to the fresh-faced blonde who is setting down a platter of muffins.

"And soon-to-be pole dance instructor." Beth sweeps her strawberry blonde hair off her shoulder and glares at all the ladies in the room. "And once I'm certified, you ladies better sign up for my first class or half-price facials at Zen and Tonic will be going the way of the dinosaurs."

"I'm allergic to exercise," Dora mumbles.

"Count me in!" Komal reaches for a muffin. "I want to learn how to twist myself into a human pretzel for fun. Plus, it might be good for tourism. You should do a demonstration at the Midsummer Festival."

"I think Mina gets enough time swinging around poles already, what with her three husbands," Isis teases.

Did I just hear that right? Three husbands? Is this another one of those inside jokes?

"Ew. *Beth.*" Komal scrunches up her face. "What's in this muffin, apart from sadness?"

"They're made with sprouted mung beans, ashwagandha, reishi, lion's mane, and I mixed in a Quinton shot for foundational vitamins and gut health."

"It tastes like a hate crime."

Beth bounces to her feet and embraces me warmly. "I'm so happy you felt called to join our coven, Winnie. If you don't mind me saying, you look a little puffy around the eyes and you're holding a lot of tension in your body. You should stop in at my clinic next time you're in the village – I have just the supplement regime to help. All natural, of course, and the first treatment is free for new book club members—"

The banter in this group is fierce. I can feel my overwhelm start to show on my face.

"Omigod, Beth, let the girl sit down before you start selling her on your magical mushrooms," Isis laughs.

"Although, seriously, Beth is the best." Celeste touches her cheek. "I go hiking a lot, and because of the harsh weather, my skin was starting to resemble a cartographical map. Two treatments of Beth's new skin serum and my cheeks look like a baby's bottom again."

I laugh nervously, desperate to relax into this warm group of friends. "I'll consider it, but I'm only in the village for six weeks. My client needs me to finish the job before his family visits. I'm a professional organiser," I explain. "Usually, I work in London with high-end clients and lifestyle influencers, but sometimes I travel wherever the mess takes me."

"Nevermore Bookshop must give you hives." Dora frowns at the piles of books, teacups, and raven feathers on the floor.

"I resent that." Mina places a device over the edge of an empty wine glass and pours the wine. The device beeps when the liquid is a centimetre from the top, and Mina stops pouring. "This place is organised chaos. You should have seen it before I moved in. It was chaos chaos. Wine, Winnie?"

"Oh, thank you." I take the glass and settle into a beanbag between Isis and Mina. "This place is a Scandinavian library compared to my client's house. He's a Renaissance man with more hobbies and artistic pursuits than he could squeeze into one lifetime, which is making *my* life interesting."

Isis and Komal exchange a look.

"Isis tells us that your client is Lord Valerian?" Celeste accidentally-on-purpose knocks Beth's muffin off her plate onto the floor. The raven swoops down to polish it off before Beth notices.

"Yes. His butler, Reginald, drove me in this evening. Lord Valerian lives so far out of the village and he has *so much stuff* that I'm staying at Black Crag Castle until the job is done."

The entire room falls silent.

"You're … living at Lord Valerian's castle?" Isis's eyes are two huge blue saucers. "Is that wise?"

"It's better than driving that winding road every day, and Alaric— er, *Lord Valerian* is a perfect gentleman." I blush when I think about seeing his wet, shirtless chest last night. "It's not a normal client relationship, but under the circumstances, I don't think I'm—"

"I mean on account of he's a vampire."

The girls fall silent.

Komal shoots Isis a disapproving look.

Are they teasing me? Because if I believed in things like vampires, I could see why they'd think—

"Isis, don't take the piss," Dora harrumphs.

Oh, they are teasing me.

"Lord Valerian's definitely a bloodsucker," says Beth with a laugh. "And a sexy one at that."

"He's straight out of one of our romance novels." Komal holds up a paranormal romance with a smokin' hot, dark-haired, coal-eyed vampire on the cover. I squint. The character *does* look a little like Alaric …

"He can sample my O negative any time he likes," says Beth.

"I think we should change the subject," says Mina.

"Let's review the facts." Isis checks off her fingers. "Brooding features and mysterious past, check. Gothic castle far from prying eyes, check. Never seen in the village before nightfall, check."

"Never?"

"Never." Maisie shakes her head. "Recently, he's been having a drink at the pub in the evenings. Mostly we just see his butler picking up supplies."

"He hasn't attended any of my yoga classes," Beth says, "so I can't confirm if he has a reflection."

"Once, he and his butler came into the market when I was buying booze," says Celeste. "He got frustrated because the automatic doors wouldn't register him. Perhaps sensors don't work on vampires?"

"Those doors are always finicky." Isis wags her finger. "Once they wouldn't let me in even when I was dancing right in front of them."

"I think that was because you were stoned, Isis."

Isis rolls her eyes. "I wasn't stoned. I was channelling the Goddess."

"I've never seen him eat," I say.

I regret my words the moment I speak them. Alaric's habits are his private business, and as much as I like these women and their silliness, I shouldn't be speaking about a client with them. I'm acting like I'm in college and trying to get in with the cool girls.

"He doesn't eat?" Isis slaps her thighs. "What did I tell you? That's a classic sign of vampirism. Only blood sustains him."

"I don't think he's a vampire," I say, laughing nervously. "He's just eccentric."

And brilliant. And quite funny. And with an arse so fine, Geralt of Rivia comes to him for workout tips.

Maisie reaches across and squeezes Mina's knee. *Something is going on here that I don't understand.*

"You know … a few months ago, the Argleton Village Tourism Board commissioned a special interest piece in the paper about castles in the area," Maisie says.

"I told you, tourists love castles. At least that's one idea of mine that Counsellor Durant couldn't disagree with." Komal munches on her second doughnut. No one has touched Beth's muffins.

"Yes, thank you, Ms Tourism Board Chair. So, anyway, I had to go through the archives to find photographs of Black Crag to include.

I found a portrait of the Lord Valerian from 1798. He looks *exactly* like your boss. Like, it's uncanny. I'll show you." Maisie whips out her phone and scrolls through her images. "Here."

I stare at the scanned newspaper article, pinching my fingers to zoom in on the grainy picture.

Okay, so that stuffy old lord *does* look an awful lot like Alaric, and if I didn't know better, I swear he's wearing the same coat Alaric wore the night we met at the pub. If I didn't know it was a painting from the 1700s, I'd swear that was him.

"That's Alaric's ancestor," I say. "It makes sense that there would be some family resemblance."

"There's family resemblance and then there's 'I've haunted this castle for four centuries without the love of a human woman and now I have the sweet, innocent organiser trapped in the tower'," Maisie says.

"I'm not trapped in the tower. And he gave me a fancy candelabra so I can run away in the night if I need to, just like this lady." I hand Maisie back her phone and point to one of the novels on the floor, whose cover shows a woman in a white nightgown, clutching a very similar candelabra and fleeing in terror from a creepy manor. "Besides, he can't be a vampire. I keep finding crucifixes everywhere, and his butler loves cooking with garlic."

Another odd look is exchanged between the women. Mina makes a slashing motion across her throat.

"Vampire or not, there is *something* about those old-fashioned clothes he wears," Beth pipes up.

"And that something is sexy," adds Komal.

"Agreed," I say, and instantly want to clamp my hand over my mouth.

What has gotten into me?

Dora glares at everyone. "Remember, there's *nothing* sexy about vampires who murder innocent men."

"Wait, what are you talking about?"

"You mean you haven't heard?" Komal slaps her knee. "Of course, you're not on the book club group chat. We'll have to remedy that.

And if Alaric is the murderer, he wouldn't exactly tell you about it. I found Danny O'Hare's body behind the Rose & Wimple the other day, and he was last seen alive at the pub the night before, having an altercation with Alaric over a woman."

That's me. The woman is me.

My stomach lurches, even though I haven't had any sprouted mung bean muffins. *That's why the police were so on guard when they questioned Alaric.* "Just because Alaric was talking to this guy doesn't mean he murdered him. I don't know, *obviously*, but maybe he was helping this mystery girl? Maybe the dead guy was bothering her and Alaric shooed him away."

With his lips.

His cool, kissable lips that I'm absolutely, definitely not thinking about right now …

My hand flies to the small graze on my neck where his teeth scraped my skin.

"We saw him in the pub that night," Isis exclaims. "He was looking all broody at the bar with his glass of red wine. He's been coming into the pub a bit lately."

"Do we think he's the murderer?!" Beth exclaims.

"No." Dora flashes Isis a look. "Remember? You had that vision which showed you it couldn't possibly be Alaric."

"Oh, yes! That's right." Isis's face twists into an unreadable expression. "Alaric's not the murderer. I know because I am a skilled psychic. I just … forgot before. Winnie's right – he was probably just shooing Danny away."

"I'd believe Winnie's version of events," Maisie says. "Danny O'Hare was a local builder, sort of a jack-of-all-trades, and he practically had his own barstool down at the Rose & Wimple. He was also a first-class wanker. Every woman in this room has had to fend off his overzealous advances. Oh, and that horrifying fact I want to tell you? Danny was exsanguinated."

The whole room gasps, myself included. "That's the horrifying fact you wanted to tell us? That wasn't in your article in the paper! If a vampire is running about, sucking people dry, then the village should know about it," Isis declares.

"I can't write that the murder was committed by a vampire," Maisie says. "Don't you remember the last time we had a vampire murder and the whole village went nuts stealing holy water from the church and keeping stakes in their handbags?"

Sorry, what?

Mina sinks lower in her chair.

"Wait a second," I say. "A vampire murder has happened before?"

"It turned out to have a rational explanation," Mina mumbles. "I'm sure this will, too. Right, Maisie?"

"Right. But it *is* all very strange. The police are stumped. Whoever the killer was, they somehow managed to follow Danny down that narrow alley and make it back past all the patrons at the pub without being seen by a single eyewitness."

"That's because the killer turned into a bat and *flew* in to make the kill."

"Isis, the killer isn't a vampire," Dora huffs.

"Then explain how Danny ended up with his veins drunk dry?" Isis's eyes dance. "I'm telling you, ladies, we have a real bloodsucker in town and if it isn't Winnie's boss—"

"Don't tell me, Isis is banging on about her vampire theories again?" a bored voice coos.

Everyone's heads turn towards the door, where an impossibly tall and elegant woman stands. She has the silken black hair and flawless dark skin of a twenty-one-year-old film star and the haughty air of a widow who pushed her husband down the stairs and got away with it.

Isis sticks her tongue out at the newcomer, who sweeps into the room like some ancient courtesan, rolls her eyes at Isis, and flops down dramatically on the one remaining beanbag, legs akimbo.

"How are you this evening, Arabella?" Isis asks, a hint of sarcasm dripping into her voice.

Arabella – perfect name – shrugs her elegant shoulders. "New liver, same eagles."

I gape at her. "Did you just make a Prometheus reference?"

Arabella smirks at me. "Hello, new girl. You're going to fit in perfectly. Yes, I've had a terrible headache from dealing with lawyers and bankers all day, and that's before I've even started my evening client meetings. I have no patience for Isis's mad theories."

"Arabella is our resident vampire expert," Isis explains. "She's one of the few humans they trust to keep their secret because she's helping them to invest their centuries of inherited wealth so they can become even richer assholes with devastating good looks—"

"Isis!" Mina, Komal, Maisie and Dora snap at the same time.

"Right, er …" Isis shrinks in her seat. "I mean, I'm sure Arabella's clients are lovely and not murderers at all."

"I'm not here to discuss my clients," Arabella huffs. "I come for one reason only – the *smut*. I for one enjoyed this chilling dark romance, although I don't think the serial killers were as imaginative as they could have been. There was a distinct lack of things shoved underneath fingernails, and *no one* got beheaded with a rusty sword—"

As Arabella leads the group in a lively discussion about *Butcher & Blackbird*, I glance around the room and find myself wishing that I were here for longer than six weeks—

What's that?

In the window behind that strange purple cloth, obscured by shadow, is the outline of a face.

Someone's watching us.

"Hey, Isis, can you see that?" I nudge her just as she pulls her arm back to throw a muffin at Beth.

"What?"

By the time Isis turns around, the face is gone.

13

Alaric

Gideon: Here's my weekly invitation that you'll ignore as usual – meet me at the Sanctus Club on Friday night. Nothing removes a stick from your arse like the sins of the flesh, and you don't have to marry a lady to have some fun for once. You could even bring along the human. That would be delightfully taboo. As long as she doesn't mind a friendly nibble ...

I CROUCH IN THE OVERGROWN GARDEN RUNNING ALONG THE SIDE OF Nevermore Bookshop, my favourite sword resting over my knees. A large stick pokes my posterior, but I don't dare shift my position to remove it.

Did she see me?

I assume not, because Winnie strikes me as someone who wouldn't keep to herself the fact that she'd caught her employer spying on her book club. If any of the Nevermore Meddling Club members knew I was outside, they'd be upon me, torches lit and claws out.

Not even my vampiric strength would save me from their wrath.

I no longer have a heart that beats with human haste, so I don't have to wait for it to stop racing. But something *is* wrong with me. I'm hot all over – something that shouldn't happen to the undead – and I'm filled with a strange, pulsing energy, even more intense than when I'm in the throes of a creative distraction.

Something has been wrong with me since Winifred Preston arrived at my home. I'm drinking twice as much as usual, but the blood doesn't have its usual effect. And despite furnishing her with a knife, I find that I can't bear the idea of letting her out of my sight with a husker on the loose.

And now I'm crouched in the garden of a bookstore like a common deviant.

Not daring to lift my head again, I scan the street, searching out every darkened nook for signs of trouble. My fingers close around the hilt of my sword, and for a moment, I am back in another century, with dust in my throat and hate in my heart …

This village may appear innocent, but I have been upon this earth too long not to fear the shadows. As long as Winifred is here in Argleton, she is in danger. From men like Danny, and from much worse creatures.

I should not care what happens to a human, not after all the things they've done to me. But the same enchantment that has me dreaming of her scent compels me to protect her.

After several minutes, I determine that no book club members are coming to stake me. I shuffle through the weeds to another window and dare another peek inside.

The book club appears to have finished. Winifred helps two of the women straighten chairs, fold blankets and stack books. Of course, she couldn't leave the meeting room in a mess.

I duck into the bushes just as the front door opens and the book club members file out. They hug and chatter on the street, clutching books and tinfoil parcels of baked treats under their arms. They head off in different directions.

Winnie is the last one out the door. She chats to Arabella Lestrange and another woman while she waits for Reginald. I duck through the other end of the garden and circle around to the parking lot of the Rose & Wimple, where my loyal butler waits for me, the boot of the car open into a yawning maw.

"You do not look well, my lord."

"It's being in close proximity to all these wretched humans," I mutter. "I shall feel better when we return to Black Crag."

"I think it is the proximity to one human in particular."

As I climb into the darkness that hugs me like a coffin, a wave of nausea hits me. I know what I have done is wrong. Winnie would not wish me to follow her and skulk in the shadows.

But when the night is filled with monsters, you need the worst monster of all on your side.

The Nevermore Murder Club and Smutty Book Coven Group Chat

Mina: I can't believe you lot. What did we SPECIFICALLY agree before last night's meeting? No supernatural talk around Winnie!

Isis: But that was before we found out she's smitten with a murderous vampire.

Dora: Isis!

Isis: Don't get me wrong. I don't think she KNOWS that she's smitten with a murderous vampire.

Beth: She didn't seem to mind. We were just teasing.

Arabella: Even though Alaric's a vampire, remember that he's not the only vampire in the village. Perhaps we should not condemn him as a murderer merely because he enjoys wearing a frock coat.

Komal: The way that frock coat hugs his arse, though ...

Celeste: Don't get her started, Arabella.

Dora: Especially not when Isis's VERY ACCURATE vision exonerates him.

Isis: Oh, that's right. I forgot about that. Alaric's not our murderer.

Mina: Well, I hope you guys didn't scare Winnie away. I like her, AND she purchased five more books from the shop, which is more than I can say for the rest of you. I'm sad that she's only here for a few weeks.

Dora: She'll be here much longer than six weeks.

Mina: Is that a prediction, or wishful thinking?

Dora: I don't do magic, remember? That's Isis's domain.

Komal: Sure, Dora.

Isis: Dora's right. On account of my amazing psychic powers and Winnie being smitten with the not-murderous vampire, I predict that she'll be sticking around. And I AM magic, so I would know.

14

Winnie

Mina: Winnie, it was so fun to see you again you last night. Isis is sorry about all her vampire talk. I'm sure your boss is totally human and a completely normal guy who just happens to look damn fine in a frock coat. We'd love to have you back at next week's book club ... that is, if you haven't decided we're all bonkers!

"Good evening, Lady Winifred, Countess of Clean. Did you enjoy the book club?" Alaric asks the next day as he enters the ballroom, his hair damp from his evening swim and his face an unreadable wall of sexy stone.

I can't decide if I'm happy or disappointed that he's wearing a shirt this time.

I managed to stay in bed until 2 pm today. I didn't sleep, as usual. The nightmares woke me around 5 am, my sheets damp with sweat, my body crawling with invisible bugs. And then I stared at the ceiling while my brain swirled around everything the book club said about Alaric – all these oddities that, if I were a character in a paranormal romance, would make me believe that I was unwittingly working for a centuries-old vampire.

But I'm *not* a character in a book. I'm a totally normal, slightly neurotic clean freak with an odd, grumpy client who is definitely not a murderer. Or a vampire.

I told myself over and over that I didn't believe Isis's nonsense, but I still couldn't make myself stop thinking about the way Alaric held me when I fell as if I weighed nothing at all, and touching the graze on my neck where his sharp teeth scraped my skin …

In the end, the only way to shut my brain up was to pick up another book from the stack Mina sold me. I started a new series the book club insisted I read – about a heroine who was going blind and worked in a magical bookshop that brought infamous fictional villains to life. The heroine had three love interests – Heathcliff from *Wuthering Heights*, Moriarty from *Sherlock Holmes*, and a shapeshifting raven named Quoth, and they solved murder mysteries around a quaint English village. Mina told me that she wrote it under a pseudonym and I could see why she hadn't put her name on it – the books were inspired by her real life (minus the magic and the fictional villains brought to life, obviously), and they were *racy*.

A blush creeps over my cheeks just thinking about them.

Or maybe that blush is caused by the intensity of Alaric's anthracite gaze, or the curl of dark hair plastered to the side of his face that my fingers itch to tuck behind his ear. Or the crazy thought that if he *were* a vampire, I might not care.

"Book club was fun," I tell him. "I haven't laughed so hard in a long time."

I hate to admit how true that is.

Patrick and I didn't laugh much. He was serious and driven, focused on building his bespoke window company, which at the time was what I *thought* I wanted in a partner. Someone who had their life together, who had career goals and valued experiences over stuff.

I did all my laughing with my oldest friend, Claire. She knows all my secrets. She's the only person I've ever trusted with the truth about Mum. Not even Patrick knew the full extent of it, although he lived with the fallout. More than once he called me a clean freak or a drill sergeant after I threw out something he wanted to keep or he found me scrubbing the bathroom in the middle of the night after one of my dreams.

But Claire had been inside Mum's house. She helped me clean the first time the council threatened to evict Mum. She could have spent her holidays in Majorca, but instead she spent them trying to convince my mother that she didn't need twenty-two tea cosies or five boxes of expired hot sauce. I thought Claire was a real friend.

Now I know better.

"I'm pleased that you had a good time." Alaric moves nearer, his leather boots clicking against the marble. "And you had no trouble in the village? No would-be murderers crashing your meeting or lurking in the shadows?"

I open my mouth to tell him about that face staring in the window, but the dark tone in his voice makes me pause. He studies me, fire flaring in the corners of his eyes. Even though the fire Reginald lit barely penetrates the chilly room, warmth pools inside me, as if the butterfly has made itself a tiny campfire.

I think of the way he leapt in to rescue me at the pub and the protective way he held me, as though I were something more to him than just a stranger.

I think of Danny O'Hare, infamous menace to women, lying in an alley with the blood drained from him.

I force a smile. "Not a murderer in sight. Besides, I have my dagger. Not that I know how to use it."

"As long as you aim the pointy end at the monster, you should be fine." Alaric's shoulders relax. "Speaking of pointy things, I got rid of the swords."

"I see that." And I saw Reginald wink at me as he handed me my evening hot chocolate, so I know he's stored them away somewhere.

"I have found someone to move the loom. They will arrive Monday evening."

"Monday?" I wince. "That's not much time to get all these tapestries out of here so they can get to it."

I'm not looking forward to manoeuvring heavy tapestries on very little sleep. I move towards the call button. "I'll get Reginald. It's going to take all three of us to move these. I don't know how you managed to roll and stack them—"

Alaric picks up the nearest rolled tapestry. I move to help him, but he tosses it over his shoulder like he's the morally-grey hero in a gothic romance and it's a damsel running from his castle. He carries it over to the patch of empty floor we cleared and unrolls it.

I gasp. "How did you do that? That thing has to weigh hundreds of pounds! I don't want you to injure yourself!"

Alaric doesn't answer. He kicks the tapestry, sending up a cloud of dust as it thumps against the marble.

I can't help it. I gasp … *again*.

It's a depiction of the valley. I recognise the curve of the stream, the rocky crag with the castle perched atop it. What I don't recognise are the knights fighting in the foreground, swords clashing, bodies twisting as they meet in the thick of battle. One horse tramples an enemy knight beneath its feet. There's a raw kind of realism to it, as if it had been rendered from memory, as if the viewer was regarding the scene from atop their own horse before they dived into the fray.

"This is the Battle of Black Crag in 1626," Alaric says. "My interpretation of it, anyway."

"Alaric, it's beautiful," I whisper. "It's as if you were there. Why do you have this rolled up? It should be on display."

"I couldn't display this." He makes a face as he points to a horse's flank. "The proportions are all wrong. And this soldier's arm is the wrong length. And this sky here? What was I *thinking?* It needs to be repaired, but I never have the time. I get distracted."

The butterfly that lives permanently in my stomach around him is joined by a friend, but their churning stirs memories I'd rather forget.

"No wonder you have trouble throwing things out, Alaric. You're a perfectionist."

He regards me, his face expectant, and there's something delicate about the stone of his flawless features. "Isn't that a good thing?" he asks.

"Yes and no. Holding yourself to a high standard *is* good, but taken to extremes, it means it's difficult to make decisions because you're afraid of getting things wrong. Perfectionism can be a way for people to avoid finishing things or, in your case, displaying them."

"Is this what a professional organiser does?" Alaric's tone is light but his eyes tell me that I've hit a nerve. "Try to get into their clients' heads?"

"Yes," I say firmly. "I'm not a psychologist, but understanding how your brain works is key to keeping the castle clean after I leave. It's the 'Sustain' part of the Winnie Wins System."

Alaric's mouth flicks down at one corner. I've seen that before, too – clients who think that my job is to come in for a day, solve all their clutter problems, and they don't have to do a thing. Many of my clients have never had to do any work on themselves.

But I don't think this is Alaric's issue. I think he's the opposite – all these hours alone with his thoughts, digging deep into these "distractions" of his; I think he knows that the mess in the castle is created by the mess inside his head, but he's afraid of what clearing up that mess might reveal.

"You're being too hard on yourself," I say softly. "These tapestries are beautiful, and even if you only see the mistakes, you should be proud of creating them. Not everyone can do this."

His lips quirk. "Really? Not everyone spends their days locked inside a grim castle teaching themselves medieval textile techniques?"

"I know, can you believe it?" I grin. "I think you should put these out where people can see them."

"No one will see them. I never have guests at the castle."

"You have me."

The words hang between us, taking on a weight and importance I hadn't intended. Alaric's eyes meet mine, and there's such vulnerability there that my thoughts scatter like pool balls after an overly enthusiastic break.

All too quickly, my gaze and memories return to his lips. I think about that moment, in the pub, when I was so lost in him that I forgot how to form sentences.

I swallow, look away. I can't think these things about my boss, about a client, and *especially* not about someone who walks the same path as my mother. I shore up my castle walls, reinforce my defences against those anthracite eyes and that infuriating half-smile.

"Once we're done with the cleanup," I say, keeping my voice bright, "I think you should have guests. I bet if you invited some of the villagers over for a party, you'd enjoy their company."

And perhaps they wouldn't accuse you of being a vampiric murderer.

Alaric looks as if he'd rather eat his tapestry.

"Fine, fine," I grin. "I've got five more weeks to convince you that it's a brilliant idea. Right now, Lord Strongman, throw that tapestry over your shoulder and let's hang it in the upstairs corridor. You have all those gaps on the walls where paintings used to live – I think we can find a home for every one of these beautiful, not-perfect tapestries."

15

Winnie

Mum: Winnie, Ken told me that Barry called the council. I'm so livid! I can't believe I ever considered them my friends. Let's see how High-And-Mighty Barry likes the doll heads I threw over the fence! When do you finish your job again? I think I might need a little help. You don't have to come in the house. I know you have FEELINGS about it, but just to drive some things to the charity shop for me? I promise that I've done so much work since you last saw it. You'll be so impressed.

"My lord, you have a visitor—" Reginald pauses as he realises Alaric isn't in the ballroom with me.

"He found a box of coloured beads and got all inspired." I shrug as I return to stacking boxes. It's Monday evening, and thanks to Alaric's tapestry-moving superpowers, the ballroom is almost ready for the loom-movers. I just have a few more boxes of tapestry tools to pack and then it's done. "I let him go to his study for a bit. His fidgeting was disrupting the organising process."

Reginald frowns at the Sleep Token riff blasting from my portable speaker. "And the buzzsaw coming out of the speakers doesn't?"

"Nope." I grin. "By the way, thank you for saving those swords for me. I don't think he's ready to be rid of them."

"I agree." Reginald's features relax, his eyes glazing over a little. "The swords are important to him. I've stacked them in one of the cells in the dungeon for when you need them. Gideon Blake is here to move the loom. I'll let him up."

I decide not to concern myself with the mention of a dungeon. *What a man keeps beneath his castle is his own business.* "Okay, do you want me to tell Alaric or—"

"I prefer not to disturb my lord during his creative pursuits." Reginald retreats. "He tends to be a little …"

"Stabby?"

"Precisely."

I grin. "Send up Gideon and his crew. I can instruct them."

A few minutes later, Reginald reappears, sweeping his arm in a grand gesture. "Gideon Blake, may I introduce Ms Winifred Preston, our professional organiser."

I look up to see an immaculately dressed man with tousled golden hair and peacock blue eyes standing in the doorway. "Call me Winnie." I stand, brushing dust from my hands before offering it to the newcomer.

Gideon regards my hand with wry amusement, his eyes sparkling with mischief. I don't know what I expected from a loom mover, but it isn't this.

"Gideon." His eyes crinkle at the edges as he clasps my hand in both of his. His touch is cool, like Alaric, but he *is* wandering around the draughty castle in a silk shirt. "I heard you need your loom relocated, or is that code for 'save me from Alaric the Cantankerous Count'?"

He says this in such a flirtatious way, with one eyebrow cocked, that I burst out laughing.

"No code. Lord Valerian needs the ballroom for his party." I peer over his shoulder. "Where are your guys?"

"My guys? You think I have a retinue of manservants following me around, catering to my every whim?" He laughs again. "Unlike your Bad-Tempered Baron, I prefer to indulge my own whims. Much more fun that way."

"I mean, where are the guys who are moving the loom?"

Gideon rolls up one sleeve, revealing elaborate tattoos of Renaissance artwork. He squeezes his bicep. "I've got two of these guys."

I snort. "You can't move this loom by yourself."

He raises an eyebrow. "Is that a challenge? What do I win if I succeed? A kiss from fair Winifred?"

Who is *this guy?*

He talks about Alaric as if they're friends … Does Alaric have friends? And he chose *this*?

"No kisses." I fold my arms. "And you're not attempting to move that loom yourself. It's got to be against health and safety regulations."

"Fine, then I'm going to make Alaric do most of the work. It's the least he can do since the poxy bastard made me help him set it up in the first place."

They are *friends. Interesting.*

"Alaric's in his study, working on an art project," I say. "I don't want to disturb him, but maybe we can get Reginald to …"

Gideon isn't listening. He circles the room, his eyes taking in the carved marble columns that I've started to clean off, the corner of the marble floor we uncovered beneath the pile of tapestries, and the neat piles of boxes I've stacked in the corner ready to be taken to the skip.

"I'm impressed, Winifred Preston. When Alaric's mother told me about this little party, I thought it would be a disaster. After all, the Duke of Dourdom hates dancing, loathes fancy dress, and is morally opposed to fun. Don't get me wrong, I enjoy a slow-motion trainwreck, especially when it involves certain members of certain royal courts. But with you at the helm, Allie has a chance to pull this off."

Allie?

Allie?

"I'm just the organiser. Alaric's the one who's done all the work."

"Is that what he's told you? Interesting." Gideon rubs his chin. "Did he tell you that I'm his party planner?"

"No."

I can't even imagine Alaric hiring a party planner. I assumed that his mother was taking care of the details. Or Reginald. Or that Alaric planned to bar the castle gates and throw boiling pitch on anyone who tried to get in.

"You're looking at the genius tasked with transforming this dusty room into a ball no one will forget. And now that I've seen the space we have to work with, I'm even more convinced this will be the event of the year." Gideon tilts his head to the side, regarding me with those fierce blue eyes. "You should be my date for the ball. We'd turn heads."

The butterflies in my stomach do a little cha-cha-cha. "Are you asking me?"

"I don't need to." He steps closer, his finger trailing a chilly line along my arm. "Surely you can feel the passion between us? This sexual fission just begging to be unleashed—"

"Gideon."

I whirl around, jerking my arm away from Gideon. Alaric looms in the doorway, glittering beads stuck to the wool of his tailored jacket, his face a storm cloud.

Gideon either doesn't notice or isn't afraid of Alaric's moods. He sweeps his arm across his body and bows deeply. "Allie, looking dapper as always. I was just chatting to your organiser about the ball—"

"Winnie doesn't want to go to the ball with you," Alaric growls.

"Winnie is standing *right here*." I plant my hands on my hips. "Thank you for the invite, Gideon," I say sweetly. "But I won't be attending the ball. I'm not really the ball-going type, and I'll be back in London by then, anyway."

"Such a pity," Gideon sighs dramatically. He moves behind me, and before I can step away, he leans in close, his breath dancing over my earlobe. "You would have made a fine date. Don't you think, Allie?"

"Get out," Alaric snaps.

"I can't leave yet." Gideon grins as he moves to the loom. He's enjoying himself far too much. "I'm moving a loom. Winnie, darling, would you bend over here for me and undo that nut?"

Alaric looks like smoke is about to pour out his ears.

"You know, Winnie." Gideon starts to unlock the clamps holding the loom together. "Some years ago Allie promised me – upon pain of an excruciating death – that I would never have to move this loom again. And yet, here we are."

"I couldn't have foreseen my mother throwing this infernal ball," Alaric mutters. His eyes never leave me as he crosses the room to help Gideon with the pins.

"Having become intimately acquainted with your mother during the party planning process, I rather believe you should have foreseen this— Are you helping me take apart this infernal contraption, or making love to it? You'll need to give that pin a bit of welly—"

Reginald slips into the room and joins me as we stand in the corner and watch Alaric and Gideon curse each other out as they take apart the loom and march it, piece by impossibly heavy piece, to its new home upstairs. By the time Alaric lifts off the warp beam, his shoulders rippling and his features stoic, with not even a droplet of sweat on his forehead, I'm the one who needs the cold shower.

"I didn't know Alaric had a friend," I whisper to Reginald as Alaric and Gideon get into a bickering match over a scuff Alaric claims Gideon made on the marble column.

"I'm not certain Gideon Blake is someone you'd want as a friend," Reginald replies. "But my lord has his strange ways, Ms Preston. I find it's best not to question them. That way lies madness."

16

Alaric

Dhampir – the abomination born from the coupling of an Upyr man and a human woman. That this is the only procreation that our kin can conceive outside of the Kiss! Corrupted by the unnatural mingling of blood, the Dhampir's hunger can never be sated. With teeth of iron, they will tear their way through their own mother's flesh, consuming her from the inside out before unleashing their horrors upon the world. They will kill indiscriminately – not for food, but for joy, and will devour the flesh of their kin. They must be prevented at all costs. Such are the strict laws pertaining to copulation with humans.

—*The Crimson Annals: Accounts of the Laws of the Upyr,*
Akakios the Younger of the Blood Ptolemy

Callista: Since I know you're not reading the news, I am informing you that the community is in uproar over this husking in our territory. Our kind fear this will expose us, that we will be hunted again. You say that you have Gideon Blake investigating on top of his duties as planner. What good is a property developer? Especially one who brazenly flouts Court customs.

Has he any leads to share? I wish to speak with him when I arrive. Arrange the meeting. And find that killer.

By the time I send Winnie to bed after our midnight dinner beside the fire, the ballroom is empty and the castle is bedecked with tapestries. I wander the halls that were once bare, cold stone, enjoying the way they now glitter with threads of gold.

I try to see my work through her eyes, to feel wonder when I look at these pieces instead of shame.

Then I think of what my mother will say when she sees my work hanging in the castle, and of Winnie leaving in four weeks, and the blood in my cold veins feels as though it is made of razor blades.

I don't want Winnie to leave. I want her laughter and her infuriating attempts to get inside my head and the way her cheeks redden sometimes when she looks at me. I want the joy she brings to this cold castle.

I want to kiss her again.

I want things no vampire should ever want from a human. I want things that will crumble my whole world to ashes.

It's best that she leaves.

She's safer back in London, far away from monsters who lurk in the shadows.

But perhaps ... perhaps I can hold onto this feeling after she's gone. My fingers itch to create. I settle at the desk in my now-tidy office, pulling out a freshly stretched canvas. Reginald appears from the shadows as I begin a sketch.

"My lord, I've prepared the car for you."

"Why? I'm not leaving the house."

"You must, my lord." Reginald regards me with his stoic gaze. "You are suffering. You need blood, and the vintage in our cellar isn't cutting it. I've made us an appointment at a feeding club. Winifred will be fine in the castle for a few hours while you—"

"I'm not going to a feeding club."

The thought of it makes me shudder. Sinking my teeth into the neck of a stranger, giving them that pleasure when there's something much closer to home that I want …

"But—"

"I said *no.*"

Reginald purses his lips. "Is this because of Winifred, my lord?"

"It's not your concern."

"You kissed her."

"I said I don't want to discuss it!"

Reginald's sigh is so quiet, it would be imperceptible if I weren't possessed of supernatural hearing. "You wish for a nightcap, my lord?"

"Thank you, Reginald. The French aristocrat tonight, I feel." I turn away, setting out my palette knives and brushes, not wanting him to read anything in my face. "You have checked on Winifred?"

"For now, she sleeps."

"Please inform me if that changes."

"As you wish, my lord."

Reginald fades into the shadows to go about his business. I return to the canvas on my easel, allowing my mind to fill in the garish white space with a vision. This is the challenge with painting, the reason it infuriates and enraptures me. When I begin, I hold a picture in my head of what I want the finished painting to look like, but as I work, that vision becomes blurry, and I can never bring back the crispness of my original idea.

This time, I'm certain my subject will remain sharp.

But before I can begin … I search my desk, trying to remember where Winnie put my phone. She left it in a tray on the corner, along with my set of castle keys. What an odd place for them to be. That woman is infuriating.

It takes me a few tries to remember how to make a call. Gideon answers on the first ring.

"Alaric Valerian himself?" He sounds amused. I hear the noise of construction in the background. "I usually hear from your dogsbody. I didn't know you knew how to use a phone. Have you called to apologise for your cruelty earlier?"

I realise I'm holding the rectangle upside down and flip it up the right way before replying.

"You were toying with me."

"I was doing you a favour, Allie. If sweet young Winifred happens to be taken with my roguish charms, then that's hardly my fault. You should bring her to my ball. The reclusive, mysterious Lord Valerian with a human on his arm – utterly taboo, completely delicious ... you'll create such a stir."

I have no desire to speak to him any further about Winnie. He may be a rake and a wastrel of the first order, but Gideon Blake would fall on a sword for me, as I would for him. (Although only if the sword is made by a master smith. I don't eviscerate myself on inferior craftsmanship.)

"What have you found out about this husking?" I ask.

Gideon sighs. "It looks bad for us. I have feelers out in the community, but either this is a rogue unknown to us, or they've frightened their kin into silence. One thing is certain – Danny O'Hare had fang marks in his neck. According to the coroner, he died from blood loss. His organs failed, he went into shock, his blood vessels literally collapsed like a house of cards. Not a beautiful death. Luckily, the police are incompetent twits – their leading theory is that the killer staged the murder to look like a vampire did it."

I snort. "That's absurd."

"I agree, but there's precedent. A few years ago there was a string of murders in the village with a similar *modus operandi*, but it turned out to be a different kind of monster. You don't remember?"

I do, vaguely. It ended up having something to do with Mina Wilde, the Nevermore Bookshop owner. But there hadn't been as many vampires living in Argleton then. Gideon's Sanctus development is attracting them to the area, which means he has a business incentive to catch this rogue vampire. The last thing either of us want is to risk courtly intervention.

"I don't pay much attention to what goes on in the village," I say. "I'm only interested this time because ..."

"... because of a certain scrummy organiser?" Gideon presses.

"Because my mother is concerned," I snap.

Gideon laughs, slow and easy. "As well she should be, as her son the lonely, grumpy lord of the castle is a prime suspect. But don't worry, I have a plan to throw them off your scent. Don't panic, Allie, we'll find who did this before they hurt anyone else, and we don't need the Mora to give this bastard the justice he deserves."

"I told you to stop calling me Allie."

Gideon laughs again. "You did, but I rarely listen to anything you say."

I hang up and drop the phone back into the tray, then swipe the tray onto the floor. Keys, phone and papers filled with doodles scatter across the rug, but I don't pick them up.

I mix my colours and absorb myself in my painting. As I work, the hunger gnaws at me, twisting my stomach into painful knots. Strawberries invade my nostrils. My skin crawls with the memory of every time she's touched me without fear.

How I have wished with a warrior's forlorn hope that someone might one day look at me like that.

Reginald can see I'm growing weak. But I can't abide the solution he proposes. Just last night he offered his neck to me, something he hasn't done for years now. He knows how I feel about it.

I'm not sure I feel the same way anymore. When I look at Winnie's neck, when I imagine the sweetness of her invading my mouth or her body melting against mine as she embraces the Kiss, I can't believe it is anything wrong, or evil. I've only known her a few short days, against my lifetimes of loneliness, but I wish that she could stay forever.

Perhaps she would want the Kiss …

No.

I cannot think such a thing. I cannot go back on the blood oath that has defined my life. I will not allow my mother to use me as a political pawn, and I will *never* curse another as I have been cursed.

So I paint and I rage and I burn from the inside out, and I hope that some solution presents itself. In my long life, I have read every book on vampire lore in the Black Crag library, so I know that there is no loophole that would allow me to pursue anything more with her than our tentative friendship.

And yet, I cannot banish her from my thoughts or my veins.

It's sometime later that I become aware of Reginald calling my name. Reluctantly, I set down my brushes and wipe the paint from my fingers. "Yes?"

"My lord, it's happening again."

I fly from the room.

Reginald calls after me. "My lord, you cannot go to her in your state—"

But I don't listen. I cross the castle in a single heartbeat and ascend the staircase to her room. Her cries reach my ears.

Who has hurt Winnie so deeply that the pain follows her into her dreams?

I think of the cruel, monstrous things I'd like to do to them.

My fingers grasp the handle. Even if she has locked the door, I can break it with a flick of my wrist. I can gather her in my arms and tell her …

Tell her what? That nightmares aren't real?

But they *are* real.

I am real.

My fingers fall from the handle. Winnie lets out another strangled sob. I ache to hold her.

Instead, I lean my back against her door. Every cry and moan that falls from her mouth renders me impotent.

What terrors have turned her nights into horror?

~

Winnie's nightmares wake her, as they have every night since she arrived at the castle, according to Reginald. A crack of light appears under the door. I hear her sigh, hear her footsteps on the rug and the water running in the bathroom. The bed creaks, and the pages of a book turn.

And then, I hear something else.

A buzzing sound.

I don't understand what the buzzing can be at first, but then Winnie moans.

This moan is different from the way she whimpers in her dreams when she is distressed and frightened.

This moan is … is …

… it's the moan she made when I kissed her.

It's the needy tremble of her body against me when my teeth scraped over her skin.

It's the sound that has haunted me every night.

It's the moan that has undone me.

My whole body tightens. Long dormant sensations clasp at my cold skin, warming me from the inside out. I taste my own blood on my tongue, rich and old and filled with dark urges.

Winnie moans again and of their own accord my hands seek my waistband. All the taboos of my kin, all the dire warnings about what can happen when a human and vampire go to bed together are drowned into insignificance by that moan.

I feel like I'm no longer in control of my body. I'm a coil of need and desperation and foolish longing.

This is not for you.

But I cannot tear myself away. My hand closes around myself. I close my eyes and draw myself out, stroking my length in cruel silence as I gorge myself in a vision of her golden eyes staring back at me, wide and burnished with pleasure. I see her full lips part, her body arch off her bed, her skin like spun silver, and …

"Alaric," Winnie whispers my name, each syllable clear as crystal to me over the buzzing of her toy. "Alaric."

I bite my lip, not realising that my fangs have dropped. The sharp pain jolts me back to reality, back to this wretched scene of me skulking in her hallway, listening to her most private ministrations, so befuddled with lust that I imagine she wants me as I want her—

"Alaric … oh!"

Her voice weaves an enchantment. The knowing of it, of what she's doing to herself in there with *my* name on her lips—

There's only a thin wooden door between us. In a moment, I could have the door off its hinges, I could be in her bed, tasting her, making her scream my name instead of whispering it. I wrench myself away from her door and force one foot in front of the other back down the stairway, disgusted with myself.

I want her so badly that I might have to stake myself through the heart just to keep her safe from *me*.

17

Alaric

Gideon: I have news, Allie. One of my informants has told me of a local vampire, Baylor Godsven of the Blood Ptolemy, who may have unnatural tastes. He got into trouble with the Mora in Finland a couple of decades ago for inappropriate relations with a human. He's now living on an estate not far from Argleton, and there have been rumours floating around about what he does to humans and vampires in his manor.

Sounds like he'd be the type to enjoy exploring a taboo like husking. Tell your mother to hold onto her tits, I will investigate. BTW, could I interest you in an investment opportunity? Guaranteed two hundred percent return, no money down ...

In my study, I draw my favoured sword from its hiding place and, with the roar of a beast who longs for things that cannot be his, I attack the towering stacks of ceramic pots. My eyes cloud with the fog of the battlefield as I hack and slash and slay – the only things I'm made for.

By the time I surface from the fog, my chest heaving, my arms aching, I'm standing amidst the ruins of my art, Winnie's moan a roar in my veins.

Reginald appears at the door, broom in hand.

"I'll clean up, my lord. She need not know a thing."

Disgusted with myself and buzzing with the thrill of my name on Winnie's lips, I return to my office to work on my newest piece. But after several hours, I give up. The painting is a failure. I feel wretched. I debate tearing the canvas to pieces, but decide to keep it – sometimes, I will take elements from discarded works to reuse on a new piece.

But likewise, I don't want to leave the painting on the desk for Winnie to see. Now I know that she … that she's attracted to me, I don't want to lower myself in her esteem by allowing her to see this worthless doodle.

Her breathy voice whispering my name pounds inside my skull as I pick up the canvas and hurry down the hall. There's a small secret room opposite the dining room that has lain empty for some years. I once used it to hide a priest escaping the wrath of Queen Elizabeth. The narrow doorway can be hidden behind a tapestry, and the way the castle walls shape around the landscape hides its presence.

I fling open the door and drop my mistake inside. I will start again tomorrow.

I cannot sleep.

Usually, when I close the lid of my coffin, I am dead to the world. (That's my little joke, since I am always dead to the world.)

Inside the velvet-lined walls of my eternal resting place, both my body and mind usually find rest.

But not today. I toss and turn. Every time I close my eyes, I hear her voice whisper my name, soft and breathy.

I hear her come apart, her moans dissolving as the pleasure claims her body. My name bursting from her pretty lips.

And I wish, I wish more than I have wished for anything else in my long life, that I could join her. She's more than a beguiling scent and delicious moan – she is brightness and celebration and laughter. She makes me feel light, as though the years I've endured are nothing but leaves floating past on an autumn breeze.

When she's here, Black Crag doesn't feel like a prison, but a home.

But she is not for me.

I made myself a promise when I took Black Crag from its last owner, when I first stood behind these stone walls and looked out at a world that wanted to burn me, that I would wall myself off. Not only would this castle protect me from the wrath of humans and my court, and enable me to create in peace, but it would be a prison to protect them from *me*.

I would never grant another human the Kiss.

I have become so content in my routines and my distractions that I've allowed myself to forget I *am* the monster, the minotaur at the centre of my maze. I let Reginald talk me into allowing Winnie inside the castle, behind my walls, and now she's inside, her sunshine and strawberry scent breaking down the defences I've built over centuries.

I never imagined that I could feel such things for a *human* ...

And worse, despite my efforts, she feels something for me, something that makes her call my name with such ardent *need* ...

But we cannot sate our hunger for each other.

And I must find a way to destroy these feelings that are more than hunger. No matter the cost.

I give up on sleep. I must come clean about who I am, what I've done, and send Winnie far away from this castle. After what I heard last night, I cannot allow her to stay.

She needs to know that she's working for a monster.

I shove aside the lid of my coffin. Many vampires have eschewed caskets for the outwardly human appearance of a bed, but ours is an ancient family and my mother is a stickler for the traditions. I spent my first century sleeping in a coffin, and even after I ran away and came to Black Crag, I found I could not give up the comfort of the darkness.

Beds with their flimsy sheets feel too exposed. I've heard enough tales of vampires staked in their beds at night by zealous villagers. The coffin, at least, offers some protection against superstitious would-be heroes.

Even with the heavy curtains closed and the lamps extinguished, the oppressive sunlight leaks into my room. We vampires will not burn up in a cloud of ash upon immediate exposure to the sun, but the burning hell-disk will make us sick. Prolonged exposure *can* kill us.

Some vampires can train themselves with short exposures to endure the sun, and some of the modern vampire clans have a higher tolerance. Years of preserving our noble bloodline have ensured our Valerian blood is more sensitive than others, and most members of the Valerian Clan shutter themselves away completely.

I have never seen the appeal of exposing myself to that raging sphere of agony … until Winnie entered my house. The more time we spend together, the more I'm loath to spend a single moment away from her.

I throw on a shirt and breeches and head down to my study to paint. I begin another three paintings and a sculpture, but they're all terrible, so I toss them in the priest's hole. I am midway through a fourth painting when I realise that Winnie should have been awake by now.

Reginald has been keeping me informed of her schedule, and she would usually have come downstairs, eaten her breakfast, and started work. Winnie is like me – she enjoys her work so much that it's the first thing she thinks of when she wakes.

At least, I used to think of my work. Now, my first thought upon waking is of *her*.

I hope she is sleeping, and that she has found some peace from her nightmares.

I drag my weakened body across the castle and climb the stairs to her bedroom. I cannot hear her music blasting from downstairs, so I assume she is still in bed. I tell myself that I will not enter her room. I simply wish to assure myself that she is safe and sleeping soundly.

My steps are slow, sluggish, dragged down by the lines of orange fire that singe my skin from through the arrow slits in the tower walls.

I am panting as I reach the landing, and discover her door flung open, and her bed empty.

"Winnie?" I call out.

I hear a muffled giggle from far away. Not inside the castle, but ...

Tentatively, I part the edge of the curtain. I wince, flinching away as a triangle of fire scorches my retinas. But I need to see her.

Winnie's window overlooks one of the two inner courtyards of the castle. This particular courtyard is one of my favourite places to sit in the evenings – the moonlight glints off a serene Medusa fountain and captures the beauty of the nocturnal flowering plants I tend. In the daylight, all is harsh and dire.

From the wild grin on Winnie's face, she doesn't think so. She and Mirabelle are playing some kind of game – chasing each other around the narrow stone edge of the fountain. As I watch, smiling at their antics, Mirabelle darts through Winnie's legs, and Winnie wobbles, her arms flailing out to the sides.

Even with the dark-tinted windows, the thin streak of sunlight burns against my skin. I drink in one final look at Winnie, then drop the curtain with a sigh.

SPLASH.

"Help!"

Winnie.

The distress in her voice has me flinging the curtains open. I shield my eyes from the burning light. It takes a moment for her to come into view. She is submerged in the fountain, which had once been a reservoir for storing water during sieges and is much deeper than it appears. Mirabelle sits on the edge, happily cleaning between her toes as Winnie flails in the water, her head disappearing beneath the surface.

She can't swim.

I fly down the staircase and through the house, pouring speed into my sluggish limbs. As a vampire, I'm fast, but I'm also dulled by the sunlight. By the time I make it outside, she's already underwater. The sun beats down on my back, hot and harsh, or perhaps that's my fear. I leap in after her, screaming for Reginald before I duck below the water's surface.

The cold liquid offers only momentary relief from the sun's wicked burn. I can barely see her through the red welts in my eyes, her body sinking like a stone down into the black depths of the reservoir.

I pour strength I do not know I possess into my legs, kicking hard. I grab her beneath the arms. She is dead weight, her head lolling, her eyes wide and lifeless.

No, please, no.

The red dots swallow my vision. My limbs are on fire, but I hug her to my chest. Her skin is supposed to be warm against mine but she's cold, so cold. I kick, hoping that I'm kicking in the right direction—

My head breaks the surface. Mirabelle yelps in distress as I send a wave over the side of the fountain, drenching her. The cruel sun beats down, and I'm screaming with agony as I haul her from the water and cradle her in my arms.

"Winnie, I've got you. Please, Winnie, wake up."

I tilt her face to mine, but she's not breathing. I don't know what to do. Humans are so fragile, their bodies so easily broken.

I don't think about how wrong it is or how I'm skirting the edges of breaking my oath to myself.

I raise my hand to my mouth and nick my index finger with my fang.

A pearl of blood pools from the cut – crimson and perfect. I pull open her cold, pale lips and smear the blood across her tongue just as Reginald rushes from the castle behind me.

"My lord, what are you doing?!"

"Winnie …" I reach for her, but the sun burns away my despair. "Drink. Please …"

Everything goes black.

18

Winnie

Mum: Winnie, if Ken tries to talk to you about the dolls, don't listen to him. He's overreacting as usual. He told the council I was terrifying local children. Can you imagine anything so absurd? I got an amazing deal at Savemart – cans of peaches for 30p each! I got two boxes. Remember when we stayed on that farm during the holidays and you were obsessed with climbing that peach tree? I'll save a box for when you get back.

I WAKE WITH A CRY AND A DEEPLY UNSETTLING SENSATION IN MY body. I reach down to slap at the imaginary bugs crawling over my legs, the dream memory of *real* bugs that had plagued my childhood. But as I slap my skin, I realise it's cold and clammy, and the sensation that woke me up is a pounding headache and a burning in my lungs like the air is made of razor blades.

My eyes adjust and I look around me. I'm not in my bedroom but slumped in my usual chair beside the roaring fire. I shiver despite the blanket wrapped around my shoulders. Alaric's chair is empty.

I jump as Reginald appears at my side. He holds out a silver tray containing a steaming mug. "Hot chocolate, ma'am. It will help warm you up. You gave us a nasty scare."

As I reach out to take the hot chocolate, I gasp.

The water.

It all comes back. I was playing with Mirabelle around the fountain and I fell in. Too late, I realised that the fountain is more like an enormous fucking subterranean crater.

Who has a fountain that deep?

I remember falling down, down, down into the darkness, the panic clawing at my skin, and two strong, cool hands grasping me, holding me steady. I remember a deep, rich voice calling for me in the darkness …

Alaric saved me.

I glance over at his empty chair, the cushion hollowed by the ghost of his body as my own chest feels hollowed out.

He saved me. Again.

I choke back the sob swelling my throat closed. All those years growing up with my mother's hoarding, I wished for some knight in shining armour to ride in and take me far away to live in his castle. But the knight never came, and I had to get myself out. And ever since, I've had to clench my fists and keep a tight grip on my life to keep myself safe …

And all the time, the knight in the castle was *here* … and he's saved me, again.

I swipe at my eyes, determined not to cry.

"Can I see Alaric?" I ask Reginald.

"Lord Valerian is resting. He may not wake for some days."

Oh no.

"Is he okay?"

The butler shakes his head. "He has a condition. He cannot be in the sun for long. He is very ill."

Wait, what?

My heart stutters.

That explains why he does everything at night, and why the castle windows are tinted and the drapes are always drawn.

But he went out in the sun and made himself sick to save *me.*

I have to see him. I need to tell him that … that he's saved me in more ways than one.

I rise to my feet. "Please take me to him."

"You cannot see him, Ms Preston, I'm sorry. He will not allow it. He needs complete rest and cannot be disturbed."

My emotions jam in my throat. *He's hurt because of me.* "Is there anything I can do?" I ask.

"You focus on staying warm and feeling better. Let me take care of Lord Valerian. I know what he needs. I shall bring you some hot soup."

As Reginald reaches out to take my empty hot chocolate, I notice a bandage on his wrist. Blood has soaked through the gauze. Did he hurt himself rescuing me, too? I feel so guilty.

But the two butterflies in my stomach dance a waltz as I think about the times Lord Alaric Valerian has swooped in to rescue me.

And then suddenly I think of Danny O'Hare murdered in the alley behind the pub.

What else would Alaric do to keep me safe?

No matter how many times I beg Reginald over the next few days, he won't tell me where Alaric's room is. "My lord will not wish you to see him in such a state, Ms Winifred."

So I get back to work. Some of my supplies were delivered this week, so I set about assembling the shelves in Alaric's study and packing his various projects into their corresponding project boxes. His winter scent clings to everything I touch, and when I place the first box on the shelves, I discover I've installed them all crooked.

I can't focus. I can't stop thinking about his cool, steady arms around me, dragging me from the water, or the fact that he's somewhere in this castle, *hurt*, because of me.

I forget the shelves and move on to Alaric's desk. His paints and palette I leave out on the table. As I'm arranging his pots in colour order, I notice that he's turned his latest artwork towards the wall. I respect his privacy and don't turn the painting around, although I'm more tempted than I'd like to admit.

I think far too much about the kiss at the pub, and about the other day when Alaric caught Gideon flirting with me, and the way he reacted. I thought at the time that maybe he felt something for me, but then he did nothing about it. Gideon left and Alaric went back to his same aloof self.

And now …

You're imagining his reaction. You want to believe that Alaric might be interested in you. But he thinks of you as the annoying professional organiser his manservant hired to tidy up after him, the one he has to constantly rescue from disaster.

And you've gone and set yourself up for another broken heart.

As I touch these objects and projects that Alaric has collected, treasured, and obsessed over, I wonder if maybe I'm not the only one who is nursing a broken heart. As if living in an actual castle is not enough, Alaric has walled himself off with stuff. Perhaps he's trying to keep his heart safe.

I can't believe he's allergic to sunlight. I hope he's going to be okay.

I'd better not tell the ladies in the Nevermore Murder Club and Smutty Book Coven about this, or they'll be even more convinced that he's a vampire.

The Nevermore Murder Club and Smutty Book Coven Group Chat

Mina: I added Winnie to our group chat since she's here for another few weeks.

Winnie: Hi everyone!

Komal: Hi Winnie!

Dora: So happy to see you in the chat, Winnie!

Beth: Hey Winnie! Don't forget that Nevermore Murder Club members get twenty percent off facials and beauty elixirs at Zen and Tonic.

Arabella: About time you got here.

Maisie: Hi Winnie!

Celeste: Welcome, Winnie!

Isis: Hi Winnie! Ladies, it's been a week. What are we doing about Danny's murder?

Komal: Throwing a party?

Beth: Drinking champagne and doing our nails?

Dora: Letting the police do their jobs?

Mina: Or ... we could ask around and see if anyone in the village knows someone who had a grudge against him.

Komal: Someone already is. I went into the pub last night with one of my tour groups, and some guy was asking Lilac about Danny. He said he was from the Sanctus Estate.

Dora: Danny probably owed him money.

Winnie: What's the Sanctus Estate?

Komal: It's that huge new development going up on the edge of Argleton, around Kings Copse Wood. I'm surprised you can't see it from the castle. It's a bloody eyesore!

Arabella: Just because the houses celebrate modern design ...

Celeste: They're fugly. And I hate that they're cutting down trees and making parts of the woods private. They're destroying habitats.

Komal: Exactly. Thank you, Celeste! It's bad for tourism. The Argleton Historical Society, Argleton Environmental Action Group and Argleton Tourism Board all tried to stop the development from going ahead, but the council wanted all that development money so they caved. If I was mayor, I'd never have allowed it!

Arabella: And why aren't you mayor again?

Dora: Arabella, don't poke the bear.

Maisie: I'll talk to Lilac, see if she has any more info for us.

Isis: Great idea. I'll make us all anti-vampire charms. I'll make Winnie's double-strength.

Winnie: I'm telling you, Alaric's not a vampire. He's just strange and aloof. Do you all actually believe in vampires, or are you just pulling my leg?

Maisie: Oh, we believe in vampires and werewolves and witches and all kinds of supernatural kookiness.

Komal: You can't not when Mina did battle with a real-life bloodsucker.

Winnie: WHAT?

Mina: Have you finished my book series yet?

Winnie: Not yet.

Mina: We are a #spoilerfreezone, so come talk to me when you get to that part.

19

Winnie

Faye: How's my star organiser? I got your 'before' photos for the gram. When you said there was a loom in the ballroom, I thought it was like a metaphor for you revenge-shagging the hot AF lord. But no, there really is a loom! This is gonna make some amazing content! Babe, when are you getting those accounts done? I would sort them but I'm having tea in Chelsea with a TOP SECRET and VERY EXCITING potential celebrity client ... :)

Another night passes when Alaric doesn't join me. The butterflies in my stomach are churning butter as I fret about how badly he's been hurt.

I turn the latest St. Vincent album up loud enough that the stones rattle, and try to do a Whirlwind on the drawing room, but it's filled with ceramic pots (although weirdly, it seems like there are slightly fewer than before, and the floor has been freshly swept). I need Alaric's help to figure out what to do with them, but Alaric isn't here because he had to be my shining knight.

Eventually, I collapse into a chair by the fire. Reginald fixes me a dinner of herb-crusted lamb shanks, tzatziki salad and garlic-lemon potatoes. It feels wrong to eat without Alaric but not wrong enough for me to refuse Reginald's cooking.

"Where did you learn to cook like this?" I ask Reginald as I spear a potato. It tastes like happiness.

"Before I was in my lord's service, I trained as a chef." Reginald beams. "It is nice to see someone enjoying my food again."

"I'm sure Lord Valerian doesn't mean to be so fussy. He must like *something* you cook." The crazy conversations about vampires with the Nevermore Murder Club and Smutty Book Coven spin around in my head. "It seems to me as if he eats nothing at all. What food does he enjoy?"

Reginald avoids my eyes. "I shall fetch dessert. And your hot chocolate." He hurries off without answering my question.

"And can I have some more clean sheets, please?" I call after him. I've been changing them after my nightmares every night and I've run out.

I turn back to the fire and sigh, staring across at the empty chair. Well, not completely empty. Mirabelle has made herself comfortable in the centre. She rolls on her back, legs in the air, directing her belly to the blazing fire while watching me with one eye.

"Meorrrw," she says.

"Exactly," I agree. "I miss him, too."

~

I wake, screaming, my mouth filling with bugs.

They're crawling over my body. I roll off the bed, my knees cracking on the wooden floor. I slap at my skin until it turns red. I tear apart the bed, stuffing the fresh sheets into the washing basket Reginald provided for me. I turn the shower on as hot as it will go and step in, scrubbing until my skin feels numb. I wrap myself in layers of cashmere and an old Clutter Queens hoodie. I will not sleep again.

I still have a stack of romance novels to get through, including the rest of Mina's series, but one look out my window tells me that it's already late in the day, and I don't want to crawl back into bed. My stomach growls. I light my candelabra and head down to the kitchen, Mirabelle trailing after me with her tail quirked up in the air like a periscope.

There is still surprisingly little food in the fridge, although I do find a small container filled with soup from the night before last. I heat the soup on the stove and place it on a tray with a couple of slices of sourdough and a spoon.

Alaric is not in his study, nor any of the rooms off the lower corridor he has dedicated to his hobbies. I think he is still in bed, recovering.

I can't stand it any longer.

He saved my life. The least I can do is visit him in his sick bed. But where IS his sick bed?

I pass the locked dining room and take the stairs as silently as possible, not wanting to alert Reginald to my plan if he's nearby. That guy is as silent as a ghost. I reach the landing on the third floor of the western wing. I haven't been here before, and after seeing the piles of books stacked in the hallway, I'm almost certain I've found Alaric's rooms.

"Alaric?" I call out quietly. I don't want to wake him if he's sleeping.

Off to my left is a sitting room, filled with two overstuffed armchairs and even more books. All the curtains are drawn tight, and the only light comes from candles flickering in the wall sconces, although I see that there are also modern lights installed. The next door is shut, but I think it might be a bathroom. My feet sink into thick, expensive rugs as I make my way to the open door at the end of the hall.

"Alaric, are you awake?"

I peer into the enormous room. It takes me a moment for my eyes to adjust to the gloom.

Huh?

I'm not standing in a bedroom, but an ancient stone chapel. Gothic windows soar towards the vaulted ribs of the painted roof. Candles flicker in four enormous chandeliers, each one placed on the four corners where the stone altar should be. Only, instead of an altar, there's a large, dark mahogany coffin.

What is this place?

I step towards the coffin, taking in the piles of clothing strewn about the two rows of pews, the empty wine glass and bottle on a bureau, and the phone dropped carelessly onto the shallow stone steps.

It looks suspiciously like Alaric's phone.

Isis's voice echoes in my head. *He's a vampire, Winnie.*

That's ridiculous. There's a reasonable explanation for all of Alaric's strange habits. There's a totally logical reason why he has a coffin in a chapel in his private suite—

My sneakers echo as they slide on the marble steps. I climb towards the coffin, my mouth in my throat, not certain what I'll see when I …

"Winifred the Great."

I whirl around. Soup splashes across the front of my hoodie.

Alaric stands in the doorway, a towel wrapped around his lower half, his eyes liquid pools of gloom. There are red splotches all over his skin that look like burn marks, but nothing as bad as I expected. The white scar running from his armpit gleams in the candlelight.

The sight of him sticks my tongue to the roof of my mouth.

"Alaric, you're up and about." I hold out the tray. "I brought you some soup."

"It is I who should be looking after you." He steps towards me, and something about the rumble of his voice makes me wonder if I'm supposed to run. "I heal quickly, Winnie."

"But not that scar?"

Alaric follows my gaze to the white scar. "No," he says sadly. "Not that one."

I bite my tongue. I have so many questions I want to ask. But my head's full of silly ideas from Isis and the Nevermore Murder Club, and I'm afraid if I open my mouth, I'll accuse him of being a vampire.

Or I'll leap on him and climb him like a haunted treehouse. It's one or the other.

Alaric regards me with guarded suspicion as he bends to retrieve his phone, sliding it beneath a pile of clothes on the pew with the ease of a predator in repose. "What are you doing up here? Reginald told you not to disturb me."

I swallow. "I wanted to make sure you were okay. You were hurt because of me. Look at your skin! I thought this was your bedroom, but I didn't mean to disturb—"

"This is the family chapel." He holds out his hand to me. "Leave the tray with me. I appreciate your thoughtfulness. Allow me to dress, and I'll meet you downstairs. I'm weak, but perhaps I can help you with the Whirlwind, as long as we keep the curtains tightly closed."

"Okay." I set the tray down on a baptismal font and slip past Alaric, down the stairs, away from the creepiness of Alaric's quarters.

What in Van Helsing's name did I just see?

20

Alaric

Gideon: How are those blue balls going, Allie? I thought you'd be interested to know, since you've been shut up in that castle during some of the most VITALLY IMPORTANT moments in history, that there is this wonderful invention called contraception – it enables a human woman to lie with whomever she chooses ... without falling pregnant. Do with that information what you will. I won't tell. Don't ever say I'm not a good friend to you.

THAT WAS CLOSE.

I'd been lying sleepless in my coffin, staring at Gideon's text as my mind whirled with possibilities, when Winnie's voice broke through my dark fantasies. I'd flown from my coffin and managed to drag my weakened body into the adjoining powder room before she saw me, where I stripped down, wrapped a towel around me, and dunked my head in the basin to appear as though I had just taken a shower.

At least my phone was now safely back in my possession. If Winnie had seen Gideon's text ...

... *what then?*

Winnie might have been frightened to see the coffin, but she would run away and never come back if she found me asleep inside it.

That's good, a sensible voice whispers inside my head. *She should run far, far away from this place. From you and the lustful thoughts you have about her every moment of every night …*

I hate myself for how much I don't want her to run.

Gideon's message reminded me that modern inventions may have gone some way to preventing Dhampir, but that's only one of two monsters dealt with. I am the other, and I am far more dangerous because of how much I want her.

Winnie waits for me in the hallway while I stamp down the beast clawing at the inside of my skin, clothe myself and comb out my coffin hair.

When I emerge to meet her, Winnie's face falls at my slow pace. "I'm so sorry. It's my fault that you're injured. I wish you didn't have to save me, but thank you all the same. I … I can't tell you what it means to me."

"You are safe in my castle, Winnie."

… or are you? Are you safe from me?

She makes a little squeak in the back of her throat. "I won't let Mirabelle lead me on adventures around the fountain again. I had no idea that it was really a portal to Hades."

"It's a cistern built to hold water when the castle was under siege. I keep the Hades portal in the basement."

I hold out my arm to her, and she slides her hand beneath mine and allows me to escort her back downstairs as I explain about the last time the castle was besieged and how it withstood. Her touch whispers against my skin. *Mine, mine, mine …*

Winnie doesn't need to know that I was there during the siege, throwing vats of burning pitch over the walls onto the enemy soldiers or slitting the throat of their commander and tossing his body from the window in her bedroom.

Or how the peasants I saved in that siege turned on me decades later when they realised I wasn't aging and burned me at the stake as a sorcerer. That betrayal still rankles. I had to wait out a generation as a shadow in the wilds, subsisting on animal blood and wayward girls taking the woodland paths to visit their grandmothers, before I could return and claim back what's mine. It took me years to scrub the human smell out of the castle walls.

"So your family lost the castle for thirty years, and then took the castle back?" Winnie follows my palatable version of the story. "You should give tours. This is so interesting, and you love history. You make it sound as if you were there."

I nod. It's on the tip of my tongue to tell her the truth, but Reginald is wrong. I've not lied to Winnie the whole time she's stayed with us, and she doesn't suspect what I truly am. If I have to say goodbye to her, we can make it another few weeks without her learning that monsters are real.

A few more weeks where I can enjoy her company and pretend that her bright smiles are for me.

But if she could be mine, then perhaps …

… perhaps she deserves the truth?

We pass by the kitchen so Winnie can make herself a coffee. I swallow down my cresting hunger, thinking of the fine vintage Reginald stores for me in the cellar, but I can't risk having a glass now, not when I'm weak and Winnie has me so twisted up.

We head to the drawing room that I've been using as my ceramic studio. Winnie pulls over two chairs and sits them opposite each other. "I realise that you're too unwell to help with the physical work today, but can you sit and tell me what to do?"

I nod.

"Good. Before we start with this room, I think it's time to do step two of the Winnie Wins System – 'Intention'."

Winnie perches on one of the chairs and indicates that I should take the other. My knees brush hers, and the contact with her warm skin reminds me of the fire licking at my skin when the peasants burned me.

"I'll do whatever you ask of me."

Yes, ask me, beg me, whisper my name like an incantation.

If you knew the things I would do to you now in that chair, if only you would ask …

Winnie's dark lips form an O of surprise. For a moment, I believe she hears my lustful thoughts. But no – she expected me to fight her on this activity. But I think she is describing a ritual, and I've lived through centuries where rituals and magic were real and dangerous.

I want to see what Winnie Preston does with magic on her fingers.

I also need to remain seated, so that I can hide my arousal in the folds of my shirt.

Winnie takes in a breath, her chest rising so her breasts brush against her lavender shirt, and I see the twin peaks of her nipples hard through the fabric.

She's cold, I remind myself as I force my gaze to her face, as I try in vain to stop myself from committing the perfect peaks of her breasts to memory. *Reginald hasn't lit the fire yet.*

"—an intention is an idea or belief that you hold to be true," Winnie is saying. I nod and nod and nod but I don't think I hear a word. "You carry it through your life and come back to it when you feel lost or overwhelmed. Intentions guide our actions so we can live by our values."

Sweet Winnie, if you knew about my intentions for your body right now …

"I can give you an example." Winnie's eyes flutter closed, her eyelashes tangling together. I lean forward an inch and press my knees to hers. I hoped the contact would ease my monstrous thoughts or quiet the hunger burning in my throat, but instead, it flares higher, burning through my kneecaps and straight into my chest.

"I would like that."

Winnie's voice trembles a little as she continues. "I haven't said much about my mother or how I grew up, but it was … not great. I spent my teenage years staying at my best friend Claire's house as often as I could and counting down the days until I could move out." She swallows, her throat moving. I'm transfixed by the artery pulsing in her long, elegant neck. "I thought once I was out of her house, all the stress of living there would just disappear. Instead, it got worse.

Claire and I lived together at uni and I couldn't deal with all the *space*. I cleaned constantly and threw out everything that wasn't nailed down … I had these awful nightmares, and I'd wake up screaming."

I open my mouth to ask her about the nightmares, the ones she still has now, but she keeps talking.

"Claire made me see a therapist, and it helped. One of the things she taught me to do was to set intentions. My intention is: 'I will allow myself to be happy.' Whenever I'm stressed or spiralling, I come back to that, and I ask myself, 'What would make me happy right now?' and I try to do that thing for myself. Does that make sense?"

I don't know what a therapist is, but it makes my breath still and my heart clench for whatever Winnie has gone through that made her, even for a moment, think she didn't deserve happiness.

"Yes," I manage to grit out, my hands balling into fists. "I understand."

"Good." She smiles that beautiful bright smile. But this time, I see the sadness on the edges. "When I leave you with this beautiful, tidy castle, I don't want you to fall back into the habits that got you to where you are. You deserve to have this space to be creative, Alaric, but Reginald's right about one thing – you could *become* a hoarder if you're not careful. I don't want that to happen to you."

The idea that Winnie might care about me sends my head spinning and the monster inside me clawing to be free.

"So we're going to set intentions for your space, and your life." Winnie places her hands on her knees, and I unclench my fists and copy her. But then she places her hands over mine, and I'm back to fantasies so monstrous that she'd personally light my funeral pyre if she could see them. "What do you want for your life?"

I want you.

I want your name on my lips again as I drive you wild.

I want to taste you. All *of you.*

I want to make you mine.

Winnie squeezes my fingers when I don't say anything. "Remember when I told you that you were a perfectionist?"

I remember every word you speak.

"It may seem odd, but often, living in mess is about control," Winnie says. "You don't have to tell me, but can you think of something traumatic that happened to you before you started accumulating stuff?"

I died on the battlefield and woke up in a castle in Germany as a monster.

I was burned at the stake by villagers I saved.

I was tortured by a witch hunter.

I was left to hang from a tree for five days and nights.

I was buried alive and had to wait for the wood of my coffin to rot before I dug my way out.

As the memories flash unbidden in my mind, my fangs push into the flesh of my lip. I can't open my mouth and risk her seeing them, so I nod.

"The traumatic thing makes you feel like the world is scary and out of your control. We can't stop people from hurting us." Her voice cracks. "But your castle and your art are things you can control. They make you feel good, and there's no risk of being hurt. So you build a physical barrier between yourself and the outside world, like the walls of a castle."

How she can spend mere days with me and yet know my heart?

I nod again. I don't trust myself to do anything else.

Winnie knits her fingers in mine, and I find myself swallowing back a well of emotion. "Trauma never goes away, Alaric. I still live with mine. The memories come up often, unexpectedly, at the worst possible times. Some people become workaholics, or turn to alcohol, to hide from their trauma. Some, like my ex, Patrick, become gym nuts because looking after your body can feel like being in control. And some people build their castle walls higher.

"But control is an *illusion*. All that stuff won't keep you safe. Only you can do that. *You are enough*." Her eyes glisten as she says this, and I'm no longer certain if she's talking to me or herself. "You are enough, Alaric. You can't hide away here forever. You're too special. You deserve a life outside of Black Crag. No matter how high you build those castle walls, someone will always get in and knock them down."

Oh Winnie, if only you knew …

"I think that your intention should be about vulnerability. You have to practise being vulnerable again and trust that even if you do get hurt, you will survive."

Her fingers are so soft in mine, so fragile. I'm not the one who is vulnerable right now. Her blood pulses at her throat, and I'm so hungry, so *feral* for her that I drive my fangs into my lip so I don't do something monstrous.

I taste my blood and it does nothing to sate my bone-deep *need*.

"I want …" I close my eyes, because looking at the care in her eyes is making it worse. "To be vulnerable."

"Good. That's your intention. Every time you feel yourself being pulled under by one of your passions, or you can't muster the strength to use the system I'm creating for you, look at yourself in the mirror and say, 'I am safe to be vulnerable,' and that should help, okay?" She tilts her head to the side. "And if it doesn't help, you can text me."

I can text her.

Because she won't be here.

Because she's leaving.

"I don't text," I grind out, sucking my lip to stop the bleeding. I force myself to my feet and jerk towards the kiln. "I do not enjoy writing with my thumbs."

"Of course you don't. Come to think of it, I've never even seen you use a phone. Well, I'll give you my postal address when I have one and you can send me a strongly-worded letter written with parchment and quill. Better?"

The only thing better *will be sating my hunger with your lips …* "Much."

21

Winnie

Isis: The Nevermore Coven are doing a little sleuthing today. Maisie has a lead on Danny's case. Want to come with? Celeste is bringing cupcakes.

"I NEED TO ASK." I SWALLOW A MOUTHFUL OF ONE OF CELESTE'S amazing cupcakes while we stare out the windows of Komal's beaten-up van at the ornate iron gates of the Sanctus Estate. "I thought you were called the Nevermore Murder Club because you liked books with a little death and righteous revenge. Are you saying that you're amateur detectives?"

It's been a week since I led Alaric through the intention-setting exercise, and he's made such amazing progress on the house. We've filled three skips and Reginald has made so many trips to the local charity shop that they now pretend to be "out to lunch" whenever he pulls up. I guess there are only so many old train sets and Victorian frock coats they can take.

Things between Alaric and me are … *interesting*. We've struck up the kind of intimate friendship that can only be forged between professional organiser and person with far too much stuff. As we unearth more of his hobbies, he tells me stories about his art and the subjects he depicts, which mostly seem to be historical battles and superstitions. For someone who never leaves his castle and seems to have a tenuous grasp of what century he lives in, Alaric's art calls upon the breadth of human experience. Every emotion – from joy and hope to sorrow and rage – is represented in his work.

But Alaric is so much more than his art. Behind that gruff exterior is a passionate man who cares deeply about the few souls he trusts (Mirabelle, Reginald, even Gideon), and has a wickedly dry sense of humour. Last night, I even caught him nodding his head along to a Siouxsie and the Banshees song.

If only my stupid ovaries would remember that he's my boss and absolutely, totally off limits, and stop spontaneously combusting every time his lips curl back into that secretive half-smile of his. It's probably a good thing I'm out with the book club tonight, because I don't know how much more I can take of Alaric's storm-filled eyes before I wear out my favourite toy.

I turn my attention back to the gates, which have remained closed since we got here.

"Don't you know that in order to have a book club, one also must do some amateur detecting? It's like a rule. We've been instrumental in solving several murder mysteries around the village." Komal licks lemon icing from her long fingers.

"Does this village attract murderers or something?" I ask, only half-joking. "Do you get a two-for-one Sunday roast at the pub if you've offed someone? Sounds like there's an awful lot of violent death for a small English village. I think I'll go back to London, the crime capital of the UK, where it's safer."

"I have theories about a magical locus in the middle of the village green. Aleister Crowley used to lead rituals on the exact spot. But whatever the reason, we should tell Lilac about the two-for-one Sunday roast idea." Isis strokes her chin. "That's genius."

"So why are we getting involved in investigating Danny's murder?"

"*Even* though no woman in this village feels an ounce of sadness at Danny's untimely demise, we suspect there might be something strange going on, and the police are hopeless." Maisie adjusts her binoculars. "When I interviewed Inspector Hayes for the paper, he told me that he's following up on several leads, which is Hayes-speak for: 'We're completely stumped.' Danny had a lot of enemies in the village. Winnie's hot vampire is top of the list since he was one of the last people seen talking to Danny in the pub, and it didn't look friendly. But he's far from the only suspect. And since Winnie has the hots for him, we owe it to her to at least attempt to clear his name."

I let out a breath I didn't realise I was holding. My cheeks flare with heat, but I don't correct Maisie. I do have the hots for Alaric. If only he felt the same …

If only he wasn't a client.

"So I spoke to Lilac and she told me the same story about the fellow asking after Danny. I drove out to Sanctus Estate earlier today and asked if Danny was working for them. The lady at their office said no, absolutely not, but my reporter's sense is tingling, so—" Maisie drops the binoculars. "It's go time."

Maisie shoves open the van door and sprints for the gates. A ludicrous red sportscar has pulled up on the other side, and the gates swing open to allow it through. I squint into the darkness and recognise Gideon's golden curls behind the wheel. He leans out the window to chat with someone at the security desk, and Maisie slips past the other side of his car and disappears into the estate.

"Shouldn't one of us follow her?" I ask.

"Not me." Komal wiggles her fingers. "My hands are sticky."

"Not me," Mina pipes up. "I have an annoying habit of crashing into things and giving us away."

"Not me. One doesn't run in heels." Arabella pulls her Prada sleep mask further over her eyes, reclining her seat back so far that Dora's knees are practically touching her ears. "Wake me when Maisie's arrested for trespassing."

Gideon drives away and the gate swings shut again. How is Maisie going to get out? I scan the area, taking in the impressive high walls and dramatic columned gate of the estate. This entrance to Sanctus Estate is down a narrow country road halfway between the village and Black Crag Castle. We're surrounded by woodland. The only other building is a small Norman keep that's been converted into a private residence back up the road. I can just make it out through the trees. Lights flicker in the tiny slits that serve as the building's only windows.

"Who lives there?" I squint at the building, wondering who, apart from Alaric, would choose to live out here in a draughty old castle. How many reclusive Lords have made Argleton their home?

"This creepy guy named Baby Gargantuan," says Komal. The girls giggle.

"Baylor," says Arabella without removing her mask. "His name is Baylor Godsven."

"Right." Isis nods. "Basil Codswallop. Now, he's *definitely* a vampire. He even wears a cape, and he doesn't seem to age. He's seen in the village even less than Alaric, but when he appears, bad things happen. That castle of his is supposedly haunted."

"People have heard and seen a lot of strange things out here," Dora says with a shudder.

"As teenagers, we used to dare each other to run up to the castle doors," Beth adds. "Until a classmate of ours came out here one night to meet her boyfriend and was never seen again."

"That's terrible!"

"Baskin Gobbins was never charged with any crime." Isis makes a face. "But that says more about the incompetence of our local bobbies than his innocence. I bet if Inspector Hayes looked in Babel Gibberwort's dungeon, they'd find human bones with fang marks in them."

"Vampires don't eat flesh," Arabella snaps.

"And you're the expert, are you? *I'm* the one making anti-vampire charms so we can stay safe—"

As they bicker about supernatural creatures, I stare at the house. It does give off a creepy, menacing vibe – so different from Black Crag, which, beneath all the dust, is beautiful in its own gothic, broody way. *Kind of like Alaric—*

A shape moves by the castle, a white blob stumbling between the trees.

"There's something out there."

Mina squints at the window. "I can't see a thing."

I glance at Mina, not sure what to say.

Komal rolls her eyes. "*Mina.*"

"Sorry, Winnie." Mina elbows me in the side. "Blind girl joke. What do you see?"

"A white shape moving towards us. It looks like a person running." I fling open the door, straining to listen. A faint voice reaches me through the dark wood. "Someone's crying for help."

Before I know what I'm doing, I've unbuckled my seatbelt and flung myself over Mina to climb out of the van. "Over here!" I yell, stepping into the trees and turning on my phone's torch.

"… on't let him …" the voice calls faintly back. The white shape stumbles and goes still. Dark shadows dance in the trees, and a cold terror creeps up my spine.

It's just the leaves moving in the wind.

But there is no wind.

Behind me, I can hear the book club ladies calling my name. But I can't shake the feeling that whoever's out there needs our help. I suck in a deep breath and pitch myself into the gloomy trees.

"Don't move," I yell. "I'm coming to you."

Branches scrape my arms. My shoes skid over slippery roots. The creeping sensation grows worse the closer I get to the keep. The white shape is moving towards me again, and I can make out the outline of a girl limping—

"Bloody hell, woman." Arabella huffs as she jogs alongside me. "I *told* you I don't run in these shoes."

I glance at her, my heart soaring with relief to have her beside me, even though I'm worried she might break her leg stomping around in the woods in those heels. But Arabella moves with the grace of a swan, which is an apt description because she also has the temper of a swan—

Just then, the girl bursts out of the trees in front of us. She grabs her knees, her whole body heaving as she fights for breath. She's young, probably early twenties, wearing a skintight white miniskirt and a single white platform trainer. Her skin is almost as pale as her clothes. Blood streaks her neck and shoulder and stains the front of her dress.

"Are you okay?" I ask, steadying her arm. She's trembling, and her skin is cold and clammy. "Did someone hurt you? We'll call the police."

"Are you … friends of his?" she gasps out.

"We're no friends of Baylor Godson," Arabella snarls, moving to the girl's other side.

I swipe back to my phone's call screen. "I've got one bar of reception. That should be enough to call—"

"*No police.* I just need to a ride back to the village." The girl's voice is hollow and strange. She straightens up and rubs her neck. When she draws her hand away, it's smeared with blood. "I met that freak bastard at the pub. He's buying the fanciest cocktails going and I think I'm in luck, right? He invites me back to his and I think right, here we go, I'll get some toff plonk and suck him off and I'll steal a gold ashtray while he's in the shower, right? But then we get back here and I must be pretty rat-arsed because I swear, he didn't even have a bed, just a bloody coffin! I tell him I ain't into no kinky shit and to take me back to the village but he chases me and bites my neck. I'm bleeding everywhere and he's laughing like a maniac and going on about how he wants to drain me, whatever that means. So I spray him with mace and make a run for it. I lost a shoe somewhere back there …" She grins absently. "I'm glad you two are here, because I feel all strange-like …"

Arabella holds out her arms as the girl collapses.

"What the hell?"

Panic churns in my gut. The man, Baylor or Basil or whatever his name is, hurt this girl. Maybe he drugged her? "We need to get her to the hospital."

"She's fine." Arabella hoists the girl higher in her arms. "She's fainted. Dora will help her."

I don't know how she does it, but Arabella manages to carry the girl back to the van without breaking a sweat or tripping in her six-inch stilettos. Beth and Isis scootch over so we can lay the girl on the backseat. Dora uses some herbs from her pocket to stop the bleeding and everyone bickers over what to do with her. I vote that we call the police, but the others want to respect her wishes not to involve Inspector Hayes, especially since the whole reason we were out there in the first place was so Maisie could stick her nose into an ongoing murder investigation—

Where's Maisie?

I look over at the Sanctus gates just as a small figure rolls over the top of the high wall and lands on her feet with a quiet thud. Isis cheers as Maisie leaps back into the van and yells, "Go, go!"

Komal stomps on the gas. The van lurches down the winding lane. I thought taking the country roads in Reginald's ridiculous car was an adventure, but Komal treats road rules more like road "suggestions" that can be discarded if the soundtrack is angry enough.

"What happened?" Komal demands over the pounding bass as she yanks the wheel hard right to drag one of the van's wheels out of the ditch. "Did you find out anything about Danny?"

"Why is there a strange girl in the back of the van?" Maisie asks.

"Don't change the subject!"

Maisie must decide it's better not to argue with the person currently scraping the van's panelling down a bramble hedgerow, because she settles back into her seat and says, "The estate is much more lively at night. There were residents everywhere, but I managed to blend in. I found the office and waited in the bushes until the lady got called away. I managed to sneak onto her computer and found Danny's payslips. It looks as if he was employed as a handyman for Sanctus, mainly to do small repair jobs and hang pictures in the houses that are completed. But that's not all I found."

Maisie's eyes blaze with triumph. We all lean forward in our seats.

"*What?*" Beth huffs.

"Danny received a disciplinary warning for behaving inappropriately towards a resident of Sanctus. They complained to the management and he was let go from the company payroll *the day he was murdered.*"

Celeste gasps. In the backseat, the girl lets out a loud snore.

"I couldn't get the name of the victim of Danny's harassment, or any of the other Sanctus residents. Those are locked down tight in a password-protected database, and I only had a moment before the woman came back inside. But it's a lead we need to follow up."

Arabella furrows her perfectly tweezed eyebrows. "What do you think happened? A billion-dollar development firm makes Danny pay for harassing one of their clients by brutally murdering him in a back alley? It doesn't make sense."

"Not yet, but we can keep digging," Maisie says.

Arabella sighs. "I suppose if I make some *discreet* inquiries with my clients at Sanctus, I might be able to unearth this woman's name. But only if the opportunity arises. Will that help?"

"We would be eternally in your debt, Arabella," Beth shouts over the girl's increasingly loud snores. "Now, what are we going to do about our slumbering friend?"

"Pub?" Komal suggests. "If she's a regular, Lilac probably knows where she lives. We'll get her home and tuck her into bed and she'll forget all about this in the morning."

"I've given her something to help calm her," Dora says. "And she's already stopped bleeding."

"And I've tucked an anti-vampire charm into her pocket," Isis says, "so Baylor will stay away from her."

"Oh, is that why it reeks in here?" Maisie scrunches up her nose. "I thought someone farted—"

As Komal careens in the direction of the village and the Nevermore Coven discuss possible murder scenarios, I turn around to watch the sleeping girl. I touch the place on my neck where Alaric's teeth scraped me. My heart stutters.

What kind of sick man would do that to her?

22

Alaric

Callista: Alaric, have you dealt with the husker yet? You know that the fiend has a taste for it now. If we do not bring them to justice, they will take another human life, risking exposing all of us. Don't pretend that you've eschewed texting as inappropriate for our kind. If I've learned to text, so can you.

"THIS ROOM PRESENTS US WITH SOME CHALLENGES," WINNIE SAYS the following week as we stand before the wall of ceramics. "Unlike the tapestries, we can't display all of these mugs. Why do you make *so many* pots?"

Winnie has brought so much joy to Black Crag, the thought of our evenings together ending fills me with dread. In moments like this, when she's too absorbed in our task to notice me, I find myself studying her, luxuriating over every detail of her lovely face and sparkling eyes, hoping to commit her to memory.

"I'll show you." I drag a bag of clay from behind the potter's wheel and tear it open.

"What are you doing?"

I'm trying to make you want to stay with me longer.

I grab a handful of clay and work it between my fingers, moulding it into a conical shape. It takes a long time for clay to warm in my cold grip. "I'm going to show you how to throw a pot."

Winnie frowns. "If we throw these pots, we'll end up with a pile of shards to clean up."

Reginald will attest to that.

"I think it would be better if—"

"Throwing a pot means to make one. Come." I beckon her with a clay-caked finger.

Winnie takes a step towards me. "I don't think that's a good idea. We're supposed to be cleaning."

"Isn't your intention that you allow yourself to be happy? Would it make you happy if I showed you how I made these pots?"

Her lip wobbles. "I'm hopeless at art. I don't like the mess of it."

"There's no such thing as being hopeless at art. Art is whatever you choose to create."

"I don't want to get my hands dirty."

"Sit."

I allow the weight of centuries to drip into my voice, but Winnie is impervious. She folds her arms. "Lord Valerian, we're supposed to be cleaning up the mess, not making more."

"If you let me show you how to make a pot, I promise that we will return to organising."

"I don't believe you for a second."

I pat the seat at the potter's wheel. A hundred emotions play across Winnie's face, but she settles into a look of grim determination. She stalks across to me and swings her leg over, straddling the wheel, her skirt bunching up around her thighs in a way that makes my throat close up and my trousers grow tight.

I fill a bowl from the pitcher of water Reginald left for her and place it beside the wheel. "Reach into the bag and pull out a handful of clay."

Winnie makes an adorable scrunched-up face as she breaks off a chunk of clay, and I show her how to work it into a cone shape. "I don't understand what's fun about squishing wet, slimy *dirt* between your fingers."

"Place it into the centre of the bat – that's the piece that turns – with the tip of the cone facing down. Now, wet your hands and get your clay a little damp. Can you feel the pedal by your foot? Give that a pump."

Winnie squeals as the wheel begins to spin. I explain how she needs to press her wrists together, opening her fingers to push on the clay as she pumps the wheel. On her first attempt, she doesn't pump fast enough and pushes her clay off the edge of the bat. On her second attempt, she pumps *too* fast and splatters wet clay across her face.

"Alaric, this is ridiculous, I can't do it!"

"Nonsense. You need to get the feel for it. More forward in your seat."

A pleasant fission shoots through my body as she obeys my command, shuffling forward and placing both feet flat on the ground. I slide in behind her, my breath catching as my body presses against hers, chest to her back, my legs framing hers.

What am I doing?

I'm torturing myself with the heat of her touch and the closeness of her body and that damned summery, strawberry scent. I shift my position so that she can't feel my hard length pressing into the curve of her arse, even though all I ache to do is press every part of my skin against her.

If Winnie's right and I collect things around me as a way of being in control, then I didn't even know what control was until I met her, because every moment that I'm close to her threatens to unravel me.

"What do I do now?"

"I'll control the speed." My voice comes out husky as my fangs slide down. I hate myself for my weakness, for being torn between what is right and what I long for whenever I close my coffin lid. "You use your hands the way I showed you. Anchor your elbows against your body and push against the clay."

Winnie nods. Her golden hair in its tight, no-nonsense ponytail shifts against me, and I'm aware of *every single detail* of her.

Her hair tickling my chest through my thin silk shirt. Her fingers in mine, skin soft but her grip firm and determined. The way she sets her jaw when she concentrates on the pot, dedicating her whole self – body and heart and mind – to whatever task she's trying to accomplish. The curve of her perfect plump arse between my thighs. The draw I feel to this woman is taking my breath away.

It takes me a moment to remember how to move my foot. I press lightly on the pedal, keeping the wheel moving at a fast but steady pace. Winnie pushes into the clay, and this time the clay complies, forming a tall cone.

"That's good. You're doing well."

I wrap my arms around her, slipping my hands in hers and showing her how to level off the top and smooth the edges as she flattens the cone. The hunger is a living thing inside me. My mind fills with such depraved, delicious, distracting thoughts that she twists against me to get my attention.

"Earth to Alaric – what do I do next?"

I want you to stop wriggling your derrière against me unless you want me to bury myself in it.

"Dig your fingers into the centre," I explain, biting my fangs into my lip. *This was a bad, bad idea.* "This will create a hole."

Winnie laughs as she presses her thumbs into the clay and it opens up, creating the hole for her pot. I wallow in the strawberry scent of her, drowning in the feeling of her warm body against mine. I never thought I'd be allowed to be close to something so sweet and perfect and *human*.

"I can't believe I did it!" After a few minutes, Winnie pulls her fingers – and mine – away. Her pot immediately implodes. "Oh, no— I didn't do it."

"That happens sometimes. The wall was a little thin. The clay could have been more centred on the bat, or you might like to bring your elbows together for more control. Would you like to try again?" I ask, shifting behind her in an attempt to hide my arousal. "Or perhaps you'd like to return to work?"

Perhaps her idea about throwing all the pots against the wall would help burn off this need …

"I want to try again." Winnie grabs a handful of clay. This time, she doesn't make a face.

"Do you want to control the pedal—"

"Please, stay with me."

Winnie drops her clay cone on the bat. I pump the pedal as she shapes her pot and hollows it. This time, when she takes her hands away, it doesn't fall.

"Alaric, look! I did it! I can't believe it. You're right, this *is* fun—"

Her scent shifts, strawberries ripening into something darker. She twists her neck to look at me, presenting me with the tantalising virgin skin of her neck and the pulsing liquid heat beneath. Her golden eyes are nearly black with pupil.

When she looks like that, I am *gone*, and I can no longer hold myself back from doing what I've dreamed about since the moment I first saw her in that pub.

I rock forward, pressing myself against her as my lips meet hers.

This kiss is nothing like the one we shared in the Rose & Wimple, when I sought only to protect her from Danny, when I had no idea how sweet the forbidden could taste.

This kiss is pure *hunger*.

I taste the softness of her mouth, flooding my tangled senses with ripe strawberries and pulsing, warm blood.

My fangs are still lowered. At any moment she could feel them or nick herself on them, and then she would know my secret. The edge of danger only makes me pull her closer. Part of me *wants* her to find them, to know me truly as I am and still to press her body to mine and moan her delicious little pleasures against my lips.

The dark, twisted part of me is ready to be vulnerable for her.

I brace myself for her to pull away, to run, to declare me the monster that I am, but then Winnie moans into my mouth, her whole body clenching with need, unfolding against me as if she's been waiting centuries for someone worthy to draw those sinful sounds from her body.

I think of her alone in the dark, facing her nightmares with the same grim determination that she brings to everything she does, and I don't recognise myself through my rage.

I will find who hurt her and I will *devour them.*

I may be a monster, but if she would be mine, I would be *her* monster—

"Alaric," Winnie breathes. "Please …"

She fists my shirt, her tiny fingers grasping, searching, as her tongue meets mine. She murmurs my name over and over, and I am so enraptured by the sound of it and the feel of her that it takes me some moments to realise she might be begging me to stop.

My undead heart stutters. I pull back. "Did I hurt you? I shouldn't have—" My sudden movement knocks the bat, and her pot slides off and topples over in a misshapen lump.

She turns to me, eyes raw. "No! Alaric, wait, please—"

"I cannot," I manage to choke out, snapping my lips closed over my fangs as I flee the room.

23

Winnie

Claire: Patrick and I are going to the country for a few days for a romantic weekend. I was hoping that when I get back, we could maybe catch up? There's something I want to ask you. It's important, and it would mean the world to me if we could meet. You're not going to hate me forever, are you?

This time, when I arrive for the weekly Nevermore Murder Club and Smutty Book Coven meeting, I push open the door to Nevermore Bookshop and head straight through to the events room, a thermos of Reginald's hot chocolate tucked under one arm.

I need distraction. I need Isis to wave her hands and chant something nonsensical to trick me into believing that I have my shit together. I need Beth to make an elixir that turns back time so I don't kiss Alaric again. I need Komal's easy authority and Arabella's snooty sarcasm and Dora's quiet kindness. I am a mess, and I just kissed my boss, and he ran away like he was Nosferatu and I was a garlic salesperson.

I need *friends*.

Alaric has been curt with me ever since the kiss. Instead of our usual banter while we sort his things, he gives me one-word answers while he works fastidiously on a painting he won't allow me to see. He refuses to eat with me by the fire, remaining in his studio after I go to bed. Yesterday, when I started moving the bags of clay out of the drawing room, I noticed several more had been opened, the clay half gone.

I don't know what to do.

Since he pulled me from the water, there's been a change in him, in *us*. I catch him watching me, his pupils blown out with unrestrained desire, and instead of being terrified or pushing back against the idea of initiating something with a client, I'm falling headfirst into him. For a long time, I've held on so tight to the life I thought I wanted that I squeezed everyone out of it, but here at Black Crag, beneath his hungry, possessive gaze, I want to surrender all control.

We've both been pretending the kiss didn't happen, but how can I ignore his possessive touch, or the fire that burns behind his anthracite eyes?

But also, how can I ignore the fact that he rejected me?

"Croak," the raven greets me from his perch above the door.

"Hi there." I hold up a small packet of freeze-dried strawberries. "I brought you a treat, *and* I promise that I won't quote any Poe at you. Although, how do you feel about Byron? Mary Oliver? Is this bard-vendetta you have Poe-specific, or do you detest all poets?"

"Croak."

"Excellent. I'm glad we've cleared that up."

"Winnie, it's so good to see you again!" Beth enters the shop behind me and practically bowls me over with her hug. "I keep worrying we'll scare you away. I made goji and kelp slice. Want to try some?"

Beth holds out a platter filled with what can only be described as mouldy anthills.

"Er … maybe later." I follow Beth into the events room.

"Everyone has been berating me about all the vampire talk in our group chat," Isis admits sheepishly as she leans in for her sandalwood-scented hug. "Which we shouldn't have given you access to until after your initiation, but Dora convinced me to make an exception."

"My initiation?"

"Oh, it's just a little ritual to welcome you officially to the Nevermore Coven. But we have to wait for a full moon early next month—"

"I can't make the initiation," Celeste says as she hands around a stack of books. "I have to visit my mother. And no, I can't get out of it."

"That's cool. We don't all need to be there for the initiation." Isis grins at me. "Well, Winnie needs to be there."

"But I'm not going to be in Argleton next month," I point out. "I've only got a couple of weeks left until Alaric's ball, and then I'll go back to London."

As I say this aloud, a wave of sadness washes over me. Going back to London will mean I can no longer exist in this liminal space. I'll have to face the fact that I have no place to live and Faye is taking advantage of me and I'm alone and my mother needs me *again*. I want to stay in Argleton and go to book club meetings and initiations and fight with Alaric about ceramics—

—and make out over a potter's wheel.

If I'm being honest.

Isis points to her head. "I'm psychic, remember? I saw a vision of you here with us as a fully-fledged member of the Nevermore Murder Club and Smutty Book Coven. *And* I saw you sticking it to your ex and your so-called friend."

What?

"Isis!" Komal shoots her a violent look before I can question her, a dent appearing between her pretty green eyes. "Ignore her, Win. Isis never knows when to shut her pie hole."

I glare at Isis. "You … know?"

Isis taps her head. "I told you. Psychic."

Dora sinks down in her beanbag, pulling her cardigan tight around her. "What Isis *means* to say is that she overheard you talking to Lilac in the pub the first night you arrived, and she's sorry for being a nosy so-and-so."

I remember a group of ladies at a table in the corner. *I bet that was the book club.*

"Are you okay, Winnie?" Beth asks, offering her plate to Komal, who takes an anthill and tosses it to the raven when Beth's not looking. "Do you need us to hex a bitch for you?"

"Let us not blame the woman for the man cheating." Celeste arranges a plate of perfect red velvet cupcakes. "That's not very feminist of us. Maybe if we cast a shrinking penis spell on him, like we did for Beth's shitty ex-boyfriend?"

I bark out a laugh.

"As head of the Historical Society, I have the key to the witch hunt display case at the Argleton museum," Komal says in a perfectly serious voice. "I bet putting his balls through a mangle will make him reassess his life choices."

Tears are starting to form as I try to hold back my giggles. "No hexes or medieval torture necessary. Yes, my fiancé and best friend cheated on me, but I'm trying my best to put it behind me and move on."

"I hope moving on means sucking face with a certain reclusive vampire?" Mina raises an eyebrow as she settles Oscar at her feet.

My cheeks flare with heat. "Alaric—er, Lord Valerian is my boss. That wouldn't be a good idea."

No, it would not.

Despite the whole Alaric rejecting me thing, I feel a stab of something like contentment hit me as I sink down into the same beanbag I sat on last week. It's as if the girls saved that spot for me – *my* usual spot in their circle. I find myself wishing again that I could stay. But that would be crazy. Even if I split off from Faye (the idea of which makes me feel ill), where would I find enough clients in Argleton?

I shove my hand in my pocket, but my phone's not there. That's right. I threw it into the fountain at Black Crag so that I didn't have to read any more texts from Claire. I like the idea of her driving herself mad texting me and never receiving a reply, and if I kept the phone, eventually, I'd have been tempted.

She sounds so sincere, so concerned about me.

That's exactly who Claire is though. She *needs* everyone to like her. A dark, vindictive part of me enjoys leaving her hanging.

I'm grateful when Mina calls the meeting to order. First, she gives us an update on the girl we rescued from Baylor Godsven. Her name is Candi and she's perfectly fine. The wound on her neck healed up and she doesn't remember a thing about that night, so she must have been drunker than we thought. Maybe it was just a drunken hook-up gone wrong.

Next, we all pull out our copies of this week's book, *Lords of Pain* by Angel Lawson and Samantha Rue. It's another dark romance, which is not normally my thing, but these writers are so compelling and the plot was so bonkers that I ate it up.

"I hate all the lords," Celeste declares. "I hope Story cuts their dicks off and eats them in front of them."

Arabella shrugs her elegant shoulders. "It's a dark romance, so that's possible."

"I'm already in love with Rath." Komal clasps her hands to her chest. "Such a tortured soul. I just want to hold him and tell him everything will be okay."

"Can we not do a dark romance next week?" Maisie asks. "I can only deal with so much morally-grey in my life."

"We can do whatever book you like, as long as it's on audiobook," Mina says. "With a sexy narrator. Maybe a hot paranormal with some growly werewolves—"

"No werewolves," Celeste shudders. "All that body hair. No, thank you."

"Okay, a hot vampire, then."

"Speaking of vampires," Isis opens her huge tote bag and starts tossing out little velvet bags. "I made these anti-vampire charms for protection."

Komal opens hers and makes a face. "It smells like an Italian pizza left on a radiator for three days."

"It *is* mostly garlic," Isis admits as she drops a velvet pouch in my lap.

"Alaric isn't a vampire!" I toss the charm into my handbag. "Remember I said before – his butler Reginald cooks with garlic all the time."

"Maybe it's so that he builds up a tolerance. Take another, just in case." Isis tosses a second stinky pouch at me, then turns to the group. "Any new information on Danny's murder to share?"

Beth raises her head from the rom-com she's reading. "Linda Derry came in for her cupping treatment today. She told me that she was walking her puppy along the path up by the Old Mill when she heard some strange noises and she says—"

"The Old Mill?" Celeste's head whips around. "Why is she walking her dogs near there? No one ever goes up there."

"Linda Derry is on the Historical Society with me," Komal says. "She always forgets to turn on her hearing aids. I'm not sure her 'strange noises' are much of a lead."

"I've found out something," Mina pipes up. "Actually, two somethings."

"Enlighten us," Arabella says in a bored voice.

Mina leans forward. "Maisie, this cannot go in the paper, okay? If the villagers hear about it, people will panic and do stupid things."

"I promise." Maisie zips her lips. "Strictly off-the-record, like my snooping in Sanctus computers."

"Exactly. Well, you all know that I'm friends with Jo, the medical examiner. She came over for dinner last night. Morrie plied her with alcohol and she accidentally let slip this little tidbit. We know that the body was exsanguinated. Jo told me that *none* of the blood was present at the scene. This is super unusual, and it means the killer took the blood with him. Pints of the stuff. Also." Mina swallows. "The only marks found on the victim's body were two small holes in the neck."

"See?!" Isis smashes her fist into her beanbag. "What did I tell you? A vampire did it. A vampire sucked Danny dry. And the only vampires we know in the village are Winnie's boyfriend, Lord Valerian, and Baylor Godsven. So I think we have a new suspect, unless there's anyone else around here packing a set of fangs."

I shudder at the memory of that dark coffin in the chapel where Alaric's bedroom should be, but then it's replaced by the cool, hungry press of Alaric's lips on mine. A blush creeps over my cheeks. "He's not my boyfriend."

"Why not?" Arabella raises one perfect eyebrow. "Bloodsucker or no, that man should be cleaning out your cobwebs with his womb broom."

"Agreed." Beth licks her lips. "I'd entangle lower beards with Alaric—"

"*Anyway*, the police aren't going to follow a supernatural lead." Isis rubs her hands together. "It's up to us to make sure the village isn't being terrorised by a hungry vamp—"

"—again—" says Mina.

"That's right, again. So we need to dig out our vampire-slaying kits, start eating a lot of garlic bread, and find the monster hiding among us—"

Excuse me, again*? Why do they keep implying that they've dealt with a supernatural menace before—*

Out of the corner of my eye, I catch movement in the window. Isis is going on about laying a vampire trap. I get to my feet, cross the room, and squint into the darkness.

Something moves on the street, just out of reach of the lights. I jump back in surprise, and all the women turn in my direction.

"Who's that?" Komal's head appears beside me. "Is there someone out there?!"

"Were they spying on our meeting?" Isis slaps her fist against the windowsill. "I'll hex their arse so far into next week that they won't be able to find it with a freaking Google Alert!"

All the women of the Nevermore Coven crowd the window, peering at the dark figure as it crosses the top of Butcher Street, heading in the general direction of the pub.

A chill runs down my spine.

Isis heaves the window open. "If we catch you spying again," she yells, "I'll turn you into a toad, and you know that I can do it!"

The meeting breaks up after that. I stay behind to help tidy up the events room and pick up a selection of books from Mina. Isis gathers the plates and wraps up the last of the cupcakes to take to her Intro to Magic class the next night. Mina's raven delicately picks out the bits of goji and kelp slice that the ladies hid behind the cushions and drops them into the rubbish.

Isis and I end up leaving at the same time. She helps me to shove my book booty into my handbag.

"This might be my true magical power – being able to shove a huge number of books into a small space," she says.

"What about you being a psychic? And the ability to turn people into toads?"

"Between you and me, I don't have a magical bone in my body." Isis waves a hand dismissively, in a way that makes me think that maybe she's trying to convince herself. "I know everything there is to know about magic, but I've never actually been able to *do* any. My sister, on the other hand …"

"What about Dora?"

Isis pauses. "Ignore me, I'm just being silly." She looks away. "Where are you heading now? Back to your vampire's lair?"

"Reginald will be waiting for me at the Rose & Wimple." I smile. "He enjoys the weekly excuse to come into the village. Alaric doesn't like to leave the castle."

But maybe I can change that.

Even if I can't make Alaric want me, at least I might be able to give him the gift of vulnerability.

"We certainly don't get many sightings of him in the village, and never during the daylight hours." Isis taps her fingers on the vampire charm she's hung around her neck. "I know I can be a little much, but it's only because I'm worried about you. Mina already defeated a vampire once before, and it nearly cost her everything—" *I still can't tell if this is a joke or not.* "I don't want anyone else I love to get hurt. But I don't have to be a real psychic to see that you're hurting right now. If you ever need to talk about anything, supernatural or not, you know where to find me."

The urge to blurt out my humiliating kiss and all the strange things I've seen at Black Crag over the last few weeks dances on my tongue. But it's mortifying enough to think that the Nevermore Murder Club know about Patrick leaving me for Claire. I'd like to maintain the illusion that I've got my life together a little longer.

Besides, everything vampiric about my boss – his aversion to sunlight, his lightning-fast reflexes, his centuries' worth of hobbies, the coffin in his private wing – has a rational explanation.

Sort of.

"Anyway, think about it. Good night, Winnie. I'll see you next week." Isis presses a card into my hand and darts off towards the other side of the green, where she and Dora live above their magical shop. I wave at her and start towards the pub.

"Winnie."

Alaric steps out from behind a streetlight. My heart leaps in my throat.

"You're …" I can't find the words. "You're outside the castle."

"It seems so."

Beneath the pale streetlamps, his alabaster skin glimmers, as though veins of gold run beneath the surface. His sharp cheekbones and strong jaw stand in stark relief, and the way he steps towards me, oozing power and possession and danger, makes me understand why dark romance heroines are so ready to be tied up in a basement and punished by the villains.

"You're in the village. People might see you?"

"Don't sound so panicked. I brought a disguise." He removes an object from his pocket and holds it under his nose. It's a small cardboard moustache. "No one will recognise me now."

Why is he even more *alluring when he's being silly? It's unfair that one man should possess so much raw sexiness.*

"You're ridiculous. What are you doing here?" I ask. "How did you get into the village?"

"I am … trying to be vulnerable. I thought you might like some supper." He holds out his arm. "Would you allow me to take you for a meal?"

The corner of his mouth quirks a little as if something he said is funny in a dark way.

He's trying to be vulnerable.

For me.

The butterflies in my stomach invite some friends over for a rager.

"Okay. Sure. I'd love to have you for supper. I mean, have supper with you! That's what I meant."

I find myself slipping my hand through his arm in an old-fashioned way that feels perfectly natural for him. Alaric leads me across the green in the direction of the pub. A chill bites in the air. How long has Alaric been standing out in the mild summer evening? His skin is as cool as ever. He shouldn't let himself get so cold. If the sunlight makes him bedridden for three days, then I can only imagine what he'll be like with man flu.

Alaric settles us into one of the outdoor tables. He gives me one of his enthusiastic lectures on the pub's history – how the building had been an inn along a popular pilgrimage route, how it had been the centre of village life for centuries and is almost definitely haunted. He doesn't answer my question about how he got into the village, but he does glare at a couple who were headed to the table beside us until they turn away. Once our territory is secure, he ducks inside, returning a few minutes later with a gin and tonic and a glass of red wine for himself, and a menu tucked under his arm.

"I think I feel like bangers and mash, but the pulled pork sliders also look good." I glance over at him. He leans one arm on the table and sips his wine. His outward appearance is one of total control, but there's a fierceness in his eyes that betrays how on edge he is. *Is he putting himself through this because of what I said to him?* "What's good here?"

"I do not know. I've never tried the food, although Reginald raves about the beef and Guinness pie."

"If it's Reginald-approved, then I'll try the pie. And a basket of Lilac's amazing loaded wedges. I may be a disaster of a human, but a plate of fried potatoes makes it better."

"You're not a disaster of a human." Alaric's dark eyes bore into mine.

I stare down at the menu. Maybe it's time for me to be vulnerable too. "Thanks, but I don't believe you. I told you that my intention is that I'm allowing myself to be happy. I try to believe that. And yet, I'm such a mess that I threw myself at a client just to try and convince myself that I'm desirable. I'm not doing a very good job of being happy."

Alaric sets down his glass. His eyes reflect a sprinkle of stars. "I was the one who trapped you against the wheel—"

I hold up a hand. "I don't want to talk about it. I think you're right and we should just pretend it never happened."

"I never said that we should pretend it never happened."

"Running out of the room in disgust said it for you." I grip my glass in shaking hands and take a long sip. My cheeks burn and I can't bring myself to look at him, so I study the dessert section of the menu. "We only have to work together for another couple of weeks and then I'll be out of your life forever—"

"You're happy when you organise," Alaric says. "You get this adorable furrow between your eyes. At first, it looks like you're irked by the objects around you, but the longer I work with you, I see that it's not frustration, but serenity. You find peace in creating order from chaos."

I think of the joy I felt after I cleaned up Professor Lewicki's office, how the organisation system I designed changed the way she taught, and then I think of the towering piles and council complaints that my mother ignores. "That might be true, but it doesn't do any good, does it?"

"What you've done for me is a miracle." Alaric's hand reaches across the menu, his cool fingers brushing mine in a way that makes the butterflies start a mosh pit. "I spend my days creating chaos from order, but I did not know what brought me joy until I met you. I do not have words for the gift you've given me."

"Oh. Well, thanks." I slide my hands into my lap. I can't look at him. I can't bear to see pity in his eyes, or something worse. Something that might give me hope. "I wish every client was like you. I love that the Clutter Queens is doing so well. I'm proud of what Faye and I built. But I got into organising because I wanted to help people who couldn't help themselves. People who hoard aren't slobs. They're struggling with overwhelming emotional issues. Their piles of stuff are piles of sadness, or piles of broken dreams, or piles of hope. They feel embarrassed, and alone, and things get worse and worse and—" *—and their children have to live for years with rats crawling over their beds at night.* "I wanted to show them that someone cares, and that there is another way. But Faye got really into Instagram decor trends and influencer culture and I got swept along with her, and now the business is so high-end that most of our clients don't even need us – they just like to show off that they have the money to hire an organiser. Being here with you is the first time I've felt truly needed in a long time. I'm not happy. But I don't know what to do about it."

The butterflies jackhammer against my heart. I've never admitted that out loud before. I've never even admitted that *to myself.*

"A wise woman once told me that you should live according to your intentions," Alaric says. "You deserve to be happy. If you're unhappy, you should leave."

My head jerks up. "I can't leave Faye. The whole business is built off my Winnie Wins System, but that's tied up in our company trademark. If I walk away, I won't be able to use it."

"She will give it up if I ask her," Alaric says firmly. "With my sword."

"That's probably not a good idea—"

I look up from the table.

No.

I choke on my drink.

It can't be.

How are Patrick and Claire, the two people I most wanted to escape when I came to Argleton, walking across the green towards us?

24

Winnie

"WINNIE, WHAT'S WRONG?" ALARIC'S DEEP VOICE CUTS THROUGH my panic.

Why are they here? How are they here? What cruel demon is torturing me, and how much do I need to bribe him to work for *me instead?*

Patrick and Claire have their heads bent together, chatting softly about some lovey couple thing that's just for them. My stomach bottoms out as they make their way towards the pub. Any second now they're going to see me, and—

I glance over at Alaric, who is watching me with dark, fierce eyes.

"Just … don't say anything. I'll do the talking." I plaster a smile on my face as I scoot around to Alaric's side of the table, sliding into the seat next to him. My skin burns where his thigh touches mine, even though he's as cool as ever.

The couple saunter towards the door of the pub, lost in their own world.

I wave. "Patrick, Claire, hi."

My ex-fiancé stops in his tracks, his fingers curling protectively around the arm of my ex-best friend. "Winnie? Is that you?"

From his tone, I deduce that his question is really, "Winnie, is that you out of the house on a weeknight, socialising and being spontaneous? Because I'm getting strong Cylon vibes."

"It sure is." My smile wobbles at the edges. "It's such a lovely night. We were just having a spot of dinner. What brings you to Argleton?"

"Um …" Patrick's face twists awkwardly. I like smooth, slick Patrick looking all flustered in the presence of Alaric. "I had to come on business, but we heard how picturesque the village was so Claire and I … well …"

"We're looking at wedding venues." Claire blurts out, her face reddening as her words knife me through the heart. "I'm sorry you found out like this. It's what I wanted to talk to you about when we got back to London. I know it's an awkward situation, but I was hoping … you might forgive me and be my maid of honour?"

Not three months ago, Claire came with me to a converted warehouse in Mayfair to sign the contract at *my* wedding venue. And then the next day, she and Patrick sat me down and told me that they'd fallen in love.

And now she's asking me to be her maid of honour?

I have no words.

No, that's a lie. I have words. None of which can be repeated in the company of a lord.

"You're … you're getting married?" I manage.

"Patrick asked me last week." Claire sheepishly holds up her hand, wiggling her fingers so the enormous rock glitters in the moonlight. "I tried to tell you, but …"

… but I threw my old phone into the fountain at Black Crag so you couldn't get ahold of me.

"Oh, well, congratulations," I managed to choke out.

"Thank you, Winnie," Patrick doesn't look at me. He stares at Alaric as if he's sprouted a second head.

"Thanks so much, doll!" Claire jumps up and down. "We're so excited. We weren't sure whether we wanted to stay in London for the wedding, but we've just seen this lovely old manor house outside the village called Lachlan Hall. It's going to be perfect. We're thinking next summer and I want—"

"You didn't say what you're doing here." Patrick frowns. "You weren't following me, were you?"

"Oh, no!" I wave a hand, frantically trying to come up with some lie that's better than the truth, that Faye forced me to come since I'm the one without a flat or a life. "I'm … um … I'm working—"

"Winifred is my betrothed," Alaric's deep voice booms in my ear.

Wait, what?

I glance over at Alaric. He sits ramrod straight, those dark eyes of his fixed on Patrick with a look I cannot fathom. A surge of gratitude washes over me.

That grumpy, aloof, sweet bastard is coming to my rescue again.

This is a bad idea.

I shouldn't let my client pretend to be my fiancé, especially after he rejected my profoundly inappropriate kiss on the potter's wheel. But in the moment, I couldn't care less.

I'm living by my intentions, and seeing Patrick's shocked face makes me very, very happy.

I lean against Alaric's cool shoulder, trying to look as if it were completely natural for me to be getting snuggly with a lord. I expect Alaric to tense, the way he did in the moment before he ran away from me. He must hate every moment of being this close to me after he made it clear he's not interested.

But he doesn't act as though he hates it. He wraps his arm around me, his fingers splayed across the small of my back, pressing me into him.

The weight of his fingers makes me feel as though this is deeper than putting on a show for Patrick, as if I've been waiting my whole life for him to declare me his.

Patrick opens his mouth, but it takes a few tries for him to make a sound. "Your …?"

"Lord Alaric Valerian, at your service." Alaric extends his free hand towards Patrick. "I'm pleased to meet you. Are you friends of Winifred from London? We must have you at the castle for tea. My soon-to-be wife enjoys entertaining, and our chef is world-class."

Alaric looks at me and *winks*, and his arm around me squeezes, and Patrick glares at him, and I think I might *die* of happiness.

"Oh, we're not friends," I say sweetly. "I used to be engaged to Patrick, but then he cheated on me with my best friend, Claire."

"I see." Alaric withdraws his hand. "In that case, I shall rescind the tea invitation."

Alaric smiles at Patrick – a wide, toothy grin that's unnatural on him and manages to look monstrous. His eyes flash with the raw possessiveness that he showed when he pretended to be my boyfriend to scare away Danny. At this angle, I can't see Alaric straight on, only the curve of his full lips as he bares his teeth. Patrick stumbles back as if he's been cursed. He looks terrified.

Oh, I love this even *more*.

"We didn't mean to hurt you." Claire's face falls. "And look, you're happily engaged too, so it all worked out okay in the end. Can't we just—"

"No, Claire, we can't just. I trusted both of you and you betrayed me."

She recoils as if I've slapped her across the face. A sensation like pride spreads across my shoulders, filling me with joyous warmth. Or maybe that's from Alaric still holding me as if I'm his.

"I read in the history of Black Crag Castle that one of my ancestor's men betrayed his betrothed. The lord hung him from the castle walls," Alaric says conversationally. "By his testicles."

Patrick's face turns white. "Perhaps we should leave them to their dinner, Claire."

"But—"

He shoves Claire inside the pub.

I smother my face with my sleeve so Patrick and Claire can't hear my laughter. "I'm sorry, you *rescind the tea invitation*? That is the sickest burn I've heard from a member of the aristocracy."

Alaric doesn't share my mirth. He also doesn't remove his arm from around my waist. "Are you okay?"

"Yes. No. I don't know." I grip the edge of the table. My hands are shaking. What's wrong with me? I'd be able to think more clearly if he wasn't glaring out at the world like he'd burn it all down for me. "I'll feel better with another gin and tonic."

Alaric disappears into the crowded pub, returning a few moments later with a pair of gin and tonics and a number on a stick. "I ordered you the pie. And a chocolate brownie," he says stiffly.

"You're my knight in shining armour."

"I'm afraid my armour is rather dulled from lack of use, but if you ask it, I shall don my suit and duel that fiend Patrick. Luckily, we will not need such a large rope for his tiny testicles—"

"The testicle-hanging isn't necessary, but appreciated." I glance in the window. Claire and Patrick have a booth along the far wall. Patrick has his head in his hands, his shoulders trembling. Claire glances up and sees me. Her face is red with misery.

Alaric wraps my fingers around the glass, and then pulls me back against him. "Then you must forget them."

I swallow gulp after gulp of G&T, wishing it would hurry up and cure the lump in my throat or the warmth spreading through my body where Alaric touches me.

"Winifred, please talk to me. I do not like it when you are quiet."

I shake my head.

"*Talk*, lest I find other ways to tempt open those lips."

The air between us charges, and I find myself transfixed by *his* lips – the fullness of the upper versus the lower, the way they press tightly together, as though he's holding something dangerous inside, and the little quirk in the corner when he catches me watching.

"Losing Patrick hurt like being stabbed repeatedly with a butter knife," I sniff, cursing myself for rambling all this personal nonsense at my boss but unable to stop. "But if I'm being completely honest with myself, I don't think I was happy with him. Not romance novel, swooning at the mere sight of him happy. He was *safe*. Everything about Patrick was the complete opposite of my mother, and I clung to that even when things in our relationship weren't perfect. I'm humiliated more than I miss him, which tells me everything I need to know. But Claire …"

Alaric presses my cheek against his chest. His lips move over my hair as he says, "You care for her."

"Claire has been my friend for so long I don't remember my life without her. We know each other's darkest secrets. She's the only one who …"

Alaric tilts his head to the side. I shake my head. I can't give him that. He already knows more about my mother than I've told anyone else other than Claire. I've laid myself bare for him too many times already, only to have him reject me. He doesn't get this, too.

"That's what hurts so much." I swallow. "Claire has been an amazing friend. She's been there for me whenever I needed her. But this time, I can't call her after this horrible thing happened because she's partially responsible for the horrible thing. Losing Patrick I could deal with, but losing my best friend, too?"

Alaric touches my cheek. I turn my head into his touch, and through the tangle of my eyelashes, I see Claire watching us. A surge of petty joy rushes through me. *That's right, Claire. I'm not going to fall apart over losing our friendship.* "I'm sorry that you had to come to my rescue again. You don't have to keep pretending to be my fiancé. I think we fooled them."

I tear myself away from him, even though severing his touch is physically painful.

"I'm used to skewering my enemies on ornately decorated swords," Alaric says as he wraps his long fingers around his glass but does not drink it. "Pretending to be your betrothed is a more pleasant form of revenge. Plus it has the added advantage of less gore on my clothes."

"I'm never certain if you're kidding or not, but I love this bloodthirsty version of you." I hold out my glass, and he clinks it with his own. His wine smells odd – heady and metallic – but I know nothing about wine so that probably means it's old and delicious. The sexual charge between us hasn't lessened now that the only parts of us touching are our thighs. Instead, all sensation in my body has focused down to that one point, to the coolness and surety of his touch, to the way he makes me feel safe and completely reckless at the same time. "Their faces when they found out that you were a lord were an absolute joy."

"A little vengeance is good for the soul." Alaric sips his wine as the food arrives, and I shovel wedges into my mouth. His eyes crinkle at the edges, and suddenly, he looks impossibly young. I never realised how old he seems sometimes, as if he's lived through ages I cannot fathom. "You're smiling. You're happy."

"I am." I feel happier than I've felt in months. But I don't want to say any more. I've already been vulnerable enough for both of us tonight. "Thank you for taking me to dinner. I know it's hard for you to leave the castle, but I hope you've had fun. And luckily, no members of the Nevermore Murder Club and Smutty Book Coven have seen you yet."

"Why is that lucky?"

"You're drinking your red wine, not eating anything, wearing that old-fashioned coat, and frightening away my ex with nothing but a smile. They already think you're a vampire. This would confirm it."

"And what if I was?" Alaric growls, his voice taking on that dark, dangerous tone he had when he told Danny to leave me alone.

I laugh. "Alaric, be serious. Vampires don't exist."

He sets down his glass. When he turns back to me, his eyes are blazing with heat. "I did not run from our kiss because I don't want you, Winnie. I ran because you're everything I've dreamed of."

Excuse me, what?

"You're fun, and bright, and beautiful, and patient. You light up a room just by walking into it. It is torture to work so closely with you, to sit beside the fire with you, when the things I long to do to your body are anything but chaste."

"Oh, um …"

The butterfly mosh pit is going *wild*. But not as wild as Alaric's stormy eyes.

"Alaric—"

"I have to tell you something about myself. Tonight. I cannot wait any longer." He takes a jagged inhale of breath. "It will make you hate me."

"I won't."

"You *will.* You will run from Black Crag Castle and never look back, and it is for the best. You are supposed to run from monsters." Alaric leans forward, his breath kissing my collarbone. "But before I tell you this truth, I want to taste you again. I want to remember what I lost."

That heated voice of his works its way into my chest. Before I can utter another word, Alaric's fingers cup my cheek, tilting my head toward him. His lips part mine and he dips his tongue inside my mouth, tasting and supping.

I must taste like potato and cheese, because he moans into my mouth as if the flavour of me is the most exquisite thing on earth. The hand on my cheek snakes around to tangle in my hair, angling my head exactly where he wants me, while his other arm wraps around me, lifting me from my stool and depositing me on his lap.

I can feel his hardness again, and even though it's obscene and we're in the pub and *what the hell am I doing*, I rock against him, chasing the exquisite *wanting* of the friction between us.

I'm suddenly terrified that Alaric is doing all this for the benefit of Patrick and Claire. I pull back, panting, searching his eyes for a truth I can cling to. His fingers on the small of my back are steady, possessive. His eyes are pure *lust.*

He presses his lips to mine again, hard and needy, and he weaves his fingers through mine, and he might as well be pushing his fingers right into my heart and clutching the tender organ in his fist.

I rise to meet him, my tongue exploring the curve of his mouth, his perfect teeth with their sharp …

Alaric pulls back, his eyes ablaze with flecks of light from the streetlights. He gathers me in his arms, lifting me off the chair and holding me against him. "Come, we will find Reginald to bring us back to the castle."

By the time Alaric deposits me in the backseat of the car, I've forgotten about Patrick and Claire entirely.

The Nevermore Murder Club and Smutty Book Coven Group Chat

Isis: You won't believe what I saw! Winnie and Lord Valerian snogging!

Maisie: Isis, rude! Winnie's on the chat!

Isis: She's not. She threw her phone in a fountain because that girl Claire kept texting her, remember? She won't have a new one yet because she's too busy sucking vampire face.

Arabella: Must you be so crass?

Isis: Yes!

Komal: I'm happy for her. That girl deserves some lovin'. Alaric being a vampire and all, he's had a lot of time to perfect his game.

Beth: Her aura has been all green and gross with sadness. A good vampire boning is just what she needs.

Arabella: Why am I even friends with you all?

25

Winnie

REGINALD TAKES THE WINDING ROADS WITH EVEN MORE RECKLESS abandon than usual. Alaric has climbed in the backseat with me, and the air between us hums with possibility. But the first time one of the car's wheels leaves the road, I break through that barrier to grip Alaric's knee so hard that I must leave crescent-shaped gouges in his flawless skin.

He watches me with that vicious, predator-like intensity that makes it almost impossible to stay on my side of the car. Reginald *has* to notice that something's changed between us, but he says nothing as he hurtles us through the countryside. Alaric places his hand over mine on his knee, his cool fingers caging in mine, and that touch alone is enough to make my stomach butterflies swoon.

By the time we finally rattle over the bridge and into the inner courtyard, I'm a puddle.

Alaric exits the car with inhuman speed. My heart sinks as I panic that he's running from me again, but then his face appears at my window. He flings open my door and pulls me from the high footplate into another dizzying kiss. The moment his lips devour me again, heat flares from my core.

He breaks our kiss to pull me inside. Reginald disappears, leaving the two of us standing in the Stabby Chic room.

My chest tightens with nerves. I've never done this before – I've never crossed a line with a client, or been with someone who felt so utterly out of my league. I feel like I'm back in university, fumbling in the darkness.

"Thank you," I whisper, "for pretending to be my fiancé. Hopefully, we won't see them around again and we won't have to—"

"I will be your betrothed any time you wish."

Betrothed. Another of Alaric's old-fashioned words that somehow sounds hot as fuck in his rich, rumbly voice. It's a word that's so essentially him – dripping with history and meaning and *power.*

He kisses me deeply one final time, before pulling away with a sharp exhale. His dark eyes drink me in, and tension pulses between us. I'm about to throw myself at him again when he speaks.

"We should stop."

I must look as gutted as I feel because he quickly adds, "Not because I don't want you. Believe me, I have lain awake dreaming of you, of the things I want to do to you. But I won't lay with you while there is a secret between us."

I exhale half a laugh. "So tell me your secret. You clearly want to."

"*Please.*" The anguish in his voice nearly undoes me. "Give me this one night, this one perfect moment, when I can believe I'm not a monster."

"You're not—"

"Goodnight, Winifred." Alaric turns and retreats to the west wing, with a final tortured glance over his shoulder, leaving me breathless and wide-eyed.

26

Alaric

I LIE ON MY BACK, STARING AT THE CLOSED LID OF MY COFFIN AS THE night fades into day. Normally, a vampire has no problem with sleep. Our sleep is not the same as humans – we do not dream. We lay down in our coffin and our bodies shut off until the sun disappears once more.

But I cannot settle myself into my dreamless sleep when Winnie Preston is occupying my every thought. Even when my eyes are open, all I see is her beautiful face, I taste her plump lips and my senses burn with sunshine and strawberries, and I remind myself how close I came to truly *tasting* her …

It took centuries of finely-honed willpower to walk away from her. My hunger for her is far from sated, but this night with Winnie has been the happiest of my long life.

Now I am counting down the hours until she wakes and I must tell her the truth.

She might stay, a foolish voice whispers inside my skull. *She wants you now. She could still want you once she learns the truth.*

You are supposed to be dead, I remind the voice. *You were supposed to die after the last time the villagers tortured me. You're not supposed to allow me to hope.*

And yet, I *hope*.

I hope for a future where Winnie stays at Black Crag, where I make art and she whirls about with her terrible music, where everything smells of sunshine and strawberries and she lets me taste her whenever I desire, and we are happy …

My supernatural hearing alerts me to Winnie stirring in her bed on the other side of the castle. A low, pained moan escapes her lips.

She's having one of her nightmares.

It takes me barely a heartbeat to find myself outside her room once more. This time, I push open the door and see her curled beneath the covers, a pained expression on her face. This close, her whimpers devastate me. I long to reach into her dream and pluck out the monster that's hurting her, but I don't have that power. Instead, I cross the room and gather her in my arms.

"Winnie, I'm with you. You're safe."

She jerks against me, her limbs flailing out to slap at her body. "Bugs … get them off me …" she whimpers, her eyes squeezed shut.

"There are no bugs." I stroke her hair. I don't know if I'm helping or making things worse.

But I remember something that helped me.

When I ran away to the Midnight Court with a skull filled with nightmares, a friend taught me to sing. I learned songs of hope and longing, songs of farewell to brothers at arms, songs of war and songs of love. I sing them to myself sometimes, when I need to remember, or when I long to forget.

I pluck one from the air and sing it for her now.

It's an old Germanic folk song about slaying monsters, one that I have sung on the battlefield many times to stir my blood for the killing. I sing and soothe her until her limbs stop jerking and her body rests easy against the pillow. She returns to sleep. I watch her for hours, making sure that she doesn't have another dream. Winnie wants me to be vulnerable. I've never felt more vulnerable than watching her suffer and knowing that there's nothing I can do.

My fingers itch to sculpt this feeling, this helplessness.

It's still a couple of hours until the sun sets, but if I keep the curtains drawn and don't overexert myself, I can work.

Compared to the secret of my blood, this art project is but a tiny lie between us. When I reveal my final artwork to her, when I can finally show her how I *truly* feel, she will not care that I have snuck around to make it happen.

I plant a gentle kiss on her hair and slip away, careful not to step into the shaft of sunlight streaming through the half-open curtains.

Winnie, what nightmares haunt you?

27

Winnie

I WAKE TO COLD MOONLIGHT STREAMING IN THROUGH THE GOTHIC windows. I rub my eyes, casting my mind back to the violent dream that woke me, but I find nothing.

Huh?

Odd.

I always remember the nightmares of towering piles and scrambling rats and bugs. Why can't I remember? Am I so sleep-deprived that I'm starting to lose my memory?

I sit upright and fumble around for my phone. 5.33 pm.

What? That can't be right.

I slept until 5.33 pm. But *how?*

Did I not have the nightmare?

I focus on my body. My skin isn't crawling. I can't feel the bugs.

My eyes fall on the pillows scattered across the bed and floor, and the person-sized indent in the mattress beside me.

Alaric was here.

The sleep-hazed memory returns to me. He held me through my nightmare.

But now he's gone.

Mortification heats my skin. Did I say or do something embarrassing?

I leap out of bed. As I hunt around in my packing cubes for the perfect 'morning after you snogged your client and he snuggles you through a nightmare' outfit, I notice a white box sitting on the table. I pick it up.

It's a brand-new phone.

My heart stutters. I flip over the box. A note is attached to the case, written in Reginald's loopy cursive.

Ms Preston

Lord Valerian asked me to pick up a new phone and number for you. His actual words were, "Winnie requires a new rectangle of annoyance, as hers has joined my ill-conceived attempts at knitting at the bottom of the cistern."

I have programmed Lord Valerian's number in it for you, although he usually will not answer or reply to texts. He did ask me not to add your playlists, but I'll leave that to your discretion.

Yours,
Reginald

Alaric got me a new phone.

It's yet another strange and wonderful way he's taken care of me, especially since he hates phones with the fire of a thousand suns. He's willing to reshape his whole life so that I can fit into it. No one has ever found me worth changing for like that before.

I could get used to this.

I throw on a soft grey jumpsuit and an oversized purple cardigan, stuff the phone in my pocket, relight the candelabra, and head downstairs.

"Alaric?" I call to the empty castle.

"Meorrw?" Mirabelle greets me on the stairs. She rubs herself around my legs then darts off before looking back at me, as if to say, "Well, hurry up, then!"

I follow her to – where else? – the study, where Alaric is hunched over his desk, brow furrowed in concentration as he dips his brush into paint and works on a small canvas.

"Hey, stranger," I say, the nerves creeping in. "What are you working on?"

"Winnie." Alaric drops his brush and leaps to his feet, his presence sucking all the oxygen from the room until I feel woozy from the sight of him. "How did you sleep?"

"Much better, thanks to you." I swallow, suddenly mortified that he saw me at my most vulnerable. I'm desperate to change the topic. "Thank you for the phone."

"I thought you might regret your impetuous overhand throw," Alaric says. The warmth in his voice glides over my body like his hands did last night. *I am so gone for this man.* "I tried to rescue the rectangle of annoyance, but it swims as well as you do."

"That was so thoughtful." I want to say more, but anything that comes out of my mouth right now is dangerous. "Um … we're okay after last night? I mean, you don't regret—"

"I regret many things in my long life, but being with you will never be one of them."

That warm fizz along my spine is back. "Oh, well. Good. I mean, me too. I have ro negets. I mean, no regrets … So, um, what are you working on?"

Alaric slams down the painting on the desk. "It's an abysmal failure. I cannot show you."

"We talked about you not being such a perfectionist."

"Yes, but tonight is not the night to begin." Alaric takes my hands in his. "Winnie, I said that there is something I need to tell you. About me."

"You sound so serious."

"This is serious." His eyes blaze as his cool fingers knit in mine. "Winnie, you must know that the time we've spent together has been some of my brightest nights upon this earth. But I fear those days have come to an end. I fear you cannot know the truth and still want me, but I owe you my vulnerability, my truth. You see, I am a—"

"My lord."

We leap apart. My chest heaves as I turn to Reginald in the doorway. He looks miserable. "I'm sorry to interrupt, but you have a visitor."

"Tell them to go away!" Alaric booms. "We're busy!"

"I wish I could, my lord. But it's your mother. She's arrived early."

28

Winnie

ALARIC STIFFENS.

I reach over and squeeze his hand. "It's too late to worry about the mess now. The ballroom and office look lovely. And the drawing room is—"

"It is not the rooms I'm concerned about." Alaric's features swim with pain. "She cannot see you here. She will smell you on me. She will know."

"What are you talking about?"

"You must leave immediately." He shoves me towards Reginald. "Take Winifred to the village. The Nevermore Coven will look after her. You can ship her things later—"

He's scaring me. "No way." I shake my head. I can still taste him on my lips and feel the oddly sharp point of his incisor against my tongue. "I'm not going anywhere."

I understand the fear in his eyes. All those years living with my mother's illness, I wished I didn't have to do it all alone. We could never have anyone over to our house, because then they'd see how we lived. I had Claire, eventually, when I told her. But she was just as young and clueless as I was.

Judging by his level of agitation, Alaric's dark secret involves his mother, and I won't abandon him to her. I can't go back to London and leave him alone, not when …

… not when he's the reason for the butterflies inside me, and the warmth kindling at the edges of my heart.

"Her car is blocking the bridge, anyway," Reginald says. "Perhaps we should—"

"Alaric Valerian!" A sultry voice booms through the castle. "Is slinking in the shadows how you greet your ravishing mother?"

Alaric's face pinches. I grab his hand and drag him into the Stabby Chic room just as an imposing woman sweeps through the doors. Her dress looks like something straight off a Paris runway – a flimsy, off-the-shoulder silk thing with a full skirt, which seems a strange choice for swanning around a freezing medieval castle. But, like him, Alaric's mother doesn't seem to feel the cold. Not a single goosebump appears on her thin, perfectly toned arms. Her hair is piled on top of her head in a mess of dark ringlets, and her makeup is absolutely flawless.

She looks young enough to be his sister. Clearly, the Valerians have no use for Beth's anti-aging elixirs.

Alaric makes a face that speaks of centuries of torment, and slinks over to her. She proffers her hand. He takes it in his, raises her delicate fingers to his lips, and kisses her knuckles.

"You smell *wretched*," she informs him. "What foul taboo have you been indulging in away from the eyes of the court?"

This woman cannot be his mother. It's impossible. She's barely older than I am.

And what does she mean by "court"?

I glance between Alaric and his mother, trying to figure out what in Dracula's name is going on. Alaric's last words about a dark secret blaze inside my skull.

His mother is really his sister? Is that the secret?

Gross, gross, gross.

That can't *be it, can it?*

"Mother, you were not due to arrive for another two weeks," Alaric scolds her lightly as he escorts her into the Stabby Chic hall. I trail behind them. "You have travelled during the daylight hours. We haven't finished preparing your rooms."

"You wouldn't turn away your own blood, Alaric Valerian. I shall arrive when I choose. Tinted window technology has come a long way. Besides, I have something important to show you, and it simply couldn't wait another day." She claps her hands. So far she has not even acknowledged my presence. It's as if she doesn't even see me. "Perdita, come here."

Another figure appears in the doorway. A woman steps into the flickering candlelight, and I stifle a gasp as I take her in. Hair like spun silk falls in sensuous curls around her heart-shaped face. A pair of wide, curious eyes in an arresting shade of baby blue fix on Alaric with cold precision, and the corner of her scarlet lips curls back into a smirk. Her crimson fishtail dress hugs her impossibly trim waist and voluptuous curves, and beneath the usually cruel light of the hall, her skin appears lustrous, speckled in silver.

She is the most beautiful woman I've ever seen.

"Hello, Alaric," the woman purrs.

A strangled noise rises from Alaric's throat. "Mother, what … what is the meaning of this?"

"Oh Alaric, you do love to tease me so. You've must remember Perdita. I'm told the two of you were once close. You must know why she's here." Alaric's mother smiles without a trace of warmth. "Perdita is to be your wife."

29

Alaric

Gideon: You should know that the Nevermore Murder Club is sniffing around Danny's death. One of them was out at our site, snooping through our files. I'll redouble my efforts, but if those meddling ladies get close to the truth, we'll have to consider measures.

Y WIFE?

No.

This is all wrong.

All these years, Callista has left me alone at Black Crag. I thought she understood that I want nothing to do with the machinations at the Nightshade Court and I have no desire to wed to suit her political aims …

But the pampered vampire princess gliding towards me with victory burning in her eyes tells me that I've been a fool.

Of course, Callista would not give up on me. She has brought Perdita to my castle, betting that I would not refuse her while her chosen bride (and my old friend) is a guest in our home. To kick Perdita out of the castle now, after she has made this trip, would invite a feud between our families, between the Nightshade and Midnight Courts. And even with my distance and disinterest in court, I know that is something we can ill-afford in the current climate.

But I will *not* marry this woman, not for blood loyalty or to save the Upyr community from civil war.

Not when my heart belongs to the remarkable human woman standing beside me, her mouth open in shock.

Panic rises in my chest as Perdita sweeps towards me. There has to be some way to salvage this mess—

A wild, desperate idea comes to me. I don't have time to ask permission, nor to talk myself out of an act so abhorred in our laws. I wrap my arms around Winnie and pull her close.

"Unfortunately, Mother, you and Princess Chastain have travelled all this way in vain. For you see, I am already engaged to be wed." I force my lips into a smile. "May I present my bride, Winnie Preston."

30

Winnie

I GUESS ALARIC'S CALLING IN HIS FAVOUR NOW.

My head spins from everything that's happened. I'm struggling to flip from the cold desperation in Alaric's voice as he started to tell me his secret to the way my body hums when he calls me his "future wife". But, after he pretended to be my fiancé for Patrick and Claire, surely the least I can do is play along with his game.

Although I doubt his mother will believe us. Why would someone choose to marry me when there are eligible ladies like Perdita around?

I squeeze against Alaric's body, wrapping my hands around his waist and glaring possessively at Perdita. I barely have to pretend at all. "Hello."

"Winifred, this is my mother, Lady Callista Valerian, matriarch of the Blood Valerian, and her guest, Perdita Chastain, Princess of the Midnight Court."

Princess?

I raise an eyebrow to Alaric. *This* must be the family secret he needs to tell me. He's some kind of royalty and he's engaged to a princess. He returns my gaze with a tilt of his chin, his mouth fixed in a firm line. It's as close to flustered as I've ever seen Alaric look.

Play along, Winnie. You'll make him explain later.

I extend a hand towards Alaric's mother. "Call me Winnie, please. I'm so happy to meet you. Alaric's told me so much about you."

A lie. Alaric has told me absolutely *nothing* about this terrifying woman. And it's probably for the best, because I might've run away from Black Crag and never come back.

Alaric's mother regards me with cold revulsion. Her lips curl back into a snarl. "*Her?* Alaric, you cannot be serious. I know you enjoy flouting our laws, but this is too low, even for you. Obviously, you cannot marry her."

Rude!

"I have prepared drinks in the sitting room." Reginald appears beside the shelves of teddy bears. "Follow me."

Alaric flashes Reginald a grateful half-smile. "Let us have drinks and we can discuss the details. Winnie, you may join us if you wish, or wait for me in your chambers. I won't be long."

"I'd love a drink."

"But weren't you saying how sleepy you were?" His eyes beg me.

"I've found a second wind." I smile. I know that Alaric's trying to get me away from them so he can do damage control, but he doesn't get to make all the rules in this fake-engagement. Plus, if I'm being honest, I'm enjoying seeing him squirm.

"It should join us," Callista sniffs. "Perhaps it can explain to us how this absurd relationship even began. Our Thralls will bring in our things."

She's calling me "it". *Excuse me?*

I can see why Alaric isn't thrilled about her visit.

Two men in their early twenties with bloodshot eyes and dopey smiles on their faces appear in the doorway, carrying between them a long crate, which they start manoeuvring up the stairs.

"Follow me." Reginald trots off in the direction of the sitting room. The two ladies float gracefully after him, their dresses kicking up clouds of dust as they sweep over the flagstones. I can practically hear the disdain dripping from Callista as she silently regards the gaps on the walls and the piles of Alaric's projects everywhere.

"I think it would be best if I found lodgings for you and Perdita somewhere else," Alaric says stiffly as he trails behind them into the room. "Winnie and I have been working on preparing rooms for you, Mother, but since you are early, we haven't quite—"

"Nonsense. I will not be removed from the castle, no matter the state it's in."

"I think Black Crag is lovely," Perdita says in a breathy, sultry voice. "It's very … traditional."

"As you'll learn, my dear, our family believes in keeping up the rituals and customs of our society." Callista fixes her son with a withering glare. "At least, *some* of us do."

"Please, do not worry – the Chastain clan have our traditionalists, too." Perdita flutters her impossibly-long eyelashes in Alaric's direction. "Personally, I enjoy life with a little bit of spice."

I'm sure you do.

Alaric's grip on my arm is a vice as he drags me into the sitting room. Reginald has uncorked two bottles – a red and a white – and placed them beside four glittering silver goblets on the table. He's fussing with the fireplace, trying to get the kindling to catch.

"Leave us, Reginald," Callista waves her hand. "We do not require the fire."

I rub the goosebumps on my arms. *How is she not freezing her tits off in that thin silk dress?*

"My betrothed needs it," Alaric says firmly. "Reginald, please finish the fire. I shall pour the drinks."

Alaric lifts the red wine and pours three glasses. I notice that the label is one of those strange old bottles in the temperature-controlled sleeves that I saw in his cellar. He reaches for the white.

"Actually, I fancy the red," I say. Alaric shakes his head softly as he hands me a glass of white. Perdita giggles as if I've said something hilarious.

"Trust me," he whispers, his breath rushing against the sensitive skin of my neck. I nod, accepting the glass. *I'll trust him … for now.*

Behind him, Callista shakes her head, her eyes venomous.

Alaric takes my hand and moves us to stand in front of the fire, our backs to the flames. Callista flicks her gaze to me with disinterest, as if I'm a bug she is hoping Reginald will notice and squash without her having to think about me again. I inch myself closer to Alaric.

Perdita circles the room, her long fingers stroking the stem of her glass. Her nails are blood red and shaped to vicious points.

"These tapestries are exquisite." She runs those blood-red talons over the fine gold threads.

"Alaric made them," I say. "He's a talented artist."

"I'm aware. I'm the one who taught him to use a paintbrush, although I see that his eye has far surpassed mine. I hope to discover many more of Alaric's talents." She smiles sweetly, but the way she strokes the stem of her glass is anything but sweet.

I'd like to dunk her head in a vat of honey.

They know each other? She taught him to paint?

"Mother, Perdita, you must be tired from the road," Alaric says. "You will have my chambers. Reginald will make them ready for you now."

"Certainly, my lord." Reginald hurries away.

"Where will you sleep?" Perdita asks, her words heavy with suggestion.

"With my love." Alaric plants a kiss on my hair that might've appeared chaste and loving, but feels like a lightning bolt straight between my thighs.

He'll what?

Perdita makes a face.

"We all have our perversions, but must you flaunt yours in front of your mother?" Callista pats the sofa beside her. "You know what you risk by fornicating with this … this—"

"Things do not have to be as they always were, Mother. Gideon has introduced me to this wonderful invention called contraception."

What is happening right now?

Why are we talking about contraception in front of his mother?

My face heats up like a fried tomato.

Callista rolls her eyes. "I don't want to hear anything more about it. Sit with me. I have much news of our predicament to impart."

Alaric lifts a questioning eyebrow to me. I clutch my wine glass like it contains all the meaning of the universe. "Go," I whisper. "I don't need you to babysit me. It's not as if Perdita bites."

"I wouldn't be so sure." With a forlorn look at me over his shoulder, Alaric strides across the room to perch next to his mother. She leans in close, whispering frantically, her elegant hands gesticulating wildly. I can't hear a word they're saying. I toss back my head and skull my wine.

And I thought my mother was difficult. At least she never tried to arrange my marriage.

"Walk with me."

I whirl around. Perdita has somehow crossed the room in a flash to stand right behind me, her tits practically brushing mine. Before I can protest, she grabs my arm in her cold hand, shoves it through hers, and starts dragging me around the perimeter of the room like we're extras in *Bridgerton*.

"You were saying that Alaric made these tapestries. Is that why there is so much stuff in the hallway and rooms?"

"Alaric's very artistic," I say proudly. "He fills his castle with his passions. He paints, sculpts, makes pottery … but I'm helping him to tame the mess. We've cleaned out the ballroom and—"

"This is excellent. My court celebrates the arts. I'm an accomplished cellist, and with my connections, I'll have his work in the finest galleries in Europe. I'm particularly enamoured with this one." She stops in front of the battle scene in the valley. "It's a wonder that he was able to capture all these precise details of this battle, almost as if he were there."

"Alaric loves history." I don't like the way she talks about him, as though she knows him better than me. *Although she probably does.* "He does his research."

"Yes, I'm quite sure he does." She gifts me with a cold smile. I catch a flash of incisor as sharp as her talons, but it's gone when I blink. *I imagined it. I must have.* "Alaric was always popular when he lived at my court. He would delight my parents with his mock battles in the throne room, and present me with the most lavish gifts that he made."

Alaric was at a royal court? I glance over at my fake-fiancé, leaning in close to his mother while she whispers fervently to him. With his aristocratic nature and his old-fashioned manners, I believe Perdita.

I also believe he would've hated it. I think I am beginning to understand why he hid himself away in this remote castle.

"Run along now, little human girl," Perdita hisses in my ear, her teeth scraping my skin. Something about her heady perfume and strange, haunting beauty scrambles my thoughts until I'm almost wishing that *she* would kiss me. "Too much is riding on this marriage for it to be undone by Alaric's stupidity. You may be his fancy – a tempting plaything he'll discard as soon as he breaks you, like one of his little hobbies – but his mother will make certain he does the right thing for his kin."

Who is she calling human girl?

"Alaric makes his own decisions," I shoot back, tearing myself away from her. "He's chosen me. You and your perky tits will have to get over it."

But my voice trembles. I'm still disarmed by her beauty. How will Alaric ever see me when she's a bonfire of golden light burning with an otherworldly glow? I fade into the shadows beside her.

"Alaric *will* be mine," she says with an easy smile, as though their love story has already been written.

I glare at Perdita, all trussed up in that beautiful dress, so certain that she belongs with the complicated man I've got to know over the last two weeks. I think of my intention. I will allow myself to be happy.

What will make me happiest right now?

I toss my wine over her head.

"Eeeee!" Perdita grabs her hair. "What's the witch done to me?"

Alaric and Callista leap to their feet. Callista rushes to Perdita's aid, calling for Reginald to assist. Alaric lifts an eyebrow at me, and a smirk tugs at the corner of his lips.

I don't want to see him smirking at me when he's *betrothed* to someone else.

I feel like I'm surrounded by piles of my mother's things, like the walls and my feelings and beautiful women and Alaric's secrets loom over me, ready to topple down at any moment and bury me alive.

I can't breathe. I need to get away.

"If you'll excuse me." I set down my empty glass. "I've got work to do. My business partner needs the accounts."

For once, I'm grateful for Faye's thoughtlessness.

"I'll escort you." Alaric offers his arm.

"Stay with your mother," I manage to choke out as I back towards the door. "You have a lot to catch up on. I'm perfectly capable of making it to my room by myself."

Alaric smiles that dazzling half-smile at me, and the stone that's lodged itself in my throat rolls around a little. "I'm in no doubt about your stair-climbing and castle-navigating abilities, Winnie. I'm concerned about what Perdita might do to you from the shadows."

"She's no match for me and my trusty knife."

Alaric glances over his shoulder as Reginald flies into the room to help Perdita. "I must kiss you goodbye."

My cheeks heat. I flash back to the amazing, toe-curling kiss we shared at the pub, and all the kisses that came after it.

I can't do *that* in front of his mother.

Especially not when I don't know what we are anymore.

Alaric misunderstands my shock as consent. He moves in, his thighs brushing mine, one hand curling around my arm. "They are watching. It will convince them that we are serious."

"Alaric—"

I don't want you to kiss me to convince your mother we're engaged.

I want you to kiss me because you want—

My thoughts are cut off by the sweep of his lips over mine, the coolness of his skin, the possessive way he grips my arm, holding me in place as he tastes me.

It feels just like the way he kissed me last night, as if I'm being swept along by a riptide, pulling me out to sea. But this isn't real. He's putting on a show.

None of it is real.

Maybe I don't care. He has me so reckless and untethered that I want to make a mess of my life, just to see what will happen. And if making a mess feels like *this*, like being swept up in the arms of a wild god, then …

Yes, my heart whispers.

No, my brain shouts.

When I withdraw, I'm breathless, panting. My cheeks redden. I'm making a fool of myself in front of Callista and Perdita, but it's impossible not to when he kisses like that. I can't bear to look at them. I don't want to know what they think of me.

I can't do this. I'm too twisted up. I don't trust myself with him, and I can't trust him when there's a secret between us.

Callista makes an aggrieved sound in her throat. Alaric whispers, "I will be with you as soon as I can get away. We need to speak *urgently*."

I nod, swallowing against the stone. I tear myself away from him and run from the room before he can see the tears beading at the corners of my eyes.

31

Winnie

I HEAD STRAIGHT TO MY ROOM AND SIT HEAVILY ON THE SIDE OF the bed. Despite the thick walls of the castle, I can hear Alaric and his mother yelling at each other. At the words "She's not one of us," fresh tears stream down my cheeks.

I'm still the dirty girl, the one who wasn't good enough for her mother to love more than her stuff. But through my humiliation, fresh questions flood my mind. *Why is Alaric's mother so young? Why did Perdita call me "human" like it was an insult? What was Alaric about to tell me before Callista interrupted?*

My infatuation with Alaric has stopped me from seeing this situation clearly. I ball my hands into fists and shove them in my eyes, trying to force myself to stop crying.

And then I glance at my phone and notice the date and time.

It's Wednesday, 6.22 pm.

I'm supposed to be going to the weekly meeting of the Nevermore Murder Club and Smutty Book Coven.

I don't know any of the women that well. It's too soon to say we're friends, but right now all I want to do is be surrounded by their bubbly energy. I imagine Celeste plying me with delicious treats and Mina handing me a tea. I imagine telling them about Alaric's mother showing up with his future wife, and him pretending that we're engaged, and all the weird stuff that's been going on. I imagine how they would listen and hug me and argue over exactly what I should do.

They would tell me to *not* be like the heroines of many of our favourite novels and rush off without letting Alaric explain.

Even though my skin crawls with invisible bugs and I have the same desperate need to flee that I had when I lived with my mum, I decide it's time to make Alaric tell me what's going on in his own words.

I'm not a prisoner in this castle. I can leave.

I hunt around for an outfit that might stand up against Perdita and Callista, eventually throwing on a wrap dress in a bright purple. I then relight the candles in my candelabra, shove my feet into a pair of patent leather ankle boots, and clomp downstairs.

As I pass by the arrow slits in the walls of the tower staircase, I see Callista and Perdita walking around the courtyard outside, their heads bent together in secret conversation, while the two young guys they brought with them walk a few steps behind. I wish I could hear what they're saying.

I check the sitting room and Alaric's study. He's not there. Nor is he in the ballroom. I contemplate heading up to his family chapel when I hear a squeaking noise coming from the drawing room where he keeps his potter's wheel.

"Damn you, Alaric." I don't want to go in there and remember when he straddled the wheel behind me and I leaned back against his hard chest and …

Nope, not thinking about it. I'm going to be strong. I'm going to get answers.

I cross the cluttered hallway and peer through the crack in the door.

He's bent over a wheel that's not spinning, his strong hands digging into a ball of clay, moulding and shaping it to his will. His brow furrows in concentration and I freeze, transfixed by the sight of him utterly enraptured with his art.

Mirabelle darts between my legs and leaps onto his lap, scattering tools and tubs of glaze. Alaric wipes his hands on a nearby towel, before reaching out and scooping her against his chest, his head lowering so she can nuzzle his chin. Their tenderness makes the butterflies in my belly dance, but I have to be strong. I can't break my resolve just because he's kissing the top of her little head—

"Alaric."

His head jerks up, his eyes reflecting the dancing candlelight. Mirabelle glares at me, as if confirming that I don't belong as part of their family.

"Winnie." His voice is clipped. "You are still here?"

"Shouldn't I be here?" My harsh voice echoes from the vaulted ceiling.

Alaric winces, as if I've wounded him. "For your safety, you should flee. But I should have known that not even my mother would frighten you."

He stands, placing Mirabelle gently onto the seat. He reaches me in two long strides, sweeping me into his arms, pressing us chest to chest so that my heart thumps against his. Every place where our bodies touch brings back flashes of our night together, of how good he made me feel.

I try to step away, but he pulls me closer, smothering me in his winter scent, and I lose the battle with my will.

Alaric grips my chin with his strong, cool fingers, angling me towards him. "I'm so sorry, Winnie. My mother, she's … She shouldn't have spoken to you like that."

He kisses me, slow and languid, taking his time as if he is savouring a fine wine, trying to commit every corner and angle of me to memory.

I emerge breathless, not wanting it to end. "You don't have to pretend, Alaric. Your mother isn't here now."

"She has eyes and ears everywhere in this castle," he whispers, gripping my chin with his strong, cool fingers. "But this kiss isn't for her."

It doesn't feel like it's for show, the way he deepens the kiss until he's drinking in my soul. He *is* like a wild god, otherworldly and chaotic and *dangerous.*

In a moment of clarity, I tear myself from him again. I back against a pillar, breathing hard. I came down here for answers, because I didn't want to leave without giving him a chance to explain. But one touch from him and I'm under his spell.

What is wrong with me?

I hold out a hand, warning him not to come closer. "Alaric, what's going on?"

"I'm sorry that I did not follow you earlier. There are things I must tell you, but my mother …" He makes a face that's a mirror image of a face I often make around *my* mother. "So I came here to work on a sculpture. But don't worry. I'll clean everything up."

"I'm not worried about the mess!" I glare at him. "You said you can explain everything. So *explain.* Tell me that everything between us isn't an act. Tell me what you were going to tell me before your mother arrived. Tell me why you don't eat, why you don't like the sunlight … why you're so reluctant to let anyone get close to you. Or otherwise I'm walking out that door right now."

"I've never lied to you, Winnie, but I have deceived you. It's the curse I must bear, the only way I have survived." Alaric's eyes flicker with a pain so intense that witnessing it steals my breath. But it's gone in a moment, replaced with his usual stony expression – his jaw squared, his eyes cold black holes, his lips set in a firm, cruel line. "Reginald warned me to tell you the truth, but I was too selfish and too smitten with you to see that he was right. I led you to believe that we are the same, but we exist in two different worlds—"

The dust fills my throat. Tears burn the corners of my eyes. *So that's it, then? He's going to marry the princess and forget about me.*

I try not to think about the words *too smitten with you.*

Because they mean nothing.

He and I are nothing.

I thought we had a connection, but I'm not part of his world. I'm still the broken, dirty girl who no one wants.

The butterflies in my stomach curl up and die, their beautiful wings turning to dust that stings the back of my throat. Suddenly all my other questions seem pointless, because *he doesn't want me.*

"I should leave." I hear the words, but they don't sound as if they're coming from my mouth. "I'll stay in the village for tonight's book club, and then I'll go back to London. You don't have to worry about me anymore. I'll send my business partner, Faye, to finish the last rooms."

I reach into my tote bag for my phone.

"Winnie, you misunderstand me." He lunges towards me, his voice frantic. "I thought we couldn't be together, that the laws of my people forbid it, and for good reason. I thought that my hunger for you could hurt you in more ways than one. But it's not *true.*"

My hand brushes the blade of the knife he gave me, slicing a long cut down my finger.

"—We can be together. All I want is for you to be mine—"

"Ow." I snap my hand out, holding my finger up to inspect the cut. "That hurt—"

I don't know how he crosses the room so fast. Alaric slams into me. My back hits the pillar with a crack that makes my teeth rattle.

Alaric pins my wrist above my head, his nails digging into my flesh. His body presses against mine again, caging me in. My other hand still holds the heavy candelabra, but he's trapped my arm so I can't swing it. I shake it, raining drops of wax on his black silk shirt, but he doesn't seem to notice.

He trembles, biting his lip as his face twists with violent, animalistic *need.*

This would be fucking hot if it weren't for the look in his eyes.

It's as if Alaric – caustic, passionate, kind Alaric – has fled his body, leaving behind a demon who has only one desire.

To *feed.*

"Alaric," I breathe. "You're hurting me."

His head jerks to the side, those eyes devouring me with predatory intent, as his mouth opens wide, his lips curling back to reveal long, pointed incisors sliding down from the roof of his mouth.

No human has teeth like that.

I'm frozen with terror as he leans in close, his tongue flicking out. He licks the blood from my fingers. His whole body shudders with pleasure, and a low hiss escapes him.

He buries his head into my shoulder, those vicious teeth poised an inch from the bare skin of my neck.

"Winnie," he whispers, his voice strained. "*Run.*"

"I—"

With a cry like the howl of the wind through the valley, Alaric tears himself from me.

"Run!"

He hurls himself across the room, upsetting bags of clay and brushes as he thrashes and claws at his own skin.

I run.

I run down the hall, wild with fear. I turn down a hallway and am immediately lost. I fling myself around corners, desperate to escape the monster behind me. I throw myself at a random door, which buckles under my weight but then swings back, resisting my desire to crash through it. A heavy chain clangs against my arm.

The dining room.

Not knowing what I'm doing but perceiving if I don't put some kind of wall between us, that monster is going to devour me, I yank the chain. It falls into my hands. The padlock was so old that it had rusted through, and I'd managed to break it free. The doors spring open.

It takes a moment for my eyes to adjust to the dim light. I slam the door, shove the wooden board through the metal bars to lock it, and thrust the candelabra in front of me. Fear rises inside me as I take in the room.

A banquet table large enough for twenty groans beneath the weight of *stuff*. I choke back the trauma of towering objects and surge forward, gabbing the nearest thing – a statue of a warrior on a horse.

It's heavy, so I lift it in my free hand, thinking it might be better than the candelabra as a weapon.

But I freeze as I notice the warrior's face.

It's Alaric.

I'd recognise those sharp cheekbones, that strong jaw, the imperious features, and that long, wavy hair swept back in the wind anywhere.

Did Alaric make a statue of *himself*? But it's covered in tarnish and looks like a medieval bronze—

Behind me, the door bangs. Alaric yells again, "Winnie, you have to leave. I don't know how much longer I can—"

His words dissolve into inhuman cries. I hear his mother's voice, soothing him.

I can't help myself. My heart hammers in my chest. I should be running for the door, but I'm drawn deeper into the room. I hold up the candelabra to several paintings stacked against the sideboard. I flip through them. Each one is a portrait from a different era, in a different style.

They're all of Alaric.

Alaric in various suits of armour, or wearing majestic cloaks, or riding horses, or looking brooding in a dark forest. Alaric with swords of every shape and size. Alaric as St Sebastian, tied naked to a stake, his body pierced with arrows. Alaric peering from the tower window while a mob approaches carrying flaming torches, his face twisted in pain. Woodcuts of Alaric as a demon dancing upon piles of skulls or drinking the blood of tortured men from a goblet.

There's even one of Alaric and Mirabelle – the wild god and his familiar.

These are the portraits removed from the walls in the castle. All those gaps in the walls were because Alaric didn't want me to see these.

They hid it all in here so I wouldn't figure it out, so I wouldn't know that Alaric has lived at Black Crag for *centuries*.

So much blood. So much death.

I spin on my heels, and the light captures a tapestry hanging from the wall. It's another scene of a battle in the valley with the castle in the background, only this time, Alaric sits astride his horse in the centre, his sword raised over his head, his face twisted in fury and two long, sharp fangs poking from his mouth, dripping with blood.

A suit of armour stands in front of the tapestry. I touch the bicep, remembering the gap in the row of armour in the Stabby Chic room. Even as my mind screams at me to run, I draw my fingers over the embossed steel. My breath fails me.

It's Alaric's armour. I recognise the curve of his bicep, his trim waist, the sinewy muscles of his legs. The suit is dented all over, and the metal crumpled beneath the armpit, where the arm meets the shoulder. Rust stains radiate across the suit from his sword hand. The blood of his enemies that he never washed away.

He killed people in this.

My vision swims. I stagger for the door, but I'm losing my grip on the candelabra and my sense. I have to get out of here.

Above me, Alaric roars, his cries shaking the castle stones.

It's true. It's all true.

My boss. My client. The guy I've been falling for all these weeks … is a *vampire.*

32

Alaric

FUCK.

The Nevermore Murder Club and Smutty Book Coven Group Chat

Beth: I might be ten minutes late for tonight's meeting. I'm in the middle of mixing up some of my soon-to-be patented anti-aging elixirs and then I need to ice the mung bean brownies.

Komal: NO.

Beth: Which part is no?

Komal: All things involving mung beans.

Isis: Beth, honey, we love you, but we beg of you, do not ice the mung bean brownies.

33

Winnie

"REGINALD!" I SCREAM AS I RACE THROUGH THE HALLS, MY chest heaving. Behind me, Alaric bellows like a wounded bear. His mother makes a sound of disapproval. A door slams so hard that the *CRACK* reverberates through the vast hallways.

Reginald appears from one of the labyrinthine hallways that bisect the main corridor. "Ms Preston, you needed something? I've just brought the car around. What are you—" He must read my fear in my face because he grabs my arm. "You've cut yourself. Come quickly. We must get you away from them."

I let Reginald drag me down the steps to the waiting car. As we tear away from the castle, I hear another almighty *CRACK* overhead, and Alaric screams.

I glance anxiously over my shoulder at the retreating driveway. "What the hell is wrong with him?!"

We reach the little gatehouse. Reginald pulls the car to a stop and ushers me inside. I collapse into a chair. Reginald has the decency to look sheepish as he takes my hand. "Nothing is wrong with Lord Valerian. He is who he is. Our kind have different means of dealing with the bloodlust—"

OUR kind?!

I shudder. "He pinned me against the wall. He told me to run. He had *fangs*. And all those portraits of him … Reginald, what *is* Alaric?"

Reginald busies himself with a first aid kit. He dabs the cut with disinfectant and places a plaster over the wound. Only then does he look at me, his eyes sad.

"He is a vampire, Ms Preston."

I sink down in the chair. "I was afraid you'd say that."

"It may not seem like it, but my lord only wishes to keep you safe. Lord Valerian's way since he left his birthplace has been to shutter himself away from the world. Which means that he hasn't trained himself to resist the call of fresh blood."

"You said 'our kind'." I whip my hand from Reginald's cool grip. "You're one of them! A—a—*vampire*."

Reginald raises his hands in surrender, as if I would have any chance against him. "I assure you that you have nothing to fear from me, Ms Preston. I am like you, but also not entirely like you. I do not drink human blood to survive. But nor am I entirely human, like you. I am what's known as a Thrall, a human kept by a vampire to run their household, watch over their slumber, and perform such duties during the daylight hours as will keep them alive. In return for my services, Lord Valerian allows me to sup of his blood."

I screw up my face. "You … drink Alaric's blood?"

"Oh, yes. It is his gift to me. Drinking gives me youth and vigour. How old do you think I am?"

I study the lines at the corner of Reginald's eyes, the scattering of grey hairs along his forehead. "Late forties?"

"I'm nearly ninety years old."

"That's impossible …"

"I assure you it's not. I look after Lord Valerian – with the modern world moving at impossible speed, he needs someone to guide him and make certain he doesn't reveal himself through his more anachronistic habits. I'm the one who has the electricity installed, makes sure he pays the council tax, arranges for a beautiful professional organiser to help him with his mess …"

"Install the internet?" I ask, as my heartbeat begins to return to a normal rhythm.

"Exactly. All these jobs I do happily, for they are trifles compared to what he offers in return. His blood …" Reginald closes his eyes for a moment, his body humming with the memory of his last feed. "You have never tasted anything so exquisite."

"Gross. No, thanks."

"I've seen the way he looks at you. I've watched him torture himself ever since you arrived at Black Crag, torn between his yearning for you and his desire to keep you safe. I told him to show you his truth, to give you a chance to understand him." Reginald tilts his head to the side. "Humans and vampires are forbidden from becoming … entangled. But more than that, Lord Valerian believes he is a monster beyond redemption, and that no one can know what he is and love him. He has not been treated kindly when people have found out what he is. Secrecy is survival to him and his kin."

I think of some of those paintings hidden in the dining room. "He was tortured, wasn't he?"

"Humans don't wish to live in the shadow of a vampire," Reginald says softly. "They prefer to burn and stake and curse rather than try to understand, to co-exist. That is why they cannot know that they've been co-existing alongside the vampire courts for all of human history. And things were not always as they are now. Lord Valerian only employed me fifty-two years ago. Before then, he did his own hunting, and things could go wrong. A vampire hunting has always been at risk of being exposed. Now, at least, he doesn't have to worry about this."

He's talking about the wine bottles in the cellar. Another piece slots into place. "You keep blood for him so he doesn't have to drink from people."

"Fresh blood is always best for vampires, but Alaric abhors the hunt. He calls it 'a violation'. Most of his kind don't agree. There were times when vampires killed indiscriminately during the hunt – draining their victims dry, or 'husking'. But this resulted in humans coming after them and staking them while they slept. New vampire laws allowed for a mutually beneficial feeding relationship, where human Thralls do their bidding and keep them safe and fed in exchange for the long life and vitality of their blood. The bite of a vampire is an ecstasy unrivalled, so I've been told." Reginald frowns. "I won't get to experience it myself. I'm unique among Thralls because my lord will not drink from me, not even these past weeks when he's been weak and suffering in your presence. He doesn't trust himself."

I swallow.

"Most vampires wouldn't react the way he did to human blood. But Alaric has always struggled with control. He's locked himself away because he doesn't want to hurt anyone, but hurt can still find him. You caught him unawares, in more ways than one. By the time I bandage you up and take you back to the castle, he will be in control of himself again."

I'm too terrified to consider such a thing. "I'm not going back to the castle."

Reginald sighs. "I understand. What do you wish to do?"

What do I wish to do?

I have no choice. I have to leave. I can't keep going with the job now that I know what Alaric is. I can't stay at Black Crag with a vampire. I have to go back to London. But maybe first …

"Take me to the village," I say. "I'm going to a meeting of the Nevermore Coven."

34

Winnie

Faye: Winnie, I'm so happy you messaged me your new number. You won't believe what's happened! You know that lunch I had with Jennifer the ITV producer? She wants to make a Clutter Queens TV show! The Winnie Wins System will more popular than KonMari! I've got a contract for squillions of dollars, but she needs to meet you ASAP – how soon can you finish up the dusty castle and get back to London?

"Winnie?" Isis throws open the door to Nevermore Bookshop. "You're early. Mina and Dora and I were just having a cup of tea—"

"You were right," I burst out. "Alaric's a vampire."

Instead of doing what I expect her to do, which is to dance around the room yelling "I told you so", Isis gathers me under her arm and ushers me inside. She calls into the gloom, "Mina, Winnie's here. We need emergency tea, stat!"

"I'm on it."

Isis drags me through to the events room and settles me into my "usual" beanbag. Mina makes me a cup of tea using her liquid level indicator. Dora takes my teacup and an open package of Wagon Wheels and arranges both on the coffee table beside me.

"It's not as good as that amazing hot chocolate you brought last week, but it'll calm your nerves," Dora says. "And please eat the last of the Wagon Wheels. We have to hide them before Celeste comes over and berates us for not waiting for her snacks."

"It's not that Celeste doesn't make the most incredible baked goods," Mina pipes up, holding out her arm towards the door so the raven can hop off and perch on the bust of some Roman dude that's sat on a shelf above it. "But sometimes, a girl just wants cheap chocolate and chemically-flavoured marshmallow."

I sip the tea. It's herbal, some kind of rich, earthy flavour that I can't place. I find myself sighing as I take another sip. *You can relax now. You're amongst friends.*

"Dora makes that blend herself," says Isis. "She's a real tea witch. You can buy it in our shop."

"I'm not a witch. Don't say that I'm a witch," Dora sounds panicked. "I just … know a bit about plants, is all. What's wrong, Winnie? You've gone all pale."

I grip the cup so hard my knuckles turn white. "What's wrong is that Alaric's a vampire."

I expect them all to laugh, or gasp, or something other than what they do, which is to nod sagely.

"Oh, honey, we know," Isis coos. "He's a walking vampire cliché."

"No, I mean he's a *real* vampire. I cut my finger today and Alaric nearly attacked me. He had these horrible fangs, and he told me to run. And the more I think about it, the more it makes sense. Alaric doesn't feel the cold. He's always cool to the touch—"

"—you've been touching him." Mina grins. "Interesting."

I decide to breeze on past the whole *touching him* thing. "He keeps his nocturnal schedule. He went out in the sunlight once to save me and it almost killed him. He seems to move with super speed and he can hear things all the way across the castle. I've never seen him eat.

I wandered into what I thought was his bedroom but it contained a coffin and … oh, gods," I cover my mouth. "The red wine Reginald pours for him every night must have been blood. I've been sitting across from him thinking we were having wine and nice conversation and all this time he's been quaffing pints of O negative and thinking about sucking my neck."

"Almost certainly." Isis licks her lips.

"Isis!"

"What? That's a sensible deduction to make."

"You're scaring her," Dora scolds.

"I'd like to go back to the 'touching him'," Mina adds. "Where *exactly* did you touch him, and how many times—"

"Mina!" Dora yells.

"Why aren't you guys more freaked out by this?" My heart hammers against my chest. "I tell you that I've been living with a literal horror movie character and you're cracking jokes."

"We already knew," Mina says.

"What?"

The three of them nod again.

"You *knew*? You should have told me."

"We did tell you!" Isis cries.

"Against our strict book club rules," Dora mumbles.

"You didn't believe us," Isis says with a hint of a smile. "That's hardly *our* fault. It would save you lots of stress and heartache if you just agreed with everything we say."

"But, how did you know?"

"We *told* you. We've had encounters with the supernatural before. If you finish my book series, you'll learn that Nevermore Bookshop is no ordinary brick-and-mortar building, and that I've done battle with a vampire," Mina says.

"Although he was a different type of vampire," Isis points out quickly. "Less hot, more bitey."

"Exactly." Mina pours some freeze-dried berries and nuts into a bowl and places it beside the raven's bust. The bird pecks greedily at his treats, making cute *nyuh-nyuh-nyuh* noises as he crunches the nuts. "That was a famous fictional vampire made entirely of clichés and evil who will never bother us again, whereas Alaric is a *real* vampire, one of many who live alongside us and are just trying to do their best in a world not built for them. Usually, the supernatural world won't bother us if we don't bother them, although in recent years, we've seen more unruly paranormal activity in Argleton. Not just vampires, but other things that storybooks tell us we should be afraid of. I have a friend over in Grimdale, Bree, who sees and talks to ghosts. And now we've got Danny's murder—"

"I think Winnie needs proof." Dora pats my arm.

"I suppose she does." Mina turns towards the raven, who taps the bust with his beak and glares at Mina.

"Croak."

"I'm sorry, Quoth. Just this once." Mina places the latest Emily Henry novel on the sofa beside her.

The raven makes a sound that might be a sigh and swoops down to land next to the book.

"Croak!"

And then he changes.

At first, the bird starts growing at an alarming rate, his talons digging into the sofa as it sags beneath his growing weight. His body contorts. His face twists and flattens, his cheeks rounding as his beak splits into a nose and lips. Bones snap and twist and organs rearrange themselves as black feathers rain down on the floor. The raven bellows as his wings fold away into his spine and his feathers retract into his skin.

The raven no longer perches on the sofa.

Instead, a beautiful, black-haired, *completely naked* man grabs the book from beside him and holds it over his crotch, where it does little to hide his majestic and very un-raven-like goods.

"It's times like this I wish Emily Henry wrote epic fantasy." The naked man flips a curtain of black hair over his shoulder and frowns at the inadequate book.

"Winnie, this is Quoth, one of my three husbands." Mina rubs the man's shoulder. "Quoth is the raven from Edgar Allen Poe's poem, brought to life by Nevermore Bookshop, which is a wee bit magical."

"Pleasure to meet you," Quoth murmurs. "I'd shake your hand, but …"

He indicates the book.

"Ah …" I try to say something, *anything*, but I can't find words.

Mina's husband is a shapeshifter. I've just witnessed real, honest-to-goddess *magic*.

Everything they've told me is true. Which means …

I wrap my arms around myself. "If this is all true, and Alaric is a vampire, then he must be the one who murdered Danny. Even the police think so. I've been living with a monster this whole time!"

"Who murdered Danny?" Komal asks as she wanders in, stopping to kiss everyone on the cheeks. She's wearing her Argleton HeliTours t-shirt. "I thought we were investigating the Sanctus Estate and this Baylor person?"

"Winnie just found out that Alaric's a vampire."

Komal pops the cork on the bottle of wine she brought. "About time. We did tell you. Wine?"

I hold up my teacup. "I'm good."

"You don't look good. You look white. I mean, you're always white, but now you're even whiter. You look like an ad for Moleskine notebooks."

"Are Moleskine notebooks a white people thing?" Mina asks.

Komal flips her hair. "If you have to ask, white girl …"

Isis quietly slides her own notebook under her bag.

"We don't believe Alaric is the murderer," Dora says. "Otherwise we never would have let you go back to the castle."

"Why not? He was angry at Danny because he was harassing me. And when Danny didn't leave me alone, Alaric pretended to be my boyfriend by … er … kissing me." My cheeks flush with heat as Komal wolf-whistles. "Reginald says that Alaric isn't used to being around humans, and that he's been struggling ever since I showed up. What if he lost control that night?"

"It's certainly plausible," Mina says. "But we've already ruled out Alaric."

"How?"

"You know that we were all at the pub that night," Komal says. "Isis went to the bar to buy a round and Danny tried it on with her. He grabbed her arm."

"Big mistake, because I'm psychic," Isis says proudly. "All I have to do is touch someone and I'll see a vision of their future. Danny grabbed my arm and I was inside his head, lying on my back in the alley, with the killer looming over me. They were in shadow, so I couldn't see them, but as they sank their fangs into my neck, I distinctly saw your vamp and his Thrall driving off in that ridiculous car."

I sink down into the beanbag, a weight lifted from me. *Alaric's not the killer.*

But I still have so many questions, so many fears. "If you saw his death, why didn't you stop it?"

Dora and Isis exchange a look.

"Because psychic visions don't come with a German train timetable," Dora says quietly. "Isis can't tell when the vision will come to pass. For all we knew, Danny could have been murdered ten years from now."

"Besides, no one is crying over his death, are they?" Isis adds.

"You didn't leave Black Crag after the police showed up to question Alaric. Look into your heart and I think you know the answer," Mina says. "The vampire I fought was an evil vampire, the most evil vampire of them all. But he was evil because people believed vampires were evil. Alaric isn't evil, is he?"

I pause. "No." I think of Alaric diving into the cistern to rescue me, buying me dinner at the pub, and pretending to be my fiancé to get back at Patrick and Claire. "But I don't know about his mother. Or his *betrothed*."

"Backtrack a little." Mina leans forward in her seat. "His *betrothed*?"

Celeste and Maisie arrive then. Celeste's arms are loaded with platters and ice cream containers filled with delicious-smelling treats. "We had a slow day in the shop, and I'm doing lots of baking in advance of going to visit Mum, so I have cheese scones, lemon meringue tarts, chocolate fondants and cherry flan. There's nothing with peanut butter, Winnie. Better eat up before Beth arrives— Oh, hi Quoth."

"Hello." Quoth waves with one hand, his other gripping the Emily Henry so hard that his knuckles have gone white.

"So, I take it Winnie knows, then?" Maisie grins at me.

"I know."

"Can I leave now?" Quoth asks. "Or at least go and put some trousers on?"

"Oh, sorry! I got distracted by the vampires and murders." Mina kisses his cheek. "Of course, you can go. I think Winnie accepts the supernatural now."

"I'm pleased. Goodnight, Winnie. I hope that next time I see you, I'll be wearing clothes." Quoth flashes me a bright, beautiful smile, then turns back into a bird and returns to his bust.

Mina picks Emily Henry off the floor and Celeste piles treats on a plate for me while I explain everything that's been happening at the castle, from Alaric pretending to be my fiancé and our steamy kisses at the pub, to his mother arriving with Perdita, and how he's roped me into being *his* fake-fiancée, to the text message I got from Faye about the incredible opportunity of making a Clutter Queens TV show, and then, finally, discovering he's a vampire and fleeing from the castle.

"So … what do you think?" I ask when I'm finished. "Do I go home to London and take the biggest opportunity of my career, or do I stay here and—"

"—fake-date the vampire."

I whip my head around. Arabella stands in the doorway, elegant hand on her hip, her frosty blue eyes studying me in an unnerving way that makes me feel as naked as Quoth had been earlier. She overheard the whole conversation.

"You should stay," Arabella says. "You *want* to stay."

"But he's a *vampire*! Why do you all seem so relaxed about this?"

"Because vampires are hot?" Komal raises an eyebrow.

"Arabella's right." Isis tosses a book over her shoulder. "Alaric hasn't hurt you in all these weeks – quite the opposite! Forget this week's book club read. You should stay and fake-date the vampire lord, and his mother can take that harpy Perdita back to whatever vampire court she came from. You're literally living in a paranormal romance novel."

"Do you *want* to go back to London?" Dora asks, cutting straight to the heart of things the way she always does.

That's a good question. I suppose when you find out that your employer is a vampire, you should make like an angry goose and get the flock out of town.

"It's what I *should* do," I say. "My mum needs my help, and this TV show is a huge deal. I may not be happy with where Faye's taking the business, but I believe the Winnie Wins System can help people. This would be my chance to show the world, but I can't do that without Faye."

"That's not true," Maisie says. "From everything you've told us, you've been running the business on your own for years."

"Maybe so, but we trademarked the Winnie Wins System. It belongs to the business. I can't use it on my own. And there's the matter of my mum. I'm worried about her blowing up her relationship with her neighbours. If the council comes around again …"

If things are that bad, is she safe in the house?

"So it sounds like you should go back to London." Komal leans forward. "But …?"

But when I think about leaving Black Crag and returning to London and the business I'm rapidly coming to resent and my mother's spat with her neighbours and the council, a sick feeling twists in my stomach.

"You guys are the supernatural experts. Am I safe at Black Crag Castle?" I ask as Arabella folds herself into a beanbag, crossing her long legs at her ankles and kicking off a pair of vicious Louboutin heels. "Alaric frightens me."

Even as I say the words, I know they're not true. I *know* Alaric would never hurt me. I believe that in my bones. I'm not afraid of his fangs and his hunger.

I afraid that if I stay, I'll fall even deeper …

"For pity's sake," Arabella sighs. "He's a vampire, not a *Strictly Come Dancing* judge. He's probably more afraid of you and your ability to get his head chopped off for breaking vampire law."

"Ignore Arabella. The rest of us do." Dora tops up my teacup. "You should ask yourself if what happened today undoes everything that's happened between you before."

"I wonder …" Komal taps her perfectly-manicured nails on the arm of her chair. "We've been noticing Alaric in the village a lot more over the last few weeks. I think he's been training himself for when you arrived, Winnie. That's probably why every time he goes to the pub he looks like he'd rather be at the dentist having his fangs extracted."

"Once, the waitress got the orders mixed up and set down a Sunday roast in front of him. I've never seen someone look so *affronted* at a Yorkshire pud," says Celeste as she takes a bite of cheese scone.

My heart twists. That was just like Alaric – to do something he hates because he thought it would help someone else.

"Reginald has lived at the castle for years, and Alaric hasn't hurt him. From what you say, Alaric hasn't even fed from him," Mina says. "That's unusual for a vampire, and it must require an insane amount of self-control. You caught Alaric by surprise with your blood today. As long as you keep your blood inside your body from now on, you should be fine."

"Unless you *want* him to bite you," Isis pipes up, with a wicked sparkle in her eyes.

"I don't want to be a vampire."

"For pity's sake, none of you have explained to her how it works?" Arabella snaps.

The book club members hang their heads in mock shame.

"For Alaric to turn you into a vampire, you and he have to exchange blood in a ceremony known as the Kiss," Arabella says in a bored voice.

"It's a lengthy and somewhat dangerous process to make a new vampire, and my understanding is that he's not allowed to do that without a licence from the Conclave – that's a ruling council of vampires from the different courts. The Conclave need to have control over who becomes a new vampire, because they can't risk oversaturating the feeding pool."

"AKA, too many fangs, not enough necks," Isis pipes up.

"When a vampire bites you, all that happens is that he gets sustenance and you both experience a rush of ecstasy. Some people have described it as 'the most exquisite rapture on Earth'." Arabella shrugs. "I wouldn't know. But you might enjoy it. It's the reason humans become Thralls."

Oh.

My cheeks flare with heat. "Well, okay, then … thanks for letting me know."

"You aren't getting much out of this fake-dating relationship if he's not even sucking on your neck." She raises one of those impossibly-perfect eyebrows. "I wonder if you'll have to explain to Alaric about contraception."

Now my whole face is burning. I remember that strange thing Alaric said to his mother. "How did you—"

"You should have your fake-fiancé explain to you about Dhampir. All I know is that it's illegal for a vampire and human to bump uglies."

"Why have you never told us this before?" Maisie leans forward.

"Because none of you have been foolish enough to fall for a vampire." Arabella glares at me. "Until now."

I sink down into my beanbag.

Beth wanders in then, a platter of green-coloured brownies covered in what look suspiciously like globs of snot tucked under her arm. "Blessed evening, sisters! I brought mung bean brownies— Oh, Winnie knows, doesn't she? Arabella's making her 'you must endure my lecture on the ways of vampires or I will do something unspeakable to you' face."

"I have no such face." Arabella glares at Beth. "Take that back, or I'll stop referring my clients to you."

"Fine, fine. I take it back. Arabella has no special 'I'm a vampire expert' face, nor any penchant for revenge. Welcome to the world of the supernatural, Winnie." Beth holds out her tray, and a waft of burnt-bean scent assaults my nostrils. "Brownie?"

"No thanks, I'm full."

"Full of Celeste's scones, are you?" Beth glares around the room as she shoves Celeste's empty platters aside to place her brownies front and centre. "The rest of you better finish these. I've been slaving over the stove for hours to get them just right and I think the cultured sea vegetable drizzle gives them a delightful zing—"

"Croooooak!" Quoth dive-bombs the table, sending brownies flying across the floor.

"Quoth!" Beth glares at him, hands on hips.

"Sorry, Beth." Mina covers her mouth, her shoulders shaking with silent laughter as Quoth hops across the table, trying to shake cultured sea vegetable drizzle off the tip of his wing.

Beth pouts as she flops into the beanbag next to Arabella. "I propose we take a vote on whether male birds should be allowed at our *girls only* book club meetings."

"Croak!"

"We'll add it to the agenda." Isis raps her knuckles against the now-empty table as she shoves the final bite of scone into her mouth. "I've already called the meeting to order. Our first item of the evening has been to encourage Winnie to stay in Argleton and bang her hot vampire boss."

"Hear hear!" everyone yells.

"Our second item of business is a very important request from Komal."

Komal stands up and taps the badge on her t-shirt that declares "Proud Member of the Argleton Tourism Board". "As you all know, I'm the organiser of this year's Midsummer Festival, which is taking place on Saturday on the village green."

"Explain for the Londoner," I say, happy for the conversation to veer away from me.

"Midsummer is the name given to the ancient European tradition of celebrating the summer solstice – the longest day of the year," explains Isis. "It's a time to embrace the warmth and abundance of summer. It's one of my favourite witchy celebrations because it's the perfect time for rituals of rebirth, healing, and fertility."

She elbows me. My cheek flush with heat, and everyone giggles.

"Midsummer Festival is so fun," Maisie says. "I cover it every year for the paper. Everyone in the village gathers on the green. There's an outdoor concert, a fete, games, and of course, the bonfire."

"Every year I make a special Midsummer Festival cake," Celeste adds. "This year, I'm experimenting with summer berries …"

"The plans are in place, and I truly believe it will be the best festival ever. But we don't have nearly enough stalls and Counsellor Durant is breathing down my neck, looking for any excuse to get rid of the festival. He actually said that people didn't want to participate in a *pagan aberration*." Komal makes a face. "I've got Celeste's cake stall, and Beth's running her natural skincare booth, and we've got Richard from the pub with his cider, but three of our regular stalls pulled out. The Argleton Naughty Knitting Society can't run their booth this year because two of their members need hip operations, and Helen Wilde is too afraid of the murderer on the loose to run her new sex toy business."

"Thank the gods," Mina whispers under her breath. I gather from their surnames that Helen must be related to her.

"Cynthia Lachlan's Jammery and that overpriced local knickknack store also declined because of the murderer." Komal folds her arms and glares around the room. "So I need the rest of you to either find the vamp responsible or help me come up with at least three new booths for this year's festival."

"Heathcliff made me promise not to do a bookstore this year," Mina says. "After last year's disaster."

"Well, you'll have to tell him to suck it up and try again. This is for *charity*."

"Maybe Winnie and Alaric will have a stall," Isis clasps her hands over her heart. "A kissing booth—"

"We're *not* pressuring Winnie." Dora elbows her sister. "If she wants to stay, we'll welcome her as an official member of the book club and help her figure out how to navigate a relationship with a vampire. But if she leaves, we'll all watch her on TV and talk about this cool Clutter Queen who we used to hang out with before she became a big-time star."

"Fine." Isis pouts, but then her face lights up. "I know – Dora and I will do our fortune-telling booth again!"

"Can't we just enjoy the festival this year?" Dora mumbles.

"Everyone loves our fortunes." Isis beams. "Besides, I'm the one who does all the work. I must channel all my energies into reading the cards, while Dora sits on her arse with the cash box and sells her herbal teas."

"If you think I contribute nothing to the affair, then you should run the booth yourself this year—"

As the girls argue about possible Midsummer Festival booths, I stare at the phone in my hands. There's a text from Reginald.

> **Reginald:** I've packed your things into the trunk. After your meeting is finished, I'll drive you home to London.

Home to London.

Far away from Alaric and his mother and Perdita, the woman she wants him to marry. Far from pottery lessons and midnight chats by the fire and listening to Alaric passionately describing the drying times of different modelling paints.

Home to the biggest opportunity of my career – a chance to get the Winnie Wins System on TV and maybe help thousands of people get their clutter under control. A chance to finally escape the obnoxious posh clients I loathe and do something that helps people.

Home to my mother, who may drive me crazy but who I love. At least she *needs* me.

Home, where I can start over again with a new flat, a blank slate.

Home, where absolutely nothing supernatural ever happens and none of my mediocre Tinder dates ever end in fangs sinking into my neck …

I should be happy to escape from Alaric and his fangs.

So why don't I feel happy?

35

Alaric

Gideon: So, did my birds-and-bloods talk help you do the horizontal greasy weasel tango with the lovely Winifred? Word at the Sanctus Club is that the Lady of Agony has arrived early. She's already summoned me to the castle to oversee my plans for the ball. Let me know if you need moral support or a new sword ...

I FILL MY GOBLET TO THE TOP ONCE MORE AND TIP MY HEAD BACK, allowing the blood to flow down my throat. I'm drinking my way through the fine vintages Reginald has procured for me to enjoy over months and years, but I don't care if I drink the castle dry.

Winnie's gone.

She's not coming back.

I've allowed the best thing that's ever happened to me slip away, all because I couldn't control myself.

All because she smells like sunshine and strawberries.

I hear my mother's tinkling laugh through the thick castle walls. She's commandeered my newly clean office for her meetings, and she's in there right now with Gideon, putting the final touches on the plan for her ball. When Reginald returns from escorting Winnie to London, he'll have to find another organiser to finish the drawing rooms in time for the ball.

The ball where mother will announce my engagement to Princess Perdita of the Blood Chastain.

I dart my tongue into the goblet, sucking out the last of the blood. This bottle came from an eighteenth century duke – a fine vintage, difficult to come by, aged so perfectly that it almost tastes fresh.

But tonight it turns to dust in my mouth.

It's for the best that she's gone.

Why had I allowed myself this delusion that she and I could have a future together? That we would live here in peace at Black Crag and sit by the fireplace every night reading books and arguing about her appalling taste in music?

She is not for me.

Even if Winnie could have loved a monster, Callista Valerian would never have allowed our union. I was a fool to believe that my mother would permit me to remain here, undisturbed, when she could use me for her own ends. All this time, I've been the chess piece she kept in reserve for her final assault across the board.

My eyes flutter closed as the glut of blood works its way through my body. Beneath it, the hunger for Winnie *burns*. She is a painting itching on the ends of my fingers, a sculpture bursting forth from a block of clay, a tapestry woven in purest gold.

And she will never look at me with love in her heart.

"You should know better than to close your eyes, son."

Callista's voice – so close she's practically on top of me – startles me, although I don't allow her to see this. She snuck into the room without me hearing her. There is a reason she is feared among vampires as the Lady of Agony.

For who fears death more than those who can live forever?

I open one eye, and am greeted by the tip of a sword an inch from my eyeball.

"You are out of practice," my mother smirks, dragging the sword across my cheek as she glides around my chair, shaving the hairs without penetrating the skin. The cold blade against me is a warning, a promise. "You have been such a disappointment to me. When I plucked you from death on that battlefield, you were full of hate and malice. Now look at you, sitting in this castle painting your little landscapes and losing your mind over a *human*, when you should be leading my army to put down this absurd rebellion. Look at this."

She picks up one of the few full bottles remaining at my feet, pulls out the cork with her teeth and sniffs. Her mouth wrinkles with distaste.

"This is foul. Death would be preferable to drinking this swill. No wonder you are weak."

Her cruelty stings, but it's far from the worst I've endured from her. I don't blink as she drags the edge of the sword over my jaw. "Vlad the Impaler didn't start impaling people until his thirties. I still have time to become the son you always wanted."

"Your time is now, son. I saw your little plaything fleeing the castle with your Thrall." She leans in close, her voice hissing against my skin. A smear of blood from her feeding earlier mars the corner of her mouth. "I take it that she found out what you are. Will you chase her down and kill her, or shall I?"

She yelps as I wrap my hand around her throat. She tries to cut me but she's too close and I'm too fast.

The warrior inside me stirs to life. The battle for Winnie's heart has been lost, but the war is not yet over.

I lift her easily, bending her wrist and flinging the sword away. She gurgles, clawing at my hand with her long, red-painted talons. Her eyes are wide in surprise. Not fear, never fear.

She *should* fear me.

I am, after all, her son.

Her *blood*.

I throw Callista across the room. She sails in a graceful arc, nearly scraping along the ceiling, before her back hits the wall with a loud *SMACK*. She crumples into a heap on the floor, momentarily stunned.

"You'll *not* hurt Winnie," I growl.

She's up and in front of me in a single human heartbeat, nose to nose, her lips curling back into a sinister smile. "There's your warrior's fire, son."

"Stay away from her."

"Your pet knows of us," she whispers. "She cannot be allowed—"

"She will not tell a soul." (Except her book club, but my mother doesn't need to know that. If Mina Wilde and Arabella Lestrange are members, then they already know.)

"Laws are laws."

She knows about contraception. She knows that if we used it, there would be no danger of a Dhampir. But she doesn't care because I'm not submitting to her will.

"Laws can be changed. I have never asked anything of you since I left the Nightshade Court. I have stayed out of your way as you blazed a path of destruction across Europe. But now you are in *my* house, and Winnie is under my protection. Hurt her and I will make certain you regret it."

My fingers close around her neck again, squeezing this time, enough so she can feel the power I wield. I may have an artist's spirit, but I have never given up on my warrior training. I know too well that one's greatest enemies will come when you believe you are safe behind your walls.

"You wouldn't *dare*," she glares back at me, her words rasping as I close off her throat. "The gravest sin a vampire could possibly commit is to kill their sire. Not even you, in your disgrace, would wish that torture upon yourself. If it weren't for me, you would have bled out, alone and forgotten, buried in the mud of that battlefield, just another nameless corpse for the archaeologists to jizz themselves over."

"You don't know me at all." My fingers tighten. The sword is within reach. I could do it. I could end her, end *this*, right now. But then

I would only be proving myself the monster. "Do not presume what I will or won't do to keep Winnie safe."

I release her, whipping out to grab the sword before she can take it again. I stab the tip into the floor, burying it several inches into the wood. The hilt quivers as I sink back into my chair.

Callista rubs her neck, and I hate the slow smile that creeps over her lips. "As you like it, son. It matters not if one human girl is screaming about vampires – they will think those smutty books she reads have addled her brain. She is gone from your life now, and as long as there is no Dhampir growing in her womb, all our plans can continue without drama."

"Host your revels if you must, but leave me out of your machinations," I growl.

"My ball needs a spectacle – a public show of the bond between the Nightshade and Midnight Courts. You *will* marry Perdita before our guests, or I shall be forced to make that spectacle the trial and execution of my son for the crime of consorting with a human." She glides towards the door. "Your choice, son."

She leaves me in a cloud of my own rage.

I don't care what happens to me. The old Alaric would welcome death, even the brutal execution dealt by the Mora for my crime. But Winnie is in danger. If Callista is willing to have me killed to make her point, then she won't hesitate to kill Winnie.

I will not allow it. I will protect Winnie, even though she doesn't want—

"Alaric."

36

Alaric

I RUB MY EYES, CERTAIN THAT I'M DREAMING HER VOICE. BUT vampires do not dream.

The blood has addled me. One of the bottles must have been corrupted, filled with hallucinogenic fungi.

It sounds so like her—

"Alaric, look at me."

I've even managed to conjure her adorable exasperation. Why must I torture myself . . .

"Alaric, damnit, if you don't turn around, I'm going to start throwing Isis's anti-vampire charms at you."

I drag my gaze to the door, and there she is. Not a hallucination, but Winnie Preston in the flesh, her arms folded across her chest and her weight on her back foot, as though preparing to run at the slightest provocation.

She's afraid.

But she's *here.*

"Your friend is a lousy witch. Those charms do nothing except fill your pockets with weeds," I murmur, rising from my chair.

"Some weeds are beautiful."

"Others are deadly."

"Deadly things can be beautiful. I brought this back." Winnie holds up the candelabra she had in her hands when she fled.

"Reginald will be pleased. Women in flowing gothic dresses are always fleeing dramatically from the castle holding them, and we're running low."

"Meerow!" Mirabelle gallops across the room and wraps herself around Winnie's legs, purring with ecstasy. Winnie kneels down to scratch her ears, her wary eyes never leaving mine.

"Hello, kitty. Did you miss me? I wasn't gone for very long."

"You're a miracle," I murmur. "A figment of my blood-drunk mind."

"I'm not a figment. I just got back from book club. Reginald is making me an iced chocolate, because it was hot outside this draughty castle, and I thought maybe we could talk."

Winnie picks up Mirabelle and takes a small step towards me. She chews on her lower lip.

"Don't come any closer," I warn, wiping my lips with the back of my hand. I'm aware of how I must look to her – the pupils of my eyes blown out, the blush in my pale skin from feeding, empty bottles scattered about my feet and my sword blade wobbling from where I buried the tip into the wooden floor.

Winnie takes another step, gripping Mirabelle tight against her chest.

"Reginald explained to me what you are," she says. "That you've been controlling your hunger around me all this time. And the book club ladies filled in some other details for me. I know you won't hurt me."

"I *did* hurt you."

The words crack against my lips. Blood swirls in my stomach. No matter how much I've gorged myself, the scent of her as she steps gingerly towards me sends me into a frenzy.

"I was afraid because I didn't understand," she says. "But now I see that you've been protecting me all along. I trust you, Alaric. I'm going to stay at Black Crag."

"You wish to stay?"

It's too wonderful to comprehend. Winnie wants to stay with *me.*

"The ball is coming up, and we still haven't finished the drawing rooms. You need them for … for feeding?" Her mouth twists. "Am I right?"

"Winnie, you can't—"

"I came here to do a job, and professional pride won't allow me to leave until it's done. We haven't even got to the 'Neutralise' and 'Sustain' parts of the Winnie Wins System yet." She raises her chin in defiance. "I dare you to find another professional organiser willing to take on this big a job at the last minute when their neck is literally on the line."

This woman. This beautiful, strange, infuriating, *impossible* woman. "There are more dangers in this house than me. You're not safe here—"

"Do you want me to leave?"

"I want you to stay. Forever."

I cannot lie to her. My arms ache to hold her.

"So …" She shrugs. "Here we are."

"Sit." I kick bottles out of the way and gesture to the chair opposite mine, the chair I now can only think of as hers. "I will tell you everything I should have told you from the moment you walked into the pub and your scent drove me to madness. Only once my tale is complete can you decide if you still wish to stay with me."

"A professional organiser doesn't desert a client," Winnie says as she settles herself into the seat. Mirabelle leaps up and settles on her lap. "It's part of our code of ethics, along with not stealing stuff and annoying said clients with our awesome cleaning playlists. But I do think I deserve the full story."

I lower myself into the seat opposite her. My hands tremble. I reach for another bottle, but decide against it. I take a breath, and, with Winnie's soft mouth and piquant scent to steady me, I begin.

"I was born in what was then known as Saxony, over five hundred years ago. I have stopped counting. My father was a blacksmith, my mother spun wool. I was the eldest of six children, and the only boy. I have been a monster so long now that I barely remember being a boy, but I do remember being happy despite our poverty. My father taught me his trade, and my mother taught me to laugh. When I wasn't in the forge, I spent my days running wild in the fields with my sisters, imagining the world beyond our village. My father was well known for his skill, and warriors came from all corners of the kingdom to have their swords made in his forge. I spent far too much time with those warriors, learning the art of the blade and the vocabulary of war.

"One day, soldiers came to our village. They descended like a heavenly host, although they brought only blood and desolation. They burned the fields where we children played. I hid in the forge while they smashed through our home. They impaled my father on his own sword, and what I saw them do to my mother and sisters, I …"

Winnie reaches out a hand to me, but I refuse it. For all the cruelties those soldiers inflicted upon my kin, I've done a thousand-fold worse, and she must know it all if she is to truly know me.

I take another breath.

"When they passed onto the next village, all they left behind were piles of ash and bone. I found the bodies of my family, and gave them what burial rites I could. And then, I strapped two of my father's finest swords to my back and set off with no purpose except revenge."

"How old were you?" Winnie's voice trembles.

"Fourteen summers," I reply. It seems I remember some things clearly.

Reginald appears, setting down an iced chocolate next to Winnie. He gathers up the empty bottles littering our feet. "I shall see that your mother doesn't disturb you," he says as he backs out of the room.

"Thank you, Reginald. Please return to light the fire for Ms Preston."

"Yes, my lord."

My Thrall closes the door lightly behind him. I force myself deeper into my memories, conjuring the acrid stench of burning bodies, the bitter taste of rage and desolation, the hollowness in my chest where my heart should reside.

"I was but one boy, and they were many, but I had the skills passed on from the finest warriors, and I wasn't tempered by age or drink or months on the march. And best – or perhaps worst – of all, I had a heart hardened by vengeance.

"I caught up with them three villages later. I waited until their battle-lust was sated, their blades dulled with dried blood, until they had taken their fill from the terrified women of the village and collapsed in a drunken stupor beside their fires. Then I stole into their camp.

"I slaughtered them in their sleep."

Winnie's mouth twists. I could sanitise this story for her, but I need her to know *everything*. She's the only person who has ever looked at me and not seen a monster, and I'm terrified that she'll never see me the same again.

But I'm more terrified of her staying because she believes I'm something I'm not.

"There was no music to my dance of death, no finesse, but it was the first time I had drawn a blade against flesh. I had nearly made my way through the whole camp when I was ambushed by one of the warriors. He had only pretended to sleep, waiting for me to get close enough to subdue. He didn't kill me, but instead he dragged me before his king, made me kneel, and told a hushed court what I had done in my rage. The king gave me two options – die immediately or join his army.

"And so, I sharpened my father's swords and became a warrior. I marched across Europe, razing villages, taking castles, tasting dirt and blood and glory. And the warrior who saved me, Hrodebert, became my dearest friend. He said that when he'd hauled me from the corpses of his comrades, he'd seen the fire of god in my eyes, and he knew I was destined for the lord's bloody work."

Reginald returns to the hall and fusses with the fire. Winnie sips her chocolate, her fingers stroking Mirabelle's soft fur. I cannot tell what she's thinking. For centuries now, everything in Black Crag has been known to me, but she is unknowable.

Once the fire is blazing and Mirabelle has stretched out across the rug between us, Reginald retreats from the room, closing the door behind him with a quiet *click*. His footsteps don't move from the door, and I know he's guarding the room, making sure neither my mother nor Perdita nor one of their Thralls disturb us.

I continue my story. "One campaign, we were to lay siege to a castle controlled by a rival king. Our intelligence led us to believe that only women and children and a small, inexperienced force held the fortress, and the bulk of the army had moved on to a more defensible position. But we were misled. Inside the castle was a force the likes of which we'd never encountered before. Vampire mercenaries, commanded by none other than Lady Callista Valerian."

Winnie gasps.

"We assaulted the walls, expecting easy victory. But none of our arrows pierced their skin. Our swords glanced off their bodies. Whenever we cut them down, they rose again. They flowed over the walls of the fortress in insurmountable numbers. Beside me, Hrodebert prayed to his god for our triumph over these demons. But gods don't listen. Callista's army surrounded us, cutting us down without mercy, and worse.

"The horrors I saw that day are forever burned behind my eyelids – my comrades screaming and begging for death as fangs sank into their necks. Their bodies going limp and their screams turning to moans as the ecstasy of the bite stole their minds. I did not know what kind of hell we had entered, but I fought with everything I had within me to drive those monsters back into the darkness. I severed the head of one as he sank his teeth into Hrodebert's neck, and that monster didn't rise again."

"I thought vampires were immortal," Winnie says.

"We do not age. We are difficult to kill. But all things, even aberrations, die in the end. There were only two ways I knew to kill a vampire – driving a wooden or silver weapon through their heart, or cutting off their head. The staking I did not learn until much later. That day, I strode through the battlefield, getting up close to evil incarnate so I could separate heads from bodies, with Hrodebert at my side.

"And then *she* came for me."

"*Callista?*" Winnie leans forward in her seat.

She tempts me with her proximity. I long to pull her into my lap, to wrap her golden hair in my fist and expose her pretty neck. I am blood-drunk and she is everything I've ever desired. The promise of her prickles in my fangs. I force the hunger down.

"Do not let her beauty fool you, Winnie. She is known among our kind as the Lady of Agony. She was not happy that we had killed some of her best warriors, so she strode onto the battlefield to deal with me in person. And I was young and foolish. I underestimated her as a woman alone, wearing nothing but a white shift splattered with dirt and blood. I drew my sword, soaked in the immortal blood of her warriors. She drew a small, jewelled dagger, a pretty trinket she still carries with her now. With that little knife she glanced aside my killing blow without breaking a sweat. She smiled down at me and I knew then that all of Hrodebert's demons and monsters were real."

I rip open my shirt, running my fingers over the raised scar beneath my armpit. "She pulled me against her chest, so that my long blade was useless, and then worked her knife through the seams in my armour, driving it home. It is the only wound my immortal body cannot heal."

"She *killed* you," Winnie whispers, her fingers reaching out towards the wound, towards *me*. I long for the warmth of her, but instead of sweeping her into my arms and kissing away the tears that gather at the corners of her eyes, I tiptoe across the knife edge of my control and close my shirt.

She will learn soon enough that I don't deserve those tears.

"I knew as soon as the blade bit my flesh that I was dying. She offered me a deal. She would save my wretched life and gift me immortality, but in return I had to swear a blood oath of fealty to her. I would disown all bonds of family and loyalty and become hers.

"I had no family left, save Hrodebert, and when the life is fleeing your body, the choice seems no choice at all. And so, she gifted me the Kiss, mingling her blood with mine, giving me the power and lineage of the Blood Valerian."

"Oh, Alaric," Winnie breathes.

"When it was done, she brought me to the Nightshade Court. The vampire population in Europe is divided amongst courtly alliances. Vampires are either born beneath the banner of a particular court, or they can swear their loyalty in a blood oath to their court of choice. The number and nature of the courts has changed over the years, but you need know only of the three that still exist today – the Nightshade Court, to which I was born, which is a court of warriors and bloodshed; the Midnight Court, Perdita's court, which is the court of pleasures and art; and the Dusk Court, the court of magic and illusion."

"I'm skipping right past this 'magic and illusion' bit, because I think I've had enough surprises for one lifetime," Winnie says. "So the courts are a form of government?"

"Yes. They do not cover specific geographic regions, although many vampires prefer to live in the vicinity of their chosen court. Each court administrates a number of services for their people, including feeding clubs, affiliated businesses, events, matching vampires with Thralls … Three representatives from each court form a governing council, the Conclave, who make laws that cover the courtly vampires. We also have a legal system, known as the Mora, which you must hope never to encounter. My mother administers the Mora, and she delights in it."

"Noted."

"Callista was true to her promise. She schooled me in combat, gave me the finest armour and weapons, made me the greatest of all her warriors. She taught me the laws and traditions of the *Upyr*, which is what we are called in the old tongue. She presented me with lavish gifts, like a gold-inlaid coffin. She allowed me to continue my father's trade, and I found pleasure in crafting weapons that I carried proudly into battle beneath the flag of the Lady of Agony."

"The swords piled in the ballroom?" Winnie raises an eyebrow.

I nod, slowly.

"I had everything, but I was miserable. All I saw of the world was pain and death and suffering. I realised that the gift she'd given me was really a curse, and I grew to hate the tasks she set me – the human armies she had me slaughter to a man, the prayers to silent gods to save them, the promising fighters she made me bring her so she could curse them, too. I envied the Midnight Court vampires who visited her, with their bright, easy smiles and their passion for beauty and colour and dance.

"One day, we were camping en route to join another lord's Nightshade regiment. We were at rest in our coffins, guarded by our Thralls, when our camp was attacked. A small band of brave human men, their bodies covered in sacred Christian symbols, swords inlaid with silver, and wooden stakes strapped to their horses, descended upon us during our sleep. They had been following us, studying us, searching out our weaknesses. That is how they knew to attack during the brightest hour of the day.

"I rose from my coffin to the sounds of my kin dying. That sun bore down on me with such violence that I could barely lift the lid of my coffin. I dragged up my sword and stumbled into the fray, swinging at the nearest attacker, only to be met by the clash of steel and my friend's familiar blue eyes."

"Hrodebert?" Winnie's eyes widen. She hugs Mirabelle so tightly that the cat gets annoyed and jumps down.

"He was older, his beard peppered with grey, but the same devout, beautiful man I'd called my friend. I was ecstatic. I had assumed he died during the siege, slain by Callista's undead army. But here he was, full of fire, his body dripping with blood. I reached out for him. 'My brother, I can't believe it's you—' and he slashed a long cut down my arm. The cut stung, but what stung worse was the hatred in his eyes.

"'You are no brother of mine!' he cried, before he swung at me again, going for my neck. Our swords sparked as they clashed. I tried to explain that I was still me, still the same Alaric he'd fought beside all those years. But he looked right through me. He saw only the evil he wished to see. He threw all his weight behind his next blow, aiming to take my head. But even with the sun beating on my back, I was stronger. I stepped around him and my battle-lust fell over my eyes. It was him or me, so I drove my blade into his side.

"He collapsed in my arms. I panicked. I missed him so much, and I was so lost and lonely and filled with guilt, so I bent to his neck and drank, pushing my wound to his mouth to pour my blood down his throat.

"I pulled him into my coffin, hiding us both from the sun while the Kiss took effect. I thought I could convince him that we weren't evil. I thought that if I had him by my side, he might bring meaning to my wretched existence. But when he woke from the Kiss, he cursed me, told me that I had made him a monster. He wept for his lost soul. The moment my back was turned, he thrust his own silver-inlaid sword through his chest rather than stay with me."

I nod to the sword sticking from the floor. Winnie's eyes widen, and a tear spills down her cheek.

"When I found him, my shame was an ocean rolling over me. I bathed his body in the Rhine and wrapped him in my cloak, and sang to him the songs my mother sang to me. I laid his sword in his hands, kissed his cold lips, and swore that I would be a better monster than I was a man.

"That same night, I fled Callista's court. I wanted to prove to Hrodebert that our kind could do more than destroy. I thought the only time in my life when I was truly happy was making swords with my father in his forge. I wanted to *create.* And so, I made my way to the seat of the Midnight Court in Vienna and threw myself at the mercy of their queen.

"The Midnight Queen saw an advantage in sheltering Callista's favourite son, and so she granted my asylum. I passed many years there, learning to paint and sculpt and sing. I met Perdita, and we would often paint or play music together. Even then, the queen wanted us to wed, but I was already growing to hate court life. So I ran from there, too.

"This time, I found myself in England, the rumoured seat of the Dusk Court, although none outside their allegiance have ever set foot in their palace, nor can even find it on a map. But I had no intention of aligning myself with vampires who wield their kind of magic. I wanted only to be left alone. I wanted to lock myself away and cause no more harm. So I disguised myself as a mercenary and found myself in the employ of an outlaw baron. I helped him to unseat a cruel lord and take that lord's castle, and then I slit the baron's throat and kept Black Crag for myself."

"And you've been here by yourself ever since?" Winnie asks in a small voice. "Apart from Reginald?"

"I found Reginald half a century ago after it became increasingly clear that I couldn't survive in the modern age without help. Before him, I had only myself and my artistic pursuits for company. I have tried to remain locked away up here, out of the way of the world, but there have been times when my hand was forced. Occasionally, armies tried to take my castle. That I could not abide. And, of course, the hunger has drawn me outside Black Crag's protective walls, although I have never made another vampire, and I never will."

"Did you …" Winnie struggles with the words. "I know that vampires used to kill …"

"I never killed my sources, Winnie. But I did not have the options of synthesised blood, feeding clubs or aging and storing the blood of deceased humans. I could not always offer the courtesy of asking for consent. I could survive for many months on the blood of the deer and wild dogs that lived in the woods, but I *am* a predator. When the hunger grew too great, I would drag highwaymen off the roads, or leap into the carriages of those who dared travel at night, and sometimes even steal into homes in the village while all were in slumber. I took only what I needed to sate my thirst, storing a little for the coming months, and tried to leave my victim safe and comfortable, with a little coin for their trouble and no trace of my feeding. Sometimes I would be seen, sometimes the villagers would find the fang marks and grow suspicious of the lord who never left his castle during the day and didn't age, and they would come for me."

"The paintings," Winnie whispers. "I saw them in the dining hall."

"Yes. Those that are not by my hand are documentations of my trials and executions. I have had many over the centuries. I have been burned alive, staked, buried in six feet of dirt, bled out, and several other tortures too imaginative and horrific to recount, but each time, I have remained. But you might see how you are the first …" My throat closes over. "The first human I have ever trusted."

"Oh, Alaric." The softness in Winnie's voice … I wish I deserved that softness. "Thank you for telling me about your life."

"Do not cry for me, Winifred. I'm no longer a man, but a monster. I have no heart, only hunger. I'm not in danger from the world. The world is in danger from me," I growl.

"That's not what I see," she says with that sad smile of hers, as another tear rolls down her cheek. "I see a man with a heart so bruised that he feels too much. If someone cuts your body, you heal. But if they injure your heart, it's like that scar from your mother's knife – you carry that wound with you always."

I find myself quite unable to speak.

"We both need to learn how to lay siege to the walls around our hearts," Winnie says. "And I think you've taken the first step in telling me your story." She looks at me with such tenderness I can barely believe it. "There's one thing I still don't understand though – why is your mother here now and why is she insisting you marry Perdita? Why does she hate the idea of our pretend engagement so much?"

Our engagement.

It takes me several shuddering breaths before I can speak again. "There is unrest within the courts. The world has changed so fast in the last century, and our society has not kept up. Now there are two rival factions within the Midnight Court – those who believe the court should become more progressive, and more invested in issues like climate change that impact vampires even more than humans. The opposing faction believe that the court has become *too* involved in human affairs, too influenced by human art and culture at the expense of our own. This faction is being stoked by forces from within the Dusk Court who seek to sow discontent for their own reasons. The Midnight Queen seeks to marry her daughter to someone in the more traditional Nightshade Court in an attempt to mollify her enemies. This will show that she respects Upyr culture. Callista's other sons have all been married off, and the eligible lords from the other ancient bloodlines are too busy sowing discord in European politics to care what happens to the Midnight Court. So I'm the only option."

"What does Callista gain from this marriage?"

"Like all the noble families of the Nightshade Court, Callista keeps a standing army of Upyr soldiers. The clans love to involve themselves in human skirmishes, settling centuries-old scores on the edges of human conflict. But modern warfare has increasingly become distasteful to our kind. We are bred for war, but in the blink of an eye wars have gone from being fought with steel and valour to drones and bombs. Not even the most powerful vampires can survive having their heads blown off. It rather takes the fun out of war. And if you're a warrior who has known only bloodshed for centuries, you start glancing around, looking for something better to fight. And you start looking at the person who made you into a war machine in the first place."

"You're talking about revolt?"

"It's possible. The Nightshade armies are growing restless. Some have already rebelled against their lords and taken their lands and castles for themselves, wiping out ancient bloodlines for the sake of boredom. Callista wishes to stop this happening to the Blood Valerian. She needs to give her army a cause they can fight in our old ways. If I'm wed to Perdita and our courts are joined in alliance, their cause will be putting down the simmering rebellion against the Midnight Queen."

Winnie rubs her eyes. This is a lot for her to learn tonight. "Okay, fine. But what does she hope to achieve with this ball?"

"My friend Gideon is building a vast property development on the edge of Argleton—"

"The Sanctus Estate. I heard about it. The Nevermore Coven thinks it might have a connection to Danny's murder."

"That is certainly likely. The estate is for vampires. The houses are specially designed to suit our needs with UV-blocking windows, blood delivery services, and secret rooms for our family heirlooms. Many high up in the Midnight Court have bought houses there – many noble clans, famous artists and even a couple of rockstars – as well as solitary vampires who've chosen not to align with a court. By hosting the ball here, she establishes herself as a friend of the court – provided she can prove that the Lady of Agony can throw a ball that will wow them. Midnight Court vampires try to outdo each other with their lavish parties, and if my mother wants to compete, she must have a spectacle. That is why she wants to surprise them with my wedding to Perdita."

"But you refused to go along with this?" Winnie asks.

I say nothing. I will not lie to her.

"Alaric, tell me." Winnie's golden eyes flicker with concern. "She's threatened you."

"If I don't go through with the wedding, then her spectacle will be my execution."

"She can't do that." Winnie's chin wobbles, and her voice breaks. Another tear slips down her cheek. "You're her son."

"I have lived for more than my allocated time on this earth, have known pain, and more pleasure—" my eyes burn into hers "—than has been my due. I'm not afraid of what she will do to me. But she knows that you know what I am, and you are not in Thrall to my blood. And she knows how much I care for you."

"I still don't understand why that's wrong," she protests.

"Any intimate relationship between human and vampire is forbidden because of the risk of Dhampir."

"What's a Dhampir?"

"A Dhampir is a different type of vampire – they aren't made from the Kiss like Upyr, but born of a human woman from the seed of a male Upyr. Dhampir aren't like me or Gideon or any other vampire you may encounter. They are demons with iron teeth, the strength of ten vampires, and insatiable hunger for blood and death. They will eat their way out of their mother's womb."

"Delightful." Winnie makes a face.

"Indeed. That is why our laws forbid any relations that might lead to the creation of a Dhampir. It's such an ingrained part of our world that very few have concerned themselves with human advancements like contraception, because the very idea of doing *that* with a human is repulsive." My fangs scrape against my lip. "Not to me."

Winnie grips the chair arms, and the tiniest, barely audible rush of air escapes her lips. But I have the hearing of a predator, and her arousal scents the air with ripe strawberries. I growl low in my throat as I struggle to hold myself down.

She dips her head, fighting her own battle with her desires. "This is why your mother hates me."

"You are dangerous, forbidden. I'm the only one who can protect you from her, but I can't do that if I'm skewered through like one of Reginald's kebabs."

"You're saying that your mother will kill me."

"She will not," I growl. "I will not allow it."

"But for us both to stay alive, you have to marry Perdita." Winnie rests her head in her hands. "You've got us into a real pickle with this fake-fiancée thing."

"I was foolish. I didn't understand the reason behind her visit and ..."

... and I wanted you to belong to me.

"Of course, we will cease that charade immediately," I say.

Her smile is a sin that will lead godly men to hell. "We don't have to."

The heart I thought long dead stutters against my chest.

"I think I have an idea to get us all out of this homicidal mother fiasco, and it's going to rely on us keeping up this fake engagement we've established."

"I can't ask you to do that, Winnie. I know that you are afraid of me."

"I'm not afraid of you, Alaric," she says firmly. "I've lived with you for nearly six weeks and you've been nothing but a gentleman. A grumpy, slightly odd gentleman, but a gentleman nonetheless. I'm afraid of *myself* and what I might do around you.

"But ..." she continues. "I signed on to whip this castle into shape, and professional pride means I can't leave until it's spotless for your guests. I'll do whatever it takes to make this ball a success, although I warn you – my fake-fiancée rate is much higher than my professional organiser rate."

"I shall pay whatever you ask."

"I was *kidding*." Winnie rolls her eyes, but her cheeks are crimson. "We need to establish some rules. I've read a lot of fake-dating romances. They all begin with a list of rules."

I enjoy her like this, all strict and businesslike, even as her arousal hangs thick in the air between us. "What are our rules?"

"I'll stay in the castle and be madly in love with you until either your mother and/or Perdita leave in disgust, as long as you keep up the charade that we're together if we bump into Patrick and Claire again," she says. "In fact, it's probably best if we pretend to be together any time we're outside the castle as well. If this village is as teeming with vamps as you claim, we don't want word to get back to your mother that we're faking."

"That is fine," I say. "I don't intend to leave the castle."

"It's nice that you think that, *husband*." Now she sounds downright *evil*. "If we're going to be a couple, then this goes both ways. I'll fake-date you, but you have to fake-date me. I like being wined and dined. I want to see you have fun outside the walls of Black Crag."

I sweep my arms, gesturing to the tapestries hanging from every wall and the small pyramid of teddy bears under the window. "I know how to have fun."

"*My* kind of fun," Winnie shoots back.

"Why don't you come and sit in my lap, wife, and I'll show you—"

"You're accompanying me to the Midsummer Festival this weekend. Those are my terms, vampire. Take them or leave them."

I sigh. "Very well. Are there any other rules I should know about?"

"Yes." Her cheeks redden further. "I think that we need to continue to be affectionate with each other in front of your mother. She doesn't seem convinced that a vampire could be attracted to a human. We have to show her otherwise. And that means …" Winnie swallows. "You have to hold my hand, be affectionate with me, kiss me."

"I have no problems kissing you, Winnie." I long to kiss her now, to taste that forbidden sunshine once more. "But will you be able to kiss me back, knowing what I am?"

"I'll manage." Winnie stares at her feet. I lick strawberries from my lips. "We have to set some boundaries about … um …"

"About what?"

"Um … feeding?" Winnie touches her neck. "It looks as though you drank your way through your stash. Do you need to …?"

I swallow, finding myself quite without words. The day Reginald installed the refrigeration system and started procuring vintage blood, I renounced drinking from humans. It's never felt right to me, even with consent.

But I've never been so tempted as when Winnie strokes her fingers over the vein above her collarbone, the same spot my teeth grazed her in the pub.

I'm a breath away from tearing strips of leather from the chair.

"The act of drinking from another being is one of utmost trust. I will never ask you to do this." I swallow again. "However, if you should decide to—"

"I plan on biting you first, vampire. To establish dominance."

I cough a laugh, before grinning, showing her my fangs.

"I'd like that."

"Gross." Winnie rises from her chair, her golden eyes sparkling with delight. She has that same look of excitement that crosses her face whenever we begin organising another corner.

I stand and take a deep bow. "I am forever in your debt, Winifred the Magnificent, my faux-future-wife. Now, will you seal our oaths to each other with a kiss?"

Winnie bites her lip.

"I'd like that." She grins. "But no funny business, vampire. I've got a pocket full of anti-you charms and I'm not afraid to use them—"

I cannot hold myself back a moment longer. I cross the divide between us in a single beat of her delicate human heart, pushing her back until she sinks into the chair, and I bend over her, all pretence of humanity washed away.

I smile down at her, fangs bared.

I let her see me, *truly* see me, for the first time.

And although Winnie's lip quivers at the sight of me, the hunger in her eyes matches mine.

I crush my mouth to hers.

The kiss hurts. It hurts because all wonderful, perfect things in this world are born from suffering. It hurts because I feel as though I have woken from the Kiss again, born anew with all my dead, necrotic tissue cut away.

I kiss her as though she really is my betrothed.

I drag her against me, my tongue diving deep as I drink in her strawberries and sunlight. She moans into my mouth and I listen to the universe shatter in that tiny, perfect sound. My shaft swells with wanting and my heart swells with hope, and I make a silent vow to myself. I will do anything, *anything*, to make Winnie mine for real.

She presses her body back against mine, her fingers reaching up to tangle in my hair as I kiss a trail from her wanton mouth along her jaw and down her neck. The hunger shoots like pain down my spine, raw and hot.

"I have contraception," she whispers. "In my toiletry bag. In my room."

This is dangerous. Dangerous because I'm considering breaking the most sacred vampire taboo. My fangs scrape over her soft skin and she smells like the summer days I haven't experienced in centuries. I'm on the very edge of control and all I have to do is bite down and send us both into a frenzy of ecstasy—I want her to feel my fangs slide into her skin.

She knows what I am and wants me anyway. No one has ever seen me the way Winnie Preston sees me, and when I'm with her I believe that I might be something more than a monster.

This woman makes me reckless.

Our bodies fit together as though the centuries that separate us don't matter, as though we're made for each other. I draw her closer, my hands roaming over her, tugging down the collar of her shirt and sniffing, scraping, licking over her skin, shuddering as I feel her blood pulse in her veins, just beneath the surface—

Even as another moan escapes her lips, her hand flies to her throat, covering her skin.

I draw away, mortified by my lack of control. But if Winnie is disgusted by me, she doesn't show it.

"You've had your kiss," she pants. "Now, claim your chair back from Mirabelle and sit down. You need to hear this plan of mine."

37

Winnie

Faye: What do you mean you're staying on in Argleton? Winnie, babe, how long does it take to sparkle up one teeny tiny castle? I know you have the hots for Mr Tall, Dark, and Vampy, but we are not going to get this opportunity again. We can't wait on this.

I could just do it without you ...?

ALARIC LISTENS INTENTLY WHILE I FORM MY PLAN. IT'S A WILD, crazy plan, with a lot of moving parts. We're going to need so much help and a metric fucktonne of luck to pull it off, and there's the little matter of the terrifying Lady of Agony and her threats—

"No," Alaric shakes his head when I finish. "Absolutely not."

His fangs have retracted now. It's a shame. I kind of like them.

I liked them scraping against my skin.

"If it goes wrong, you'll be *literally* risking your neck in a room filled with hungry, lascivious vampires, at least one of whom has killed a human."

"But I'll have my handsome fake-fiancé to save me." I smile.

I'm quite proud of this plan. I think it's one of the best ideas I've had since the Winnie Wins System. Which Faye is going to pretend is all her idea on national TV, and there's not a thing I can do about it since we both own the trademark.

But I'm not going to think about that.

Alaric scowls. His hand closes around my arm and pulls me close. So close that every breath I take tastes of him.

"If we must do it this way, I will not be leaving your side until the ball is over, my *betrothed*."

"Um ... yes. Good." The way he says *my betrothed* makes the butterflies in my stomach dance a little conga line straight between my thighs.

Now that I know what Alaric is, the weight of him makes sense to me. Not a physical weight, but the emotional weight of five hundred years of *yearning* all concentrated on me. It's heady and addictive being the focus of such a man's attention, especially when he kisses me like *that*.

Especially when us being together is forbidden.

Which is exactly why I need some distance between us now.

You'd get plenty of distance if you were in London, the sensible voice inside my head screams.

But I can't leave now. I can't go back to my normal life knowing what I know, especially now that a crazy lady vampire intends to kill me.

And I can't leave Alaric to face this alone. Not when I can help. This is the biggest mess I've ever tried to clean up, but if I can do this, I can do *anything*.

I place my fingers over Alaric's hand and try to prise them off my arm.

"This is going to work. The Nevermore Murder Club and Smutty Book Coven will come through for us. You haven't met these ladies, but they can do anything. The hardest part is going to be getting your mother to agree. Call her now."

I can't help it. I love a new project, and this is much more important than cleaning up Alaric's castle. It's about cleaning up his *life*. I want to get started.

"If I propose this ludicrous idea and she refuses, I may have to kill her. In addition to all the pots we still need to sort, you'll have to clean the blood out of the carpet." Alaric sighs. "Reginald?"

Reginald appears a moment later, bowing deeply. "My lord."

"Where is my mother? Bring her to us. We wish to speak to her."

"She and Perdita left to visit an artist on the Sanctus Estate. She says not to expect her until early morning, and she left her Thralls behind as she says they will feast at the party."

"When did she leave?"

"Around the time you stabbed Hrodebert."

Alaric sighs. "And you remained on guard at the door because ..."

"Because I trust your mother about as much as I trust German vampires to make a decent blood pudding," Reginald says. "Which is to say, not at all."

"You were listening."

"I'm sorry, my lord. It's only that I don't want Ms Preston to leave." Reginald beams at me. "If I may say so, I think her plan has merit—"

"Very well! We shall have an audience with Callista tomorrow. For now, my future wife is yawning. Reginald, if you could bring Winnie some more candles for her candelabra, she shall retire to her room to sleep." Alaric moves silently towards the door. "I will walk with you."

"I'm sleepy, not maimed. I can walk myself."

"Even if my mother isn't in the castle, her Thralls are here. I don't trust them. You agreed that I am to remain by your side at all times."

I roll my eyes, but the butterflies are doing a sultry little salsa number.

Reginald hands me a fresh candelabra lit with flickering candles, and we begin our meandering walk through the castle, Mirabelle trotting ahead of us with her tail held high. Alaric doesn't sweep me into his arms this time, and I admit I'm a little disappointed. He walks stiffly, his eyes fixed on me. His fingers find their way to the small of my back as he guides me through the narrow hallways and darkened corners.

We reach the top of the stairs.

"Well, goodnight," I say. "Don't let the coffin bugs bite."

"Sweet dreams, Winifred Preston."

I push open the door to my room and set down the candelabra. When I turn around, Alaric is standing behind me. The sight of such raw emotion on his usually stony countenance startles me.

"What are you doing?"

Alaric's eyes are fathomless voids. "I … I am trying to commit every moment with you to memory, so I may revisit these days and nights long after you're gone."

That might be the strangest and most romantic thing anyone has ever said to me. I swallow down the lump in my throat.

I want him.

I surge up on my toes, pressing my lips to his. He starts, and makes a noise of surprise, but it takes barely a second before he is wrapping his arms around my waist, lifting me up to his chest, his lips firm and possessive as he carries me with no effort, as though I weigh less than a feather.

"Winnie, I—"

I hold up a finger to his lips. "You asked me what would make me happy. This, you, tonight – that's what I want."

"We should—"

I shut him up with a kiss. Every sensation amplifies – the roar of the fire warm on my back, the coolness of his body as he presses himself against me, the taste of winter spices and haunted places in the rough, breathless kiss that has us both panting, the hard length of him pressing against my thigh.

Is he … um … *that* big?

"You are tough to resist," he murmurs, his hands gripping my arms.

"So don't resist."

His lips crush against me, breaking through every last bit of willpower that I possess. My hands slide into his hair, tangling my fingers in those long curls. A low groan slips from his lips. He wraps his hands around me, pressing us together so I can feel his chest press against mine with every ragged breath, and spins me around so I'm the one with my back against the door, his weight against me, caging me in. As if there was any chance I'd run from him.

His lips trail down my neck as he laughs, sending goosebumps down my body. "If I'd known that plotting against my mother was the way to get you into bed, I'd have introduced you on the first day."

A laugh bubbles up inside me, bursting warm against his lips. "That's a lie. You didn't want me when we first met. You thought I was an annoyance sent by Reginald to colour-code your teddy bears and throw away your swords."

"Winnie, from the moment I smelt you in the pub, you have possessed me utterly. I am already yours."

His voice is so serious, it makes my heart hum in the back of my throat. "Next thing you know, you'll tell me that you've organised all your paintbrushes by size, and you'll have my panties on the floor."

"Are you telling me that if I talk about the benefits of clear storage containers over opaque, I will finally see what you've been hiding under your blouse?" His hands skim the hem of my shirt.

"Lord Valerian, you don't need to talk *that* dirty to me." I place my hand on the toned plane of his chest, pushing him back so I have enough space to peel off my dress and toss it to the floor.

I can't believe I did that.

I've never stripped in front of a guy before, never made such a bold move. And now I'm standing here in my purple lace bra and knickers, fighting the urge to cover my lumpy bits, second-guessing my boldness.

Alaric's eyes *feast* on my body, as if he's been alone in this castle for *centuries* and has forgotten what tits look like. I stop feeling nervous and self-conscious, and start wanting him to look at me some more.

"Winifred." He whispers my name with reverence as he reaches for me. I gasp a little at his cool touch as he runs his fingers delicately, slowly over the lace of my bra, across my stomach, over the curve of my breast. Softly, gently, trembling as he holds back *something*.

I shiver at his touch, wanting more than slow and light. I want him to devour me.

I grab the back of his head and pull his lips to mine, tasting his spicy winter scent as he pushes me against the door with such force that the wood creaks. The sumptuous fabric of his old-fashioned coat does little to hide the hard lines of his body or his arousal.

That's more like it.

There are way too many clothes on both of us.

Keeping my lips on his, my fingers make their way down his chest and to his belt, trying to undo the leather contraption.

What the heck? Is this thing from the seventeenth century? Why so many clasps and things?

Alaric laughs into my mouth before pressing his forehead to mine. "Let me help you with that, wife."

"I thought I was your fake-fiancée?"

"You are. But since we're pretending, it pleases me to pretend you're my wife."

As soon as the dreaded belt falls to the floor, I meet his gaze, falling into those dark, fathomless eyes. My chest fills with helium as I make quick work of unbuttoning his pants and unsheathing his cock.

Um, excuse me, how is this thing *real?*

I try to wrap my fingers around the shaft, but barely get around it. I pump my fist, slowly, stroking his length, feeling the raised vein and beautifully-shaped head, already wet with his desire for me.

"Winnie …" Alaric moans, his eyes drifting shut.

"Lord Valerian, it is an injustice that you've been hiding this away in a draughty old castle," I scold him as I stroke him again. "The women of Argleton should have been worshipping *this*."

"There's only one woman I want," he growls, his lips crushing mine. His hand cups me behind my head, fingers winding in my hair as I stroke him and try not to worry about how he's going to fit inside me.

A string of German curse words leaves his lips as he tilts his head back. I love him like this, stiff Alaric all undone by me. I drop to my knees, coming face to face, well, face to purple head, with the literal monster he's been hiding all this time.

It's even more glorious to look at – hard and swollen, with those lovely veins running down the length of it. Slowly, I lick the tip, lapping up the bit of precum that has gathered there. It tastes like him, like winter and darkness.

"Winnie." He says my name like a prayer as he grabs the back of my head, running his fingers through my hair. Usually I hate when guys do that, but with him, it's different. I like him on the edge of control, all tense and wound up and dangerous, because I know he'll never hurt me.

I'm safe with him.

"You like that?" I ask, swirling my tongue just along his head.

"Very much," he says, his words shaky.

Relaxing my throat, I slowly take in his cock, inch by exquisite inch, relishing in the feel of his thighs vibrating around my face as I take him as far as I can go. I lick and suck every bit of him ... well, the bit I can get in my mouth, which honestly isn't much.

The way his thighs shake and his muscles clench and he raggedly calls my name makes me want to keep going, but he fists my hair, forcing my head back so that I'm looking up into his dark stare.

"As much as I love the feel of your mouth on me, *I* am the one who is in charge. I need to know how you taste before I come undone."

I don't protest as Alaric scoops me off the floor and drops me on the bed.

He steps out of his trousers as he comes at me. He shrugs off his coat and tugs off his shirt, tossing them carelessly aside so he's standing over me, completely naked. It's my turn to drink him in.

He looks like a Michelangelo sculpture – all ropy muscles and smooth, marble skin. His burns from the sunlight have completely healed. The only part of him that isn't raw Renaissance perfection is the jagged white scar stretching from beneath his armpit.

Alaric jerks me to the edge of the bed and peels away my purple knickers. My skin sizzles wherever his cool fingers touch me. He spreads my legs wide, dips his head low between my thighs, and inhales deeply. If Patrick had ever sniffed me, I'd have kicked him off the bed, but when Alaric does it I feel like a goddess. Especially when he growls out, "Fuck, Winnie, you will drive men to ruin. I bet you taste just as sweet as you smell."

I can't even tease him about swearing because he pries my thighs further apart. His heated gaze meets mine as he leans over me, lips inches from exactly where I want them to be. "You deserve to be worshipped, Winnie, and I'm not stopping until you come all over my tongue."

I whimper, ready for him to devour me. But he doesn't move, a slow smile crossing his face.

"You say that you deserve to be happy. Will this make you happy?"

"Y-y-yes." I buck my hips against him, trying to make him stop talking and give me what I'm aching for. But I should have known that Lord Alaric Valerian has finely honed the art of seduction as he has all other artistic pursuits, and I'm to go along with his deliciously devious plan.

"Then tell me that you deserve it. Tell me that you deserve this worship, or I won't suck on this beautiful swollen bud," he says, trailing a finger down my wet centre. His lips quirk in that glorious half-smile of his.

"Worship me," I manage to breathe.

"Good girl," he growls before diving his tongue straight into my centre.

A gasp leaves my mouth as my body quivers under his touch. My whole back is alive with goosebumps as he drags me across the linen duvet, lifting my hips off the bed so he can devour me all the easier.

And he does devour me. That's the only way to describe the wanton relish with which he feasts between my legs, the way his tongue laves over me, sucking and nibbling and licking until I'm a mess of nerve endings and pleasure and *want*.

His eyes never leave mine. Those two obsidian orbs are a direct line to his soul as he watches every moan, every twitch, every time I clasp the duvet or arch my back off the bed.

The intimacy of it makes me feel like I swallowed a hummingbird. I want to look away, but for a moment I believe magic is real because Alaric has me bewitched.

He wants to see everything. He wants to watch me fall apart.

Stars form behind my eyes as he picks up the speed of his tongue, adding in his fingers to the same rhythm as he hums against me.

My head falls back, my orgasm building low and warm in my stomach, the butterflies dancing their mating dance.

Alaric moans against me, sucking my clit into his mouth.

Sparks fly through me, and I let out a low moan, my whole body pulsating as I come around his greedy tongue.

He laps up every bit of me like I'm the sweetest dessert before kissing a trail up my stomach and stopping at the lace of my bra.

"I can't believe this infernal contraption is still on," he murmurs, laying a trail of cool kisses across my breast. "Still, I am grateful it is flimsier than a corset."

RIIIIP. With one hand, he tears the fabric, and the two halves of my bra fall to my sides.

"Alaric," I gasp, looking up to meet his grin. "That was my *favourite* bra."

"I'll buy you a new one. I'll buy you all the frilly, lacy, not-corsets you desire as long as I can keep worshipping you and making you mine, *wife*." Alaric folds himself over me, holding himself off me with his elbows on the bed, his legs tangled with mine and the length of him nudging my hip. He nuzzles one breast, stroking the other with those strong, cool fingers.

He is still so *cold*. Between the heat of the fire and the amazing things he's doing to my body, I feel like I'm lying in an oven. But then his mouth clamps around my nipple, sucking hard enough to send a jolt of fire through my chest.

My hips move against him, grinding, seeking the heat that he stokes inside me. I'm hot enough for both of us.

Alaric laughs his rumbling, delighted laugh as he stares at me in wonder. He rolls my nipple between his fingers. "You like that, Winnie?"

"Yes," I murmur as his lips slide to the other nipple, giving it the same wonderful treatment. "I want to feel your cock inside me."

He growls, his eyes locking with mine.

"We need ... uh ... the contraception? Is that what it's called?"

I roll my eyes. "Yes, Alaric. Grab the condoms from my bag."

"Condoms?"

"Don't tell me you don't know what a condom is?"

Alaric shakes his head.

My shoulders sag. "Okay. Hold all your filthy thoughts, my lord."

Alaric rolls off me and I slip off the sheets. I feel his eyes boring into me as I cross the room, and can't resist giving my arse a wiggle that results in a low moan from the bed. I riffle around in my toiletries. I keep all my travel things organised in a clever case with individual compartments for everything, and Patrick and I used to use condoms before I went on the pill, so there should be ...

Ah-hah! Winnie the organiser wins again! I grab a strip of gold packets and head back to the bed. Alaric has rolled over, resting on one hip, the other knee raised, watching me with curiosity. I kneel beside him and lay out the gold packets like an offering.

How can he be this good in bed and *not* know what a condom is? Vampires are an eternal mystery.

Alaric looks down at the packets, then fists himself, his lip twisting with confusion.

"You intend to crown it with gold?"

I laugh, shaking my head as I open the packet, throwing it to the side and taking out the latex. I slide it over his shaft, stroking him slowly.

"See? It stops any little Alarics getting out."

"So you cannot become with child?"

"Yes, so there's no risk of Dhampir."

Alaric's eyes drift closed, lashes tangling together as I roll the condom as far as it will go. Candlelight flickers across his cheeks, highlighting his sharp cheekbones and the cruel slant of his lips. He lets out a sigh that aches with wanting.

His eyes fly open as he grabs my hips, pulling me back to him so our lips meet again. He crushes my body with his, rolling over me until I'm beneath him again, skin against cool skin.

"Now you are *mine*," he whispers, his voice tight with hunger and everything he's held back.

I can taste myself on his tongue still, and it's kind of hot, thinking about how much he enjoyed himself. I lap up his tongue and press further against him, letting him know how badly I want this.

How badly I want *him*.

I lean back into the pillows. A dark curl flops over Alaric's eye as he notches himself between my thighs. His monster cock nudges at my entrance, sending a flicker of unease along my spine.

"I don't know how you're going to fit," I say, worry creeping into my voice.

"We take it slow," Alaric whispers as he kisses my forehead. "The night belongs to us."

And then I'm no longer worrying, no longer *thinking*, because he's pushing inside me, and it's tight, *so tight*, but he feels amazing. I press my legs into the bed and breathe through the stretch as he works his way in, a little at a time, swallowing my whimpers with his kiss. His fingers knit in mine, and he murmurs beautiful words that make me feel powerful even as more than my body is cleaved into pieces.

"Winnie, you are made for me," he moans, gripping onto the headboard. "You are perfect."

"I cannot believe—" My words become gasps as he drives his hips forward, filling me to the hilt.

He was the one who was supposed to be vulnerable, but right now, I'm the one whose heart is splitting at the seams. I'm the one who feels the prick of tears behind my eyes even as my body revels in the magic of him.

And then he starts to move. He draws out slowly and thrusts back in, piercing me with an exquisite sigh that makes me wonder if he's not being vulnerable now, too, if he's not trying to show me a piece of him that no one else has got to see.

"I've got you, Winnie." His body cages mine, his fingers squeeze, his lips tease along my jaw. "You're safe with me."

"Alaric," I moan, not realising how beautiful those words could be. I meet his rhythm as he thrusts hard inside me, each stretch more exquisite than the last.

"That's it, Winnie. Take me, take all of me," he growls, sliding his fingers between us and using my own wetness as lubrication as he rubs me in rough, teasing circles while he slams into me. "Come undone for me."

I do. Every last knot inside me falls open. I'm exposed – mind, blood, sinew, organs, heart … it's all laid bare for him. His teeth scrape against my neck and my whole body shakes as my orgasm erupts. I call out his name, grinding my hips to meet his over and over again.

He follows me in a slew of German curse words before he stills against me. Even through the latex, I feel him spilling into me. I moan again, my heated pussy almost unable to take any more.

Alaric drags his lips from my neck. Even though he's just come, the hunger in his eyes is *wretched*. His body shakes, and I know that there's something of me I haven't yet given him.

He's being gentle with me.

The heat he'd stoked inside me starts to burn again as he trails light, cool kisses over my breasts and then up my neck, his shoulders shuddering as he licks and nips at my skin.

"You're amazing. Do you know that?"

I find it hard to speak, hard to *breathe*, while he's still inside me, his monster cock giving the occasional little jerk.

"I lost myself for a moment there." He grips my chin, forcing me to meet his dark stare. "But then I opened my eyes, and here you were. Not an illusion, but real. Winnie Preston in my bed, writhing beneath me and calling my name from those pretty lips. Magic."

"Technically, it's *my* bed."

"*Technically*, all things in Black Crag Castle belong to me." His eyelashes tangle together as he blinks. "Even you."

His words send hot fizz down my spine. "I'm yours tonight."

"Then if you are mine, tell me that you know you are amazing."

"I can't say it while you're still inside me," I manage to squeak.

That infuriating close-lipped smile bears down on me. "Say it."

I sigh. "Fine. I'm amazing."

Alaric's head bobs down, sucking my nipple into his mouth until I gasp and writhe some more. "I did it. I did what you said!"

"You did," he laughs, looking up at me. "That's my good wife."

I cry out in protest as he slides out of me and leaps from the bed. Alaric peels off the condom, staring at it with a wrinkled nose before tossing it in the rubbish bin beneath the table.

"You're supposed to tie the end so Reginald doesn't get a gross surprise when he cleans the room," I tell him.

"Reginald has dealt with far worse things," he says as he disappears into the bathroom. I lie on the bed, warm from the fire and my two orgasms, missing the reassuring weight and coolness of him. I hear the water running.

I guess the condom was too much, and he needed to clean up.

My eyes feel heavy, and I swear I could go to sleep right here. Maybe the dreams wouldn't even bother me tonight …

But before I can drift off, Alaric is back. He scoops me off the bed, pressing me into his chest as he carries me across the room.

"Alaric, what are you doing?" I squeal.

The scent of lavender permeates the air. He walks both of us into the shower, his broad shoulders almost touching the sides of the glass door. Warm water sluices over us. He leans me against the wall, running a soapy flannel over my sore and heated body.

"I never said I was done worshipping you," he murmurs, his fingers darting between my legs again.

"You don't have to," I whisper.

His dark stare locks on mine. "But I want to. I want such dark and wild things from you, Winnie, you cannot imagine."

He holds me against that wall, kissing my protests away as his fingers work their magic until I come apart for him once more.

~

When I emerge from the bathroom a few minutes later, Alaric is sitting in one of the chairs at the window. Moonlight falls over his face as he reads a book.

"The bathroom's free if you—"

"Hmmm." He turns a page.

I march over and snatch the book from his hands. My skin flushes as I realise that it's next week's smutty vampire book club pick, and the page Alaric's reading is a particularly racy scene between the vampire prince and his human bride …

"I was reading that."

"You're a vampire who's lived for over five hundred years. There's nothing in that book you haven't done before."

"That's not true. Page sixty-four was *most* enlightening."

My ears are burning. I drop the book onto the nightstand and jab a finger at the bathroom. "Get in there and brush your fangs or whatever it is vampires need to do so we can go to sleep."

Alaric flashes me one final infuriating smirk before shutting the bathroom door behind him.

By the time he returns to my room, I'm beneath the sheets and struggling to keep my eyes open. "I know this is usually the time when you get up and do things, but I need a night off. Someone wore me out."

"I understand. You must rest." He pulls the covers up to my neck and lays a chaste kiss on my forehead. He picks up his coat and starts for the door.

"Alaric?"

He turns.

I lift up the corner of the duvet. "Will you stay with me tonight?"

"I do not sleep during the midnight hours."

"Fine, then will you lay beside me and stare at the ceiling while I sleep?"

He smiles, dropping his coat and pulling back the sheets. There's a slight heat in his skin from the shower water as he presses against me, his arms wrapping around my waist.

"I will stay because it pleases you," he whispers in my ear. "I cannot say no to you, my wife."

Alaric clicks off his light.

"Alaric?"

"Mmm?" His voice rumbles through my chest.

"If you bit me, would it hurt? Does it leave a scar? Arabella from book club said it's pleasurable, but is it pleasurable like a nice day at the beach or like a party drug? Can people get addicted? Can you do it anywhere or does it have to be on the neck—"

"Go to sleep, Winnie," he whispers. "I will *never* hurt you."

"What if I want you to?"

My heart thuds against my ribs.

His breath rasps.

"Alaric?"

"I suggest you sleep, wife, and stop tempting me with dangerous words."

"But—"

"*Sleep*," he growls. "Sleep, and forget what you are asking."

38

Alaric

Gideon: That is a crazy plan, but I love it. I'll be at the castle first thing in the evening. Together, we can persuade the Lady of Agony to accept this bonkers scheme. Oh, and Allie, watch yourself. I'm not concerned about your stabby matriarch as much as I am about your fragile little heart around that human not-wife of yours.

WINNIE HAS STAGED A HOSTILE TAKEOVER OF MY SIDE OF THE bed.

In all my years as a vampire, that is not a sentence I ever expected to think aloud. But that's precisely what's happened.

First, she spoke of biting, and left me aroused and starved and wanting while she slipped into slumber. Then, she wriggled towards me in her sleep until she was fully on my side of the bed, my arm trapped beneath her head, giving my hands nowhere to rest but her tiny, breakable body. She is so deep in sleep that she doesn't know she's crept into the clutches of a monster.

The things I dream of doing to her while I watch the vein in her neck pulse are beastly.

I remain as still as I can, fighting a battle against my darkest desires, certain that the tiniest movement will awaken the beast inside me that hungers for her. My shaft jabs against her thigh in an unseemly way, and my fangs have dropped.

I will not. I cannot.

What if I want you to?

She didn't mean it. She doesn't know what she's saying.

The nightmares have threatened to claim her twice already. During the first one, she began inching her way across the bed like a homicidal caterpillar. But as soon as she settled against me, she calmed, and fell deeper into sleep.

"I've got you, Winnie," I whispered. "I won't let anything hurt you, not even in your dreams."

The second nightmare was worse, and she thrashed and whimpered in my arms, slapping her body as she cried out. I held her and sang softly the words of an old Germanic song Hrodebert taught me – a song of forlorn love – and she settled once more.

There's a pool of her drool on my arm. I'm transfixed by the vein in her neck, the ebb and flow of blood being pushed through her body …

I can't lie here a moment longer, or I will do something we both regret.

I need to take all this raw, inhuman *need* and channel it somewhere.

She's so settled in sleep that she doesn't wake as I pull my arm from beneath her. I fly from the room, down the stairs to my study, and back again, my arms filled with supplies and my ears pricked for the sounds of my mother's Thralls. When I return, Winnie is where I left her, her beauty unchanged, immaculate.

As silently as I can, I move my chair away from the spear of sunlight piercing the gap in the curtains into the darkest corner of the tower. I sharpen my favourite charcoal and fill page after page with sketches. Each image I toss away the moment I've finished it, for none of them are quite right. I'll take them down to the priest hole before Winnie wakes.

Drawing is the only way to control the hunger.

Having her in my bed was everything I have ever wanted, and it should be enough. I don't want to hunger for her the way I do. But now that I've vowed to make her mine, and my skin is drenched in her sunlight and strawberry scent, my need has increased tenfold.

Loving her will destroy me utterly. But I am more than ready to be ruined.

39

Winnie

Mum: The bloody council bloody lady bloody came over. She wanted to come inside but I wouldn't let her. Can you imagine the nerve! She stood on the street and snapped photos, so I threw all those doll heads at her. Haha, now she won't come back. And you said those doll heads were rubbish.

I WAKE TO FADING SUNLIGHT ON MY FACE AND THE MEMORY OF A song with words I don't understand.

My eyes fall on the mess of pillows scattered across the bed and floor, and the person-sized indent in the bed beside me.

Alaric slept here.

Alaric slept here because I *went to bed with him*. Because he gave me the best orgasm of my life three times over and whispered all those filthy *things* in his gravelly voice …

That beautiful sad song in a language I don't understand plays across my memory.

I slept through the night again. I didn't have the nightmares.

I didn't have nightmares because Alaric was here.

I roll out of bed, surprised at how good I feel. This is what a proper night's sleep feels like. Or rather, a proper day's sleep. My phone says it's nearly 5 pm. Alaric will be having his evening swim right around now.

And when he gets back, we can confront Callista and take a shot at catching a killer, saving his head from being disassociated with his body, and ending a regressive ancient vampire law.

Just, you know, a typical day for a professional organiser.

I find a tray of fresh bread, preserves, hard-boiled eggs and pastries at the foot of my bed, with a note from Reginald explaining that while Lady Callista is staying in the house, he'll have to serve my meals in my room.

Okay, sure.

I also notice that one of the chairs under the window has been moved into the corner by the bathroom. There are a couple of charcoal sticks on the floor beside it, but no other signs of Alaric.

I throw on wide-leg trousers and a cute purple cap-sleeve tee, stuff my face with pastries, shove my feet into my Ugg boots, and fling open the door.

I stifle a scream.

"Good afternoon, Ms Preston," Reginald says from his position on the landing. "My lord apologises that he could not be here when you awoke. He had some business to attend to, so I'm taking over his guard duties. I'll escort you to the ballroom. I'm sure he'll be eager to see you."

"Thanks, Reginald."

As we approach the ballroom, I hear a faint swooshing noise. *I suppose his mother has him working on preparations for the ball.*

Reginald pushes the doors open, and I peer into the gloom.

My heart leaps into my throat.

Alaric dances across the vast marble ballroom, his long fingers wrapped around an enormous sword. He is majestic as he steps and lunges and parries an invisible foe, the sword glinting as it slices through air.

Remember how I said I always dreamed of a knight in shining armour coming to rescue me?

Now that dream is weaving a deadly dance in front of my eyes, and he is *majestic*.

And hot AF.

Hot like a lovechild of Aragorn and Geralt of Rivia.

Alaric must hear my lady parts gasping, because he whirls around and stops short when he sees me. The sword clatters to the floor.

"My wife." He's upon me in a moment, his hands gripping my forearms, dragging me into the room. "I'm sorry that I wasn't there when you woke again. But I needed to practise. I trust you slept well."

"I had a great sleep." I swallow. I don't want to explain about the nightmares, that last night is only the second time in three months where I've slept through the night. And most of the day. I especially don't want to explain when he's so close to a weapon that could have my clothes cut off in a matter of *moments*. "Your mother didn't try to suck me dry, so I'd say luck is on our side."

"She'll be awake shortly. As soon as Gideon arrives, we'll speak with her." He frowns at his discarded blade, as though this is somehow its fault. "I am aggrieved that I couldn't keep you safe from her without this absurd plan."

I press my forehead against his, wishing we could stay in this moment, that we could be Winnie and Alaric again, but I'm dangerously close to falling for this man, and I can't be distracted from said plan. "You've saved my ass three times now. I owe you."

"You owe me nothing." He brushes his thumb over my lower lip and chases it with his mouth. His tongue slakes across mine, a spear of dark magic that makes me long for the kind of chaos that only he can give me, the kind of chaos that's wrong and right all at once.

It's difficult to pull away, but I do it, my feet sliding across the polished marble floor. Questions burn on my tongue, but he's being so *Alaric* that I don't want to ask them yet. I want more tiny pieces of him before this fragile thing between us withers.

I fight to catch my breath. "Why did you suddenly need to swing a sword around?"

"I'm training," he says seriously. "For the next time I meet Patrick."

Why does that make my knees weak?

"Maybe don't kill him," I suggest. "Just maim him a little. Can I try?"

"Certainly." He spins me around. His arms wrap around me as he presses his chest into my back. "My wife shouldn't need me to maim her enemies for her. Pick up the sword."

I bend down and pick up the large, two-handed sword. Bending drives my hips back into Alaric. He lets out a hiss as his fingers dig into my hips, and a cheeky part of me likes hearing him lose control. I purposefully grind myself against him as my fingers close around the hilt of the sword. I'm rewarded by a low groan.

I'm dancing with a monster.

I'm making things messy.

But I don't care.

The sword is lighter than I expect, the leather hilt worn and the blade chipped in places. This sword has seen battle.

No wonder Alaric didn't want to get rid of his swords. They're part of his story. I wonder what battles this weapon has seen? I wonder if . . .

My questions die as I straighten up and feel a very different type of sword dig into my thigh.

"Legs wider." Alaric's commanding voice brushes against my ear.

He kicks my foot out. Now his thighs are pressed into mine, and I can feel *everything*.

Oh, he is *not* playing fair.

Alaric places his large hands over my much smaller ones and shows me how to grip the hilt of the sword. His voice rumbles through me as he explains how to keep a firm grip with the top hand, but to keep the other looser so that I can wind the blade.

His cool hands move over mine as he describes the different stances and guards. He nudges my feet, forcing me to move, and he moves with me, our bodies locked in a deadly dance as we step and spin across the ballroom, the sword blade whipping in front of me. Every touch brings back flashes of our night together, of how good he made me feel.

It doesn't matter how good he makes you feel. You are too fragile for this. You can't just jump into a relationship with the first supernatural creature you meet, especially after you've just been dumped by Patrick.

Don't make a mess of your heart, Winnie.

"Winnie," Alaric breathes, his chest heaving as he struggles for breath. "I must tell you that I—"

"Pardon me. Don't let me interrupt. I'm here for the show."

I leap away from Alaric, the sword flying from my fingers. Alaric catches it midair and whirls around to face the intruder.

Gideon leans against the door, wearing an impeccable grey suit, his blond hair slicked up in a trendy style, and his eyes crinkling at the edges with suppressed laughter.

"Winnie Preston, it's so lovely to see you still hanging around." Gideon winks at me. "I see you've got Allie to give you his weapon."

"What makes you so sure I didn't win it off him in a fair fight?" I cock an eyebrow in return.

"Call me Allie *one more time* and you will learn how difficult it is to conduct business with your ribcage inverted," Alaric growls at his friend.

"Don't tease me with a good time." Gideon crosses the room and slots my arm in his. "I'm here to offer my services as bodyguard and party planner. But since the old bat is still hanging upside down from the roof somewhere, I want to see the magic you've worked on Allie's mess."

"She doesn't really turn into a bat, does she?"

Gideon laughs. "Oh, poor, sweet Winifred."

Alaric stomps behind us as I show Gideon the work we've done in the ballroom. Gideon's eyes widen as I walk him through the rooms, explaining the organising system and how Winnie Wins works. "Our next step is 'Neutralise', which is all about making a game out of tidying up and disrupting all the little habits that contribute to clutter."

"I am in awe." Gideon bows so low that his forehead touches the floor. "You know, if you wanted to stick around Argleton, I have a business opportunity for you."

"You sound like you want to recruit me into a pyramid scheme."

"The only pyramids I like are dusty old ones filled with treasures ripe for the taking," Gideon says. "I'm merely *suggesting* that your skills may be uniquely suited for my members. As more vampires give up their crumbling castles and embrace modern living on the Sanctus Estate, they find themselves at a loss for what to do with their stuff. Even those who lack Alaric's proclivities find themselves with rooms full of ephemera acquired through decades and centuries of immortal life. If you could prevent the more lascivious ones from sucking on your delectable neck, perhaps you could make a name for yourself as a vampire-clutter-cleaning specialist."

"She's not interested," Alaric says stiffly as we leave the ballroom and enter the pottery studio.

"I think Winnie can speak for herself." Gideon tweaks Alaric's cheek. I can practically see smoke coming out of Alaric's ears.

"Thanks for the offer," I say quickly. "But I already have more business than I can handle in London." *Although, it would help if my business partner didn't keep heaping more work on me and hogging all the credit.*

"If you change your mind, you know where to find me. I assure you that my members pay handsomely. But if they offer to share a drink with you, you can politely make an exit." Gideon nods to the sword in Alaric's hand. "Or take the not-so-polite route."

"No one is going anywhere near Winnie's neck," Alaric growls.

"Tell that to our killer, if Winnie's plan goes off."

"The only room we have left to organise is this one." I gesture to the kiln, trying to get them off the subject before Alaric turns his friend into an attractive platter of sushi. "It adjoins the ballroom, so I understand you'll need it for feeding during the event. We're moving the kiln and wheel to another room, but the only thing that's stumping me is what to do with all the pots and mugs. They're far too pretty just to throw away—"

"Perhaps Alaric might offer them to Perdita as a wedding gift. Although they will need an army of Thralls between them to fill them with sweet nectar."

I whirl around. Callista has snuck up behind us, completely silently. Alaric darts across the room to stand in front of me.

Callista's smile to her son is cold. "Your Thrall informs me that you wish to see me. Have you made a decision about the ball?"

Alaric's fingers knit in mine. "I will not marry Perdita at the ball. You'll have to find another way to forge this alliance."

She sighs. "Very well. I am disappointed. You were once my favourite warrior. It's been a long time since I had to stick one of my children's heads on a spike on the castle walls, but it's always an effective deterrent for rebellion. I really should do it more often."

"You're not going to execute Alaric, either," I say, trying to keep my voice steady. "We have another plan."

"Alaric, it's speaking." Callista makes a face. "You should tell it not to do that, lest it finds its tongue ripped out."

Alaric's hand rests on the sword at his side in a way that is both threatening and *insanely* hot.

Not engaged to a vampire. Fake-engaged only.

"You will listen to what my betrothed has to say."

"Are you trying to make me ill before my evening drink?" Callista snaps her fingers, and her Thrall appears in the doorway, swaying slightly on his feet. He pulls down the collar of his shirt, and my stomach churns.

She's not going to feed in front of us, is she?

"I think you'll like this plan, Lady Valerian." Gideon pulls over a wingback chair for her. "It will appeal to your flair for the dramatic. And I personally would prefer both Alaric and Winnie to keep their heads attached to their bodies. They are ever such delightful company."

Callista makes another face, but she settles herself into the chair. The Thrall kneels at her side, but she contents herself with petting his head like a puppy.

"We have a way for you to create your spectacle at the ball *and* solidify your alliance with the Midnight Court without killing Alaric or forcing him to marry Perdita," I explain. "You will unmask the vampire murderer who is hiding in this community."

"You can administer the Mora at the ball," Alaric says, a hint of disgust in his voice.

Callista narrows her eyes at me. "You do know what I enjoy, son. I'm listening."

"We know that a vampire murdered Danny O'Hare by way of husking," Gideon says. "That vampire has thus far escaped both human and vampiric justice. But as we know, once a vampire husks a human, their hunger cannot be sated any other way. The killer hasn't struck again, but they will find it difficult to resist. And as they have done this husking in broad moonlight, knowing their actions would be noticed by our kin, they are the type who thrives on being the centre of attention. They will not miss your ball. After all, you've invited anyone who's anyone in the vampire world. They will enjoy listening to the gossip, knowing that they are safe ... until they're not. When the time is right, you will unmask the killer for everyone to see."

"You'll be the heroine," I add.

Callista licks her lips. Her fingers play with the Thrall's neck. "And who, precisely, will I be unmasking?"

"We don't know yet, but we have suspects," Gideon says.

"*And* a way to draw the killer out of hiding," I point to my own chest. "Fresh human blood, ripe for the taking. We'll have human staff at the ball, listening and gathering information, tempting the killer out of hiding. And not just any humans – we'll have the Nevermore Murder Club and Smutty Book Coven – the best amateur supernatural detectives the world has ever known."

Probably the *only* amateur supernatural detectives the world has ever known, but Callista doesn't need to be reminded of that.

"You propose to be bait for this killer?" Callista's eyes burn into me. "And to bring more un-Thralled humans to my ball?"

Alaric's jaw works, but he doesn't protest. I square my shoulders and meet Callista's cold gaze. "I do."

"And my son will have you on his arm?" Her nails dig into the Thrall's flesh. "A human as his ... *betrothed*, in direct violation of our laws."

"Unlike the taboo of husking, the restrictions on human/vampire relations have been outdated for years," Gideon says easily. "The law is to prevent the risk of Dhampir, but now that there are many ways to ensure a human woman cannot become pregnant, the law is no longer required."

"*Contraception*," Alaric says proudly, as if the word itself is magical.

I suppose, in a way, it is.

"Vampire and human relations are a hot topic right now. I know your conservative court will baulk at the idea of changing this law, but it's already being discussed in progressive circles and considered by the Midnight Court," Gideon explains. "The Americans have already done away with their Dhampir restrictions."

Alaric explained to me that American vampires didn't fall under the court system, but had split off decades ago and were looked after by a large and influential tech company.

"I don't care what those crazed capitalists do," Callista spits.

"No, but you do care about making this Nightshade Court and Midnight Court alliance work, and if the Lady of Agony shows her approval for a human and Upyr relationship while also administering the Mora to a known husker, that will send a message to all factions that while you have no issues dealing out justice in accordance with our savage ancient laws, you are willing to bend to accommodate new ways for our kind to exist in the world," Gideon explains. "My members will be as impressed by your progressive thinking as they are by your brutality. It will play well for you politically, even more so than if you were to wed Alaric and Perdita."

"Opening the doors to human and vampire relations could have many other benefits, too," I add. "New alliances, business opportunities, maybe even wars that need vampire mercenaries – you could keep those rebels too busy and sated by bloodlust to think about crossing you."

Alaric's eyes fall on me, dark with surprise. I grin at him. I've learned a little about psychology dealing with my clients. *I know how to make spoiled, rich bitches do things they don't want to do.*

I've just never tried it on a warlordess before.

"It *has* been a long time since I've administered the Mora." Callista's tongue licks her lips. "Although I am disgusted by the idea of humans and vampires lying together, it is a small price to pay to solidify my power. Very well, since Gideon and Alaric seem convinced this will work, I am willing to try it. But the killer *must* be unmasked by the Witching Hour or I will choose another head to place upon my favourite spike."

She smiles at me. Cold fear drips down my spine.

"And what of Perdita?" Alaric asks.

"She has campaigned for a relaxing of the rules regarding human relations, although I believe it's because she wishes to keep some flimsy human artist as a pet. Leave it to me to convince her to go along with this wild plan."

"Thank you, Mother." Alaric offers her a bow of his head, although his eyes never leave her face.

"Now that we have decided, make your plans as you will. If you'll excuse me," Callista rises, snapping her fingers for her Thrall to follow. "I'll need to sharpen my sword. But first, it's time for breakfast."

She sweeps out of the room, leaving a cold spot behind her.

Alaric stares at me with awe. "I don't know how you convinced her."

I grin. "I'm magical."

"Now we just have to get this book club to agree to help us."

"They'll agree," I say, although I sound more certain than I feel. "They cannot resist a supernatural mystery. All we have to do is lay the perfect vampire trap."

The Nevermore Murder Club and Smutty Book Coven Group Chat

Komal: Winnie, you volunteered us to WHAT?

40

Winnie

Mum: Winnie, it's not fair, I've been doing so well with my cleaning, but the council lady came again and she's issued me with a notice that says they're going to condemn the house if I don't make it the way she wants it.

GRIMDALE SEXUAL HEALTH CLINIC: Winifred Preston, thank you for booking your appointment for a non-hormonal copper IUD. We look forward to helping you manage your sexual health.

Now that we have our plan for the ball, all I have to do is convince the ladies in the Nevermore Murder Club and Smutty Book Coven to help us. I've given them the broad strokes over the group chat, but I plan to lay on the Winnie Wins charm at the Midsummer Festival. I offered up Alaric and myself as volunteers and told them we'd treat them all to dinner at the pub afterwards. I'm hoping that if they spend some time with him (and he pays for all the drinks), they'll like him as much as I do and agree to be vampire bait to help him.

For now, we need to make sure that the castle is ready for the ball. And that means breaking the back of our final room. After my appointment at the Grimdale Sexual Health Clinic to get an IUD put in (because you can never be too careful when you're sleeping with a hot vampire who could impregnate you with an iron-toothed monster) I put on my Get Shit Done playlist and Alaric and I sort the last of his sculpting tools, throw out the broken ones, and stack the clay neatly in a room near the back of the castle.

All that's left to do now is find some use for the towering wall of ceramic pots.

"She agreed to that too easily," Alaric says as he regards the mugs.

"Your mother? You're being a pessimist. She loves you in her own violent, terrifying way. I don't believe she was really going to kill you—"

My phone beeps. It's my mother again.

Mum: I tried to apologise to Ken. I left a box of Reggae Reggae Sauce from Savemart on his front step, because I know it's his favourite. But he tossed the carton over the fence. Can you believe it? The nerve of some people. I can't believe I ever considered them friends.

I tap out a vaguely supportive message. There's no point explaining to my mother that Ken probably saw a box of unsolicited BBQ sauce on his porch as a threat, not a peace offering.

"Someone's messaging you a lot?" Alaric's nostrils flare. "It's not Patrick, is it?"

"Jealous, husband?"

"I am jealous of the sun, for it kisses your skin where I cannot. I am jealous of that coffee you're drinking, for it touches your lips ..."

"Okay, okay, I get the idea. It's my mother." I tap out another message dissuading her from writing WANKER in Reggae Reggae Sauce across his front window. "Difficult mothers aren't just for vampires, you know."

"Tell me about her."

"I—" The words *I can't* catch on my lips. Alaric spilled his heart to me beside the fire. He gave me everything, making sure that I knew all the darkest corners of his soul before I made my choice to stay. I should trust him enough to give him this tiny piece of me. "She's a hoarder."

"Like me?" Alaric raises an eyebrow.

"Not quite like you. She's not an artist like you. She's a compulsive shopper. She goes to the shops and whatever she sees, whether it's forty dented cans of mustard or a bright yellow umbrella, she tells herself that it will change her life. She gets such a thrill from finding a bargain or buying someone the perfect gift, but by the time she gets home the thrill has worn off so the bargain goes in one of her towering piles or the gift never makes it to the receiver. But the thing that makes her worse is that she hoards memories."

"Memories?"

"My mother sees a thousand connections between objects and thoughts and feelings and memories that I don't. You're like her in that way. Only she stores her memories and dreams in objects. So to her, if you throw away the object, you throw away all the happy things associated with it, or the future she imagines for herself. Each item she collects is part of an ideal world she's creating for herself. Which makes your life difficult when you're her daughter and you're being crushed beneath piles of your own childhood drawings and school textbooks."

Reginald appears silently at my side and hands me a mug of his famous chocolate, iced instead of hot, since the night is warm. I wrap my fingers around the mug, letting the spicy, sweet scent steady me against the bitter memories.

"She has always been messy, but it was just part of her personality. She's so much fun. We never had a lot of money growing up, but she always tried to make everything special for me. She would spend hours doing crafts with me, or inventing wild games, or decorating cakes with pick 'n' mix lollies into whatever animal or cartoon character I was obsessed with that year. Those early years, I remember Dad being beautifully, giddily in love with her. He called her his 'wild spirit'."

"To be that in love is a precious thing," Alaric says sombrely. His eyes are fractured obsidian shards.

"Precious things can break." I force back a tear that itches the corner of my eye. "Dad was injured in his factory job before I was born, which meant he got a payout so we bought our small house, and he was on a benefit so he didn't have to work. Mum worked part-time at a shoe shop, so they were home with me a lot. I didn't have a lot of friends but I was never lonely because I always had them to play with.

"I think the hoarding started when my dad decided he didn't want to sit around at home any longer. He got a job driving lorries. He was away from home a lot, and when he was home, he was tired and cranky. Everything about Mum seemed to annoy him. I think in the beginning, she started buying things to cheer herself up, but it became this vicious cycle she couldn't snap out of. Dad would come home and there would be another pile of boxes in the hall or on the sofa, and they'd fight, and she'd go out and buy more boxes, and so on. But even then it was manageable. We could still use the kitchen and bathroom. She kept her clutter out of the bedrooms.

"I don't remember a specific time when things got worse. My mum started to obsess about keeping mementos. I remember once, my dad wanted to get rid of an old vacuum cleaner that no longer worked and Mum wouldn't let him because they'd been given it as a wedding gift from my cousin, and throwing it out was like throwing away their entire marriage.

"In the end, that's exactly what he did. I woke up one morning for school and he was gone and Mum was crying. And after that, the hoarding got worse. She filled the hallway, so we had to climb over boxes to get to our bedrooms. She stacked so many Savemart boxes in the kitchen and it became so riddled with cobwebs and maggots that we couldn't get to the fridge or oven, so most of our meals were take-aways or crackers and cheese. I had to keep making excuses for why I couldn't have friends over to the house so they didn't see the way we lived. I could hear rodents moving through the stacks of papers while I slept. The winter before I left, the floor in her bedroom rotted through and her bed fell into the sitting room." I take a deep breath and try to resist the shame this story stirs in me. "I left the day I turned eighteen, but that house still has a chokehold on me. I worry about her constantly. She's always sick and the neighbours complain and every time I try to clean she gets upset that I'm throwing away her things and ..." Suddenly, through the trauma of sharing this with Alaric, a light switches on in my brain about something completely different. "*That's it!*"

"What's it?"

I raise my mug to my lips as I stare at the rows and rows of perfect little ceramic pots. The idea forms in my head. Another brilliant Winnie Wins idea.

"I have figured out how you're going to keep your end of our bargain."

Alaric looks pained. "I've already agreed to attend this absurd pagan festival."

"Yes, but attending is passive, and we need to disrupt your habits. So we're going to *participate*. I don't want to throw your ceramics away. They're beautiful. But there are more here than we could hope to use in a lifetime. Even one of your lifetimes. But *other* people could use them—"

"Stop thinking what you're thinking this moment."

"I am a *genius*. This will be a good lesson for you if you're really serious about changing your ways." I pick up my phone and dial. "Hey, Komal, it's Winnie. Listen, do you have room for another stall at the Midsummer Festival ...?"

41

Alaric

Callista: Perdita is concerned about her own position in court. She's determined to go ahead with the marriage and fight together with you to change the vampire/human laws. She says that you can keep your human toy at court with you if you return as her husband. It is a reasonable offer, Alaric. If you want this to go your way, you and your human toy will have to step up your efforts to convince Perdita to reject you.

"We could skip this part of the plan if you wish," I tell Winnie as my hand closes around the handle of the dining room door. Perdita's tinkling laugh pierces the thick wood.

Winnie's lip wobbles, but she squares her shoulders. "Part of the job of your fake-fiancée is scaring away the woman who wants to be your *real* fiancée, and I take pride in a job well done. We need Perdita to decide this marriage isn't for her, and the only thing I can think of is to show her that you can't be trusted to keep up appearances at court."

"I won't allow either of them to hurt you, and if at any time you wish to retreat, we can—"

"Alaric, open the damn door."

I push open the wooden entryway to the dining room. It's brightly lit by a row of long column candles resting on mismatched silver holders down the centre of the banquet table. My mother sits at the head, and Perdita at her side, her chair pushed back from the table and her long fingers wrapped around the neck of her cello as she draws the bow across the strings.

I recognise the song she plays – a mournful tune we wrote together when I first arrived in her court, many moons ago. A song that always makes me think of Hrodebert and all that I've lost. Her eyes flutter open, and she dares a thin smile as she draws her bow across the final note.

Perdita is still playing for keeps.

I don't want to put her in an untenable position by rejecting her. I want her to come out of this with everything she wants as well. Perdita deserves that much for agreeing to our mothers' wild marriage scheme in the first place.

I pull Winnie towards the other end of the table. Mother's and Perdita's Thralls move around the room, lighting candles and trying in vain to stack the paintings and artefacts I hid from Winnie into the corner.

Perdita wrinkles her nose as she sees Winnie. "The human is still here?"

"Of course. She is to be my wife." I pull out a chair for Winnie, before lowering myself into one beside her, placing my sword on the table in front of us both. Perdita must be reminded that she is a guest in *my* house, and I'm still a warrior of the Nightshade Court. "I thought Winnie might enjoy hearing the songs of my *past*."

I hiss the final word. During my years at the Midnight Court, I considered Perdita a friend, although I'd been careful to keep my heart safe from her as I hadn't with Hrodebert. I was her pupil in the ways of art and music and creativity, and in return I listened to her complaints about the machinations of court. She never wanted a husband, least of all a brutish outcast of the Nightshade Court. Her tastes run to her own sex. But she is the daughter of a queen – she has always accepted she will not marry for love, whereas I cannot entertain a union of convenience.

I want the whole world to know that Winnie belongs to me, and I to her, wholly and utterly.

"Play for us, Perdita," my mother orders.

"I'm bored of music. It must be time for supper." Perdita snaps her fingers, calling over her Thrall. Callista narrows her eyes, not pleased to be disobeyed.

Beside me, Winnie stiffens. Perdita smirks as she bids her Thrall to kneel beside her. He does this with the excited, stupefied look that all Midnight Court Thralls wear, a look that entranced me when I first arrived there but now makes me sick. Being in Thrall to pleasure is still a form of servitude.

Perdita obviously aims to frighten Winnie away, but I know she has a strength within her that Perdita cannot fathom.

And it's good that Winnie sees this, because the other night it seemed as if she was … curious. I need her to know what a vampire bite can do to a human, how addictive it can become.

I need her to understand because if she asks me again, I won't be able to resist her …

Perdita lowers her lips to her Thrall's neck. Her fangs drop, and she pricks his skin, sighing with pleasure as her fangs sink into his flesh.

The room bursts with the scent of fresh blood. My nails claw at the armrests of the chair. That hot, rich scent mingles with Winnie's strawberries and sunshine, and it takes every ounce of strength I possess not to throw the chair aside, fold her into my arms, and drink until we're both moaning with ecstasy.

Fresh blood …

It's been so long, and I am so weak for her …

I dare a look at Winnie. She sits ramrod straight, her gaze fixed on the Thrall's neck, where Perdita sucks with abandon, making little mewling noises in her throat. The Thrall's eyes roll back in his head, and he lets out a low moan of pleasure that makes my toes curl inside my boots.

Winnie's lips purse. She digs her nails into her palm. But is she afraid … or …

"A little supper sounds delightful." Callista snaps her fingers, bidding her Thrall to kneel. She sinks her fangs roughly into his neck, her throat working as she sucks down her fill. The air is so thick with bloodscent that I'm grinding my fangs against my lower teeth.

Winnie lets out a low whimper that shoots through my body and into my shaft, which tents indecently in my breeches. I can't move my hands to adjust myself or I will do something I regret.

The hunger is a beast tearing at my stomach, eating me from the inside.

My mother shoves her Thrall away and leans back with a happy sigh, not bothering to wipe the blood from her lips. She smirks at me as she holds her goblet beneath him while his blood flows freely from the wound, capturing every drop, knowing that each crimson tear falling from his neck drives me to the brink.

She wants to see me falter, to remind me of the monster I am inside. She still believes that Winnie could not love a monster. And as much as I hope otherwise, I truly expect Winnie to run for the door any moment now and never come back.

"Care to join us, son?" Callista holds up the goblet. "We can toast your unconventional engagement. Unless your little wife-to-be has changed her mind?"

I give Winnie another moment to make her choice. It's all I can give her before the hunger becomes too much. But she doesn't move from beside me.

A faint moan escapes her lips. The same moan she made the first time I kissed her.

And I am *gone*.

"Certainly, we will join you, Mother."

I snap out my hand and wrap my fingers around Winnie's small wrist, yanking her out of her chair and into my lap. She wriggles a little, settling her knees on either side of me. Her eyes widen as she feels the obscenity of me between her legs, with my mother and my arranged fiancée in the room with us.

Every brush of her against my needy skin is exquisite torture.

"Alaric—"

"Trust me," I whisper, my voice hoarse with bloodlust.

I tilt her head towards me, wrapping my fingers against her neck. Every movement is agonising for all the things I want to do to her. A vein pulses beneath her skin, so hot and ripe and delicious. But I have made her a promise, so I must sate my hunger with whatever she can give me.

I bend and capture her lips in mine, white-hot need coursing through me. Her mouth tastes sweet, so sweet. It's been centuries since I've tasted fresh strawberries bursting on my tongue, but she makes me remember. She makes me wish for things I cannot have with a hunger that is *more* than I can bear.

I am floating, dizzy and drowning in sweetness, my hands roaming over her body in worship. The little moans she makes in my mouth are so needy that I almost believe she craves a monster.

But does Perdita believe it? Does she know this show is also for her, to convince her that marrying me means wedding a vampire so saturated in sin and forbidden desire that she will never recover her reputation?

Winnie's fingers twine in my hair, pulling me closer. She grinds against me, pushing my head down towards her neck, her head falling back so that my fangs scrape her skin and I yearn, I want, I *crave* …

This woman will ruin me …

"I've lost my appetite." Perdita kicks her Thrall away and storms from the room.

"Careful, son." Callista stands to leave, setting the goblet of blood down beside me as she walks to the door. "Remember how easily you can break your toys."

Her two Thralls crawl after her on their hands and knees, and the door clicks shut behind them.

The blood in the goblet and the scent of strawberries threaten to drive me over the abyss of my control. I drop my arms back to the chair, tearing the leather to ribbons.

"Winnie," I breathe against her soft, warm skin. "You should leave. This was a mistake. I can't control myself for long. The blood …"

"I want to know," she whispers. "I want to know what it means to have all of you, Alaric. Because I don't think you're a monster. I don't think anything about this is wrong."

I try to push her off, but she clings to me and I'm so *weak* for her. Her blood pulses beneath my lips and all I have to do to taste it is to lean forward and press my fangs against her. "I don't want to take from you—"

"It's not taking if I give it freely. It's what a good fiancée would do for her betrothed."

I shove her again, but she crawls over my lap and I can't deny her any longer. I tear away from her neck and crush my lips to hers, giving her a final chance to leave because I no longer have the strength to force her away.

When her tongue caresses mine, a guttural groan escapes from deep in my throat.

One taste of her isn't enough anymore.

Wrapping my arms around her waist, I pull her close, her body moulding against mine like two pieces of the same sculpture fitting together in perfect harmony.

My shaft presses against her belly button, and the little vixen teases me, wriggling against me, poking the monster who has lain dormant for so long.

A low growl forms in my throat as I topple into the void. The world shrinks away, my vision narrowing as her heartbeat thuds in my ears.

I lunge forward, pulling her against me before pushing her back against the table, crushing her body with mine as I crawl toward her neck, my tongue reaching out to taste …

… blood.

Just a drop and I'm roaring, bucking against her, brutal and beastly and lost in my hunger. But that one taste gives me strength, clarity. I remember that I didn't bite her yet. I blink and Winnie comes into focus beneath me, her golden eyes hooded with lust and a streak of red soaking her shirt.

Inhaling the air, I try to still myself.

This isn't her scent. That isn't her blood.

My eyes follow the trail. I must have upset the chalice when I flipped her onto the table.

Winnie's eyes flicker to the blood on her shirt.

"Is this what you want?" she asks breathlessly.

My gaze narrows back to hers. Her chest heaves as she skims her fingers against the still warm blood now gliding down her neck.

She swipes the thick liquid down her chest, pulling her shirt further down to expose the expanse of her cleavage peeking out of her lacy bra.

"Do you want to bite me, Alaric?"

"Winnie, I want everything you have to give me," I whisper, running my fingers down the swell of her breasts. "Your blood, your soul, your heart."

"The second and third aren't up for grabs just yet, but tonight, you can have my blood." She dares a tiny smile. "I consent. I want to know what it feels like. What I taste like to you."

Keeping my eyes on hers, I bend down, running my tongue along her skin, lapping up the trail of drying blood.

It takes the edge off. It makes me groan and makes my shaft twitch.

But it doesn't sate my hunger. It doesn't taste like strawberries and sunshine.

I know how badly I want to taste her. How much pleasure we'll both get from it.

But I also know how to make it even more worth the wait.

Winnie rolls her head to the side, exposing the exquisite curve of her neck and that tempting vein just above her collarbone. But I ignore it, licking a trail of blood from her breast, chasing it with little nips, careful not to break her skin with my fangs just yet. My fingers work open the buttons of her shirt as I continue my descent down her stomach.

"Aren't you going to bite my neck?" she asks, goosebumps prickling her skin. "Don't you want to?"

She actually sounds hurt, as if I'm rejecting her. As if I could ever deny her.

"Oh, Winnie, the things I want where you're concerned would terrify you. I have imagined this night in such exquisite detail that I half wonder if I've dreamed you into being. So yes, I will bite you, but I wish to savour you like a fine wine, and that means you're going to have to be a good girl and wait."

I bow my head and continue my trail down her stomach, kissing the bare skin where her trousers are belted around her perfect waist.

"I … I don't understand. I thought that …" Her voice catches as I unhook her leather belt and slowly pull her trousers over her voluptuous hips, torturing myself with the slow reveal of her body. Her petals are bare to me, and when the scent of her arousal fills the air, I let out another low growl of satisfaction.

"No panties, Winnie?"

"No," she manages to gulp.

"You're going to be the death of me," I whisper as I slowly run my tongue down the centre of her.

"Too—Oh! Too late, vampire."

Her joke falls limp from her lips, replaced by another gasp as I dip my tongue against her, tasting the sweetness of her juices. How is it that I can no longer taste food and yet she is the finest feast?

I have to keep my fangs from piercing her delicate skin. To bite her here, on her first time, would be cruel. But now that I taste her, I wonder if perhaps I have that kind of cruelty in me.

Winnie whimpers as her thighs tremble around me.

I want to devour every part of her, but I take my time, licking just the sides of her mound then the softest swipe against her centre.

"Alaric, please," she begs, bucking her hips, pushing herself closer to my lips.

"Please what, *Bonne Vivante* Winifred?" I trail my finger down her wet entrance, prolonging the exquisite torture.

"Please let me come," she pants.

"No, I don't think so." I run the tip of my finger around her entrance again, dragging it out.

Her eyes flutter closed as she leans her head back. "This is torture."

"Torture, is it? Do you mean, in the same way you have tortured me since you arrived, strutting around my castle with your exquisite scent, driving me to such agonising hunger that I barely recognise myself? That kind of torture?"

"Y-y-yes …"

I smile as I blow a small breath just over her entrance.

Winnie's hands go to my head, gripping the tendrils of my hair, trying in vain to push me down.

But I don't give in that easy.

"Such a greedy little thing," I tsk.

In a movement too quick for her to register, I grip her wrists, pinning them above her head with one hand. I lean her to the side, her hips at an angle so I can still hold her down while having access to her beautiful pussy.

She wriggles her hands against mine, trying to free herself, but I have five hundred years of supernatural strength and experience against her.

Laughing, I breathe against her mound. "Still so greedy."

"Please, Alaric, please."

"Since you asked so nicely, I'll give you a little taste."

I run my tongue down her slit. Her hands may be trapped, but her legs come up to wrap around me, trying to clamp my face against her. But I'm not giving her what she wants.

I press lightly on her stomach with my free hand, pinning her to the table. I slowly run my tongue up and down, just enough to get her worked up before pulling back and glaring sternly at her.

She whimpers, pushing her hips up again as if she can somehow pull an orgasm from the air.

"You're so beautiful like this," I murmur, hooking one finger inside her. She's so soft, so unbelievably warm. So *alive.*

The vein in her neck bulges as she cries, arching her back, but I pull out again, licking her arousal from my fingers.

I could torment her all night like this, listening to those moans of frustration. But sucking sunshine from my fingers flares my hunger to the brink. I cannot hold back any longer.

Diving back into her pussy, I lap up every bit of her sweetness, feeling her thighs begin to shake around me.

Her moans begin to intensify and I know this is the moment.

While keeping my eyes locked on hers, I slowly lick up to her clit, circling it with my lips before piercing the very tip of the hardened bud with my fangs.

My mouth fills with her essence, sharp and sweet and more delicious than I could ever have imagined. She tastes of every good memory, every perfect day, every stolen happiness rushing at me all at once. I could drown in her ambrosia and call it the sweetest death.

I have waited, I have wanted, but in all my darkest imaginings, I couldn't have dreamed of such perfection.

Winnie's cries fill my ears as she comes hard around me, the mixture of her arousal and blood filling my lips – the closest to heaven a monster like me will ever get.

She pushes her pussy closer, her thighs pulsing around me as she continues coming all over my face. More of her blood spills into my mouth, the pleasure of it nearly sending me over the edge of my own release.

I want nothing more than to keep tasting her forever.

To sup my fill of her nectar.

It takes everything I have to pull back, wiping her arousal and blood from my chin.

I'm sick. I've become everything I've long despised about my kin. Winnie should be running for the hills right now.

But I'm not certain I believe myself anymore, not when the woman I love is still writhing beneath me, lost in the throes of bloodthrall. Not when her lips fall open and she lets out those delicious little moans as she rides out the exquisite pleasure of a vampire's bite.

I could watch Winnie like this for hours. If I kept drinking from her, she'd sustain her release for hours. But I don't want to scare her with that just yet.

Instead, I collapse into the ruined chair, my own arousal swollen and painful as I give her space to return to me. I lick every last morsel of her from my lips. There is a smear of blood on her inner thigh, which I lean in and clean for her, but otherwise, the tiny wound has already closed over thanks to the properties of my saliva.

"That was …" she breathes, her chest heaving.

"Mmmmm."

"I don't remember *that* on page sixty-four."

My laugh is cut off as she lunges for me, sliding off the end of the table and straddling my hips on the chair as she crushes her lips to mine.

I shouldn't give in, I know. Winnie needs time to rest, for her human body to recover from the blood loss and what she's just experienced. But it's impossible to say no to that hot mouth on mine, those perfect breasts pushing against my chest, and her heartbeat roaring in my ears.

I wrap my arms around her, pulling her naked body closer to mine.

She paws at my clothes, peeling off my shirt as she slides to the floor so I can shove off my pants and underwear.

Before I can protest, her mouth is on my hardened cock, swallowing the whole thing as she bobs her head up and down, those dark eyes never leaving mine.

"Fuck, Winnie," I mutter, pumping my hips to fuck that beautiful face of hers.

But as close as I am, I don't want to finish there.

"I want to be inside you, *wife*."

Winnie doesn't say a word as her eyes lock on mine. Candlelight sparkles in her golden irises. I reach for one of the golden packets I put in my pocket after our first night together, but she stays my hand.

"I have a gift for you," she grins. "We don't need a condom."

I darken. "The risk of Dhampir—"

"I *know*, Alaric. That's why I had a copper IUD installed. It's another type of contraception, and it's even more effective. It's a little device that stays inside me and makes sure I don't get pregnant."

I'm so shocked that I lean back in the chair, studying her. "You have a contraception *inside* you?"

She nods, her body taut with desire.

I can barely speak through my hunger. "I can feel all of you, bare, without restraint?"

In response, Winnie stands and mounts me, inch by exquisite inch, sliding her wetness down my cock.

I grip hard onto her hips, guiding her. I know she wants it fast by the way she slides against me, but I need it slow. I need to take my time and feel every inch of her.

Winnie lets out a gasp as she rocks her hips and I slide home.

"You are exquisite." I wrap my arms around her, pressing her against my chest, her racing human heart against my immortal one. "I wish I had eternity to worship every inch of you."

"You *do* have all of eternity," she huffs as she grinds down against me.

"True, but *you* don't. I have only a blink of an eye to hold you." I choke back the emotion swelling in my chest as she rides me hard, drawing me nearer to release. "I have one blink to show you what you're missing."

"Alaric, you—"

I sink my teeth into her neck.

The sensation is of falling. I fall through starlight as her blood rushes between my lips. I tumble like an autumn leaf, tossed on a crimson river, drenched in sunlight and the blush of summer's first fruit.

Winnie quakes around me as the bloodthrall carries her along her own crimson river. Her screams fill my ears as my mouth fills with her blood.

Ecstasy.

I can't hold it in anymore as I grip hard onto her hips, spilling myself into her as I suck as much blood as I dare to take from her.

It costs me my soul to pull away. I lick at her wound to seal it before I collapse against her, breathing in the fresh warmth of her flesh as she gasps and shudders against me, still suspended in her own pleasure.

Winnie clings to me as her cries quieten. The scent of her blood and arousal tickles my nostrils. Her heart rate slows until we are beating in sync, her chest rising and falling against mine.

I reach beneath the table for the cord to ring for Reginald. The bell tinkles deeper in the house.

"Why did you do that?" Her eyes widen, but she makes no move to grab her clothing. "He'll see us like this—"

"He'll leave some food outside the doors. You need to eat something. You've lost blood." I bow my head with remorse. "More blood than I should have taken, I'm so sorry. You tasted so good, I … I had to fight for control."

"If tasting my blood feels like *that*, you can have more."

"Don't tempt me, human," I growl, my fingers digging into her hips.

"Now that you mention it, food does sound good." Winnie rests her head on my shoulder, her eyes fluttering closed. I stroke her hair, humming softly to her and listening for the sound of Reginald leaving a tray of food in the hall.

"That was … Wow," she murmurs, her body slackening against mine.

"We can do this every night," I whisper back, twisting her golden hair in my fingers. "If you stay at Black Crag with me."

"As your fake-fiancée?" Her voice is slurred as sleep begins to pull her under.

I pause, terrified to say what I'm about to confess. "As my everything."

But Winnie doesn't answer. She's sound asleep.

Everything about this night is perfect.

Even the exquisite torture of it – the night will end, and unless I can convince her otherwise, after the ball Winnie will return to London and I'll never see or taste her sunshine again.

But at least there are no secrets between us anymore … save one.

That I am hopelessly in love with Winnie Preston, and the monster in me wishes for an eternity that can never be.

42

Alaric

"It's perfect," Winnie says as she watches Reginald set down his enormous cast-iron pot and fiddle with the knobs on the portable stove. I set down a cooler of ice, which Winnie suggested in case people want their chocolate cold instead of hot. "We'll be the most popular booth of the Midsummer Festival," she announces.

"As I feared." I glare at Reginald, who is pointedly *not* looking in my direction. He's been avoiding me ever since he agreed to Winnie's crazy suggestion. I could not refuse either of them, especially not with my mother watching our every move.

She hasn't spoken to me since she left the dining room, but I overheard her and Perdita while they were on their evening walk. Perdita is growing concerned that I am too soaked in perversion to be a good fit at court, and that the proposed marriage may have the opposite effect than her mother wished. "I can't risk the future of the Blood Chastain on Alaric's unpredictable nature."

"I thought the Midnight Queen sought to be more progressive?" My mother's smile could shatter bone. "Improve our relations with humans?"

"Indeed. But I think this would be a step too far, even for her." Perdita paused. "And for me. I think you are right, Callista. I renounce my claim on Alaric, and I shall attend the ball as a representative of the queen to observe our new allies at work."

Winnie's crazy plan is working. If only I could find it in me to feel pleased. But every hour closer to the ball is an hour closer to putting her in danger, and another hour closer to Winnie inevitably leaving Black Crag.

Callista and Perdita are here tonight, dressed in their finery with no heed for the heat the humans feel in the air. They wander slowly around the village green, chatting with Gideon and his friends and clients. I wonder if among the crowd who flutter around Gideon like carnivorous butterflies is Danny's killer.

I wonder if they're whispering about Lord Alaric Valerian out in public with an un-Thralled human. I wonder if they all know about *contraception*.

Seeing me and Winnie together, openly in love, will make them even more excited for the ball. More fodder drawing the husker into the light.

Winnie is, of course, oblivious to the bloodsucker politics swirling around her. She affixes her handmade sign to our booth and declares us officially open for business. A small crowd has already gathered on the green to peruse the stalls and put their orders in at the pub.

"Why is the iced hot chocolate so expensive?" a grey-haired man complains as he squints at Winnie's handwritten sign. I wonder what he'd taste like drizzled over ice cream.

"Because you get a handmade ceramic mug with it, and you get to keep the mug," Winnie smiles, undeterred by my future dessert's rudeness.

"Oh, how fun! I'll have mine hot." A woman selects a mug with a speckled green glaze from the stack I've laid out on the table and hands it to Reginald. He fills it to the brim with hot chocolate, drops in two homemade marshmallows, and passes it back to her.

"I guess I'll have one, too. Iced, thanks." The man choses a dark blue glazed mug with two handles and reluctantly hands over his cash to Winnie. But when he takes a sip of Reginald's chocolate, his whole face lights up.

"Pearl!" He waves at a lady over at the tea cosy stall. "You have to try this!"

Soon, we have a crowd of people around our table, exclaiming over the mugs as they choose their favourites. Warmth fills my chest. Reginald beams as they praise his chocolate, and Winnie is in the centre of it all, matching mugs to people's outfits and using words like "bespoke" and "artisanal". Two old ladies even come back for seconds.

"You must be Winnie, the newest member of the Nevermore Murder Club and Smutty Book Coven." One of the old ladies with blue-rinsed hair and a large carpet bag slurps her chocolate happily. "I'm Mabel Ellis, honorary lifetime member of the coven. I haven't been able to get to any meetings lately, thanks to this bung hip, but it won't stop me enjoying the festival. Oh, I must go, there's Mina and her lovely man, Heathcliff. I bet he'll want to say hello."

A line quickly forms at our booth. Reginald is pouring chocolate over ice as fast as his human arms can ladle and Winnie is so busy dealing with cash and dishing out marshmallows that people start asking *me* about the cups. Winnie promised me that I wouldn't have to talk to humans if I didn't want to, but I find myself picking up pots and showing off my favourite details.

I haven't shown another soul my work apart from Reginald and Winnie since I left the Midnight Court. It's quite intoxicating seeing humans enjoying my art without the promise of bloodthrall.

Not *quite* as intoxicating as Winnie's strawberry scent swirling around me or the bright smile she flashes me every time she catches me looking at her. Even as sated as I am by that taste of her blood, I find myself always turning back to her, as if she is my true north.

"Hello, Winnie." A startlingly beautiful man with a waterfall of black hair steps up to our table. Mina Wilde's hand is threaded through his arm, and her guide dog stoically waits as they peruse my table. Two small human children pause behind them, transfixed I presume by Mina's dog. "These pots are beautiful. Can Mina pick them up?"

"Hi, Quoth, Mina. Of course you can touch them. They're for using, not just for show. Alaric made them," Winnie calls over her shoulder as she turns to serve another customer.

"You made these?" The little girl's eyes bug out of her head. "All of them? Wow! You must just spend all of eternity making pots."

"That's true."

"I want to make a pot. Could you teach me?" her little brother asks.

"Your hands are too small," I say. "You could perhaps make a cup for a mouse."

"I want to make a cup for a mouse!" he says, his face screwing up in determination.

Winnie beams at me. I dare to wonder if perhaps I'm doing okay at talking to humans.

"These are beautiful." Mina runs her fingers over a textured pot. "I love the way they feel in my hands. We'll take four. Quoth, help me choose mugs for Morrie and Heathcliff."

"This one is perfect for Morrie," Quoth says as he picks up a tall pot with an icy blue glaze. "And that red one in your hand for Heathcliff. You know, Lord Valerian—"

"Call him Alaric," Winnie says, turning away before I can correct her.

"—Alaric." Quoth's silken hair falls over his eyes. "I'm an artist too, although I mainly work with paint. I've been experimenting with sculpture, since it's the medium Mina can still experience, but I have a long way to go before I'm as competent as you."

"A couple of centuries, at least," Mina says with a laugh.

"*Anyway*," Quoth continues. "I have a small gallery opposite Nevermore Bookshop. We display local artists and don't charge a rip-off commission. If you have more of these mugs, I'd love to have them in the gallery."

"I don't think that would be—"

"That would be amazing, Quoth!" Winnie cuts in. "I'll have Reginald drop you off a carload tomorrow."

As Quoth and Mina and the two kids wander away with their mugs of chocolate, that strange sensation settles in my chest once more. *My work displayed in a gallery alongside human artists? That should be abhorrent to me, so why do I feel so warm?*

Because I like the way it brightens Winnie's smile when I make an effort to be in the world.

Because if I want her to love me, I have to make her friends at least tolerate me.

Because … maybe I *want* her friends to tolerate me.

From across the green, my mother glares at me. According to her, we don't fraternise with our food.

I find myself smiling and waving at her, eliciting a deeper scowl. Tonight, not even the Lady of Agony can frighten me. I like talking to the villagers. They ask questions about the cups and how I made them. They praise Reginald's iced hot chocolate recipe with increasingly poetic epithets, and I believe his face might be in danger of breaking from smiling so hard.

Reginald has dedicated his long life to looking after my every need. It pleases me to see him put himself first for once.

And Winnie … she is radiant beneath the flickering glow of the torches and fairy lights that illuminate the green. She's wearing a floral blouse with a silk handkerchief tied around her neck, hiding the two pinpricks of my fang marks that haven't yet completely healed. Every time I see that scarf I taste her on my tongue again, and my shaft stiffens. She has not said anything about my rash words begging her to stay, but she has not declined, either.

She waves to her friends in the Nevermore Coven, who are busy with their own stalls or, in the case of Komal Ahuja, rushing about yelling instructions into a megaphone and shooting a devilish glare at a man in the corner. Winnie promises to introduce me properly to everyone later. I cannot decide if I'm honoured to meet her friends or terrified.

I'm still not certain we should be involving these humans in a ball hosted by the Lady of Agony, no matter how much experience with supernatural sleuthing they claim to have. But Winnie is convinced they are essential to her plan.

And the more time she spends with them, the more she smiles and that faraway look in her eyes dims.

Beside me, Winnie stiffens. I glance up, alert for danger.

Is the killer in our midst?

Worse. Patrick and Claire are here. They're eating cotton candy and laughing as they stride arm in arm up to our stall.

"Oh, look at these!" Claire picks up one of the taller mugs that I'd decorated with a bright pink glaze dribbled over the rim, as if a unicorn has thrown up inside. "These are adorable! And after I drink my chocolate, I can keep the cup? That's so clever—Oh, hi, Winnie!"

Claire beams at Winnie as if she only just noticed her, but I am certain Claire saw Winnie across the green.

Winnie's fingers seek mine beneath the table. I give her hand a squeeze. My fangs drop.

"Er, hi, Winnie." Patrick takes a step back. His eyes flick to me, and he quickly looks away. "And Albert, was it?"

"Alaric," I growl, lifting the corner of my lip to give him a glimpse of fang.

Patrick shudders.

"Darling, we have to get some mugs for our new place." Claire sifts through the pink-hued ones. "I think a set of six, for when we have friends like Winnie and Alaric over for dinner—"

I don't miss the desperate look Patrick shoots Winnie over his fiancée's shoulder. I may have been shut away from the world for centuries, but I *know* the meaning in that look. Patrick likes to *win*. He is a different type of collector than I am. I have a house filled with objects because they're safer and more interesting than people. Patrick likes to collect things – and people – to say that he owns them. He likes to feel as though he has the best prize. He's wondering if maybe he gave Winnie up too soon.

Winnie, thankfully, is blissfully unaware of her effect on Patrick. She stirs the hot chocolate, chatting away to the villagers lining up at our booth as if it's the most natural thing in the world. Beside her, I feel awkward – too tall, too dark, too undead.

I'd feel better with a sword in my hand.

And Patrick's head on a spike.

I am more like my mother than I like to admit.

I thought that when I bared my fangs at him last time, that would be enough to keep him away from Winnie. But this human doesn't know when to quit.

Patrick pays for two cups of hot chocolate and a set of six mugs. As he hands over his money, he leans in and whispers something to Winnie. He doesn't realise that with my superior senses, I hear every word.

"Winnie, can I meet you by the bookshop when the bonfire starts? Everyone will be distracted."

"Why?"

"I can't tell you now, but it's important. You need to come alone. I have something to tell you about your boyfriend and the murder that happened here a few weeks ago."

Winnie fumbles the cup she's holding. I catch it midair before it smashes on the ground, my eyes never leaving her face. She studies Patrick with a mixture of curiosity and … is that longing? Fear?

She nods, and returns to plonking marshmallows into people's drinks. But I can't return to my easy chatter with the humans. I glare at the back of Patrick's head, imagining how great it would look mounted above my fireplace.

43

Winnie

Mum: When are you coming back to live with me, darling? I've cleared the boxes out of your room. It's all clean and devoid of personality, just the way you like it. Oh, except for the sundresses. I've left a bunch on your bed. You'll thank me when you're married and pregnant.

Alaric goes all surly after Claire and Patrick stop by. I can't say I blame him. He would have overheard Patrick begging me to meet him later. Patrick isn't acting like himself. I watch him as Claire drags him over to Beth's Zen and Tonic stall. His eyes dart all around and he keeps his arm protectively around Claire's waist.

He was never touchy-feely like that with me.

But more than that, he looks spooked, as if he thinks a monster is about to leap out from behind the tea cosy stall and eviscerate him.

It's a good thing I convinced Alaric to leave his sword at home.

I turn back to Alaric, who scowls at Patrick's back. But then a little girl asks him to help her pick a mug, and he selects one of the slightly lopsided ones with a beautiful teal glaze that matches the ribbon in her hair.

"It's a fairy pot," she cries, handing the pot to Reginald so he can fill it with ice and chocolate. "For mixing spells."

"Of course," Alaric says. "But remember that fairies are tricksy, so you have to drink all your chocolate, or they will turn it into something gross, like boogers." The girl giggles.

"Attention, everyone!" Komal calls into her megaphone. "Please gather in the centre of the green. Stallholders, please close up shop for the next half hour. We will be lighting the bonfire in ten minutes. Ten minutes until the bonfire!"

"Would you like to watch the bonfire?" Alaric asks, his eyes black voids.

"I'd love that. But … are you okay? It doesn't remind you of, you know …" I lower my voice to a whisper. "Being burned alive?"

"Fire can heal as well as destroy, Winnie. I want to be wherever you are." He holds out his hand. "Shall we?"

I can feel the cool of his skin on my fingers. Reginald places a hot chocolate in my other hand and we wander through the villagers to find a place on the edge of the green. I can't help but notice that he's positioned us just opposite the entrance to Butcher Street, only a few steps from Nevermore Bookshop.

I glance around the crowd. I see Claire over by Beth and Isis, who are holding out torches for Gideon to light. She sees me and waves. Patrick isn't with her.

Is he already waiting for me at the bookstore? I glance over my shoulder, but the street is in shadow. I can't see a thing.

I turn back to the green. The villagers have piled wood and old pallets into a conical-shaped bonfire in the centre. School-children have placed little cloth dolls they made amongst the wood – offerings they burn for good luck for the year ahead. Atop the fire, someone has fixed a wooden silhouette of a man. I glance at Alaric, but he stares stoically ahead, unfazed.

Komal reads out a speech about the traditions of Midsummer Festival, and both Isis and the local parish priest offer blessings. Isis is in her element, capturing everyone's attention in a gold velvet dress that dances in the firelight, her head wreathed in a circlet of orange wildflowers. Maisie moves around the action, snapping pictures for the Gazette.

Beth joins Isis at the front of the crowd, their faces glowing as Dora lights their torches. Komal stands to the side, wearing her volunteer firefighter uniform, in case the blaze gets out of control.

Isis and Beth touch their flames to the petrol-soaked wood, and the fire roars to life. The heat smacks me in the face and I stagger back. Everyone cheers, and the pub band strikes up a jig that has Isis pulling people from the crowd to dance.

I pat Alaric's arm. "I'm just going to pop off for a sec. Don't let Isis coerce you into dancing. I want the first dance when I get back."

"Of course, my wife. Is everything okay?"

I know we're supposed to be pretending, but I wish he'd stop calling me that. It makes the butterflies dance every time. "Yes. I just need some air. I'll be back in a second."

His gaze lingers on my face. He nods. "Say hello to Patrick for me."

"I knew you heard him. You're not going to try and go with me?" I must've mistaken that jealous spark in his eyes.

Alaric doesn't take his eyes off the fire. "You may be my betrothed, but I do not command you, nor would I ever try. I can only warn you to be careful. Know that I am here, and I will fly to your rescue if you call my name."

"Thank you," I breathe.

Why does every word from this man's mouth sound like poetry?

As I hurry off towards Nevermore Bookshop, I can't stop thinking about the other night. I tug down the silk scarf around my neck and touch my fingers to the skin beneath, feeling the tiny bumps where Alaric's fangs bit me. A wave of pleasure sweeps my body simply from the memory.

That whole night was just … *wow.*

When I walked into that room with Alaric, I intended only to put on the best act of my life so that Perdita would be disgusted and not want to marry him. But at some point between that first breathtaking kiss and him *biting my fucking clit* I stopped acting.

I have been kidding myself.

This might have started as a fun infatuation, but I have fallen for that surly vampire *so damn hard.*

So hard that whenever I think of going back to London, I get a horrible queasy feeling in my gut, and it has nothing to do with my deteriorating relationship with Faye or my mother's sundress obsession.

I don't *want* to leave him.

And I'm *terrified.* Especially after Patrick …

Patrick. Where is he?

I'm standing in front of the bookshop, staring up at that strange interior. All the lights are off because Mina dragged her three husbands out for the evening. I'm itching to get back to the festival and Patrick is *nowhere.*

"Patrick?" I walk around the side of the shop, down the narrow alley that separates it from Celeste's bakery next door. "It's cooler over here away from the fire. I don't particularly care for freezing my tits off while I wait for you to—oh, *no.*"

My foot nudges a crumpled object on the ground. I pull my phone from my pocket and shine the light down, my stomach sinking into my shoes and my heart ramming itself up my throat.

Patrick lies across the alley at an awkward angle, his glassy eyes peering up at me. A smear of blood mars his perfect cheekbone, and he has a pair of fresh puncture wounds in his neck.

I scream.

The Nevermore Murder Club and Smutty Book Coven Group Chat

Isis: LADIES, DROP WHAT YOU'RE DOING. THERE'S BEEN ANOTHER MURDER!

Celeste: We know, Isis. We're all RIGHT HERE, waiting to give our statements to the police.

Beth: Well, Arabella isn't here. She never comes to these village things.

Arabella: That's because I haven't been hit over the head by the village pride stick. Do you need me, or can I stay tucked up in bed?

Isis: We're fine, Arabella. We'll message you if any of us need bail money. Sorry, I figured that it would be easier to talk in our chat so the police don't hear our theories.

Isis: There's no denying that it's a vampire. We all saw those fang marks. Danny's killer has struck again.

Komal: We know, Isis. We shouldn't all be on our phones like this. It might look suspicious.

Isis: Why? No one suspects us. Well, maybe Beth.

Arabella: Beth is rather shady.

Maisie: Beth doesn't have an alibi. She wasn't at her booth when Winnie screamed.

Beth: Hey, leave me out of this! I went to my car to get some more of my elixirs. They'd been selling really well until the murderer had to come along and ruin everything.

Komal: At least you'll still have a job after this! My first year as the chair of the Midsummer Festival and I've got a dead body. Councillor Durant will never let me within three feet of a village event again!

Dora: Panicking isn't going to do us any good.

Mina: Dora's right. We need to approach this rationally. We don't want to miss any important clues that could help us unmask the killer at the ball. Maisie, see if you can get any useful information out of the police. I'll go chat to my friend Jo, the medical examiner. Isis and Dora, do you have eyes on our main suspect?

Dora: She's standing over by the church, talking to that developer fellow from Sanctus Estate.

Winnie: His name's Gideon Blake. He's a friend of Alaric. Well ... I'm not sure if "friend" is the right term.

Dora: Are you doing okay, Winnie?

Winnie: I'm shaken up, but I'm okay. I'm worried about Claire. She must be so upset.

Beth: Why do you care about the harlot? I thought we hexed her?

Maisie: BETH!

44

Winnie

Faye: You're mad, Winnie. Why are you staying in a dusty old castle when we have a literal TV show in the works? Sometimes I just don't understand you.

I'M NEARLY ASLEEP ON MY FEET BY THE TIME THE POLICE SECURE the scene and get around to interviewing me about discovering Patrick's body. Alaric remains by my side the whole time, filling in details about our evening that I can't remember. The image I hold in my mind is Patrick's pale face frozen in terror and those two bloodied fang marks in his neck.

Patrick – I'm so, so sorry.

We have to catch this killer before they get anyone else.

"—and where were you around the time Ms Preston found the deceased's body?" DS Wilson's pen whirls across her pad.

"I was watching the bonfire when Winnie went to meet Patrick. I stood with Gideon Blake. He will confirm this. Patrick came to our booth earlier and asked to speak to Winnie privately." Alaric's jaw works, his hand firmly and possessively in the small of my back.

"And did that upset you, that Winifred was speaking to her ex-boyfriend?"

Alaric's smile is all teeth. "My fiancée may speak with whomever she chooses."

"Fiancée?" DS Wilson's gaze darts from Alaric to me, and back again. "You two are *engaged?* Didn't you only meet a month ago?"

"Our love came unannounced in the night, knocking down walls and lighting candles in the gloom," Alaric says simply, as if he's discussing the laundry, as though every exquisite word is fact.

I nod as if I'm not moved by his words. DS Wilson scribbles something else down, then turns to me.

"Ms Preston, you said that Patrick had recently dumped you, is that correct?"

"We broke up a few months ago, yes," I say frostily.

"What caused the breakup?"

"He cheated on me with Claire."

"I understand from his fiancée, Ms Dempsey, that you were taking this breakup rather poorly."

Really, Claire? Because I haven't answered your texts?

I glare over DS Wilson's shoulder at Claire. "Ms Dempsey has been my best friend since I was six years old, and she and my ex-fiancé were seeing each other behind my back for months. I wasn't thrilled, no, but I think I'm handling it quite well, considering. I haven't been sending him vicious texts or slashing his tires or hiding in his closet covered in whipped cream. Look, I know that I'm a suspect because I found the body and I was the one going to meet Patrick in a darkened alley, and I know you have Alaric as a suspect for the first murder, but he has an alibi in this case, so I'm begging you, please, *please* find who did this. Patrick didn't deserve this."

Tears well in my eyes. Patrick may have treated me badly, but he was a bright young guy with a thriving business and a geeky wine hobby and a whole future ahead of him. I loved him once and, even on my darkest nights after the breakup, I never wished for *this*.

"We'll be conducting a full investigation, don't you worry." Wilson snaps her notebook shut and regards me and Alaric with a knowing stare. "Ms Preston, both victims spoke to you within minutes of their deaths. If you think of anything you haven't told us, you know where to find me. While our investigation is ongoing, neither of you are to leave the village."

Great. My ex-fiancé is killed by a vampire and they suspect me.

Alaric pulls me close as Wilson stalks away. I sink into his arms, comforted by the strength of his body around me and the cool blade I feel in his pocket.

"I'm sorry for this, Winnie."

"You're not sorry," I sniff. "You wanted to hang Patrick from the battlements by his testicles."

"I'm sorry that you're upset. Shall I have Reginald take us home?"

I nod. Alaric wraps me tighter in his cool embrace. I burrow into his shirt, breathing his spicy winter scent and allowing the grief to flood over me. I hear Alaric murmuring softly, and realise that he's speaking to Reginald on his phone, telling him to pack up the stall and bring the car around.

I look up at him silhouetted in the pale moonlight, his jaw tight, his eyes flecks of cool obsidian as he remains on alert for a possible murderer skulking in the shadows. For an ancient vampire warlord, he can be so *sweet.* My chest tightens.

Even though there's a vampire killer on the loose, I've never felt safer than here in his arms.

A raven perches on the guttering above us, silently watching the scene unfold. It tilts its head toward me in greeting before flying off into the night. Reginald pulls up ten minutes later, and he and Alaric bundle me into the car.

Once settled into the backseat, Alaric pulls me against him again, stroking my hair while the tears finally spill over. I barely notice the harrowing drive back to Black Crag until Reginald pulls up in the inner courtyard.

"Get her inside," Reginald says. "I'll see to everything else."

Alaric lifts me out of the car, carrying me into the castle as though I weigh nothing at all. His brow furrows in concern.

"Are you okay?" he asks me as he settles me into my usual chair in the sitting room. "You're paler than the poor vegan whom Gideon once gave the Kiss."

I shudder. "Poor guy. What happened to him?"

"He was most aggrieved at having to drink human blood." Alaric kneels in front of the fire and starts stacking the logs. Something about seeing Lord Valerian performing this small manual task he usually leaves to Reginald makes me cry harder.

"Alaric, did you hurt Patrick?"

I didn't mean to blurt it out like that. His face collapses. I wish I could take the words back.

"I know that you must ask this question," he says, not looking at me. "I am, after all, the monster."

"No, I didn't mean … it's just that Patrick and Danny hurt me, and now they're both dead. I can't help but think that I'm at the centre of this and …"

"… and I am your monster."

I am your monster.

His words are caustic and soft and sad. But they make me feel anything but. They make my throat close over. They make me feel loved, adored.

Safe.

"If I were to kill Patrick, it would be face to face, in a fair fight," Alaric says. "Well, mostly fair. I know you don't understand all our laws and customs, so you cannot see a difference between the heinous things I have done and the heinous thing done to Patrick, but there *is* a vast difference. I have a difficult time believing *any* vampire capable of such a crime. Husking is an unspeakable act, one of our most forbidden atrocities. The Upyr responsible deserves whatever tortures my mother dreams up—"

Alaric breaks off mid-sentence. He leaps to his feet like a cat, his dark eyes scanning the room.

"Alaric, what's wrong?"

"There's someone in my castle."

"What?"

"I can *smell* them." He sniffs the air. "They smell like … patchouli."

Wait a second …

Alaric crosses the room with silent steps and thrusts an arm behind one of his enormous tapestries, pulling out a handful of strawberry-blonde hair to which is attached an Isis.

"Unhand me, vampire!" Isis grabs for one of her necklaces. "I have a charm to make me impervious to you! No, wait, that one's for werewolves … gimme a sec here …"

Isis starts furiously sorting through her necklaces. Alaric looks confused.

"Give it up, sis. None of those charms work." Dora emerges from behind the same tapestry, picking a cobweb from her hair. "Valerian, you should really dust behind these things."

"You—" Alaric starts.

"I suppose we should join the party." Maisie drags Mina and Oscar out from the tapestry behind my chair.

Celeste crawls out from inside the towering liquor cabinet, and Beth and Komal sheepishly wave from behind a third tapestry. Alaric looks like his head's about to explode.

"The whole Nevermore Coven is here?" I ask as Komal flops down beside Dora, her volunteer firefighter jacket covered in bonfire soot.

"Everyone except Arabella. She says she doesn't do surprise drop-ins on vampires, but really it's because she's just painted her nails and she doesn't want to move before they dry," Komal says.

"They dragged me along, too."

I yelp in surprise as Gideon pokes his head out from inside a large decorative urn.

"Hello, lovely Winifred. Sorry, Allie," Gideon shrugs. "They forced me to drive them over here, said they had to speak with you urgently. And I have your spare key, so …"

"You could have refused them," Alaric snaps.

"We're not good with no," Komal supplies. "Is this the hospitality we get for literally sticking our necks out for you?"

"What are you all doing *in my castle*?" Alaric's hands ball into fists. "Winnie's had a harrowing night. She should rest—"

"Rest is for the dead. Present company excepted." Isis finally gets her necklaces untangled. "The murderous vampire killed again tonight. We have to stop them before they hurt anyone else, so we're here to strategise."

Reginald appears in the doorway, a tray containing a hot chocolate and a glass of blood in his hands. His face pales in shock as he sees all the people. "My lord, I didn't know we had guests. And so *many* guests. And someone lit the fire. That's *my* job."

Gideon vaults out of the urn and grabs the blood from the tray. "Thanks, Jeeves. If we could get a round of hot chocolate for the ladies of the Nevermore Murder Club and Smutty Book Coven. And while you're at it, bring us a couple of bottles of Allie's finest vintage Dutch Prince."

"And maybe something hot to eat?" Isis pipes up.

"Winnie tells us you make amazing mince pies." Celeste rubs her stomach.

"I'm a raw vegan, but I'd make an exception for a mince pie," Beth adds. "That's how much Winnie raves about them."

Reginald disappears, looking a little shell-shocked. Alaric passes me the hot chocolate while Gideon settles himself into his chair. Mirabelle appears in the doorway and leaps onto the back of the sofa, hissing at Oscar as if warning him not to leave his dog smell on her favourite rug.

"This plan of yours for the ball," Alaric says. "I presume it's foolhardy and dangerous."

"How did you know that?" Mina looks aghast.

"It's almost as if our reputation precedes us," says Komal with a smile.

"We've been speaking to Gideon, who knows everyone who's anyone in the local vamp community—"

"He has even better contacts than Arabella, and he's infinitely less bitchy," adds Isis.

"—and we've come up with two top suspects," explains Maisie. "Arabella's client – Alyra Maythorn of the Blood Kincaid. Danny made advances at her while he worked as a handyman at Sanctus, and she was at the pub on the night of the murder. She was also at the Midsummer Festival, and I saw her having a heated conversation with Patrick shortly before the bonfire. But the second is someone Winnie brought to our attention."

"Baylor Godsven of the Blood Ptolemy." Gideon settles back into the chair, stretching his long legs across the rug. Beside me, Alaric's fingers curl into my arm. "He doesn't live on the estate, but in a large property near the village of Grimdale. He's been in trouble with the Mora before for sneaking into the bedrooms of young humans at night and doing things that are best not repeated in the company of ladies."

"I resent that," Komal makes a face. "I'm hardly a lady."

"We rescued a girl who was running from his castle," I say. "She said he wanted to 'drain her dry'."

"Yes, and my sources inform me that there are dark rumours about what Baylor gets up to on his estate with humans … who may not always consent. He's been outspoken in court politics about going back to the 'good old days' when vampires held dominion in Europe, and ridding ourselves of the laws we have to keep us secret and 'subservient' – his words, not mine. It's believable that Baylor's grown bold enough to try husking, although why he would risk the Mora by doing it out in the open is still beyond me … but perhaps that's half the thrill for him—Allie, how do you drink this swill?" Gideon makes a face and tosses the rest of the blood into the fire, where it sizzles and sparks. "I don't suppose any of you fine ladies feel like letting me have a little suck? I promise I'll make it fun for you too."

I self-consciously tug on my silk scarf. Alaric walks over to Gideon and shoves him roughly back in the chair. He snatches the empty goblet from Gideon's hands and sets it down on the table.

"I apologise for the rudeness of my friend. I hope it will not reflect poorly on my hosting or on my fiancée, Winifred. She enjoys your company and does not wish to be ostracised on account of my aloofness."

"We're cool, Vlad." Isis props her tie-dye Dr Martens on Alaric's antique coffee table. His jaw ticks, but he doesn't say a thing.

"Was this Baylor at the pub the night of Danny's death? Did you see him this evening at the festival?" Alaric growls at Gideon.

Gideon shakes his head. "No sightings at either location, although if he were there, he'd be skulking in the shadows, waiting for the perfect opportunity to snatch a human …"

I shudder, thinking of poor Patrick, grabbed in the dark and drained dry.

"Both Alyra and Baylor have RSVPed for the ball," Gideon says softly.

"All you have are two vampires with possible motives and no evidence," Alaric says. "There could be others with some motive we cannot guess. My mother will not invoke the Mora on flimsy evidence."

"We know that. That's why we're going to gather evidence at the ball. I'll make a powerful truth potion," says Isis. "We will mix this into the blood cocktails that we'll distribute to the guests."

"You'll distribute? Human servants delivering blood cocktails to my guests?" Callista appears in the doorway, her dress sweeping behind her as she enters the room and stands in front of the fire.

Isis gasps, and Maisie does a funny little curtsey. I understand – Callista's cold, deadly beauty is disconcerting, especially when you know of all her dark and callous deeds.

"Y-y-yes, ma'am."

"I prefer 'my lady', if you please." Callista licks her lips. "I think my guests will be tickled by the prospect, and your scents will draw out the husker. You are all un-Thralled, without the mark of another vampire in your blood. In a room already brimming with hedonism, they will find it impossible to resist. But there are risks."

She sounds delighted by the prospect of risks, but I pat my tote bag, where my knife sits safely inside. "We'll be ready to fight this husker off, if required. We'll make sure everyone is armed."

"We will focus our attention on the two suspects with the aim of eliciting a confession or incriminating evidence, which we will record," Maisie says. "We all have hidden cameras and recording devices we can hide on our bodies."

"Where did you all get spy equipment from?" I ask.

"From the internet," Mina shrugs. "By way of my husband, Moriarty."

"Moriarty, as in the fictional villain of Arthur Conan Doyle—" My eyebrows must be lost in my hairline by now.

"One and the same." Mina smiles. "Morrie's a big fan of the internet. Lots of opportunities for skullduggery and shenanigans."

"Enough about Mina's fictional husbands. Back to the plan!" Isis regards Callista with an attempt at a confident smile, but ends up looking like she's lost in a carnival horror maze and desperately needs the bathroom. "When we catch the killer, Alaric and Gideon will drag them in front of you in a big show, lots of grunting and bulging muscles and such, you will do your vampy justice act and ... *voilà*! No more murderer."

"Indeed." Callista's smile could break glass.

"What about the police?"

Every pair of eyes in the room swivels to look at Reginald, who stands in the doorway holding a silver tray groaning beneath the weight of hot chocolates, goblets filled with blood, and an enormous stack of steaming mince pies.

I didn't realise how hungry I am until those meat pies hit my nostrils. I grab one as Reginald sets the tray down, tossing it between my hands so the pastry doesn't burn my fingers.

"What *about* the police?" Alaric asks.

"Even if you bring the murderer to justice, my lord, the police won't know that, and we cannot allow them to continue to suspect you or Ms Preston."

Reginald raises a valid point. I remember DS Wilson's determined face as she scribbled on her pad. She definitely thinks I have something to do with the two murders.

"We have a plan for that, too," Beth pipes up.

Alaric looks tired. "Which is?"

"It's best you don't know the details. Plausible deniability and whatnot. But we'll make sure that the police don't look at Alaric or Winnie again."

"I want it known that I think this plan is terrible," Alaric declares.

"Your protest is noted, Count Duckula. Now, be quiet. We're almost out of your hair." Isis raps her fingers on the back of the sofa. Mirabelle sniffs her chipped purple polish. "The only unknown is this princess. Is she going to be a problem?"

"Perdita will be helping me with the Mora as a representative of the Midnight Court. She will not be in attendance as Alaric's fiancée." Callista's face screws up. "That dubious honour will be going to Winifred."

Alaric turns to me, and the firelight catches in his eyes. He kneels beside my chair, taking my hand in his. "It will be my pleasure to have you at my side, wife," he whispers, the deep timbre of his voice rattling against my ribcage.

Why, why do I find myself wishing those words were real? Why does the way he says "wife" make my knees tremble?

Why did I agree to this pretend engagement when I *knew* my heart was all mixed up?

I guess I'm going to a vampire ball.

And then a horrible thought crosses my mind.

"What am I going to wear?"

45

Winnie

Harudha: Winnie, I'm very happy that you're seeing someone new, but unfortunately, I don't know any therapists who specialise in 'fake-dating supernatural monsters'. Are you sure you don't need to book an appointment with me?

"I HAVE A SURPRISE FOR YOU."

I startle as Alaric's towering form looms over me. Curse all vampires and their ability to move silently like a cat stalking a box. What is he doing in here anyway? He's *supposed* to be helping Reginald with the chairs, but none of us have seen him all evening.

"I don't have time for surprises." I gesture to the dust covering my favourite blazer, the teetering pile of ceramic mugs, and the Get Shit Done playlist blasting from my portable speaker. "I have to get these last pots boxed up for Quoth, and then Gideon needs help hanging the decorations in the ballroom and *where have you been?* You were supposed to get up hours ago. You haven't even had your swim yet and we need you to—"

Alaric clasps my hand. "I've been awake. I've been in my studio. Come."

"Alaric—"

He pulls me to my feet. I manage to set down the pot I'm wrapping before he drags me away.

"Alaric, what is it that can't wait?"

He doesn't say a word as he tugs me into the small courtyard containing the cistern. My panic rises, remembering the water closing over me, but he skirts the edge of the cistern and pulls me through a narrow passage between the overgrown garden beds. Lichen-covered stone rises on both sides of us as he leads me down narrow, slippery steps, winding between the towers and through an older wing of the castle where ruins crumble away down the hillside. I've never been to this part of the castle before, and I'm terrified that I might make a wrong step and end up in the ravine far below. But Alaric moves with casual ease. He knows every stone by heart.

We reach another set of stairs carved into the bedrock itself. I grip Alaric's hand as I press my back to the rock and shuffle down sideways.

"Keep your eyes on me, Winnie." His cool hand in mine is steady. "Don't look down."

"Excellent advice. Have you thought about teaching?"

"One more step and you're there."

My foot slips on wet rock and I scream as I go flying. He catches me in his arms, holding me against his cool chest as my jelly legs give out. He scoops me up and carries me to—

"What do you think?" he beams.

I work my jaw, but I can't find the words. I had no idea that a place so beautiful could exist, especially not clinging precariously to the side of a castle.

A small stone temple with a columned portico and carvings of Dionysus and his dancing maenads and satyrs is carved into the rock of the cliff itself. In front of it is a large, rectangular pool with a small fountain that burbles in the corner. The water laps invitingly at the edges and spills down over two smaller pools further down the cliffside. Surrounding the main pool are statues of angels and winged beasts, ivy twisting over their weatherworn features. One side of the pool is open to the valley, and there are rocky platforms where you can sit and admire the view. Despite the chill in the air, steam rises from the water.

And *someone* who was supposed to be helping with ball preparations has lit at least a hundred flickering candles around the edges and placed a picnic basket and towels on the steps of the temple.

"Wow. What is this?"

"This is the castle grotto. It was built by the lord who owned the castle before me."

"The one you skewered?"

"Actually, I tossed him from the castle walls," Alaric says, like it's no big thing. "He used to host extravagant parties here. The pools are fed from a natural spring, and by lighting a fire in an oven inside the temple, I can heat the water. I thought you might like to join me for my evening swim."

My body seizes. "No, thank you."

"Winnie, you told me when I set my intention for our work that no matter how high you build your castle walls, someone will always knock them down."

"I did say that."

"Then allow me to help you dismantle your walls."

Damn him. "I don't have a swimming costume." I back away from the water.

"You do not need one. It is only you and me and the moonlight."

A faint mew echoes from inside the temple. Mirabelle pokes her head from behind a dancing satyr.

"And Mirabelle," Alaric says with a laugh. "The little minx followed us down here."

He strips off his clothes, the planes of his sculpted body practically glowing in the moonlight as he walks down the temple steps, submerging himself up to his waist. His cock bobs on the surface of the water, half-hard already.

I swallow. He's doing this on purpose. He knows I'm weak for him.

But does he know how weak? Does he know how much I want to stay?

Alaric turns to me, beckoning me with a single finger. A slow, remote smile plays over his lips, and I catch the glint of one of his fangs. He's not hiding himself around me anymore.

He's naked in more ways than one.

My fingers move of their own accord, pulling my dust-streaked shirt over my head. Underneath, I'm wearing a blood-red bra with black lace details. Alaric sucks in a breath.

"This is what you get for ruining my *favourite* bra," I growl at him. He manages to look both delighted and suitably chastised.

"Remind me to destroy all your corsetry from now on."

My heart is hammering against my chest. He must be able to hear it. I kick off my trousers and fold them neatly on top of my shirt. Then I find Alaric's clothes and fold them, too. And I roll his socks together. And I should probably try and get the dust off this shirt—

"Winifred," Alaric's voice rumbles, closer now. "You are stalling."

I swallow hard and turn back to him. I keep my eyes locked on his as I reach behind me with trembling fingers and undo the clasp of my bra. Hunger prowls in a dangerous shadow behind his eyes as he watches.

With shaking legs, I step out of my panties. Now we're both naked. Alaric holds out his hands to me. My legs tremble as I step into the water. It's deliciously warm. I reach for him and he clasps my hand in his, his skin cooler than the water – solid and reassuring as stone.

"I've got you. Take another step."

The next step is easier, and the one after, and before I know it I'm in the water up to my waist, my body pressed against his. Alaric wraps his arms around me, burying his face in my hair, our bodies fitting together like we were made for each other.

"You're trembling," he whispers. "You don't need to be afraid, Winnie. I'll never let anyone or anything hurt you."

"I know," I whisper back. And I do know it. I have never felt so safe with anyone before.

But I'm also *terrified.*

I was supposed to be safe with my mother, and I wasn't. I thought I was safe with Patrick, but that was also a lie. I *want* to trust this beautiful, deadly vampire who holds me so tenderly, as if he's afraid of breaking me. But I'm terrified that I won't be able to survive being broken by him.

And then I think of all the times he has saved me, how he has been in the shadows when I needed him, how he has upended his life and changed his habits because of my trauma. He has bent his ancient will to fit me into his life.

And I think that maybe he needs me to save him even more. He needs to believe that he isn't a monster, that someone sees past his fangs to the bright jewel of his heart.

"I don't know what to do now," I say, and I mean it about swimming and also about us.

"Lean back," Alaric's dark voice commands me. "I have you. I will not let you go."

I will not let you go.

His fingers press into the small of my back as he angles my body so that I'm facing sideways to him. His other hand goes beneath my chin, tilting my head back so my body is forced to follow. A cool breeze blows across my exposed neck, and Alaric sucks in a breath.

I suck in a few shallow breaths as the water swirls around me. My legs bend beneath me. Alaric wraps his arm around my back as my feet lift off the bottom. Water rushes over my torso and I fling out my arms, fighting to put my feet back down again. Alaric's face appears in my vision, his dark hair draping around his face.

"Hold onto me if you're afraid. The water cannot hurt you. I will let go of you and you will float, but it will only work if you keep your body relaxed."

How can anyone *relax* when all that's holding them up is a quivering wet mess that has tried to kill them once before?

But something in the way Alaric says *you will float*, as if commanding the water to obey his will, stirs me. This is a man who has waded into battles that now adorn history books and medieval tapestries. I'll show him that I can be brave, too.

I try to remember the slow breathing techniques that Harudha taught me. I start at my toes and work my way up my body, focusing on the soft lapping of the water and the warmth and the cooling resistance of Alaric's arm around me. I relax, my eyes wide open, watching his face for a sign that I'm in trouble.

Alaric may not have seen the sun for centuries, but his smile is pure sunlight.

The butterflies swim laps across my belly.

Alaric slowly peels his arm from around me. His eyes never stray from mine.

"That's it," he murmurs. "You're floating. You're doing it, Winnie. I knew you could. You can do anything."

The way he says it, with the surety of ages, makes the butterflies flutter in my chest. I reach my arm up to touch him, and this unbalances me. I tip sideways and water closes over my face.

"Argh!" Panic rises through my chest as I flail, kicking my legs, trying to find the bottom again.

But then his arms go around me, and he pulls my head from the water and presses his lips to mine.

The water heats to a million degrees.

My chest feels as if someone's kicked it in. His cool lips do nothing to ease the heat pooling low in my belly. Before, when he's kissed me, I've tasted his hunger, but now, I taste something deeper.

I study him, wide-eyed, as I press my body into him and kiss him back. He is so beautiful that it hurts to look at him, like trying to glimpse the sun. Water clings to his skin in cool droplets. Stars shimmer in his eyes – reflections of the Milky Way above us in their inky depths.

He pulls away, breathing heavily. "I know it's hard for you to let me see your weakness," he murmurs. "You have always had to be so strong. You're the one who cleans up everyone's mess, so you never get to be a mess yourself. Well, I want to love you whether you are a quiet day or a raging hurricane. I want you to fall apart for me so I can love every piece of you. Give me your wounds, Winnie, and I will bleed for you."

I want to love you.

How can I be afraid of loving him when he speaks like this?

But I *am* afraid. I'm afraid that I might sink beneath the tumult of his love. I'm even more afraid that I might float.

I can't find words to voice my fears, so I pour them into him with our kiss. And he takes them and swallows them down for me. *My monster.*

And then, the kiss is no longer sweet, no longer stained with pretty poetry. It's hot and hard and possessive. It's his fingers tugging my hair, his teeth scraping my lip, his huge hands everywhere all at once, driving me wild.

Alaric spins me around and pushes me against the side of the pool, caging my body with his arms. I look out over the cliffs into the valley beyond, everything shadowed and shrouded in fog. I can't escape him even if I want to, and I definitely don't want to. His cock brushes against my arse and I gasp a little, pushing back against him until he lets out a pained groan.

"Naughty humans who tease me like that might find themselves bitten," he growls, scraping his fangs over my neck.

In response, I wiggle even harder.

He pins me against the rocks, kicking my legs apart. I'm no longer touching the bottom, but I know that he won't let me drown. He slides his length between my thighs to tease my entrance, and I hear myself make that needy little groan again.

"I am utterly lost when you make that sound," he growls against my ear.

In a single stroke, Alaric pierces me from behind, driving up inside me with such force it expels the air from my lungs. I gasp and grip the rocks as Alaric draws back and slams into me again.

"You feel amazing, Winnie. You *are* amazing."

The way he says it, the hard edges of his voice blasted away, I *know*. He loves me. And the reality of that slams into me with his next punishing thrust.

He loves me.

And maybe I can't say it back yet, but …

But maybe …

"If this is swimming," I grin, "I think I like it."

In response, he dives his other hand beneath the water to circle my clit. His cool touch beneath the toasty water is too much. My last doubts and questions fall away, because how can anything bad for me feel *this* good? Alaric swirls and circles as he spears me from behind, and I'm floating and falling all at once.

My orgasm is yanked from the soles of my feet, from the deepest chambers of my heart, offered up on the altar of this wild god, this monster who only wants to worship me.

I come around him with moans and splashes, staring over the edge into the dark valley below. The night steals my cries and the stars bear witness as Alaric sinks his teeth into my neck. Euphoria rushes my head, stealing away the last of my fears as I come a second time and he rides his pleasure to its peak.

He licks my wound closed as he collapses against me, his body cooling the ecstasy that courses through me. I can see why vampires must be careful, why they have rules. Humans could ruin themselves over the pleasure of their bite.

The stars shimmer their approval. Alaric is still rigid inside me. He sings softly, an old song in a language I don't understand, but I don't have to know the words to hear the worship in it.

He cuts off the song.

"Stay with me," he says, his breath cool against my ear.

I wiggle my arse against him. "I'm not exactly running away."

"Good. Don't go back to London after the ball. Stay at Black Crag with me."

I go rigid.

The old, familiar fear clenches around my heart. I see towers of stuff, rooms filled with shifting papers, a rat in the peanut butter.

"I don't know if I'm ready," I say. "I haven't lived with someone since I left Mum's house. I never even lived with Patrick. I have issues. You'll find out—"

"You have nightmares," he says. "I've heard them. The first night, I came running, certain that you were in danger before I realised the truth. I've listened through the door when you had them." He loosens his grip on me so I can lower my legs. I lean back against him, and he kisses the top of my head. "I'm sorry for breaking your trust like that, but I couldn't bear the thought of you enduring the nightmares alone."

A blush creeps over my cheeks as I remember what I sometimes do with my purple vibrator after a nightmare to calm myself down. "Did you ever … hear anything else?"

"Oh, no, absolutely not," he says stoically. "Definitely not anything that would appear on page sixty-four of one of your books."

Great. Just wonderful.

"I dream about my mother's house – only it's monstrous, filled with things that want to crawl all over me or eat me or bury me alive. And I can't get back to sleep until I've cleaned the whole room and scrubbed my skin raw."

"Reginald did mention that you keep asking for clean sheets," Alaric says. "I thought it was just normal human behaviour."

"I am anything but normal," I sigh. "But it's strange. On the nights you've been in my bed, I didn't have the nightmares. I slept right through."

"You still had them, but I held you and sang to you, and they passed."

Of course, it was Alaric saving me again.

"Okay," I say.

"Okay?"

"Okay. I'll stay on at Black Crag with you." My heart hammers against my ribs. "On three conditions."

"I accept."

"You don't even know what the conditions are."

"I don't need to."

"One – you have to keep working on cleaning up the castle and keep your projects contained within their rooms. I can't—" I swallow. "I can't live in a place that reminds me of my mother's house."

"I can do this."

"Two – you have to explain everything about vampires to me. I need to know *everything*. I can't have any more secrets between us."

"No secrets." Alaric sighs deeply. "And what is number three?"

"That Reginald must make me hot chocolate every single night."

Alaric kisses my neck over the spot where he bit me, sending a fission of pleasure through my veins. "I agree to your terms. Do you wish me to make a blood oath?"

"No. But you could come inside me again."

We kiss and talk and fuck and kiss some more, until my conscience gets the better of me, and I drag Alaric out of the water so that we can go back and help.

As we walk back, I glance up at the ancient walls – walls designed to keep the castle's occupants safe from enemies. Alaric and I have our walls, too. We wouldn't have survived without them.

So much is still unanswered. There is no work for me in Argleton, the business I've poured all of myself into is back in London. And I'm still triggered by Alaric's mess.

But with Alaric's cool fingers laced in mine, London feels a million miles away.

Maybe we can pull our walls down together, and build something beautiful in their place?

Maybe this cold, impenetrable castle with its cold, impenetrable Lord could be my home?

46

Alaric

Perdita: I think what you're doing is very brave. Foolish, but brave. Despite all the trouble our mothers' arrangement has caused, I want you to be happy, Alaric. I just hope you know what you're doing.

I HUM TO MYSELF AS I ADD ANOTHER LAYER OF GESSO TO MY PAINTING. She's staying. She's staying at Black Crag with me.

After we returned from the grotto, I tucked Winnie into bed. She needs all her strength before the ball tomorrow, but I'm too bursting with joy to have any hope of falling asleep beside her. She won't need me to sing her through her nightmares for another hour or so yet, so I have come to my study to work on yet another attempt at a painting. This one is a work of cubism in the style of Marcel Duchamp, but it's not going any better than the others—

"Hello, Alaric."

I tear myself from my easel. I find my mother in the chair opposite my desk, her dress streaked with her Thrall's blood and a self-satisfied smirk playing across her lips. Mirabelle stomps along the desk, plonks herself down in front of the Lady of Agony and furiously cleans her behind as if to protest the malevolent woman usurping her chair.

I have no clue how long she's been sitting there.

"I see you are hard at work on your pointless fancies, as always," she says, reaching for the cat with a hungry glint in her eye.

"Art is never pointless." I pick up Mirabelle and place her gently on my lap as I sit down. "What do you want?"

"I'll keep this brief," she says. "I'm leaving for Germany after the ball. Perdita has agreed to return with me. She will visit our court before returning to her home in Italy."

"I've already told you that I'm not leaving Black Crag."

She snorts. "Of course you aren't. I do not wish you to accompany us."

Her words hang heavy between us.

"Do you mean—"

"Winnie has proven to me that though she is but a breakable human, she has the fire of a Valerian warrior in her veins. If all goes well at the ball, finding the killer and bringing him to justice will do more for my reputation than this marriage ever could. She was right about our law, too. I'm drafting a contraception amendment right now. It's a genius political move. I am anxious to return to my castle and continue the work of building this alliance and putting down the stirring rebellion. Winifred is a worthy match for you, my son."

"You mean—"

"It's been more than five centuries since I gave you the Kiss," she says. "And still I have not learned that I cannot control you. I see that you have made your choice, and although Perdita is of the Blood Chastain and the match would be politically useful, I will not stand in the way of your happiness, Alaric. You have been unhappy for so long. I see now that many things in our world must change, so you will lead the way. I will bless the union between you and Winnie. And if our kin should have something to say of it, then they will fear the wrath of the Lady of Agony."

She smiles then, a genuine smile, terrifying for its cold brutality.

"Thank you, Mother," I say, with genuine warmth.

"I am excited to plan another extravagant ball." She flashes me a chilling smile. "You may set a date. Sooner is preferred. It would be politically advantageous."

My heart stutters. "We haven't discussed a wedding—"

My words die away as Callista removes an envelope from the folds of her dress, sealed with red wax and the Valerian family crest, and holds it out to me.

"Not your wedding, son. I refer, of course, to the date for Winnie's Kiss. It took much convincing on a pre-sunrise Zoom call, but I have secured the permission of the Conclave."

The red seal burns in my retinas.

I shake my head. "I won't turn Winnie into one of us."

"Alaric, you *must*."

I stand, tipping Mirabelle unceremoniously onto the floor.

"Don't be so naive, Alaric. Our kind will accept a human on your arm, but only if they know she will become one of us. You do not understand how fragile our position is. You wish to stand against me to marry this human? This I respect. I can see now that your love for her is real and not merely a way for you to wriggle out of your responsibilities to our family. But we have *laws*, and the son of a noble bloodline is not exempt."

I bow my head. "I won't do it. It is Winnie's choice, her life, not mine."

"A vampire and a human *cannot* wed. She cannot live here with you until she is dust and bones. Why do you think this rule exists, Alaric? It's to protect *you*. What will happen to your heart when Winnie ages and you do not? What will happen to you after she dies an old woman and you live on, eternally youthful, your heart shattered into a million pieces? Stronger Upyr than you have been driven mad by their desolation. You consign yourself to an eternity of misery for one short human lifetime of happiness. It is unthinkable, and I don't say that lightly. Unlike contraception, there is no cure for mortality."

"I don't care."

Callista's dress crinkles as she leans back in her chair. "Turn her, Alaric, or I shall do it myself."

"You will not touch her."

"A marriage between a vampire and a human is an aberration. It would be like a wolf marrying a lamb. If you truly wish to bind your soul to hers, then she must be one of us. As your mother, I will do that which you cannot. You may hate me for a century or two, but I'm used to your ire."

Memories flare hot against the insides of my skull. Callista pulling me to her breast on the battlefield, spilling her blood into my mouth as she drank from me, the waves of agony and ecstasy that pulsed through my body as my soul died and I was reborn a monster.

The idea of her fangs anywhere *near* Winnie …

"You would issue an ultimatum to your son?" I rasp.

"Would you expect anything less from me?" My mother smiles, and her sharp incisors glint in the candlelight. "I do this for your own good, Alaric. She is not one of us. But she could be. Turn her, or I will do it myself."

She leaves me then, her skirts rustling as she glides from the room. My nails tear at the leather of the chair. I made Winnie a promise, but how can I tell her this? How can I explain?

Winnie's bright smile burns behind my eyes. I love her with the kind of fierce, reckless love that I have always believed impossible for a monster like me.

I love her, but she cannot survive me.

I love her too much to make her like me.

What am I to do?

47

Winnie

Faye: OF COURSE I'm going to use Winnie Wins on the show. I sold the show based on the concept! Just because your name is on the system doesn't mean you own it. It's part of our brand, and if you're not willing to do what it takes for this business to succeed, then I'll have to do it myself. When you come to your senses we're going to have a serious talk about your future with Clutter Queens.

"Ow."

My hand flies to my head as Beth jabs another bobby pin into my skull.

"Hold still, Winnie. I know what I'm doing."

"Yes. I loved your work on *Hellraiser*, but you're turning me into a slice of Swiss cheese. Ow."

"A *sexy* Swiss cheese." Beth grins as she twirls my chair around.

I gasp. Beth is a magician. She's twisted my hair into an elaborate style that frames my face with wisps floating free like I'm a fae princess. She's rubbed one of her serums into my skin and I'm glowing, and the subtle sparkles she's added around my eyes and across my cheeks only add to the mystical effect.

"Alaric won't know what hit him." Komal grins as she tugs on black dress trousers.

"Now, for the finishing touch." Arabella lifts the lid from an old-fashioned garment box. "I bought this in Paris, but it doesn't fit me. And since you've volunteered us all as the help and I'm stuck in these degrading polyester trousers ... you may as well have it."

Arabella unfurls a dress that leaves my jaw on the ground. It's made of some kind of shimmering golden material that catches the light and reflects a rainbow of colours. It's cut on the bias with sheer panels placed in the most scandalous arrangement, and as far as I can tell, there is no back to the garment at all – just a series of strings.

"What do you think?" She grins.

"Wh-wh-where's the rest of it?"

Arabella shoves me and the dress into the bathroom. "If you don't put that dress on, I will come in there and do it for you."

My heart hammering, I shuck off my clothes and try to sort through the tangle of straps. Outside, I can hear the Nevermore Murder Club chatting away as they pull on their servers uniforms and check their spy cameras are concealed and working perfectly. Mina's husband Morrie is hiding in a secret room off the library, monitoring all the equipment.

Everyone is here except for Celeste, who had to see her mother so couldn't make it. They're all excited to meet a room full of vampires who view them as snacks and unmask the murderer once and for all.

Please, don't let this be a big mistake.

I manage to pull the dress over my head and get the straps laid mostly correctly. I smooth down the front and dare a peek at myself in the mirror.

Okay. The dress looks good.

Damn good.

The sheer panels run down the sides and pierce across my stomach, flowing and dipping in just the right places to show off my curves. I turn around, and the thin laces crisscross my back, giving glimpses of skin along a low slit that reaches nearly to my arse. If I bend over in the wrong company, I could give some poor old vampire a heart attack.

Can I really go to a vampire ball on the full moon in this?

"Are you ready to come out?" Mina calls.

"Yeah, we want to see!"

"If you are climbing out a window to escape wearing that dress, I'd like to point out that this tower is several stories above a shark-infested moat," adds Arabella.

"There are no sharks," says Dora. "Winnie, please don't believe her. There are *no sharks*."

"After you fall several stories into a moat, whether there are sharks or not is a moot point," Arabella huffs.

"I'm not climbing out the window." I grip the door handle. "I'm coming out. Please don't laugh."

I step into the bedroom. Seven heads turn to me. One by one, their mouths fall open.

"Winnie Preston, you *fox*," Isis screeches.

"Alaric's gonna wish he died again," Komal purrs.

"I am a fashion *genius*," Arabella preens. "That dress was made for you."

"I believe it was made for *you*," I point out. "Maybe I should change …"

"Don't give her a moment to second-guess herself." Komal shoves me towards the door. "Alaric is waiting downstairs. And we need to get to the kitchens and start making those blood cocktails. Isis, do you have the truth potion?"

"Dora's got it. Apparently, I can't be trusted with breakable vials." Isis makes a face as she plonks down on the bed, knocking over her purse and sending an avalanche of makeup and crystal necklaces off the side of the bed.

Dora fishes around in her purse and pulls out the potion.

"I'll take that." Arabella holds out her hand. "Since I'm mixing the drinks."

Arabella would only agree to help tonight if she could stay in the kitchens and mix the cocktails. She said she couldn't have any of her clients in the room see her in a uniform or her business would be ruined.

Mina picks up Oscar's lead. The ladies crowd around the mirror for one final fit check before herding me down the narrow tower staircase. Alaric waits at the bottom, Mirabelle simpering around his ankles. When I see him, the butterflies in my belly practise their Olympic diving routine.

He's wearing an immaculately tailored suit. It's not his usual anachronistic style, but a fashionable cut with modern lines in a crisp, soft fabric. He must've paid a fortune to have it made so quickly to his exact measurements, because this suit hugs him so perfectly it should be illegal. The flickering light from the candelabra in his hands makes the sharp lines of his cheekbones stand in high relief. He's too beautiful to be real.

And he's *mine.*

"Most Reverend Winifred." His eyes widen to black holes. "You are exquisite. No one will be able to keep their eyes off you tonight."

"Or their fangs," Arabella supplies from behind me.

"They wouldn't dare," Alaric growls.

"Yeah, it's just *our* necks on the line," Isis chirps.

Alaric holds out the candelabra to me. "I brought you a gift. In case you need to run away."

I raise an eyebrow. "I thought you ran out of these? On account of all the maidens?"

"I had Reginald order several more. A certain professional organiser has made us appreciate the value in being prepared."

Alaric tucks my hand under his.

"Don't leave my sight," he whispers. "Remember, to the guests in this room, you are food. The only thing stopping them from biting you is the fact that I have claimed you."

"Have you?" I whisper. "Claimed me?"

"Sweet Winifred, it's you who have claimed me." Alaric draws my hand to his mouth, pressing my knuckles to his cool lips. The way his eyes roam over me makes me feel like I'm wearing nothing at all and he's kissing something much more intimate than my fingers. "In this dress, I am utterly at your mercy."

As we weave our way through the castle, the murmur of voices rises from below. Alaric's portraits and suit of armour are back in their places on the walls, freshly dusted. I love being surrounded by these depictions of him from different times – tiny windows into his life.

Reginald is at the door, greeting guests and taking their coats. Gideon sweeps them through the house, talking a mile a minute so no one has a chance to peer into any of the adjoining rooms and see the mess that we haven't yet cleaned up. I'm excited to get stuck into those rooms once tonight is over.

Because I'm staying.

Black Crag is going to be *my* home, too.

I'm giddy with the idea of it, and terrified. I don't know what I'm going to do for money. Faye's become hostile ever since I suggested that she do the show alone and not use Winnie Wins. But Alaric's creative energy is infectious, and he has my head spinning with ideas. Maybe I'll write a book, like Marie Kondo. Maybe I'll put a desk beside his in the study and we can spend our evenings in a frenzy of creative energy, as long as everything is tidied away at the end of the night.

As we drop the girls at the kitchen and glide along the hallway together, I twist my head, admiring what we've achieved. The hallway is empty of boxes and art supplies. Everything is clean and tidy and *perfect*. The golden threads of Alaric's tapestries glitter in the candle-light. Voices and laughter and music drift from the ballroom, and, despite the danger beyond those doors, I find myself excited to be on Alaric's arm in Arabella's pretty dress.

Alaric doesn't look quite as excited. This is a big step for him, to go from seeing practically no one to hosting an extravagant ball. And that's aside from the danger of tonight's plan. His eyes gaze forward, hardened and resolute. If this is what he looked like before striding into battle, he must have sent his enemies running in terror before even drawing his sword.

I squeeze his arm. "You can do this. I'm right here at your side."

"That's what I'm afraid of."

Alaric sucks in a deep breath and pushes open the doors.

We sweep into the room, carried by the swell of the music and the rush of voices. I gasp as I take in the finished ballroom. I hadn't had a chance to see it since Gideon and Alaric finished decorating.

I don't see the dusty, cramped space I encountered on my first night here.

In the centre of the floor, a raised dais draped in ivy and golden fronds houses a lively band playing galloping music on fiddle, double bass and a couple of wind instruments I don't recognise. The musicians play naked, their bodies painted with glittering gold, their hair pinned beneath golden wreaths. Around them, couples and groups spin and twirl in an ocean of swirling colours beneath a canopy of glittering fairy lights and glowing spheres.

Alaric's golden-threaded tapestries line two walls. Vampires crowd in front of them, snapping photos using the electronic photo booths Gideon set up. Apparently, that thing about vampires not showing up in pictures is false.

The butterflies in my stomach flutter nervously as I take in Callista's guests. I had no idea to expect so many vampires. Everywhere I look, my eyes are drenched in the sight of rich, sumptuous gowns and impeccably tailored or excessively flamboyant suits – some fiercely modern, others pulled from the trunks of ancient royal wardrobes. Even without fangs on display, there is something otherworldly about them – their skin is too flawless, their eyes are too bright, too sharp, and their smiles far too smug.

The raw, primal *power* in the room has a heaviness that makes me feel drunk, even though I'm too nervous to touch a drop. My fingers tighten around Alaric's arm.

I'm going to be eaten alive. What are we doing?

Callista sweeps over to us, wearing a crimson dress that's straight out of a Dracula movie, her lips painted a matching colour. The lipstick looks wet, as if she's painted her lips in fresh blood.

"My son, you came. I had my doubts." She leans in, kissing both his cheeks. "And Winnie Preston, stepping bravely into a nest of vipers. But who will offer the poison bite?"

Before I can answer, she takes Alaric's arm and drags us over to a circle of vampires. The only one I recognise is Gideon, who looks utterly edible in a grey suit and shimmering golden waistcoat that makes his hair look like a halo.

"Ms Preston, I heard congratulations are in order," he says, that mischievous glint in his eyes. "Now that you're intending to stay in Argleton, what can I do to convince you to work with my clients?"

"Oh, Gideon, you jest!" A woman in a purple velvet fishtail dress slaps him playfully on the arm. "What could one of us possibly want from a human apart from the nectar of her veins?"

My stomach lurches. I force a smile on my face.

"My *fiancée* is a professional organiser, and tonight's ball would not have been possible without her." Alaric sweeps his arm around, indicating the room. "You know what some of us are like. Over the centuries we accumulate the ephemera of an immortal life. This very room used to be filled to the brim with my various obsessions. But Winnie has worked her magic and now look at it."

"Callista, you never told us your son was a comedian." A man in a matching pinstriped purple velvet suit leans in to kiss Callista's cheeks. "Alaric called this woman his fiancée."

"Yes, Alaric and Winnie are to be wed," Callista says. "I thought you would approve, Bernard, as you have long campaigned in the Midnight Court for restrictions on human and vampire interactions to be lifted."

"I …" The man looks lost for words. "I didn't know the Lady of Agony shared our beliefs. Because of course, since the invention of contraception, the danger of Dhampir is nearly nonexistent. As prominent Nightshade blood, you have always advocated for a return to our traditions—"

"Yes, well." Callista flashes me a tight-lipped smile. "Perhaps some traditions need to change."

"We couldn't agree more, and we're very happy to meet you both." The woman extends her hand for Alaric to kiss. "You must be excited, Lord Valerian. You haven't sired a vampire before, have you? It's the most beautiful ceremony."

I turn to Alaric who has gone, if possible, even paler. "What's she talking about? What ceremony?"

"Please, don't concern yourself with it. I would not do anything that you do not wish."

"Oh, Alaric, quit teasing the girl." The man laughs. "You know you cannot take a human as a *wife*. It's absurd. You'd have what, fifty years together if you're lucky? I assume you will seek permission from the Conclave to give her the Kiss—"

My heart hammers a mile a minute. "Alaric, is this true—"

"So, Callista, will you be staying on in Argleton?" Gideon cuts in, flashing Alaric a stern look. "I still have a few homes unsold in my Sanctus Estate, and for such a majestic lady I would make you a good deal—"

"I toured your estate at a party last week, but I don't much care for modern architecture." Callista makes a face. "There aren't even any gargoyles. Honestly, Gideon, it can't be that expensive to slap up a gargoyle or two. This used to be a *proper* country."

Panic creeps along my spine. "Alaric, what's this about a ceremony—"

"Fancy a drink?" Isis pops up between us, thrusting her tray at the vampires. As they leap on the glasses filled with crimson liquid, she hisses in my ear, "Meet me by the ugly baby statue. I have an update."

I nod. I know exactly which statue she means.

Isis darts away before the vampires can replace their empty glasses on her tray.

"Excuse me," I force a smile. "I have to go to the bathroom."

"Winnie, wait." Alaric chases after me. I duck through the crowd, trying not to draw attention to myself as I head for the fat cherub flanking the door between the ballroom and drawing room. Alaric catches me beneath the statue. He grabs my wrist, whirling me around so we are chest to chest.

"Please, Winnie, don't listen to anything they say. They mean to unnerve you, because your presence has startled them and they need to be in control—"

"Is what she said true – if we were to be married, you have to turn me into … into one of you?"

His face twists with frustration. "I can explain—"

"You should have told me this when you asked me to stay." I shove him away. "I don't want to be a vampire, Alaric. Don't you get that this changes everything?"

The hurt stabs the butterflies, killing them dead. How could he not tell me this? How could he hate what he is and yet expect me to just give up my human life like it's no big deal?

I *know* my argument is reasonable, my anger justified. But Alaric's face crumples, his lordly mask falling away.

And I know that not even this ancient, immortal warrior is impervious to wounds.

"As you wish." His voice is hard as steel.

"Alaric, I didn't mean—"

"There you are." Isis appears, completely oblivious to the tension crackling between us. "I wasn't supposed to take so long but I got waylaid by a bunch of blooddrunk fangsters wanting refills. Callista's friends are chugging it back like … well, like vampires at a blood bank. At this rate, everyone in the room has had some truth potion by now. *And* I have news—"

"Is everything okay?" Komal appears on my other side. She's come from the direction of the kitchen dumbwaiter, her tray filled with glasses brimming with blood. Alaric's eyes drop to the red liquid, his eyes flashing.

He lied to me. He said he would never hurt me, but he's going to make me like him. After everything he told me about how much he hates what his mother did, he wants to do the same to me …

I think I'm going to be sick.

"What did you want to tell us?" I snap at Isis. I need this to be done so I can get out of here.

"I've identified Baylor Godsven." Isis shifts some of Komal's full glasses to her tray. "See that man over my right shoulder? No, *don't look*. I don't want him to think that I'm talking about him. Laugh at something I just said."

I throw back my head and force a laugh. Alaric chuckles beside me, but his features are grave, his laughter a harsh bark. He hisses at Isis, "Be careful around him. It's possible he's already husked two people. If he's the murderer, his hunger will be a demon gnawing at his stomach. He might snap at any moment."

"Oh, I think he's already snapped. He's a man of dark proclivities," Isis smirks. "Or so he informed me while he tried to shove his hand down my shirt."

Alaric's dark eyes become storm clouds. "That *beast*. I shall see him out immediately."

I can't bear to look at him. Is this chivalry all an act for my benefit?

"No, Alaric," Isis laughs. "This is what I wanted! I'll use my womanly wiles to get that confession out of him. I bet a guy like him gets off on the thrill."

"I've found someone, too." Komal nods to a woman in a circle in the corner of the room. "You know her, Alaric? Her name is Eleanor Mock of the Blood Alexandre. According to the secrets she's spilling after three cocktails, she was sired without consent by a now-dead vampire. According to what I hear, this horny old vamp sired at least ten women before he met the justice of the Mora. What if she's taking revenge on men who prey on women?"

"Patrick would never hurt a woman," I cry, flashing a glare at Alaric, who turns away.

"But he did cheat on you, didn't he?"

I nod. "But how would she know about that?"

"Oh, Winnie, this is a small village. She probably heard us all talking about what a wanker he is at the pub." Isis rolls her eyes. "We did that a lot."

"Because he *was* a wanker," Komal adds, lifting her half-empty tray onto her shoulder. "I'm going to get back there and see what else she feels like confessing."

"And I'll stick close to Mr Dark Proclivities." Isis sashays her hips and breaks out her most dazzling smile. "Have fun, you kids. We'll keep you informed."

"Isis, wait—"

She darts away, leaving me alone with Alaric.

I glance at the door. "I'm going to leave. I don't think I can stand this a moment longer—"

"Please Winnie … Please don't leave." He looks around the room, both of us conscious of every set of eyes on us. "Dance with me. Let me explain?"

He holds his hand out. Do I imagine it, or are his fingers trembling a little?

"I don't want to dance. I am trying hard to hold it together right now, but if you drag me into the middle of this room and put on a show for these vamps after what you just told me, I am going to *lose my shit.*"

"I would never make a spectacle of you." His eyes have gone back to being hard chips of obsidian. "If you leave this ballroom, I cannot protect you. And somewhere in this castle is a vampire who longs for a neck as beautiful as yours. I wish only to explain what you heard, and it will be safer on the dance floor with everyone around us."

A knife twists in my gut, severing butterfly wings as I clasp Alaric's hand and allow him to pull me onto the dance floor. My body is numb where he touches me. He sweeps me into his arms as the band begins a slow, mournful tune …

Wait a second …

"Is this …" I raise an eyebrow. "… 'Rain' by Sleep Token? This is on my Get Shit Done playlist. You *hate* this song."

"You have opened my eyes to new wonders, Winnie Preston," he says as his fingers find the hollow of my back. He presses me against him, our hearts thudding against each other – two beats of mine to every one of his.

Alaric's cool fingers knit in mine as he holds my hand up and spins us slowly, his feet moving between mine with easy grace. For a moment, I forget the anger in my heart.

He can dance.

Of course he can dance. He's had several lifetimes to learn.

Alaric's cheek grazes mine. His skin is as cool as stone, which is what I need my heart to be right now. A stone, impervious to his tricks.

"We have many laws about humans," he whispers. "Some are to protect you from us. Others are to protect us from you. Most of us old enough have been persecuted at one time or another. But this law is for everyone.

"A vampire and a human cannot make vows to each other until they are both Upyr. As much as a couple may love each other, eventually immortality will come between them. The human will beg to live forever, or the vampire will resent their love aging while they remain unchanged. Eventually, time will rob the couple of their happiness, and the vampire will bury his beloved and must continue, enduring, long after his love becomes dust. To know love and to lose it is a fate worse than death, which is why relationships like ours are forbidden even if we stayed out of each other's beds."

His words sink in. I can't believe I never considered what it means to be with a vampire. Alaric won't age. He'll still look this fucking devastating in a hundred years. And in a hundred years, I'll be dead. What we have now feels so real and unbreakable, but time itself would tear us apart.

How could I be so stupid?

My dress tightens like an iron maiden closing around me.

"When were you going to tell me this?" I choke out.

"I didn't think to tell you because I have no intention of ever granting you the Kiss. I made a vow that I would never sire a vampire. My mother calls this life a gift, but I never believed that … that is, until I met you." His cheek shifts against mine, sparking fire in my skin. "If I died on that battlefield, I never would have met you. Eternity was worth the wait for you, Winnie Preston."

My eyes burn with unwept tears. Damn him and his pretty words. "But you must have a system, right? For choosing who gets to be a new vampire? Surely you have to grow the population at some point?"

"Normally, a vampire couple will apply to the Conclave for a licence to sire offspring, and that couple will choose an appropriate human to continue their bloodline. There have been occasions when an Upyr has fallen for a human and successfully petitioned the Conclave for the right to sire them. But it is not common, especially not among the courtly classes, for they don't like to introduce new blood. I do not care what Perdita or anyone in this room says, you have nothing to fear from me—"

Don't you understand? I want to scream at him. *I have* everything *to fear from you.*

"I said I would stay on three conditions," I murmur. "One of those conditions was that you told me *everything*."

"And I will tell you everything. I will give you every book about vampire lore in the library. We have an eternity together for you to unpack the mysteries of my kind."

No, we don't. That's the whole point.

I need my life to have rules and order. I need to be able to control things. But your world … I don't understand it. I can't control it.

What if I wanted this? What if I chose you over mortality? Why didn't you give me a choice?

What if I agreed and then we broke up? What if I asked you to do this, but you refused, and I resented you? What if—

"—Patrick's body … pity about … absolutely delicious …"

My ears prick up. I nudge Alaric's arm, steering him closer to the voice that laughed Patrick's name.

"Winnie, please." Alaric's voice cracks with pain. "You know how I feel about you. I would never—"

"Sssshh, I heard—"

"Sorry to break up the party." Komal tugs on my arm, startling me out of Alaric's embrace and the conversation I'd overheard. "We have a problem. I can't find Isis."

48

Alaric

WINNIE'S FINGERS DIG INTO MY ARM. "ALARIC."

I scan the room, searching every face for the annoying witch or the vampire she was spying on. I can't see either of them. "They're not in the ballroom. Did you see her go off with him?"

"No, but—"

I grab Winnie and haul her off the dance floor. Her words thud against my skull.

I don't want to be a vampire.

This changes everything.

Winnie made me feel like I was worthy of love. But I cannot get the disgust in her voice out of my head. For all her words, she looks at me and sees a monster.

She doesn't want to be like me. She doesn't want *me.*

And I cannot flee this room. I cannot let loose the monster within me that she so fears, who now claws and scratches at my skin, desperate to take back what he has lost.

I have to deal with the killer first.

Guests call out to me, wanting us to join their groups. Everyone is curious about the human girl on my arm and what it means for our laws and my mother's courtly interests, but I don't care that I'm snubbing them.

There is a predator in my house, and even though he's got the annoying witch, and I'd sort of love to lock her in a dark, soundproof room, she's under *my* protection.

This monster will not allow such sacrilege in his house.

I veer away from the main doors. If Isis passed through them, her scent is overwhelmed by the vampires milling around, drenched in their expensive perfumes. I doubt he'd try to take her through the crowd and risk being seen spiriting away a human. I drag Winnie toward the side doors, where we spoke with Komal and Isis only a few songs ago. I stand under the doorway and sniff.

Winnie's strawberry scent briefly distracts me, my heart flayed open by her rejection, but I catch a whiff of Isis's patchouli perfume. "This way."

"Alaric, slow down. We can't—"

I drop Winnie's hand, realising that I've been dragging her faster than a human could possibly run, that I'm further proving that she should never have trusted me. "I'm sorry. He's taken her down this hallway. I can smell her—"

I sprint around the corner, following the scent. But right in front of the dining room, I lose it. It's as though she disappeared into thin air.

A faint sound reaches my ears. A suckling noise and a woman's whimper. "Please, no ..."

She's in my priest hole!

I don't know how Baylor knew of its existence, but he's taken Isis inside my secret room to pursue his wickedness. I tear the tapestry from the wall, revealing the hidden doorway. Winnie grabs the handle, but Baylor has locked it from the inside. I left the key back in my study, but we don't have time for such niceties.

I tear the door from the hinges.

"Well, that's hot," a breathy voice whispers behind me. Winnie's friend Beth. Members of the Nevermore Coven crowd into the hall as

Winnie directs a candelabra into the gloomy maw of the room. This time, they all hear Isis's whimper.

"She's in there!" Winnie surges forward.

Panic seizes me. "No, let me—"

But it's too late. Winnie shoves her way into the room just as piles of art supplies and half-finished sculptures rain down on her.

49

Winnie

"ARGH!" I THROW UP MY ARMS AS PAPERS, CANVASES, WOODEN frames and, for some reason, several tubes of glitter topple down on me. "Alaric, what *is* this?"

I stagger back as the avalanche of stuff fans across the floor. Broken pottery crunches under my feet. The itch of dust tickles my nostrils. Bile rises in my throat as I catch glimpses of half-finished paintings – my own likeness peering back at me from literally *hundreds* of dusty canvases.

I whirl around, and everywhere I look, I see my face. In one, I'm sitting in a castle window with Mirabelle in my lap, watching the moon rise over the valley. In another, I'm a seventeenth century queen with an intricately embroidered gown. In a mixed-media piece, my eyes are glass beads.

There are clay sculptures, and bronze castings, and even a cross stitch. All of me. All of them packed haphazardly into this secret room. And those are only the ones near the entrance.

I whip out my arm, thrusting the candelabra into the gloom, and I see that the entire secret room is stacked almost to the ceiling. Only a narrow gap leads through the centre, the path invisible in the gloom. I hear another whimper.

Isis is back there.

She's buried under all this stuff. She's suffocating. Bugs are crawling all over her.

The world spins. My skin prickles. I slap at the bugs crawling up my legs, tearing at my dress, trying to get them off me. It's infected. *I'm* infected—

Strong fingers wrap around my wrist. "You're okay, Winnie."

It's Gideon. And he looks more serious than I've ever seen him. But his features are fading in my vision, blurring as I fight to stay in the moment. I'm being dragged into my nightmares by the musty scent, the sound of piles creaking and rodents burrowing, the crinkle of *things* beneath my feet.

"What's the matter with her?" Someone shakes me. "Hey, Winnie? What's happening? You've gone white."

I turn to Alaric. His jaw trembles as he stands shin-deep in broken art projects. The king of his mountain of stuff.

His *treasure.*

And I realise that I've uncovered the biggest lie of all.

He hasn't got better. He hasn't given up on his hoarding ways. He's been hiding everything away in this room, hoping that I'd never find it, trying to manipulate me into believing this could work.

The Winnie Wins System is a complete failure.

I'm *a complete failure.*

I couldn't stop my mum from ruining our home. I couldn't stop Patrick from cheating.

I couldn't even help Alaric.

He's been lying to me all this time.

"Winnie, I can explain …" He sweeps his hand over the broken frames. "These were all for you. I was trying to—"

My heart thrums in my ears, an ocean of trauma that sweeps away Alaric's excuses. The stuff rushes up at me, and I grip Gideon's arm, certain I'm going to pass out.

But the nausea recedes, and I remember why we're here.

"Isis is in there, and he's hurting her," I hiss through gritted teeth. "Someone has to clean up."

Gideon drops my arm and darts through the hole in front of me. Komal tries to haul me back but I duck under her and fling myself after him. I have to turn sideways to fit through the gap. Piles of stuff brush my skin, and the invisible bugs crawl all over me. I shut my eyes and urge myself forward.

It's just rubbish. It can't hurt you. It's just stuff—

I feel my way through the horror, listening for Gideon's footsteps and the horrific slurping sound that must be a vampire feeding. But it's almost drowned out by the groaning of the piles and the crunch and scrape of papers beneath my feet.

During the worst years of her hoarding – the two years before I left – my mother's house was like this.

The panic rises in my chest. My ears ring. I can't hear the slurping anymore, just grunts and groans and scuffles, but I don't know what's real and what's a memory.

But Isis is in there. I have to get to her. I can't let the mess claim her, too.

"Winnie, it's okay. Back up. I got her." A dark shape lurches towards me. Rough hands pull me out of the dark tunnel so that Gideon can come out. He waddles sideways, sending more glitter raining down onto the gathered women as he lays Isis gently at their feet. Dora drops beside her, cradling her sister's body in her arms.

I stagger back from my friend's glassy eyes, the horror rising in my throat.

Is she …

"She's alive," Gideon breathes. "But a few more minutes and she wouldn't be. She's lost a lot of blood."

"She's still bleeding," Maisie gasps, pointing to the dark stain on Isis's neck.

"It will stop in a moment. I've licked the wound."

Komal whacks him over the head with her tray. "How dare you?"

"Ow! I was *helping*. Vampire saliva closes a wound quickly." Gideon rubs his head where Komal hit him. "I thought you knew all about vampires."

"I didn't know that your version of first aid was to go around licking things!"

"Where's Baylor?" Alaric demands, his eyes so stormy that I'm afraid of what he might do.

"He's still in there. He's subdued, for now."

Alaric plunges into the room. Gideon picks up Isis and carries her through to the sitting room. He sinks onto the sofa, holding Isis against his body, as he orders Maisie to find something sweet for her to eat.

I slump down beside her, knitting my fingers in hers. Isis's eyelashes flutter, and she makes a gasping sound.

"I caught him," she croaks out. "I knew it was him. Witch's instinct …"

"You're amazing, Isis. But you have to rest now. We're going to get you something to eat."

She claws at the camera hidden in the button on her shirt. "I got it all. He said that he wanted to taste me as he took my life."

"Fuck, Isis." Dora elbows me out of the way. "I can't believe we agreed to this crazy plan. I could have lost you."

I stagger back, letting Dora take care of her sister. Maisie runs in with a cup of Reginald's hot chocolate, which she passes to Isis. The other book club members – except Arabella, who probably doesn't know yet – crowd around. My stomach churns with shame.

I can't believe I put them all in danger. And all because—

… all because I wanted to protect Alaric. I wanted to clean up everything for him so we could be together. But it was a lie.

I whirl around and stagger from the room.

"Winnie, wait—" Gideon calls, but no one comes after me as I fumble my way back to the hidden room. Alaric has dragged out Baylor's limp body, and he's handing him off to Callista's Thralls. His eyes blaze as he sees me.

"Mina's husband has already handed over Isis's evidence to my mother. She's preparing for the Mora, and they'll bring him to the ballroom." Alaric's jaw works. "I'm so pleased we got to your friend in time."

"No thanks to you." I gesture to the avalanche of stuff strewn across the hallway. "What is this?"

"It's me."

He says it matter-of-factly, as if he's discussing the weather.

"But … I thought you were over this." I toe a box in disbelief. "We did all that work cleaning your rooms. We got rid of all that stuff. I made you a *system*."

"And you did a beautiful job. That's why I hid these things here. I've been so overwhelmed by your presence, I needed an outlet. So I would sneak away and paint or sculpt or …" Alaric brushes glitter from my bare shoulder. His touch makes me shudder. "I wanted to give you a gift, to capture something of your beauty and brilliance in my work, but nothing was perfect, so I hid them away. But now you've agreed to stay here with me. We can clean this up, together. We'll play your music and put things in boxes and everything will be perfect again."

"No." I shake my head. Tears stream down my cheeks. "It won't."

"Winnie—"

"We're not meant to be together." I struggle to get the words out through my sobs. "We're too different. *This* is who you are, and I can't live with it. And you can't live with me as I am. Your laws won't allow it. We tried to make this work but our walls are just too high."

"Love tears down walls, Winnie." His voice chokes with emotion.

"Don't you see? I can't love *this*. I can't be with someone who needs me to clean up their mess." I turn away from him. I can't bear for him to see me cry. "We have to get back to the ball. We don't want to keep the vampires waiting."

50

Alaric

Callista: I grow impatient. The Witching Hour approaches. Where is my killer?

WINNIE RUNS BACK TO HER FRIENDS. THOSE TEARS SPILLING down her beautiful cheeks haunt me – tears I know I caused.

I hid these things away precisely so I wouldn't cause her pain. And still, I have caused her pain. I broke the two vows I made to her when I asked her to stay.

I long to go after her, to attempt to explain, to see if what I have broken between us can be repaired. But she is right about me. I *am* a monster. She is right to run.

My castle is in uproar and I am needed. Gideon comes for me, his face grave. Reginald takes us to my study, where he brought Baylor. I dig my fang into the pad of my thumb, relishing the pain. I rub the wound against Baylor's lip, rousing him from the stupor Gideon had placed him in – my friend is a fellow adept at an ancient form of vampiric martial arts that can subdue one of our kin. Gideon and I pin his arms and drag him to the ballroom. He barely has the energy to struggle.

As we enter, the room falls deathly silent.

Silent as a tomb.

The band has been dismissed and Callista stands on the band dais, her arms raised for attention. Perdita stands behind her, holding a tablet towards the crowd where Isis's camera footage plays on an endless loop. The only sounds in the room are the scrape of Baylor's body against the marble and his voice rasping on the tape.

"I want to taste you as I take your life. I bet you are the sweetest delight."

Disgusting.

He deserves the hell that awaits him.

I cannot help but feel that I deserve it, too.

Hundreds of vampiric eyes watch as we toss the struggling Baylor at my mother's feet. I scan the room for Winnie and see her huddling in the corner with the women from the Nevermore Coven minus Arabella and Dora, who are taking Isis home. I admire the grim set of her jaw, her determination to witness this justice for her friend even though she is upset and frightened and I have broken her heart.

My body knows it's too late – I have broken us. But my heart leaps when her golden eyes meet mine.

She quickly looks away.

"A grave crime was committed during our revels – the third such crime committed within our community in the last month." My voice booms around the vast room. I let my words drip with the blood and dust of the battlefield, with every vile act I've committed and every torture I've endured. They must all know that I will not tolerate monsters in my house. *I'm* the top beast here. "Our justice must be swift. I call upon the ancient Rite of the Mora to judge this man."

"Yesssss." A hiss echoes through the crowd, the vipers coiling to strike.

"Who will judge our court?" I call.

"I will judge." Callista steps forward, her features alight with relish. "Lady Callista Valerian, of the Blood Valerian, for the Nightshade Court."

"I will judge." Perdita's staccato voice rings like music through the silent hall. "Princess Perdita Chastain, of the Blood Chastain, for the Midnight Court."

I draw back in surprise. I didn't know Perdita had undergone the rites to administer the Mora. She has more bravery than I credit her for.

"Have we a qualified representative from the Dusk Court?" calls my mother.

It's a loaded question. Members of the Dusk Court usually prefer not to reveal themselves—

"Here," a voice calls from the back of the crowd.

Vampires shuffle aside, granting the representative a clear path. A woman in a midnight dress dotted with a galaxy of gems and a diamond-studded mask over her face steps forward into the light. Something about her is familiar to me, although I cannot place it. She lifts the mask to reveal—

"Lilac?" I hear Winnie gasp from across the room.

Of course.

In the weeks that she's been serving me during Reginald's forced village outings, I've never once asked Lilac about her court affiliations. Like me, she favours drinking in silence, and I got the sense she's in Argleton for the same reasons I am – to live free of court interference. But it stands to reason she is from the court of potion masters and magicians – after all, she does mix a mean blood cocktail.

The Rose & Wimple bartender turns to me with a sad smile. "Hello, Alaric. I've been impressed with the cocktails at this party. Next time, though, I think you should go lighter on the truth potion. It leaves an aniseed aftertaste that isn't to my liking."

"Truth potion?" Bernard cries.

Spitting sounds echo around the room as vampires deposit their half-drunk cocktails back into their glasses.

"A necessary evil to unmask the killer in our midst," Callista says. "Dusk Court, will you judge?"

"I will judge." Lilac's voice rings clear. "Lilac Elisaria of the Blood Ptolemy, for the Dusk Court."

Blood Ptolemy? That means—

"This man is my sire," Lilac adds, her mouth twisting into a grim smirk. "I will see him brought to justice."

A gasp circles the room. It's rare for a vampire to turn against her sire. But the Mora allows for those of the same blood to judge. I catch the eye of Eleanor Mock of the Blood Alexandre, Komal's suspect. She nods once to Lilac. A nod of accord between them.

So Lilac's siring was nonconsensual. Another vile crime for which Baylor should suffer.

Lilac steps onto the dais alongside Callista and Perdita. Gideon appears behind them, placing two goblets onto a small table, and lays a long blade across them. Callista's blade. I'd recognise it anywhere.

Callista carries the tools of the Mora with her whenever she travels, in case she be given the opportunity to wield them.

I turn to the shocked faces of the crowd. I have seen my mother administer the Mora so many times that the rite is burned onto my soul, but many in this room have led privileged lives, sheltered from the brutality of Upyr justice.

My gaze finds Winnie again, but her golden eyes are focused on Callista and that shimmering blade.

I long to go to her, to hold her close and assure her that Baylor's evil is behind us. But she's no longer mine to hold. I thought I had torn down every wall between us, but instead, I buried our love in rubble.

Very well. If I am the monster …

I kick Baylor's slumped figure, seizing his neck and thrusting it upward. He stares up at the judges, his lip curled back in an impertinent sneer.

"This man has broken our first sacred law," I cry. "He took blood from a human woman, who was in my employ, without her consent and with the intention of drinking her dry. He has dared do this tonight, in our presence, beneath the roof of a fellow Upyr, because his thirst prevents him from thinking clearly. Because he has already husked two other humans."

Baylor tosses back his head and laughs. The harsh sound echoes through the ballroom. He doesn't say a word in his defence, just cackles until his cheeks redden and his whole body convulses.

"You're fools and liars, every one of you." He licks the dried blood from his lips. "I'm guilty of many of your so-called crimes, but I'm not the only one among you brave enough to embrace my true nature. You sit up here in your lofty houses, with your courtly rituals and your high ideals, and you think yourselves civilised. But *civilisation* is a human concept. We are predators, and they are our *prey*. You all wish you had the stomach for what I did—"

"Enough." My mother presses her foot into his face. The heel of her glittering shoe drives straight through his eye. Blood splatters across the marble, and Baylor does not laugh any longer. His cackles become shrieks of pain.

Callista calls over his cries, "Midnight Court, you may now pass judgement."

Perdita steps up to the goblets. She raises her left hand, stretching out her long, delicate fingers towards Baylor. She brings her wrist to her mouth and bites down.

She holds her wrist over the left cup, allowing droplets of her blood to splatter over the blade of the sword before collecting inside the chalice.

"Guilty," Perdita announces, her clear, musical voice ringing out over Baylor's cries.

Lilac goes next. There is nothing delicate about her as she slashes a long cut across her arm with one fang and squeezes a gush of blood over the sword and into the left cup.

"Guilty, you vile *bastard*."

My mother takes her turn, taking her time to smear her blood along the blade before dribbling it into the left chalice. "Guilty," she announces. "Dusk Court, would you like to do the honours?"

Interesting. The Lady of Agony is softening. This is one of her favourite parts of the Mora.

"Hell yes." Lilac picks up the sword. "I'm going to enjoy this. I think I'll make you eat your own testicles, you fucker."

The wound in Baylor's eye has already started to heal over, but now his screams are those of terror. His bravado cannot hold in the face of what's about to happen to him. He crawls over the floor, trailing blood from his eye. I jerk him back and pin him down while Gideon forces his mouth open. He laughs and shrieks as we force him to drink the blood of the Mora.

"You have flouted the sacred laws of the three courts, and now you carry their justice within you," Callista intones as Gideon and I haul Baylor to his feet. "You have been judged and found wanting. What is about to happen to you is your fault."

Lilac's pretty lips curl back into a snarl as she draws back her arm and drives the blade straight through Baylor's chest.

The blade slides through easily, a perfect thrust through the gaps of his ribcage. The tip emerges out of Baylor's back, sending a spray of crimson in an arc across the marble. He falls to his knees, trying to speak, but blood bubbles up between his lips.

"The rest of the ceremony will be performed in the dungeon," Callista declares as Gideon and I start to drag Baylor away. "Those who wish to observe it, follow us. Those who do not may continue the festivities."

Lilac practically skips behind us, singing a traditional Dusk song that's laden with unspoken magic. I lose sight of Winnie in the chaos as a line of vampires follows us as though we're the pied pipers of carnage out the double doors of the ballroom, along the hall, and down the narrow staircase into the castle dungeons, where Reginald has already prepared a room for the final piece of the ceremony.

"Are you staying for this?" Gideon asks as we haul Baylor onto a wooden rack and secure him. The sword still protrudes from his chest. The wound will not close because of the blood of the three courts on the blade.

"I must find Winnie."

"Right answer, friend." Gideon's hand rests on my shoulder. He opens his mouth to say something, then seems to think better of it, which is just as well because everything Gideon has ever said about

Winnie makes me want to poke a straw through his back and sip out his spinal fluid.

He pats my shoulder again and turns back to his grisly task. I hurry up the stairs. The band has started up again, and sounds of merriment echo through the castle. I scan the ballroom, but she's nowhere to be seen. None of the other book club members are there, either. Poor Reginald is trying to hold down the fort while angry, thirsty vampires surround him, demanding another round of cocktails without the truth serum.

Where is she?

I hurry through the castle, fearing it may be too late when I hear Beth's distinctive laughter from the entrance hall. I arrive as the remaining members of the Nevermore Murder Club and Smutty Book Coven are pulling on their coats. Winnie doesn't have a coat on the rack, so she pulls my winter cloak from the cupboard and drapes it over her shoulders, fiddling with the silver clasp. Her golden hair has fallen loose from its stays, cascading over her shoulders in dishevelled waves.

"Winnie." I reach out to her, but she holds up a hand to stop me, her features drawn.

"That was quite a show," Komal says. "I don't suppose you'd consider administering the Mora on my good friend Counsellor Durant, for the crime of being a complete bellend?"

"What will happen to Baylor?" Beth asks.

"Do you truly wish to know?"

All the ladies – even Winnie – nod furiously.

"He has been taken to a room in the dungeons, where Lilac will use the sword to dismember him. He'll be cut into nine pieces. Each of the three who administered the Mora will take three pieces of him back to their Court to be placed in a special Hall of Justice they reserve for such things. The blood he drank and the blood smeared on the sword will mean that he cannot heal from the wounds but also, that he will never truly die. He will continue existing, severed from his body, with no chance of being put together again, as the ages of the world pass him by."

"Good," Mina growls. "He deserves it for what he did to Danny and Patrick, and what he tried on Isis."

"It's *brutal*," Beth breathes.

"That is vampire justice."

"Remind me never to piss you off," Komal murmurs.

"You humans do that simply by existing, but as long as you are friends of Winnie, you are safe."

My joke falls flat, with only Komal managing a faint smile.

"On that cheery note, we'll be on our way." Mina checks Oscar's harness before tipping her beret to me. "Alaric, thank you for your hospitality, and for helping us to catch the murderer. And thank you for saving Isis."

I shake my head. "The credit for saving your friend goes to Winnie and Gideon."

"That's not true. We never would have found Isis in that secret room if you hadn't sniffed her out," Winnie says stiffly.

The other book club members exchange a look.

"Ladies, I think we'll just … admire the painting on that stone wall over there." Komal shoves everyone out the door, and throws a hard glare at me over her shoulder. "Come outside when you're ready, Winnie."

A moment later, Winnie and I are alone in the entrance hall. She tugs on the corner of my cloak as she kicks off her heels and shoves her feet into a pair of Reginald's Wellington boots, refusing to look at me.

"You should get to bed," Winnie says, her voice full of faux cheer as she braces herself against the chill of the night air. "It's nearly sunrise."

"I can't leave us like this. Winnie, about that room—"

She shakes her head. "I've had my fill of secrets tonight. I'm going with them. I need to see if Isis is okay."

"Winnie, please, stay with me. We can talk about this."

"I've already talked." Her voice rises. "I told you about my mother, about why I am the way I am. You've seen my nightmares about the bugs and the piles of things falling on me. I actually *believed* I was safe with you. That I could make a home here. But you took a part of that home and turned it into a *nightmare*. A nightmare that you expect me to clean up. Just once, I wish I could trust someone in my life. I wish I was worth making a change for—"

"You are worth *everything*," I growl. I'm desperate, my pulse pounding in my ears. Her strawberry perfume reeks of fear and anger. "I would give anything to make things right, Winnie. I'm not the same as your mother. I was making you a gift to show you how I feel—"

"But that's not what I need!" she cries. "I *told* you what I need. You made an oath, remember? You keep this place tidy and you tell me the truth. And one night later those promises are both ashes and dust."

"I didn't tell you about the Kiss because I will never do that to you." I reach for her, craving her warmth, certain that in my arms she'll remember that I'm hers. "And I was right to refuse it, since you do not wish to become a monster."

"No." Her eyes flash. "I don't."

And there it is – the wound that she had stitched closed in me bursting open.

Monsters don't hurt as humans do.

We hurt worse, because our skin is tougher, our hearts harder, so the knife that cuts deep must be drenched in poison.

Who can love a monster?

"You have made your decision, then."

"I have." Winnie tugs the hood of my cloak over her head, her eyes flashing.

"But I love you."

The words crack on my tongue, a sentiment I never imagined possible for me. They're supposed to be the most powerful words in the world, but the moment they fall from my lips, they collapse into dust.

Winnie shakes her head. "I'm sorry, Alaric. I know I'm hurting you. That's the problem. The person you love should make you the best version of yourself, but we make each other *worse*. And I can't spend the rest of my life cleaning up your mess."

"Then you should leave. Forever. You aren't wanted here."

My rib cage is tearing open. I love her, but she cannot survive me. I love her too much to make her like me. So I will make sure she is safe from me, no matter the cost.

"Alaric—" She steps back, her eyes flooding with tears.

"You. Aren't. Wanted." I punctuate each word with a flash of fang. "You breezed into my castle with your loud music and your ideals and your *system*, and you took everything I am and organised it into neat little boxes to make me into someone who was palatable to you. But it was all pretend. You're afraid of me because I see you, I see everything you've tried to hide from the world. But you never saw me. You only saw a project – someone you could fix the way you could never fix your mother."

"You're being cruel."

"You are shocked? I am showing you who I truly am, Winifred. You were right – there is no Winnie Wins system to fix what is broken between us. You can't spend your short human life cleaning up messes and hiding away from the world."

She gasps as tears spring from her eyes and begin to trickle down her cheeks. She whirls on her heel and sprints outside, desperate to get away from me.

I can smell the salt of her tears.

She doesn't look back.

51

Winnie

Dora: We've taken Isis to her flat. We'll see you all there once vampire justice has been done.

WE CROWD INTO KOMAL'S GIANT ARGLETON HELITOURS MINIVAN and she careens back in the direction of the village, dodging around the vampires crowding the road as they start to head back to their homes before the sun comes up.

Thankfully, the members of the Nevermore Coven are too busy holding on for their lives to notice the tears cascading down my face—

"Are you okay?" Beth squeezes my thigh. "You're crying."

"I'm in fear for my life."

"Don't worry. Komal flies helicopters, and that's way scarier. At least in a car, we're already attached to the earth."

Maisie squeezes my knee. "Oh, Winnie, honey. Whatever is wrong, you two will fix it."

We can't fix this.

I didn't realise until that moment that I'd been waiting for him to fight for me. Alaric the warrior, who swore that he would never let anything hurt me again, would come swooping in, sword swinging, and make it all better.

Instead, he's driven a stake into my heart.

Alaric can't be what I need, and I'll never be what he needs.

I swipe at my tears. "I'm just worried about Isis."

"We all are. And when this is over, you can tell us the real reason you're crying," Mina says.

I wish my tears were for Isis, but crowding out my concern for my friend and the ordeal she's just suffered are the bugs crawling over my skin.

I close my eyes, but I see the piles of Alaric's stuff sliding across the floor. All those images of me, crumpled and distorted, shoved on top of each other in that room.

I remember squeezing through that narrow tunnel into the dark gloom.

The memories duel against my old trauma – things that I thought I'd forgiven my mother for but still appear in my nightmares.

The first time I returned after moving out and discovered the whole house was accessible only by dark, narrow corridors lined with precarious piles of stuff.

The hours and hours I've spent sorting and tossing and scrubbing and fighting with her over bags of rubbish, and six weeks later the house is the same again.

The downstairs bathroom and kitchen that we stopped using because something was leaking but we couldn't find it in the mess, so when we stood on the floors they were like sponges, and Mum wouldn't hire a contractor because she didn't want anyone to see how we lived.

Lying on my bed, staring at the ceiling, trying to sleep as I heard mice shuffle through the papers that had taken up residence in my once immaculate room.

That's what I was going back to if I stayed with Alaric. And if I became a vampire, too, I would face an *eternity* of it.

And that wouldn't be fair on him, either. He needs his art the way I need my storage containers.

I never even made him an art studio in the castle. I cleaned and organised and hid away his mess, but I didn't make a space to celebrate the joy of his creative spirit. No wonder he hid everything away. I made him feel guilty about who he is.

We're not meant to be.

I open my eyes as the car pulls over. We're in front of Spell The Tea, the witchy shop that Isis and Dora own together. Komal unlocks the side door with a key – Nevermore Coven members are the kind of friends who have spare keys to each other's homes – and we push our way through the crowded storage room of the shop to reach the staircase that accesses the flat above.

It takes everything in me to force myself up that staircase. The back of the shop is almost as bad as one of Alaric's rooms, and my trauma is too close to the surface tonight. But as we emerge into Isis's apartment, I breathe a sigh of relief to find that it's not as chaotic and cluttered as I pictured. The walls are painted in calming greys and pale blues, the floorboards have been whitewashed and covered with a pretty teal rug, and apart from a few too many crystals and candles crowding the bookshelf and nightstand, the place is relatively tidy.

Isis and Dora are cuddled on the couch beneath a fluffy teal blanket, while Arabella fusses in the kitchen, swearing under her breath as she searches Isis's cupboards. "If you want the bloody biscuits, you need to tell me where you keep them."

"They're in the biscuit tin, Arabella. That's where normal people keep their biscuits."

"This monstrosity?" Arabella shakes a ceramic laughing vampire at Isis, who manages a small giggle.

Arabella tugs off the lid and nearly drops the hideous jar when the vampire starts singing, "I vant to suck your blood."

Isis's weak laugh becomes a full-on cackle.

"How are you, Isis?" Komal, Mina and Maisie run straight to her side. Oscar sits obediently beside the couch as Mina squeezes under the blanket for a hug. Out the window, the sun begins to peek above the rooftops.

Alaric will be tucked up in his coffin now. I hope he's—

No. Stop thinking about Alaric.

If I think about him, I'll bring the dead butterflies back to life. I'll remember how safe I felt in his arms. I'll talk myself out of leaving.

And I can't do that. I've spent my whole life being a spectator, sticking to the rules, keeping everything neat and tidy so no one notices that I'm a mess inside. I can't do that anymore.

"Isis seems to have recovered from her ordeal *just fine*." Arabella slams down a plate of biscuits and a cup of tea with such force that the table wobbles.

"I feel a little woozy, and my neck stings, but otherwise, I'll live." Isis sits up and picks up the teacup. "Thank you for saving me, Winnie."

"I'm just happy we found you in time." Fresh tears well in my eyes at the thought that I'd put my new friends in danger. I drop Alaric's heavy, fur-trimmed cloak on the floor. "I'm so sorry that I suggested this plan. I didn't mean to—"

"Nonsense, Winnie. Don't you blame yourself for that man's evil. Besides, that is far from the most dangerous plan we've ever pulled off," Maisie says. "Remember when we decided to help that palaeontologist excavate those fairy remains and accidentally cursed Dora?"

"I'll never forget it," Dora shudders.

"Or when you lot decided to blackmail the head of the vampire mafia and I had to use all of my connections to bail you out of his secret dungeon?" Arabella rolls her eyes.

"She'll never let us live that one down," moans Komal.

Dora leans over to press her hand to Isis' forehead. Her arm brushes mine. Dora stiffens.

"Winnie ..." Dora's chest heaves. "Your mother needs you."

I grit my teeth. "She really doesn't."

"Have you had a call from her?"

I pull out my phone. There aren't any of her usual nonsensical texts about the Council, which is odd. What's more odd, there are several missed calls from Ken, Mum's neighbour. My stomach twists.

"My mother can wait until we know Isis is okay."

"I'm *fine*," Isis says. "And we caught the bad guy, so no one else is going to be hurt. Tonight was a triumph. You all must be tired. We haven't slept all night. But I think I'd like one of your healing teas, Dora. The one that makes people feel safe. I … I don't think I'll be able to fall asleep without it."

Isis's eyelashes flutter against her cheeks. I hate seeing her like this, so listless and frightened – the opposite of the boisterous, overconfident witch I've come to adore.

"Of course, sis. I'll need some fresh yarrow. I have some in my garden." Dora slides her arm from beneath her sister and lays Isis's head on one of her teal pillows. Seeing the love between them is the last straw.

My tears spill over.

Even though I knew better, I still *wished*.

I'm still that same lost little girl wishing that her mother would wake up and see her.

That her father would walk through the door again.

That her fiancé would truly love her.

That her monster, her vampire knight, would ride to her rescue.

But now that final hope is *gone*.

I collapse into the sofa, my body folding in on itself.

"Winnie, we've got you," a kind voice says. My friends wrap their arms around me. "It's okay to cry. Let it out. We're here for you."

Through the fog of tears, I'm dimly aware of my phone ringing again. I fumble for it, but Dora takes it from my hand and answers for me.

I shake my head. "I don't want to talk to him."

"It's not Alaric. It's someone named Ken."

A surge of adrenaline hits me, almost knocking me to the ground. *All those missed calls.* I press the phone to my ear and try to keep my voice steady. "Hi, Ken, I'm sorry that I—"

"Winnie, you'd better come home, love." Ken's voice cracks. "There's been a fire."

52

Winnie

Mina: Let us know when you get to London safe, Winnie. The Nevermore Murder Club are thinking of you. Isis is concocting a good luck spell for you as I type!

"IS THIS THE PLACE?" THE DRIVER CALLS BACK TO ME AS HE PULLS in behind a red fire truck.

Rain pelts the windows of the taxi. I squint out at the end of the row of red-brick townhouses – or, at least, where my mum's townhouse *should* be.

I'm still expecting to see the grimy white trim, windows blacked out from stuff piled inside, and the wisteria clogging the junkyard that is the front garden and crawling up the siding in a possessed-house-sinking-into-the-swamp-from-whence-it-came way.

Instead, I'm greeted by a pile of smoking rubble, a bunch of firefighters and police officers, and neighbours milling around in their dressing gowns. Bricks topple from the walls of Ken's house next door. His sitting room is open to the elements. I can still see the canasta game he and Barry had set up at the dining room table.

“This is the place, thank you.”

I pay the driver and drag my suitcase onto the pavement. He doesn’t offer to help. I don’t blame him. I wouldn’t want to leave the dry comfort of a cab for this disaster.

Water splashes up my trousers as I manoeuvre my case up the wonky steps, lifting it over a swelling carton of magazines and a stack of no less than seven broken pairs of rollerblades. I drop the case in a pile of wisteria.

Broken shards of my heart thud against my chest.

“Mum?”

She blinks from beneath the blanket the paramedics have wrapped around her shoulders. She’s wearing a threadbare t-shirt and soiled bunny rabbit slippers. Her eyes are hollow, haunted. “You came,” she croaks.

“Of course I came.” I wrap her in my arms. I’m shocked at how thin she is beneath her enormous shirt, her bones sticking from her skin.

“Oh, Winnie, it was awful. I was asleep. Ken and Barry were up late because it was Barry’s birthday and they were mid-way through a bottle of wine when Ken smelled smoke and called the fire department. If he hadn’t banged on the window, I wouldn’t have got out in time. The fire-lady over there says they think it started in the kitchen. It was probably that old microwave. You were always telling me to get rid of it—”

“Shhhh, don’t worry about it.” I press her to me. “I’m just glad you’re okay.”

“Poor Ken,” she sniffs. “They’ve said his house is probably condemned as well.”

“He’ll forgive you.” I’m not sure that he will, but we’ll deal with that later. “He’ll have insurance. The important thing is that no one got hurt. And it looks like the fire is almost out.”

“I lost everything, Winnie. All our memories. My whole life was in that house.” Her lip trembles. Tears streak her cheeks. “I don’t know what to do.”

"Let's not think about that now. I see someone's brought you a cup of tea." I pick a cup off the fence post next to her and realise it's empty. "I'll find someone to refill this for you. Everything's better after a cup of tea."

I notice she's clinging to a small, rectangular object.

"I found this in the rubble," she sniffs, holding it out to me. "The council lady can't force me to get rid of it now."

It's a framed photograph. The glass has smashed and the wooden frame is stained with soot, but the image inside is preserved. It's a photo of me, posing with Mum and Dad in Santa's grotto at Hamleys on Regent Street. One of the last photos of us all together before he left.

A hard lump forms in my throat.

All the years I have let this house rule my nightmares, and now it's gone.

Someone has taken my soul and put it through one of those old-fashioned clothes manglers.

Mum strokes the frame, peering up at me with childlike innocence. I try to remember when our relationship did this one-eighty and I became the grown-up and her the child, but it's too long ago now to recall.

"It's going to be okay, Mum." I force my lips into a smile. "I'm here. I'll look after you."

53

Winnie

One month later

> **Faye:** Winnie, I got a job through this morning and they asked for you specifically. That's a bit rude – I hope you're not telling clients to do that. We are supposed to be partners. But I suppose it's okay just this once since I have some promo for the TV show to shoot today. I'll also need you to brainstorm some ideas for a new clutter anagram. People are going to be confused by Winnie Wins because my name isn't Winnie! Ta, doll!

"YOU BETTER NOT BE GETTING RID OF ANY OF MY STUFF," MUM calls out as I drag four heavy tote bags filled with Savemart purchases into the hallway, where the hotel manager waits to whisk them away to the tip.

Clack-clack-clack go the keys on the typewriter she rescued from someone's skip bin the other day, burrowing into my skull.

"Of course not." I shut the door as quietly as possible and start shifting cups around our small kitchenette. "I'm making a cup of tea. Do you want one?"

Clack-clackity-clack. She's in the middle of writing her memoir.

"Sure, thank you, honey. You're always so considerate." *Clack-clack-clack.* "I've had such an interesting life. When I publish this, I'll be rich and famous and we won't even need to wait on the silly insurance to get a new house. It's going to be amazing."

Clack-clack-clackity-CLACK-CLACK.

Stab me with a rusty spoon.

I push a bunch of half-empty cereal cartons off the bench I cleaned two hours ago and unearth the kettle. As I lift the lid on the jar containing the tea bags, a little mouse pokes his head out and wiggles his whiskers at me.

I wish I could say that mouse made me scream, but the truth is that I'm now used to seeing them again and hearing their little rodent feet scurrying around at night. The hotel isn't exactly top-of-the-line, but it's all I can afford.

I replace the lid of the tea tin and hunt out another stash of teabags in the cupboard that bear no signs of teeth marks, while Mum clacks away in the bedroom. As I bring her tea through to her, she flips on the telly. An ad for the *Clutter Queen* show blares from the screen, Faye's grinning face mocking me.

"Turn that off before I pull a Keith Moon and toss the telly out the window."

"But this place doesn't have a swimming pool. All you'd do is drop it on the cafe awning downstairs." Mum flips the channels. "I don't understand why you're not on the show. I thought you and Faye were business partners."

I thought so, too.

Another mouse scurries along the skirting board behind the tallboy. I yelp and dart into the bathroom, slamming the door behind me.

I can't live like this anymore.

I've been sharing this small hotel suite with Mum for the last month. The rebuild on her and Ken and Barry's places can't begin until the insurance pays out, and they're dragging their heels. So, for now, she's homeless.

At least I managed to drag her to a doctor after she wouldn't stop coughing, and she's been diagnosed with a severe respiratory illness from the dust and mould that accumulated in her old place. She also hasn't cooked for herself for nearly two decades, since her hoarding put the kitchen out of commission, so she's severely malnourished and can barely fend for herself. This means that when I'm not working, I'm nurse, chef, maid, and amateur psychologist. She needs my help, and I don't exactly have anywhere else to go.

Being busy is good. I'm helping Mum and it keeps my mind off a forlorn castle and a certain grumpy, beautiful vampire …

But some days, I can't see how I'll ever dig us out of this hole. Like today.

I sit on the closed lid of the loo and try to sob into my hands so Mum doesn't hear me.

I miss Alaric. I miss him so badly that the pain is physical – a constant tightness in my chest, like the butterflies are being stretched on a rack. I miss his wry humour and his rare laugh and the way he made me feel safe … until he didn't.

I miss having friends like the Nevermore Murder Club and Smutty Book Coven. I miss being able to sink into a comfy beanbag and unload my problems on empathetic women.

I miss laughing.

I miss Black Crag's creepy, gothic beauty.

I miss Reginald's hot chocolate.

I miss Mirabelle's mischievous nature and mouse-catching abilities.

I miss Alaric. I might've mentioned that.

I miss *myself.*

I don't know who I am anymore. I'm not the same person who left on that train to Argleton, but I don't recognise this new Winnie, either. She's like a stained glass window that's been smashed to pieces and put back together by a stoned squirrel.

Clack-clack-clackity-clack-clack.

Inside the walls of this motel room, I've lost Winnie. Every day when I come home from work there are more Savemart boxes and piles of random papers. The cleaning staff complained to management about the state of our room, so on top of everything else I now have to try and sneak her stuff out so we don't lose the room.

Mum switches to the Home Shopping channel. I dab my eyes several times until I'm calm enough to move, then smooth down my outfit and exit the bathroom.

"I have to go to a job."

"What about your tea? You left it on the tallboy."

"You have it." I square my shoulders and plaster a smile on my face. "I don't need tea. I'm fuelled by my torn cuticles and feminine rage."

I dash outside before she can waylay me to read her memoir. While I wait for my Uber, I pull up my bank account app and stare at the number, wishing it was bigger. I've been working ten hours a day, taking on as many Clutter Queens jobs as I can fit in (which is all of the jobs, since Faye is busy with the TV show). I'm trying to save enough money to get Mum into a flat of her own so I don't have to listen to typewriter keys pounding in my skull.

At least the work keeps me occupied; it keeps me from thinking about *him*.

Because when I think too much, I start to wonder if maybe we could have found a way through the gulf that divides us. I begin to ask myself if my trauma made me overreact to his secret room, or if my visceral reaction to the idea of the Kiss is more about my fear of committing to someone who might let me down. I bet that's what Harudha would say if I could still afford to see her.

But then I'll remember that Alaric *did* let me down, and he was supposed to be the one thing in the world that was safe.

And the worst part is, I can't even talk to the Nevermore Murder Club and Smutty Book Coven about it all.

At first, the girls sent me nearly daily updates from Argleton. But after I didn't answer them, they slowly stopped texting. Last week they removed me from the group chat.

That stung, but it's for the best. They were a fun part of my life for a while, but my world is Mum and insurance companies and trying to save my business relationship. I can't be distracted by supernatural shenanigans and book clubs. It's not as if I have any time to read anymore, and I shouldn't be thinking about …

I bet Alaric went to Europe with Perdita. Is Black Crag falling into disrepair with him gone? Does Reginald live there by himself? I imagine he's keeping the silver polished and Mirabelle fed until Alaric and his beautiful vampire wife return next summer to enjoy hosting balls and swimming in the grotto …

No. I jam my fists into my eyes. *Don't torture yourself.*

Alaric isn't mine. He never was.

This was always how it was supposed to be.

~

When I arrive at the new client's Belgravia house, I suck in an awed breath. Even by Clutter Queens standards, this house is hella posh. All of the fancy windows appear mirrored, throwing back reflections of the tidy street. I wonder briefly if Patrick might have installed them. His company made bespoke windows and he worked on several old houses in this neighbourhood. I shove the thought away.

I check for mouse droppings or cereal crumbs on my coat, smooth down my hair as best I can, and reach for the bell.

"Oh, thank the gods. I was terrified you wouldn't show." A woman throws open the door before I ring. She tugs a black veil down over her face like a sinister Victorian widow. Her comically large beaded earrings make a tinkling sound as she darts forward. "Come in quickly. I have to get out of the sun."

She's a vampire.

I don't know what gives away her secret. Perhaps it's the alabaster pallor of her skin beneath the veil or the excruciating beauty of her voluptuous figure. Possibly it's the ancient tilt of her eyes, as if she has seen through eons and has too many stories to tell. But when she wraps her long fingers around my arm to drag me inside, and I feel the coolness of her undead skin, I know that I'm right.

She slams the door behind me. Inside, the house is bright, even though the windows are so dark they are practically blacked out. Expertly placed lighting illuminates large pieces of modern artwork against crisp white walls. The old Victorian house has been gutted and reimagined as a modern open plan space – architectural features like ornate cornices and plaster details sharing space with a dazzling floating glass staircase and steel industrial design. Every space has been tastefully adorned with designer furniture and yet more artwork.

"You must be Winnie. I'm Viviana. Welcome to my home." Viviana sweeps her arm dramatically around. "I'm told that you have a way with people like me, that you can help us to celebrate the life we have lived while enabling us to let go of what we no longer need to carry."

Who said that about me? But it's rude to ask, so instead I nod vigorously. "Thank you for trusting me. You have a beautiful home. Perhaps you could show me where you need my help."

Viviana leads me down a wide corridor to what is clearly intended to be a bedroom, but it's packed with stuff. I bite back the bile sticking in my throat at the sight of those stacks and piles.

Viviana called me because she wants to get rid of her stuff. Unlike certain other vampires that shall not be mentioned, she wants *to change.*

"My wife and I have had our application accepted by the Conclave," she says. "We are siring a new vampire."

"You're giving someone the Kiss?" I can't help the fission of curiosity running down my spine.

"We are! Not a child, you understand. That's not allowed. But they will be *our* child, someone who has been let down by their human life and deserves another chance. They will need to live with us while they adjust to their new form, so I'm making this room ready for them." She smiles wistfully. "My wife and I have carted these objects around many homes over our lifetime. Each one of them is a memory from our lives together, but it's time to clear them out to make room for new memories. It's such a big job and I haven't been able to face it. I'm afraid—"

"I can help you," I assure her. "I have a system, the Winnie Wins System, although I'm not sure it's quite the right thing here. But let's get started and we'll see where we end up."

~

I work with Viviana for hours, long into the night, and I enjoy myself so much that I don't even need to pull out one of my playlists. She pours herself a glass of blood, orders Indian on UberEats for me, and makes herself comfortable on a Timothy Oulton pouf while I hold up each object for her to make her decisions.

It takes a long time because, for every piece I hold up, Viviana has a story to tell me about where she acquired it and its significance to one of her many lovers. But I love every moment. She draws me in with her stories – the places she's travelled, the world history she's been part of, and her literal eternal zest for life and adventure. And now she's on the cusp of another adventure – siring a new vampire with her love. For the first time since I was at Black Crag, I feel the insatiable itch of doing good work. Work that *helps* someone, even if that someone is a rich, vivacious vampire.

I realise at some point during hour three that part of my job is to be a witness for memories. Viviana needs to touch each object, to speak its significance, and only once this is done can she release it.

"I have an idea," I say.

Viviana helps me clear a wall in her hallway. We place each item in front of it as though it's a piece of art, and I snap a photo with my phone. I'll put them in an album for her, so she can return to the pieces and their memories without needing to physically keep the items.

"This is working, Winnie." Viviana pours herself another glass and clicks a button near the window so the glass becomes opaque, letting in a square of pale moonlight. "I've been staring at this room for months, willing myself to begin, but it seemed so daunting to sift through all these memories. You make it so manageable. And you never make me feel silly for carrying these things around for years."

I wish I had done the same for Alaric. I made him so afraid of being himself that he created a secret room to hide his heart from me.

"Thank *you* for sharing your life with me," I say. "This has been a special job. Now, what about this jewellery box? The markings on the bottom look French—"

"Oh, that." Viviana's hand flies to her mouth. I'm surprised to see tears spring in the vampire's eyes. "I didn't expect …"

"Are you okay?" I quickly set it down. "Do you need a moment alone?"

"It's fine." She waves her hand in front of her face. "It was centuries ago. It's simply that … I loved a human once. The great love of my life."

My heart hammers against my chest. "You did?"

"This was during my early days as an Upyr, before many of the rules we have today about what is right and proper for vampire and human relations. I was in the French court and I met a woman there – the most remarkable woman, with a voice like stardust and the most impeccable taste for the finer things in life. She gave me that jewellery box so that I would remember her. She wanted me to give her the Kiss. *Begged* me for it. But I refused her."

"Why?"

I shouldn't pry, but I'm so curious about it, and Alaric never told me a thing except how much he hated his mother for giving him the Kiss.

"I told her that I loved her as she was and I didn't want her to become a monster like me. Finally, she grew tired of asking and married another. I haven't thought of her in such a long time, but oh …" Viviana turns the box in her fingers, her voice shaking. "You see … I realised decades later that I lied to her. I didn't refuse her because I was afraid of turning her into a monster. I was afraid that if she knew the joy of eternal life, then she would have no need of me anymore. I didn't believe that love could endure over centuries. In time, everything crumbles. Walls, civilisations, hearts. I was so scared of losing her that I ended up driving her away."

The hard lump in my throat makes it difficult to get words out. "I'm sorry."

"Don't be." Viviana hands me the jewellery box. "I want you to keep this, Winnie. Let it remind you to never be too stubborn or too afraid to love. Things that break can be repaired, and become all the more beautiful for the cracks. Eternity is a long time for regrets."

I shouldn't accept such a gift from a client, especially not one dripping with rubies and gold filigree, but once she places it in my hand I find it impossible to let it go.

"Thank you," I whisper, forcing back the tears pricking in my own eyes.

Eternity is a long time for regrets.

In time, everything crumbles …

… even walls as high as mountains.

By the time Viviana ushers me out the door, it's close to midnight. We've made a serious dent in her collections and I've agreed to return next week. I struggle to accept her praise. My mind is hundreds of miles away, in a gloomy castle perched atop a rocky crag, sitting in front of a cosy fire across from a man whose fathomless eyes still haunt my dreams.

With the jewellery box under my arm, I return to the motel, my skin already crawling with invisible bugs – bugs that I cannot seem to banish. I slide my key into the lock but can't quite convince myself to turn it, to walk back into the living nightmare that is my life.

But as I'm debating heading out to drink myself into a stupor, I hear my mother's voice inside … and another voice as well.

She's arguing with the telly.

But I can't shake the timbre of that other voice. Even through the door, it courses through my body, curling my toes and waking the butterflies from their deep slumber.

It's a voice that absolutely *shouldn't be here.*

It's Alaric.

54

Winnie

What's he doing here?

He's supposed to be in Argleton.

Why is he in this shitty hotel talking to my mother?

My hand trembles as I shove the key in the lock and turn the handle as quietly as possible, slipping inside without announcing myself. My heart leaps into my throat as I huddle in the kitchen, careful not to stand on the pile of crinkly papers Mum has acquired since I left, and strain my ears to the bedroom.

I *need* to know what they're saying.

"—I don't even know why I'm like this," Mum sniffs. "I try so hard to be normal, but then I see something and I tell myself, 'That's it. That's what I need. That thing will change my life.' Part of me knows that's not true, but another part of me *doesn't.* But I can't make both sides of me agree."

From where I'm standing, I see them both. Mum's lying on the bed, her filthy bunny slippers that she refuses to get rid of perched on the TV cabinet. She has a box of tissues beside her and a whole row of teacups on the bedside table. Alaric sits across from her, one leg tucked beneath him, his aristocratic clothes all rumpled and his head bent toward her, listening with that intense expression of his. He has a mug in his hands, but he doesn't drink from it.

Seeing him winds me. I can't breathe.

Alaric is here, *in my hotel room, talking to my mother.*

"—Winnie hates me," my mother is saying. "I don't blame her. I tried so hard to give her a good life after her father left, but everything I tried was a failure. I don't blame her for moving away."

What?

The slightest breeze could knock me over. My mother has never, *ever* spoken like that before. She brushes off my father leaving as no big deal. She says that she was going to kick him out anyway. She claims that if she had "more free time" or a "better system", then she'd get on top of her hoarding.

I thought she loved her stuff more than she loves me.

"I understand. I too built a wall of things around me," Alaric says. "A fortification so high and deep that no one could break through and hurt me. But someone *did* break through. Your daughter. And she showed me the joy that comes with tearing down the walls."

"It's too late for me." Mum honks into her tissue.

"You are still breathing. It is not too late. You still have your daughter, who made her whole career out of helping people just like you, all because she feels as though she failed you. I've been reading a book about our condition. We are not doomed to live like this, driving away the people we love. We can change, but only if we have someone called a therapist, and also support and empathy, and Winnie is ready to give you both, you have only to ask."

The tears burst, running in silent rivers down my cheeks.

"Your daughter is decisive," Alaric continues. "She's like a modern automobile. She tells herself she wants to do something and she does it. It's one of the many qualities that I most adore about her. But you and I are more like my butler's car. We need a lot of love and coaxing to get revved up for such a task, and even then, we never do exactly what we're supposed to do."

Mum smiles over her tissue. "And sometimes I think the devil's behind the wheel."

"Exactly." Alaric smiles back, and it's so soft and sad that my chest can't take the pain of it. "All the world sees when they look in on our lives is chaos and junk. But Winnie sees our creativity and our pain and our *hope*. She's the first person who ever truly saw me, and she found me worthy of her trust and her love, which some might argue was a foolish thing to do. Winnie has so much love and grace to give that I didn't appreciate her gift until I had broken it beyond repair. But you're her mother. She loves you unconditionally, and she wants so badly to help you. She's waiting in the kitchen, and I'd love it if we could tell her that you'll try therapy and you'll try loving her the way she deserves. Because she's worth it."

I let out a loud sob.

He … he …

I can't believe he came here to say this to her.

"Winnie?" Mum shoves her tissues under her pillow and hops off the bed. "Are you in there? You didn't make a peep. I was just having a cup of tea with your friend Alaric."

"I—" I gasp through my sobs, furiously wiping at the snot running from my nose as I step into the doorway of the bedroom. "Mum, I—"

"Oh, Winnie, there's no need for all this crying." Mum's eyes dart nervously to the kitchen. She's uncomfortable with displays of emotion. She doesn't like to think that I heard what she said to Alaric. "Do you need a cup of tea? Tea makes everything better."

For once, I don't want to push down these emotions. I'm sick of tidying away my feelings into neat little boxes to make other people happy. "Mum, can you give us a moment alone?"

Mum looks as though she wants to argue, but she twists her face into a faux smile. "I'll just go and put the kettle on."

It's a lie, of course. Mum can't find the kettle in the disaster of a kitchenette. She shuffles out of the room and closes the door behind her, leaving me and Alaric alone, although I bet every storage container I own that she has her ear to the door, listening in on every word.

Alaric stands. He's so tall that he has to stoop a little to avoid hitting his head on the grimy light. The sight of him standing amongst my mother's accumulated piles of crap, his clothes so out of place, his features pinched tight, drives me to ruin.

He's even more beautiful than I remember.

A warrior out of time, his noble steed long ago retired, but he's still here … fighting … but for what?

Alaric nods to three boxes of paperback novels and a couple of old toasters stacked at the foot of the bed. "This is how you grew up?"

Beneath the gentle question, I catch a tentative plea. *Is this what I did to you? Is this how deeply I hurt you?*

I swallow once, twice. "She goes out shopping while I'm at work. She thinks that she's helping – setting us up with the things she needs after the fire took it all. If I didn't throw most of the junk out while she's asleep, this room would be filled by now."

"Winnie, I—" His Adam's apple bobs. When he raises his eyes to meet mine, they're swimming with pain. "I never meant to hurt you like this. The moment you walked into this room, you shrank. You became less of yourself. I never saw you shrink at Black Crag until you found that secret room. I am sick to my heart that I made you feel like that."

I stare at the boxes because if I keep looking into his eyes, I will collapse. Shame burns white-hot in my throat, on the back of my neck, in the pit of my stomach. I don't want to feel this way about my own mother. But Alaric's right – I'm shrinking, and I don't know how to stop.

"You shouldn't be here," I mumble. "Perdita is probably wondering where you are."

"I am precisely where I need to be," he answers. "And Perdita is back in Italy, where she belongs. I came to give you something. I presume you haven't opened that pretty box in your hands?"

I glance down at the jewellery box Viviana gave me. I'd forgotten I was holding it. "No."

"Good. Don't open it yet. Your gift is inside, but I'm afraid it won't make much sense without the second half." He pauses to visibly collect himself. "Winnie, I have so many things to say to you. Most of them are apologies. If you wish me to leave and never return, I will walk out that door right now. I know you cannot trust my word, but please trust that much."

"How did you get a gift inside—" The butterflies are back ... and they're flamenco dancing. "*You* arranged the job with Viviana? But *why*?"

Instead of explaining, Alaric steps around the corner of the bed, over the boxes, to stand in front of me. The air between us fizzes with static – the magic that drew me to him from the moment we met still dancing on, even though the music has died.

I can't look at his eyes, so I stare at his perfectly shiny shoes. *That looks like Reginald's work.*

"I'm here because I couldn't face eternity without explaining why I broke us." Alaric clears his throat. "All the time you lived at Black Crag, I grew more afraid. Afraid that I would let slip my true nature, and you would see my fangs and run. But you didn't run, Winnie. You saw something beneath the monster, and that something made you laugh and made you feel safe. I have never met anyone who looked at me the way you did, as if I was their harbour during a storm. I wanted to prove that I was worthy of you."

"Alaric—"

"You turned me completely inside out. I'd never felt this way about anyone before. I was frightened and ecstatic and frenzied and terrified and completely in awe of you. I knew I could never be worthy of your love, but I wanted you to know that the gifts you'd given me would endure long after your heart stopped beating. So I made painting after painting of you, but nothing came out right. Then I thought to try a sculpture. On my moonlight walks down to the grotto, I found flowers the colour of your golden eyes. I dried them on a rack in the cellar and made wreaths, but they were flimsy, dead things. I kept objects you touched because they felt like holding little pieces of you. I found myself ordering gold glitter from the internet like a vampire possessed. I grew *obsessed* with my task to make something that captured *you*. I planned it as a gift to you, but now I see that I was making this art for me – because I knew I could never keep you and I wanted to hold you in my heart for eternity. Each time I fell short, I hid away the evidence in that room so you wouldn't see that I failed you."

Oh, Alaric.

"I should have just told you how I felt," his voice cracks. "I was so engrossed in my project that I didn't consider how you might react when you saw the secret room. I hid those things away, and I hid the truth about the Kiss, because I was so terrified that if you knew these bad, rotten, monstrous things about me, you would leave. As everyone I trust leaves. In the end, I drove you away, not because I'm a monster, but because I'm *me*."

I'm not prepared for the pain in his voice, for the way his words tremble in the space between us, so raw and sad and hopeless. More tears spill down my cheeks.

"Don't you see?" I breathe through my tears. "This is exactly why I left. Because you shouldn't have to change who you are for me. You have this wonderful creative mind and you shouldn't have to shove it away into a secret room because of my trauma. You are right about something – I *do* shrink. I hold myself back when things get tough, because the only way I survived growing up was by curling into a ball and waiting it out. But I don't have to do that anymore. I don't have to change, and neither do you. We're perfect the way we are, but that doesn't mean we're perfect together. And I'm not just talking about being a vampire and a human. We never would have worked."

"I disagree," he says in that rich, commanding tone that I've longed to hear again. "I love to obsess over details and make big, messy art. You love to organise. It may seem as if we are incompatible, but perhaps what we truly are is—Ah, that other half of my gift has arrived."

"The what?"

My head jerks up, and I meet his eye. It's a mistake, because I'm trying to hold onto the shattered pieces of my heart, and those dark, expressive orbs have me in their spell.

A knock sounds on the door.

Email from Claire Dempsey to Winnie Preston

Subject: You left the clutter queens!

Winnie,

I just saw on Faye's insta that you're no longer in business with her! I'm so happy. She was totally taking advantage of you.

If you read this far, I'M SO SORRY about everything.

I never meant to hurt you. Patrick and I just happened. I know you might not ever speak to me again, and I'd understand that, but I hope you read this because I have to tell you something about Lord Valerian, and you might not like it.

Patrick had to go to Argleton to meet with a new client, and I tagged along to look at wedding venues. But the client insisted on having their meetings in the middle of the night. Weird, right? Well, it gets weirder.

After the meeting, Patrick was shaky and listless and kept rubbing his neck and muttering strange things. And then he saw you with Lord Valerian and he got even more freaked out. He kept saying that he needed to warn you, that Lord Valerian was "one of them". I think that's what he was trying to do at the Midsummer Festival.

Patrick's client was the Sanctus Estate. I don't know what any of this means, but I hope it isn't bad. I just thought you should know.

Miss you,

Claire

55

Winnie

"MY VISITORS HAVE ARRIVED." ALARIC SKIRTS AROUND ME TO answer the door.

Panic seizes me. If the manager is already pissed about Mum's mess, he won't appreciate us ignoring his "no gatherings" rule at one in the morning. "It's awfully presumptuous for you to invite your own visitors into *my* hotel room—"

Alaric flings open the door. Into our tiny room traipses the entire Nevermore Murder Club and Smutty Book Coven.

"Winnie!" Isis throws her arms around me, her crystal necklaces clanking against my ribs. "We're so happy to see you again! Your aura is all muddled up. You need one of Dora's herbal teas."

"We missed you." Mina and Oscar burrow in beside Isis. Her arms encircle me. "No one stays behind to help me pick up after the meeting anymore."

"I brought you a box of cupcakes because I know you'll be eating junk London food." Celeste dumps an enormous Glazed and Confused bakery box on the kitchenette counter before joining the hug. "Avocado toast and healthy smoothies and salads without any cheese. Gross."

"And I added some of my famous mung bean brownies," Beth says as she leaps into the fray. "If you soak them in your tea, you can get them soft enough to bite."

Dora places a package of tea on top of the box and silently joins the embrace.

"I stole your parking space out front." Komal kisses my cheeks as she squeezes me tight. "The hotel manager said he'd never seen someone park quite as jauntily as me. Can you believe I shaved thirty-eight minutes off the Google Maps driving time?"

"I've never been so frightened for my life, and I spent a summer internship at journalism school reporting from an actual war zone." Maisie has to slide her arms around my hips to fit herself into the chaos.

"This place is an absolute dump," Arabella sniffs as she stalks the perimeter of the room like a panther. She's wearing an absurd wide-brimmed floppy designer hat that she does not remove even though she keeps bending the brim against the walls. As she passes me, she dares a quick kiss to the top of my head.

My heart fills with warmth. After a month in London, I'd started to wonder if I imagined them all – this chaotic, wonderful, supportive group of friends who have my back.

"What are you all doing here?" I laugh, squeezing them so hard my arms might fall off.

"Alaric asked us to come," Maisie says. "He said you and your mum might need some help moving into your new homes."

"Maisie, shhhh!" Dora hisses.

"I wish," I laugh. "We'll be living here for a while. Mum's insurance hasn't come through yet, and I can't afford a place on my own until she's all settled—"

Isis glares at Alaric. "You haven't told her yet? What are you waiting for? Unlike you, we don't have all of eternity."

Alaric taps the box that's still clutched in my hand. "Open it."

"There better not be a ring in this box." I glare at them all. "This isn't a smutty romance novel. Over-the-top gestures don't work in real life when there are issues that—"

"Just open it, Winnie!" Komal laughs.

I lift the lid. Inside the box, nestled on a bed of gold velvet, are two sets of keys – each one attached to a small, hand-carved wooden charm.

"I met a wood carver years ago in Vienna and he taught me his trade. I'm afraid I'm still an amateur. I cut the wood from the forest at Black Crag," Alaric says. "I made the sunflower for your mother, and the butterfly wings for you, because you are Wing Commander Winifred. The keys are for your new homes."

"New …" I stare at the gift in confusion. "What are you talking about?"

"Quoth sold all my pots," Alaric says. "He came to the castle and took away a bunch of my paintings and tapestries to sell, too. I ended up with all this modern money and no clue what to do with it. Reginald has been managing my accounts as well as he could, but since Arabella demanded to take over, she's made it quite clear that I have enough money to last several eternities, and I should probably start spending some of it on things that make me happy. And the only thing that makes me happy is you, Winnie. So I have bought your mother a new house. It's a little two-bedroom unit in a small gated community in Reading for people who struggle with different mental health issues. They offer a range of support services for residents, including an on-site therapist and a weekly cleaning service. The house has a small garden and a room for hobbies—"

"I have a *house?*" Mum emerges from the kitchen to snatch the sunflower key out of my hand. "I mean, I don't know that I need this weekly cleaning service, but I can't wait to see my new home!"

I notice that the centre of the sunflower is a googly eye. I can't stop the laugh that bursts out of me.

He bought my mother a house?!

But then what's the second keyring for?

A tiny, hopeful corner of a smile tugs at Alaric's lips. He nods to the second keyring, which contains two keys. "The girls helped me choose a place for you. It's in Highgate, overlooking the ancient cemetery. It includes a generous second bedroom that I thought you could use as an office for when you open your own organising business." Alaric's eyes burn into mine. "Which you absolutely should do. Viviana has been blowing up my annoying rectangle with praise for you ever since you left her. She says she has at least five friends who desperately need your services."

"Wait, Viviana told you—"

"There are people who need you, Winifred the Magnificent." Alaric's lip tugs closer to a full smile. "You don't need the Winnie Wins System to work your magic. And it's time you realised that."

I touch the beautiful carved wing, the butterflies inside me flapping like hummingbirds. "A house? I don't know if I can accept this—"

"Speak for yourself." Mum grins, fisting her key. "Komal, was it? You'd better start that van of yours. I'm going to look at my new pad!"

56

Winnie

IN NO TIME AT ALL, THE GIRLS HAVE SHOVED MUM'S NEWLY ACCUmulated possessions into the back of Komal's van. I notice Dora dumping the paperbacks into the recycling bin and flash her a grateful smile.

We pile into the van. "Where are we going, boss?" Komal asks Alaric. He takes out his phone and pinches the screen to zoom into the map to show her.

"You ... you're using a map? On your *phone?*" I can't believe it.

"I have changed my opinion about the annoying rectangle." Alaric shrugs.

"Who are you and what have you done with Alaric Valerian?"

His grin could melt the polar ice.

Komal tears off down the road, angry rock music that would be right at home on my Get Shit Done playlist blaring from the tinny speakers. The girls sing along while Isis tells my mother's fortune and Alaric ...

... Alaric smiles and laughs and jokes with them. He even sings along with a couple of songs he recognises from my playlist, his deep, rumbling tenor giving me a serious lady boner. He's learning to let down his guard around other people and have *fun*. I'm not the only one who's changed.

It's 2 am when we arrive at the new house. Alaric has a gate and door code ready for Mum, who leaps out of the van to type them in. She flings the door open and gasps. (Like mother, like daughter.)

"Winnie, come look!"

I follow her inside. She turns all the lights on and stands in the middle of the room, spinning in wild circles. "It's beautiful! I can't believe it's all mine!"

It's strange to see her in a room with crisp white walls and a floor that isn't hidden beneath mouldy papers.

Strange, and wonderful.

Maybe this is just what she needs – a place that's truly hers, away from memories of my father, away from the idea of a perfect childhood she wishes she'd given me. I know that a new house won't fix her desire to hoard, but for the first time since I left her house at eighteen, hope fills my heart when I look at her.

Maybe, with my support and love, and with a team of professionals who will help her manage her hoarding, my mum could be free of her stuff.

The Nevermore Coven marches inside, carrying the boxes of things Mum has already acquired that I haven't managed to sort yet. Maisie and Celeste get to work stacking the kitchen shelves with groceries they brought with them, while Komal and Mina fold new towels (I resist the urge to run over and colour-code them) and discretely whittle down Mum's overzealous crockery purchases. Isis and Beth re-arrange the furniture to make it, in their words, "Feng Shui AF". Arabella perches on a bar stool, filing her nails and calling out wan encouragement.

Alaric looms in the doorway, surveying the scene with furrowed brows. His eyes flick to me, and the corner of his mouth quirks into a question I don't yet have an answer for.

"Thank you," I whisper. "You don't know what this means to me, what you've done."

"I have done nothing."

"Alaric." I elbow him in the side. "You bought my mother a *house*. You convinced all my friends to go along with your crazy scheme and drive down here in the middle of the night to move her in. You convinced my mother to go to *therapy*, something that she's never before agreed to. I don't know why you did all this when your wife is waiting for you in Italy—"

"I never married Perdita."

I raise an eyebrow. "But—"

"I've had only one wife who matters to me, and she never agreed to marry me for real."

"Why are you two still hanging around?" Komal tosses her keys to Alaric. "We've got this. Go show Winnie her place."

That's right. I'd been so preoccupied with Mum that I'd forgotten Alaric said he got me a place too.

My eyes widen in surprise at the keys in Alaric's hand. "Can you even drive?"

"I am a centuries-old vampire prince from one of the most noble bloodlines of the Nightshade Court." Alaric holds out the keys to me. "I have no clue how to work that infernal contraption. You will drive. I will work the map *and* choose the playlist."

~

Alaric may be able to read a map on his phone now, but he hasn't fully grasped the concept of traffic because he leads me on a zig-zagging journey across the city before yelling at me to pull over in front of an old Victorian brick factory.

"Alaric, this isn't a house." I frown at the old brick facade as Alaric fumbles with the keys. The place is beautiful in a derelict, industrial way, but I don't see …

Oh.

Alaric holds open the enormous factory door so I can glimpse that magazine-worthy interior. Whatever genius designed this place kept the high ceilings and period features, including the old pipes and brick pillars, but they've installed a contemporary interior with glass, steel and richly veined marble surfaces. A comfy corner sofa stretches around a central fireplace that's already ablaze, and warm lighting and cosy rugs make the huge open-plan space feel homely.

"Viviana gave me the name of her architect, and he happened to be about to put this place on the market when I called," Alaric says as he drops the keys back into my hand. "The moment I saw it, I thought it screamed Her Most Majestic Madame Winifred."

Heat from the fire warms my face as I walk through the galley kitchen, running my fingers over the marble benchtop, touching the shiny new coffee machine, and kicking off my shoes to feel the soft rugs beneath my toes. I notice little details:

A record player and a bunch of records stacked on a shelf. All bands from my Get Shit Done playlist.

A stack of vampire romance novels beside them, bookmarks marking page sixty-four.

A purple container on the kitchen counter labelled 'Reginald's Hot Chocolate Mix.'

A series of storage baskets beneath the coffee table, just waiting to be filled.

A large painting placed between two of the high windows, taking up nearly the whole wall, of the night sky over the valley, with Black Crag silhouetted in the distance.

And in the centre of the glass-and-steel dining room table stands a silver candelabra, identical to the ones I had to carry around the halls of Black Crag.

He sees me.

A lump of something like *yearning* rises in my throat.

"—there's a master bedroom on the mezzanine upstairs." Alaric waves his hand at the floor above the kitchen. "Down this hallway is a guest bathroom and two rooms. One has its own entrance, and would be perfect for your storefront—"

I'm dangerously close to crying. "You put this together … for me?"

He shrugs. "All you've ever wanted is a home, Winnie. If it couldn't be with me, I thought, perhaps …"

He trails off, instead gesturing to the vast open space, the blazing fire, that cursed candelabra.

I step towards him. "Did you have help with the decor? I've noticed a distinct lack of Stabby Chic."

"Reginald and Arabella helped with the details. She says that my 'Mary Shelley meets Bernard Black' aesthetic wouldn't work for you. Do you like it?"

"I …" I swallow, my eyes stinging as I blink furiously. If I say anything more, I will burst into tears. I stare down at the keys in my hand. The one Alaric used in the front door is shiny and new, but the second is an old, clunky thing. "What's this second key for? The garage?"

"The second key is for Black Crag."

My heart stutters.

Neither of us speaks. The way Alaric's eyes study me, it's like being burned from the inside out.

Finally, he swallows, his Adam's apple bobbing.

"So many times over the years I have wondered why I endure, why I continue on this earth when I so hate what I am and what I've done. The answer is the same reason I'm standing here today – *hope*. Hope isn't some passive dream, Winnie – the hope inside me has claws and teeth and blood boiling in her veins. That key is my hope. I bought this house for you because you deserve a home that's just yours, a home that isn't built on bloodshed and haunted memories, a place where you are safe to soar. But I …" He swallows again. "I wish that you didn't want it, because you already have a home. With me."

The keys fall from my fingers.

"Alaric …" I breathe.

But I can't find words for this sensation in my chest – a blooming, as if the butterflies inside me were never butterflies at all. All this time, they've been caterpillars making their first shambling journeys, spinning their cocoons from the shards of my old, discarded life.

Now they are unfurling, blooming, becoming wonders of bright colour.

I cross the rug in two steps and throw myself at him. He starts, caught off guard, but catches me, because he's always there to catch me. Because I'm safe with him. I'm home in his arms.

When he kisses me, it's like Celeste's warm caramel sauce drizzled straight into my veins.

I've spent my whole life running from the trauma of not being able to trust someone who loves me, who was supposed to take care of me but couldn't. That fucks with your head.

But in Alaric's arms, I realise something about myself. Avoiding pain *is* a kind of hurt you inflict on yourself. Even someone like Alaric who has been through more hurt than anyone should have to endure is still here, ready to lay his heart at my feet knowing that I might choose to stamp it into mush.

I live with hope, too – hope with blood under her nails and dirt in her hair. I am *ready* to have my heart broken, because humans aren't perfect and neither are vampires. We're all sacks of skin and memories, dragging our mess around with us. Sometimes that mess is things, and sometimes it's feelings, and sometimes it's memories that aren't all happy.

I've spent my whole life trying to tidy away the mess and I've missed the beauty in it – until him. Until he showed me that not all mess is a sign of weakness. That I can be messy and loud and creative and bold and I can fuck up a hundred times and he will always be there for me, because that's what love is.

"I love you," I whisper against his lips, and the whisper becomes a cry as tears finally pour down my cheeks. "I love you, and I'm afraid."

"I'm afraid too," he whispers back. "But that's half the fun."

We crash together in a tsunami of lips and teeth and fangs and hope. His kisses are so wild and desperate that we have to breathe together to survive them. Somehow, we end up on the sofa in front of the roaring fire, our clothes thrown across the tiled floor and our hands all over each other. The white scar below his armpit glows faintly in the firelight, a reminder that all victories are hard-fought and won with blood.

When Alaric wraps his lips around my clit, my heart surrenders before my body, as if I have been waiting to be his. His fang pierces me again, driving me to such pleasure that my cries ring from the high ceiling.

After I've come again and he's spilt himself inside me with the roar of a monster untamed, he holds me tenderly, placing a pillow behind my head and wrapping fuzzy blankets around us both. We watch the fire together as the minutes tick closer to sunrise.

"What are we going to do?" I ask.

"Right now? I'm going to make you scream my name one more time before the sun rises and I have to go to sleep. I've put black-out curtains in the bedroom so—"

"No, I mean, I said I love you, but nothing has changed. You're a vampire and I'm a human. Our love is still forbidden."

Alaric stills.

I prod him. "We have to talk about it."

"We do not."

"We should have talked about the Kiss ages ago. If you'd told me, I would have had time to consider it. I could have told you that it ..." I swallow down the weight of my words. "That it doesn't repulse me. That I could be interested. Maybe."

"I won't do it. I won't make you into a monster, Winnie."

"When I get back, we're going to work on your self-esteem. Why are you so determined to believe that all vampires are monsters?" I rest my head on his chest, listening to the slow, steady thud of his heart. I squeeze him as hard as I can, but it's like squeezing stone. "You have regrets. We all do. That doesn't make you unredeemable. It makes you more human than many of my kin. I don't hate what you are, Alaric. I'm not afraid of you. I'm not afraid of being like you. I think that you're wonderful. And the idea of spending eternity with you makes me happier than a two-for-one sale on storage containers."

"You mean it?" His voice trembles. He brushes a strand of hair from my face, his eyes wide with awe.

"You make me happier than a big mess, a loud playlist, and a mug of Reginald's hot chocolate." I grin. "So yes, I would be honoured to share eternity with you. But I'd like some time to see how things go first. I have a lot of changes to make in my life, and that might be one too many all at once."

"What changes?" He sounds wary.

"I'm retiring the Winnie Wins System."

"You can't do that. It's yours. It's—"

"Faye can have it. It's outdated. *Passé*." My grin broadens. "I'm instigating the Winnie Loves System. It's a brand new approach to cleaning, and it's all mine."

Alaric's lips flatten into the long-suffering look he wears whenever I talk about tidying. "And what, I'm afraid to ask, is the Winnie Loves System?"

"I haven't exactly figured out all the letters yet, but it's going to be brilliant."

"What's the V?"

"Why are you so concerned about the V?"

"V is not a common letter." Alaric frowns. "If your new system is going to endure for all eternity, then it needs to figure out a viable V word."

"The V stands for 'Very Naughty Vampires Who Don't Listen To Their Professional Organisers Go To Bed Alone'." I stick my tongue out at him.

"That's a *terrible* system."

"I'm kidding. It stands for 'Very Much is How Much I Love You'. Just roll with it." I laugh when Alaric makes a face. "I'll figure it out. I'll have all of eternity."

"But that part is true?" His breath grazes my cheek. "About loving me?"

"That part is true."

"The way you rise from the ashes, Winnie the Majestic, even a phoenix is in awe of you," he murmurs as he leans in to kiss me again.

From the New Dracluttera Website: The Winnie Loves System

Welcome to Dracluttera – the first-ever professional organising service for the Upyr community. If your home is being swallowed by possessions you've acquired over a century (or more! We don't judge!) then take advantage of our discreet, supportive and empathetic clutter-clearing services.

No mess is too large for us to handle with our unique Winnie Loves System, designed by professional organiser Winnie Preston. We'll help you to:

Live: *Step one is about envisioning the life you want by focusing on your ideal future self, instead of looking back at the past. You have all of eternity ahead of you – what kind of vampire do you want to be? Is your stuff holding you back, or is it an important part of your growth?*

Organise: *Step two is to sort your possessions, throw out or give away the things that no longer serve you, and arrange what's left into an easy-to-use system.*

Vampy: *In this step, we celebrate how far you've come along your journey to clutter-free living! We do something fun together, whether it's making some blood cocktails, going shopping for a new coffin lining, or buying that Alaric Valerian painting you've been eyeing off (link to his shop here). The goal is to empower you to keep going even when things are difficult.*

Evocation: *This step is about speaking and preserving your memories so you no longer have to store them in objects. We'll show you different techniques to safeguard your legacy.*

Support: *This is the most critical step of all. For you to sustain your new clutter-free life, you need a support system of family, friends and professionals who will keep you accountable and lift you up when you have setbacks. You'll also be able to join our online support group for vampire hoarders, and even attend night-time clutter seminars.*

Here at Dracluttera, we want every Upyr to succeed and thrive! Contact Winnie today for a no-obligation quote. And yes, we do accept payment in ancient gold coins and/or particularly beautiful jewellery.

57

Winnie

Komal: I don't care how tired you are from moving or how much you want to shag your hot vampire boyfriend after he wakes up from his day nap, we'd better see you at book club tonight! (And this probably goes without saying, but DO NOT EAT Beth's carrot cake. It contains things that no carrot cake should ever contain.)

"Do you really like it?"

"I told you I like it. What will it take to make you believe me, human?" Alaric growls. "Perhaps if I tie you to it and lick you all over your body until you beg for mercy? Then would you believe that I like it?"

"Maybe." I grin. "Or maybe you'd have to bite me, to really convince me."

Alaric sits across from me in front of the blazing fire, his dark gaze drawn upwards by the large display case I've installed along one wall of the sitting room. It houses a selection of his swords and weapons.

I understand now why he was holding onto them. Each one of them is a part of his story. They bear the scars of the battles he's fought.

Even though the scars on his soul will never heal, they are part of his story. Part of what makes him the vampire I fell in love with.

Things that break can be repaired, and become all the more beautiful for the cracks. Even hearts. Even souls.

Not every chapter of our stories is smutty or nice or bloodless, but who are we without the history we carry around with us?

Alaric lifts his goblet to his mouth, taking a deep sip. His eyes drop to my face, heavy with pleasure, flecked with golden firelight. "What did you do with the rest of the swords?" he asks.

"They're in trunks down in the dungeon. I thought maybe you could make them into a sculpture or add another wing to the Stabby Chic hall. Ooh, better yet, we could use them to decorate the walls of my office! That way, when new clients walk in, they'll know that they'd better listen to me … or else."

"But if you're ever called to go through with your threat, your unruly client would quickly discover that you have two left feet and can barely swing a blade."

"I'm sure that with an eternity to practise, I'll be able to stab something. Maybe not my target, but *something*. It would help if my swordmaster could get through a lesson without grinding his giant vampire cock into me and fucking me against his loom."

Alaric raises a dark slash of eyebrow. "Is that a complaint … or a request?"

I snuggle deeper into my chair. Alaric has just arisen from his nap, but I've been busy all day, moving my things back into the castle and arranging my new office desk in the bay window of the library. If I'm going to see Dracluttera clients in Argleton as well as London, then I need a place to work, and I couldn't ask for more than the scenic view down the valley from my very own *Beauty and the Beast* library.

And speaking of my beast …

Alaric may be sipping his blood like he has no other care in the world, but I can tell from the way his eyebrow twitches that he's excited to get to his creative wing of the castle and work on his new project. He's putting together an art exhibition with Quoth – after the success of Alaric's moonscapes, they think they might be able to get a London gallery interested. And Komal has asked him if she can install his model of Argleton in the tourist office, so he wants to give it a fresh coat of paint.

It's amazing how tidy Black Crag is now that Alaric has outlets for his passions. He gets such a thrill from seeing people enjoy his work, and then he takes that thrill out on my body. We all win.

Especially me.

Eternity is a long time for regrets.

We decided to keep the house in London. I'll go down there every few weeks to see clients and Alaric and I will stay in the city and practise being in the world. He's yet to experience the joy of late-night gallery openings, fast food, escape rooms and terrible musical productions, but I intend to show him *everything*.

And as for my Kiss, we haven't set a date yet, but we're talking about it, getting used to the idea. I'm not ready yet, but I think I will be soon.

"Gideon has been talking you up to everyone on the Sanctus Estate. My mother and Perdita have been spreading the word at their respective courts. I think you'll have no end of clients willing to pay top dollar for Dracluttera services. That is, if you don't mind avoiding garlic before client meetings?" Alaric raises an eyebrow.

I tilt my G&T towards him. "I don't know. I *do* love garlic, especially in Reginald's cooking. But not as much as I love you."

"Reginald is so pleased to have you back." Alaric sets down his empty goblet. "He loves having someone to cook for. You know that when he found out you left, he yelled at me."

"I don't believe it." Reginald has never raised his voice above a polite murmur. *Never.*

"It's true. He called me a most colourful assortment of names, none of which can be repeated in the company of a lady." Alaric's tongue lashes against his lower lip, licking up a droplet of blood. "It was his idea to give you the key to Black Crag. He always believed you'd come back. He even helped me clean out the priest hole. Well, most of it."

"Most of it?" A familiar worry stabs my chest. I don't want surprises when piles of stuff are concerned.

"Yes. We decided to save this." Alaric reaches into his pocket and pulls out a fist. "I made it in my forge."

He unfolds from his chair, and as he stalks across the rug towards me there's something of the predator in his eyes. But then he drops to his knees in front of me, holding out his hand.

He unfolds his long fingers to reveal a ring.

I gasp, my usual reaction to anything when Alaric is involved. The ring is *perfect.* It has a rough, organic surface, and the gold bears the deep lustre of age. A large, blood-red ruby in the rough shape of a heart sits at the centre.

I tear my eyes from the stone to look at Alaric. The firelight bathes his high cheekbones, his alabaster skin and the firm line of his mouth. The black depths of his eyes reach inside me – deep and sharp and hard as anthracite, creating a perch for the butterflies that never seem to stop dancing when he's near me.

"A wise person told me once that I should be more vulnerable." His lip quirks a little. "That no matter how high I built my castle walls, someone would tear them down. That someone was you, Winnie. You sieged straight into my heart and razed those walls to dust, and I laid down my arms and let you do it because I didn't even realise how desperately I wanted to be free. I have everything I ever dared to wish for and more, all because of you, and all I want is to give you everything you deserve. You told me once that your intention for your life is to allow yourself to be happy. And I hope, I wish, that maybe, you could be happy with me, as my wife."

My heart and my lips answer at the same time. "Hell yes!"

I fall into him and he falls into me and we're hugging and kissing and crying and laughing and it's *perfect.* He pulls me down onto the rug with him, rolling me beneath him, pressing the hard planes of his body against mine as he slots the ring onto my finger, and I can't believe he's mine *forever.*

Forever is a long time, but I'm ready.

"Patrick was working for the Sanctus Estate?" Isis shrieks. "That connects him to Danny. They were both getting their necks sucked, and they both knew vampires existed. How did we not know this?"

I'm back in my favourite beanbag, munching on one of Celeste's red velvet cupcakes with a mug of tea in my other hand, while Beth tries in vain to get everyone to try one of her cordyceps-infused wheatgrass jellies. The ladies of the Nevermore Murder Club and Smutty Book Coven are spread out around me, enjoying two of their favourite pastimes – discussing a supernatural mystery and teasing each other mercilessly as only good friends can.

And now they're *my* friends. I can't believe how lucky I am.

"It hardly matters," Arabella says. "We caught the killer."

"It *does* matter, because even if Baylor killed Patrick, Claire's email tells us someone on the Sanctus Estate was drinking from him without his consent," Dora says. "Maybe we can't trust this Gideon Blake."

"I don't trust anyone with the name Gideon," Arabella thrusts her nose in the air. "That name has been ruined forever for me."

"Ex-boyfriend?" Komal smirks.

"Something like that."

"I can't believe it never occurred to me that Patrick could be connected to the estate," I say. "Patrick's work was making bespoke windows, and of course a vampire property development would require special sun-resistant glass."

"I don't blame you, Winnie. You were distracted by the hot vampire lord." Isis glares at Maisie. "*Some* people, whose literal job it is to *investigate*, should have uncovered that information."

Our resident gumshoe throws up her hands in mock surrender. "Patrick's firm wasn't going to release information about his clients to the press. And we caught the murderer, remember?"

"Yes, but if someone at Sanctus is hiring humans to work on the estate, using them as food, and at least two of those humans have ended up husked, we should probably investigate."

"I know!" Isis pipes up. "One of us gets a job there and seduces Gideon into telling them the truth. I vote Beth."

"Excuse me?" Beth glares at Isis. "Why me? What about you?"

"I'm too important." Isis puffs out her chest. "I'm the psychic. My skills are needed elsewhere. The only skill you bring to the table is pole dancing, which will come in handy for the seduction—"

I shake my head. "We're not using humans as vampire bait again."

"Sanctus are looking for buyers for the remaining houses, right?" Maisie says. "Someone who lived there could get right up close to the action and figure out what's going on."

"But none of us are vampires except for Alaric," I point out. "And my betrothed is many things, but a skilled and cunning spy is not one of them."

"Fine." Arabella sighs. "I will do it."

All eyes swivel to her.

"What makes you think you're going to be able to infiltrate a community of rich, snobby vampires?" Isis asks.

"Because," – Arabella flicks her hair over her shoulder – "as a vampire myself, I've purchased a home in the Sanctus Estate."

EPILOGUE

The Killer

I WATCH FROM THE SHADOWS AS WINNIE LEAVES THE BOOKSHOP, jogging up the street to where her vampire and his butler await her.

Things worked out peachy in the end. But the Nevermore Coven is not out of danger yet.

There will be vampires who don't approve of Lord Valerian flaunting his relationship with a human. Some of those vampires may take matters into their own fangs.

The Nevermore Coven are feeling smug about their victory. They brought Baylor to justice. A fitting end for a vile creature.

What they don't know is that Baylor, while guilty of many transgressions, is innocent of these *particular* crimes.

The Nevermore Murder Club and Smutty Book Coven is not the only source of justice in this village. I too am ridding the world of vile creatures.

I'm here, in the shadows.

I'm watching.

My fangs are sharp.

I've only just begun.

Join the Newsletter for Updates

Read a bonus scene from Winnie's initiation into the Nevermore Murder Club and Smutty Book Coven, as well as Winnie's 'Get Shit Done' playlist, in the *Cabinet of Curiosities*, a Steffanie Holmes compendium of short stories and bonus scenes, which you can get when you sign up for updates with the Steffanie Holmes newsletter.

www.steffanieholmes.com/newsletter

I love to talk to my readers, so come join us for some spooky fun!

Love, lust and graveyard dust.

Steff

Acknowledgements

AUTHORS FIND THE ORIGIN STORIES OF THEIR NOVELS INCREDIBLY boring. Most of mine begin with "The muse visited me in the shower and gifted me this bonkers idea …" which suggests either that my muse enjoys some perverse proclivities, or that she has a thing for kiwifruit-scented body lotion.

If you're the sort of person who reads acknowledgement pages, you might enjoy the origin story of *Fangs for Nothing*. One night, I was lying on the sofa under a pile of cats, as one does, when my husband bounced in, declaring that he's come up with "a brilliant plan".

(Last time my husband had a brilliant plan, he built 60% of a garden wall before he lost interest and took up making things on a lathe. So, I am wary of brilliant plans.)

This time, his brilliant plan is to knock out a wall of our house to add an extension to house his model trains. He is trying to convince me of the merits of this plan by showing me how we could also add a pole dancing studio for me and space to store all the puzzles I procured during the first COVID-19 lockdown.

And while I'm hiding under the blankets trying not to imagine what colour I'd paint my pole studio, I find myself thinking, *At least we're not vampires. Imagine if we had a whole castle and centuries to fill it with our various hobbies.*

And so, Lord Alaric was born.

I have my husband to thank for Alaric's kindness and dark eyes and how dashing he looks swinging a sword around (mmmmm). But I can't blame Alaric's love of stuff solely on him. This story is as much about my pile of half-completed art projects and cross stitch as it is about model trains.

Thank you to all the readers who fell in love with Winnie and Alaric and the Nevermore Coven when I first indie published this book. Thank you for giving these characters a home in your hearts and on your Kindles.

This version of the book wouldn't exist without Anthea, who contacted me out of the blue because she fell in love with the world of Nevermore Bookshop, and changed the trajectory of my author career forever. Thanks also to the amazing team at Atria Australia, HarperCollins New Zealand, and all the booksellers who have enthusiastically championed this kooky, spooky romance about a grumpy vampire artist and the human who goes Marie Kondo on his heart.

Winnie and Alaric wouldn't exist without the keen editorial eyes of Becca Mysoor, Meg Cooper, and my husband, James. To Katherine and Celia for taking a loving machete to all my precious adjectives and making this story even better.

Many people support me and believe in me, even when I struggle to believe in myself. My family – my mum and dad and sister Belinda. The writers with whom I've celebrated and commiserated – Erin, Danielle, Kelly, Selena, Angel, Vic, Rachel, Kim, Isa, Amber, Mel, Marie, Devy, Elisabeth, and all the others I've missed. To AK and Nalini for the "HELP, I've got an offer. What do I do?" advice. To the bogans, my brothers and sisters of metal, for keeping me grounded. I apologise for the volume of our shenanigans that end up in my books. (That's a lie. I'm not sorry.)

Always, to my cantankerous drummer husband, who is everything. Every hero I write is a piece of you and what you mean to me.

And, lastly, to Socrates, for the eleven pivotal scenes deleted when you jumped on the keyboard. I didn't need them anyway. I'm not supposed to have a favourite cat, but you're totally the favourite, even when you're a dick.

Steff

About the Author

Steffanie Holmes is the *USA Today* bestselling author of kooky, spooky paranormal, cosy fantasy and gothic romance. Her books feature clever, witty heroines, secret societies, quirky villages where nothing is as it seems, creepy old mansions and alpha males who *always* get what they want.

Legally blind since birth, Steffanie received the 2017 Attitude Award for Artistic Achievement. She was also a finalist for a 2018 Women of Influence award.

Steffanie lives in New Zealand with her husband, a horde of cantankerous cats, and their medieval sword collection.

www.ingramcontent.com/pod-product-compliance
Lightning Source LLC
Chambersburg PA
CBHW011124110326
40840CB00001B/29

* 9 7 8 1 7 6 1 6 3 3 9 1 1 *